THE BONNY LAD

Jonathan Tulloch lives in the north-east of England with his wife and child. His first novel, *The Season Ticket*, won the Betty Trask Prize and was released as the feature film *Purely Belter*. A prize-winning short story writer, *The Bonny Lad* is his second novel.

D1352942

ALSO BY JONATHAN TULLOCH

The Season Ticket

Jonathan Tulloch

THE BONNY LAD

VINTAGE

Published by Vintage 2002

2 4 6 8 10 9 7 5 3 1

First published in Great Britain by
Jonathan Cape 2001

Vintage
Random House, 20 Vauxhall Bridge Road,
London SW1V 2SA

Random House Australia (Pty) Limited
20 Alfred Street, Milsons Point, Sydney
New South Wales 2061, Australia

Random House New Zealand Limited
18 Poland Road, Glenfield,
Auckland 10, New Zealand

Random House (Pty) Limited
Endulini, 5A Jubilee Road, Parktown 2193,
South Africa

The Random House Group Limited Reg. No. 954009
www.randomhouse.co.uk

A CIP catalogue record for this book
is available from the British Library

ISBN 0 09 928456 1

Papers used by Random House are natural, recyclable
products made from wood grown in sustainable forests.
The manufacturing processes conform to the environ-
mental regulations of the country of origin

Printed and bound in Great Britain by
Bookmarque Ltd, Croydon, Surrey

For Aidan

Towards evening on a cold, early spring afternoon, a single-decker bus was droning its weary way across the Metropolitan Borough of Gateshead.

Skirting the silent, wide-open grassland spaces where industry once boomed and meandering through shrinking housing estates, the bus followed the course of the River Team, muddy lung of the Tyne. It passed under the shadow of an immense, rocket-shaped tower block, and came to the junction of two defunct colliery railway lines. Turning, it began to rattle up a hill, trailing one of the dismantled lines. The engine toiled with the gradient, while the driver pumped gear changes.

About halfway down the bus sat a woman and a little boy. The woman stared without expression through the window; the child gazed fixedly down the aisle. During the bus's slow journey through the borough, many passengers had got on and then off, yet these two had remained in their seats, never once looking at each other. Four or five inches of the chewed foam upholstery separated them, but as it climbed the long hill, the bus vibrated so vigorously that the tips of their elbows drew close, like the noses of two people squaring up, or about to kiss.

At the next stop all the other passengers got off, leaving only the woman and the boy. No one else was waiting to climb on board. Not for the first time the driver's eye appeared in the mirror as he scrutinised them. 'What stop was it yus were wanting again?' he asked the woman. She did not seem to hear him. Folding his arms, he leant wearily over his wheel. 'Where yus gannin', pet?' His voice was gentle. 'Ye cannet stop on here all day, y'kna. Anyway, there's only two places this bus gans to. There and back. And yus've already been to one of them.' Still there was no response. Yawning, the driver straightened up, his eye again searching for them in the mirror. 'Ah kna it's a circle line, hinny, but there's better merry-gan-roonds for the bairn doon at the Metro Centre.' Raising himself up from his seat, the driver turned to face the silent pair. 'Ha'way, pet, yer ticket ran oot miles back. Ye'll get done, y'kna. Me an' all.' Still receiving no reply, the driver shrugged, and sitting back down, set off once more to labour slowly up the hill.

The woman was painfully thin, her face bone-pale. Her sweatshirt and jogging trousers were grey, worn to a shine at elbow and knee. Her brown hair, flecked here and there with the tired gold of an old peroxide, straggled lankly between prominent shoulder blades. Red plastic court shoes pinched into the flesh of her instep. Her eyes were dark with heavily applied make-up and exhaustion; in her glaringly white face they were like the black, unseeing eyes of a Pierrot doll. The child beside her was very young, about six years of age. His huge blue eyes peered fearlessly through an unruly fringe of thick red hair. A fading scar ran the length of a grubby cheek. His hands rested tensely at his sides as though clenching a pair of guns. He sat as motionless as the woman, except that every so often he would jerk his head sharply, and heedless of the obvious pain, chew at a swollen bottom lip like a little snared animal gnawing at its paw caught in a trap.

The bus shuddered to its next stop, its doors gasping open. Among the new passengers was a chattering group of elderly women who, having shown their passes, fluttered down the aisle together like a flock of starlings. They alighted on the seats in front of the woman and child. Drawn to the little boy, they immediately turned to him. 'Ee, what a lovely bairn,' chirped one of the new arrivals.

'Look at all them ginga locks,' a second cooed.

A third, the one sitting directly in front of the boy, leant right over to him. 'A proper bobby-dazzler.'

Neither the woman nor the boy seemed to hear or see them.

'Isn't he canny?' they continued.

'What a picture.'

'Such a bonny lad,' they all chorused. 'Ye must be so proud of him,' they said to the mother.

She did not reply.

Reaching the steepest incline so far on the lengthy hill, the bus slowed to a crawl. 'Ha'way,' the driver called out, his face smiling in the mirror. 'Thems with two legs and all their own teeth get oot and push!' The passengers laughed. And the pensioners turned away from the mother and boy to give their attention to the driver. 'Giddy-up, dobbin!' he shouted, striking the window with an open palm and whinnying like a horse.

'Giddy-up, dobbin,' laughed the pensioners among themselves.

'Yus kna why ah call this auld jalopy dobbin, divven't yus, Elsie?' the driver called.

Elsie, the old woman sitting directly in front of the boy, shook her head good-naturedly. 'Gan on, tell wor,' she smiled.

'Then ah'll have to tell yus aboot me auld granda,' he continued with mock seriousness. ''Cos it was him what started it. He used to work doon the pit up on the hill there. Know the one?'

With the fluency of a well-known ritual, the elderly women replied as one. 'Why aye.'

The driver laughed. 'He worked the ponies. The ones that used to pull the coal doon the hill to the staithes on the Tyne. In wagons, but. This was in the days before steam power of course.'

'Of course.' The pensioners were now joined by some of the other passengers.

'When he was retired,' the driver continued, shouting over the bus's struggling, 'he used to like gannin' doon the hill for a pint or three, and ah'd pick him up on me last roond and bring him back up. Ee, lad, he used to say, cannet ye gan nee faster, auld dobbin used to pull livelier than this. What, ah asked, auld dobbin what ye used to lead up and doon the hill for forty years? The very same, he said, and always pulling a wagon o' coal.' The driver paused, his eye large in the mirror as he pretended to assess his passengers' reaction. 'What's the matter, divven't yus believe wor?'

'Ee, ye've got more patter than the rain,' chuckled Elsie.

The driver beamed. 'Is that a proposal or what? Ha'way, Elsie, ah'll turn this bugger roond and head for Gretna Green before ye've time to change yer mind. Why not? Ah'll be drawing me pension an' all by the time we get there in this thing. As me Uncle Wally used to say . . .'

The engine suddenly throttled as the bus mounted a speed ramp, and the driver's words were drowned out. The engine continued to groan loudly. The pensioners turned back to the little boy. 'Ee, he's that lovely.'

'Such blue eyes.'

'And red hair.'

'What a bonny, bonny lad.'

'D'yus want him?' The woman's voice was dry and flat. In the silence that followed her interruption, she narrowed and widened her eyes as though trying to focus on the faces of the pensioners. ''Cos ye can have him if ye want. Ah'm at me wits' end with him. Kna what ah mean? Me wits' end.' The elderly women shrank back, exchanging nervous glances. 'Divven't get wor wrang,' she continued. 'Ah love him to bits, me. Ah just cannet cope. He's a pure terror. Ah kna yus wouldn't think it to look at him. But he is. And ah divven't kna what to dee with him no more.' The woman paused for a moment and

4

stared at the back of the pensioners' heads with the same limpet passivity with which she had stared through the window for so long. 'Ah tell ye what,' she said, louder now, but still as tonelessly. 'A week. Ah'll come back in a week. If ye take him, ah swear doon, ah'll come back for him in a week.'

Reaching a temporary traffic light, the bus ground to a halt. The driver glanced in his mirror and then cleared his throat. Everyone was staring at the strange woman and child. 'Did ah ever tell yus aboot me cousin Doddy?' the driver asked. There was little response from the disconcerted passengers. A pneumatic drill began to spit from the adjacent roadworks. The driver raised his voice. 'He worked all his life at the post office then just packed it in. Didn't care what he did instead. Sweep the road, take the dole, play centre half for Sunderland. It was all the same to him as long as he nivver had to set foot inside a post office again. Stamps, stamps, stamps; breakfast, dinner and tea. The Queen came to wor post office, he told us one day, and when every other bugger what was introduced to her curtsied or bowed, me he said, ah leant doon and licked her neck. Couldn't help it. Just saw her face and thought she was a stamp. Force of habit after all them years.' The driver scanned his cargo in the mirror. 'What's the matter; divven't yus believe wor?'

There were only a few half-hearted chuckles, just audible above the drill. The woman continued to stare doggedly at the pensioners. 'Ha'way,' she begged. 'Just for a day. A night. Just until ah find somewhere else for him. Ah'll come back first thing.' Reaching out, the woman tapped Elsie on the back. 'Will ye take him for just an hour?'

Utterly bemused, Elsie turned round. 'But pet,' she began uncertainly, 'he's such a bonny lad.'

The woman shook her head. 'Ah've telt yus, he's a menace.'

'Surely he cannet be all that bad . . .'

At that moment, the boy suddenly moved. Jerking his head violently, he gnawed ravenously at his bottom lip. Then he lunged forward. It seemed that he was going to clash his head viciously against the metal bar on the back of Elsie's seat but at the last instant he lifted his chin and, in a movement of great fluidity, reached out for the bar and pulled himself up. Slowly he raised himself to the old woman's face. He smiled. Elsie gasped with pleasure. The boy's smile grew as he leant right over to the old woman as though offering her a secret. 'What is it, pet lamb?' she asked. But his voice was drowned out by the moan of the drill. 'Ye can tell Elsie all aboot it,' she whispered. He spoke again, but still his words could not be made out. She smiled encouragement. 'Ha'way, bonny lad.'

The drill stopped abruptly, and in the sudden quiet the boy's voice reverberated loudly. 'Gis a tab, auld wifie, man.'

The traffic light changed, and the bus pulled away. The boy was about to speak again when a hand reached up and yanked him down. 'See what ah mean?' the woman rasped in general appeal. 'He's always deeing this to us. Showing us up. Ah've told him ah divven't kna how many times, but he nivver takes a blind bit of notice.' She turned to the child. 'Ha'way, Sonny Gee, sit doon and divven't cause a scene.' But as soon as the woman released her grip on him, Sonny Gee lifted himself back up on the bar. She thrust him down once more. This struggle repeated itself a number of times as the bus continued to rattle up the hill. 'Dee as yus're frigging well telt,' the woman said after pulling him down with great force. The bus pulled in at the next stop. No one left, a few came on. The vehicle moved off, sweeping abruptly down one of the declivities on the undulating hillside. Sonny Gee began creeping back up the bar. Inch by inch, he raised himself until he was only a nose length from the back of the pensioner's neck. The woman did not seem to notice him as her eyes moved over the rest of the passengers. 'Where are we anyhow?' she asked. Everybody looked away. Sonny Gee reached out to finger one of Elsie's blue-rinsed curls. 'Cannet neebody tell us where we are?' the woman continued. Going

6

from one averted face to the next, she fixed on a teenager. 'Will ye not tell wor where this friggin' bus is gannin', lad?'

The teenager blushed. 'Lobley Hill,' he replied without looking.

'Eh?'

'Lobley Hill.'

The boy had begun pulling the pensioner's hair. 'Ha'way, auld wifie, gis a tab. Ah kna ye've got thems. Saw ye smokin' a one before ye got on. Yer hair stinky-stinks o' it an' all.'

'Lobley Hill?' The woman spoke slowly. For the first time her face seemed to glimmer briefly with life as she glanced out of the window. The bus, having reached the plateau on the top of the hill, was passing an open green space whose drumlin-like mounds, newly planted with saplings, stretched into the rising distance. It was the old Watergate Colliery, recently converted to a forest park by a European Community grant.

The woman rose and pushed the boy out from the seat. She pressed the bell. 'At last,' quipped the driver. 'Thought ye two were gonnae bring a paternity suit against wor.'

The woman took a few steps down the aisle, but when she looked back, the boy had sat back down. 'Ha'way,' she called.

'Na,' he replied.

As the woman stood in the aisle staring at him, the motion of the bus caused her head to sway slightly and her arms to lift at the elbows, increasing her resemblance to a puppet. 'Ha'way,' she repeated. Sonny Gee had reached out to Elsie again, and was playing with her hair. 'Ha'way, Sonny Gee, leave the auld lady's hair alone.'

'If yus divven't give us a one then ah'll . . .' the boy was saying to Elsie, '. . . then ah'll pull doon me pants and pooh all awer yer blue hair.'

The passengers gasped with shock. 'Ye oot here now!' demanded the woman. Grabbing him round the throat she yanked him to his feet, but in a movement of stunning agility

7

Sonny Gee slipped from her grip and threw his hands out to grab the metal bar. She pounced on him, seizing him by the shoulders. For a full thirty seconds neither of them gave an inch, until, with a final jolting tear at the little boy's wrists, his hold was ripped free. Hurled back, he struck his head against the glass of the window. 'What yous all looking at?' demanded the woman, staggering as she dragged Sonny Gee to his feet. 'Nivver had a barney with a one of yer own bairns before?' The bus turned a corner on which stood a large church, its bricks the same red as the houses of the estate around it. The woman seemed to look at the church for an instant before turning back to the boy. 'Ye friggin' workie ticket,' she said, pulling the boy down the aisle.

The bus stopped. The woman and boy got off, followed by Elsie and the other pensioners. The boy tugged at the woman's hand as Elsie went by, but she kept tight hold of him.

'Junky,' said one of the passengers left on the bus as it pulled away. 'Junky.'

'Aye,' sighed the driver. 'It's the bairn ye've got to feel sorry for. Ah mean, what chance has he got? A lad like that. What chance has he got?'

The woman and child stood by the bus stop until all the other passengers had gone. 'Ha'way,' the woman said, moving away at last.

The afternoon was ebbing into a bitter evening. A chewing wind blew, and the boy shivered in his threadbare Newcastle United football top and shorts. 'Where we gannin'?' he asked.

'Ye should have brought yer fleece,' the woman said.

'Where ye taking wor this time?' Sonny Gee asked once more.

'Ah told yus it was gonnae be cold. Ye should have brought yer little fleece.'

Sonny Gee clamped his jaws tightly to prevent them from chattering. 'Ah'm not cold, me,' he said. They walked on through the wind, passing red-brick houses whose untidy front gardens were littered with broken toys and loose carrier bags. 'Ah'm not cold,' repeated the boy with a soft vehemence. 'And me fleece isn't little.'

After they had come about a hundred yards from the bus stop, the woman slowed. Staring ahead at the church on the corner, she seemed lost in thought at the sight of it. Then she reached the mouth of a cut, and with one last look at the church, turned down it.

The cut was long and twisting. It ran between two high wooden fences, and was dark like a tunnel. A heavy smell of creosote filled the air. The wind moaned restlessly through the knots and splinters of the wood, and the ash of the path deadened their footfalls. As they walked, a cat yowled from somewhere just ahead, but each time they turned one of the corners, it was never there.

At last they came to a lone street light. The lamp-post was old and stark as a dead tree; its light was broken. Graffiti filled the fence around it. A wheelie bin lay on its side, its lid had been torn off and rested among empty cans of lager. The woman stopped and leant heavily against the lamp-post. 'Where we gannin'?' Sonny Gee asked.

The woman did not reply. She brought out a little compact mirror from her jogging trousers, and opening it, stared at herself. The glass of the mirror was cracked, shattering her reflection into fragments. She gazed deeply at the image with a blank air as though puzzled by what she saw.

'Why cannet ah just stay at Audrey's again, or Gemma's?' the boy asked. 'It's mint at Gemma's.'

'Because they cannet have ye this time,' she said.

'Ah'll gan to that Maureen wifie's then. Or Sandra's . . .'

'Neeone else'll have ye, man Sonny Gee,' the woman interrupted him. Taking out a lipstick, she began to apply it. Her hand shook slightly. 'This is the only place left.'

Sonny Gee stared at her suspiciously as she finished with the lipstick and began to pull a comb through her hair. Half of the teeth of the comb were missing. 'Where is it then?' he demanded. 'Will it have a geet big telly and that? Will there be any dogs there or owt? Will . . .'

'Ye'll find oot when we get there,' the woman interrupted. 'So stop gannin' on.' She stared closely at the boy. He was hugging himself in the cold, the flesh of his bare arms and legs were puckered with goose bumps. In the cut, the evening had already arrived. The air felt dismal. 'Ye should have brought yer little fleece,' she said.

'It's not little,' he retorted. 'And ah'm not cold.'

When she had finished combing her hair, she looked at her reflection one more time and then put away the compact. 'Now you,' she said to the boy.

'Na,' he replied.

'Aye.'

'Na.'

'Aye, Sonny Gee.'

'Na.'

There was a brief struggle but the woman overpowered him. The boy's thick red hair crackled with static as the comb was hauled through it. 'Such lovely hair,' the woman said, her hand growing more gentle. 'What the lasses wouldn't give for this hair.'

'Fuck off,' the boy spluttered, wrenching himself free.

The woman restrained him. 'It's God's truth. Ye're such a bonny lad. Such a lovely, bonny lad.'

'Ah'm nee lass,' muttered the boy.

'Nivver said ye were,' said the woman, continuing to comb his hair.

'Y'kna that lad what lives on Old Parsonage Road?' Sonny Gee asked. 'Him what does kick-boxing; that chaver what reckons he's geet hard? Well, ah battered him. He's eleven, but ah smashed him in the goolie-goolies.' The boy waited, challengingly. He thrust out a bottom lip, but suddenly it began to quiver. His voice grew strangely quiet, like a baby left to cry for too long. 'Why do ah have to keep gannin' away, Mam?'

The woman put the comb away. Then she looked closely at the boy. 'It'll be nice,' she began. 'Where ah'm taking ye. It'll be nice. Anyway, it's just for a bit. It's always just for a bit, eh? A little while then ye can come back.'

'But why do ah have to keep gannin'?'

'Ye kna why.'

For an instant, the boy seemed close to tears and his teeth nibbled at his bottom lip, then he raised his head and jutted his chin out aggressively. 'When ah grow up, ah'm gonnae kill him. That Macca. Ah'm gonnae kill him.'

His mother shook her head wearily. 'That's why ye have to keep gannin' away. Ye wind him up summink rotten. He needs a bit time to cool down. If only yus'd make an effort to get on with him then ye wouldn't have to keep on gannin' away.'

The boy's aggression flickered then died like a flame. 'Why divven't ye send *him* away then?' he asked quietly.

The woman sighed, then with a sudden spurt of energy, she spat on the cuff of her sweatshirt and began rubbing it vigorously against Sonny Gee's face. 'Divven't ye twist aboot,' she told him. 'Ah want ye clean for where ye're gannin'.'

'Where am ah gannin'?' the boy asked.

Without replying, the woman drew his hands out, turning them palm upwards. They were pitted with dirt. 'How d'yus get them that clarty?' Tutting, she let go of the hands, and they fell to the boy's side. 'Keep them behind yer back. Where we're gannin'. Keep them hands hidden.' Wetting her fingers, she began to flatten his hair, which had already sprung back after the combing. Gently, she pushed the hair out of his eyes, and then, with a sigh, reached into a pocket and brought out a packet of Superkings. She opened the crushed gold and black box, and flicked suspiciously at the filters. 'Ye been helping yersel' again?' she asked. Sonny Gee shook his head. 'Who has then, the friggin' tooth fairy?'

'That Macca took them, ah saw him. He's always twocking yer tabs.'

The woman tensed with frustration. 'Ye're still at it, aren't ye? Nee matter what ah tell ye. It's small wonder, he cannet stand the sight o' yus.'

'Well ah cannet *sit* the sight o' him,' the boy spat back.

'Aye, well, he's my boyfriend,' she shot back, 'so ye better get used to him.' Placing a cigarette in her mouth, the woman searched her other pockets for the lighter. She couldn't find it. 'Ha'way, man Sonny Gee, give it back. Me lighter. Give it back noo. Ah've told ye before not to play with lighters.'

The boy's eyes widened with innocence. 'Ah haven't touched it.'

'And ah suppose it wasn't ye what set fire to them mattresses in the backyard?'

The boy shrugged. 'Na.'

'Ye're a friggin' arsonist, ye. Ye'll end up burning doon the whole block of bedsits one o' these days. Ha'way, give it back. Ah kna ye've got it.'

There was a pause. Shivering, the boy rubbed his eyes with the heel of his hand. His voice was suddenly small once more. 'Mam, cannet ye and me gan away? Cannet ye and me leave Macca?'

Replacing the cigarette, the woman crammed the packet back in her pocket. Her anger was dissipated on a sigh. 'Oh aye,' she said exhaustedly. 'And where could ye and me gan?'

'With them birds,' the boy said, simply.

'Eh?'

'The birds.'

She shook her head sadly. 'Ye're not back on aboot them birds again, are ye? It does me heed in. Honestly, man Sonny Gee, it's divvy talk.'

'It isn't.'

'Where d'ye get it from? How can ye live with birds? Ye just cannet. It doesn't make sense.'

The boy nodded adamantly. 'Ye can. Ye can live with the birds. We could gan there with them. Ye and me. Together. Nee Macca. Just us.'

The woman stared at the boy for a while with a puzzled air. 'D'ye think ah like having to send ye away? But what else can ah dee? Ye wind Macca up till he snaps. Ye kna ye dee.' She broke off. Then, impulsively, she threw her arms wide open. 'Ha'way, ye daft beggar, give us a love.' The boy held back, but his mother advanced on him. He struggled for a while before allowing himself to be taken. The embrace continued for a few, awkward moments, and then broke. Standing apart, mother and son walked on.

The cut gave way on to a piece of open ground. They walked along a paved path running between a row of retired miners' cottages and countless washing lines strung between tall metal poles. It was an enclosed place, with another cut at the far end the only other access. The whole area was surrounded by a thick beech hedge. From each chimney of the row, smoke drifted up into the gathering evening.

'This is shite,' said the boy dubiously as they walked along the terrace. 'Ah'm not stopping here.'

The woman stopped at a cottage about halfway down the row. She seemed to stare at it for a long time before pushing open the gate. The heels of her shoes clicked uncertainly down the short concrete path leading to the rough red wood of a front door. The boy watched her from the gate. After taking a deep breath, she raised a hand to knock. There was no reply. After some hesitation, she steeled herself and knocked for the second time. When there was still no answer, she seemed to sag and sank slowly to the doorstep, until she was sitting on it with her back leaning against the coarse wood of the door. 'Where we gannin' noo?' Sonny Gee called.

The woman looked back down the row of cottages to the cut. 'Neewhere,' she said defeatedly.

'Why?'

''Cos there isn't neewhere else left to gan. Ah told ye, neeone else'll have ye.'

'What we gonnae dee then?'

She shrugged. 'We're gonnae wait.'

The boy came down the path, and squeezing past her, pushed deftly against the door. His fingers probed the jamb. 'Ah could get in there,' he told her. Moving over to the window which peered out from the cottage like an eye, its sight blurred by the cataract of a thick net curtain, he stood on his tiptoes and gazed within. Turning to the window ledge, he ran a hand over its length. 'Ah could get in there an' all.' He rattled the pane. 'Easy-peasy get in there.' Shaking his head, he walked back down the path, and climbing on to the gate, began to swing to and fro.

'Git doon,' the woman said.

Sonny Gee swung a few more times, making the hinges groan, and then jumped off. Cupping his hands, he blew on them. He jumped up and down for a while, and then climbed back on to the gate.

'Ah telt ye to get doon from there.'

From the mouth of the cut, a ginger cat appeared. It watched the boy jump down once more. Sonny Gee stared at it for a while, then got back on to the gate. The wind was sharpening as the light faded.

'If ah have to come awer there ah'll make ye feel sorry,' the woman said, looking up. Her voice softened a little. 'Ah told yus ye should have brought yer little fleece. Ye're freezing. Come here and sit doon.' Sonny Gee walked slowly towards her. 'Give it another knock,' his mother said.

'Nee point,' Sonny Gee replied, pausing halfway down the path.

'Eh?'

'Ah can see him.' Sonny Gee pointed at the net curtains.
His mother pulled herself quickly to her feet. 'Where?'

'He's gone now.'

'If ye're working yer ticket again . . .'

'Ah'm not,' interrupted the boy. 'Listen.'

They waited in silence for a few seconds and then a bolt slid,
a chain rattled and the door inched open. A pair of eyes peered
out warily through the narrow gap. Slowly, the door opened
more fully.

2

He was an old man. His shoulders were rounded, and his body stooped forward in the frame of the door. He stood there blinking in the wind, his lips mumbling with silent bewilderment. As though utterly bemused by the presence of his visitors, he stared at them blankly for a while, then turned and disappeared back into the house.

After some hesitation, the woman followed him through the open door. Slowly, she walked down a narrow passage and entered a room in which an armchair and a two-seater settee were grouped round the glowing embers of a small coal fire. On the far side of the room there was a table at a window. The old man stood with his back to the window, his hands resting on the table. The fingers of these hands were twisted as though with arthritis. The woollen green cardigan he wore was holed at both elbows. Without moving, the woman and the old man stared at each for a long time.

'Ah'm not stopping here,' said Sonny Gee, suddenly bursting into the room. 'Ah've had a look and it's shite.'

'Shh,' said the woman sharply, taking him by the hand.

At last, the old man moved. Reaching into the pocket of his cardigan, he fumbled for a long time before bringing out a pair of glasses. The spectacles seemed tiny in his misshapen hands, their golden wire frame fragile, and it was only with great effort that he was able to control his clumsy movements enough to lift them to his face. With the glasses on, he studied the woman and the boy in turn, but still he seemed unable to place them. Shuffling slowly to the armchair, he lowered himself heavily into it. After a few moments, the woman sat on

16

the settee, pulling Sonny Gee down beside her. A clock ticked from a sideboard. From time to time, the fire cracked. 'So,' began the old man at last. 'It's ye.'

'Aye,' replied the woman.

'He's got a fire,' Sonny Gee said, pointing at the coals. 'He's lit a fire inside.' The boy rose from the settee, only to be firmly pushed down. This happened again. And then once more, before Sonny Gee slumped back petulantly. 'Ah'm not stopping here,' he mumbled quietly.

On a number of occasions the old man seemed about to speak, but each time the words dried on his lips. He wore battered slippers on his feet. A pair of heavy black boots stood on the hearth stone. 'Why ye here?' he asked eventually.

'Came to see ye,' the woman replied.

'Why?' His voice was low and expressionless.

'To see how yus are.'

'Why?'

The woman raised her hands and shrugged. 'It's been so lang.'

'What is it yus're after?'

'How d'yus kna ah'm after anything?'

An abrasive snort escaped the tight compression of the old man's jaws. 'What is it yus're after?' he repeated heavily.

The woman floundered for a few moments, and then turned to the boy beside her who was staring at the fire in fascination. 'Ah've brought this one to see ye,' she said. But the old man did not look at the boy. His hands kneaded the rests of the armchair like a pair of searching claws. 'Ye look thin,' the woman said. 'And yer hands, they look knackt. Isn't there nee compensation gannin'? To help yus oot. For auld pitmen an' that?'

The old man blinked. 'Ah'll be lang gan by the time they get roond to me.'

'But ah heard . . .'

'What d'ye kna aboot it?' he shot back. The room echoed

with his hostility. Then slowly the old man began to lever himself to his feet. Standing, he gazed bemusedly around the room. It was growing darker at the window, and the fire cast the only light in the room. 'Ah'll put the kettle on,' he said, quietly now, and shambling over to a smoked-glass door which was behind the armchair, disappeared through it into a tiny kitchen.

Left alone, the woman scrambled for her cigarettes. Kneeling on the hearthrug, she held one out to the fire. It burst into flame, and she had to shake the flame out before putting it in her mouth. The red tip of the cigarette glowed as she sucked on it greedily. 'Gis a tab, man Mam,' the boy demanded, grabbing the cigarettes.

'Not ye,' she said, snatching the packet away.

'Why?'

''Cos ah say.'

In the kitchen, the old man could be heard filling a kettle.

'You're having a one,' said the boy.

'Ah'm a adult. Tabs are nee good for bairns like ye.'

'But ye give us one the other day.'

'That was to stop ye deeing me heed in.'

The boy paused to think. 'Well, give us a one now, or ah'll dee it in for yus good and proper.'

Casting an anxious glance at the kitchen door, the woman raised a warning finger. 'Keep yer voice doon,' she hissed. 'Ah told ye, yus've got to make a good impression.'

'Gis a tab then.'

'Na.'

'He won't mind,' said the boy. 'That auld gadgie. Not if he gans lighting fires inside.'

'Ah telt ye, ah'm not giving ye nee tab.'

'Aye, ye are.' The boy opened his mouth to shout, but before he could get a sound out, his mother had clamped a hand over his mouth. He struggled violently, kicking and punching with the lithe desperation of a cornered weasel. 'If ye divven't give us a tab ah'll not stop here,' he seethed. 'Ah'll . . .'

'Here then,' the woman said, throwing a cigarette at him. 'And ah hope it chokes ye.' From the kitchen came the circumspect little song of a gas ring. 'Divven't let him see, mind,' she added, pointing at the smoked-glass door. 'The moment he comes in, hoy it on the fireback.'

'Who is he? That gadgie mista. Who is he?' the boy asked. Taking a huge gulp on her cigarette, the woman shuddered slightly as she blew out the smoke. Tetchily, she tapped her arms with two fingers. With a quick, intelligent eye, Sonny Gee looked round the room. 'What's that?' he asked, pointing at an object on the mantelpiece. It was an old miner's lamp, its brass glowing with the firelight.

'Divven't start with yer questions now, man.'

'But what is it?'

Inhaling deeply again, the woman glanced at the mantelpiece. 'An ornament.'

'What's a ormanent?'

'Ornament, man, ye divvy.'

'Aye, well, what's a one of them?'

'They remind ye.'

'What of?'

'Things.'

'What things?'

The woman shrugged. 'Ah divven't kna. They're just things people have to remind them.'

'Are they worth owt?'

'Depends.'

Sonny Gee paused thoughtfully as he leant over to the fire. He held his cigarette carefully over an ember so that it didn't flare. 'Have we got a ormanent?'

The woman inhaled deeply and a stream of smoke coursed into her eyes. Smarting with pain, she twisted her face. 'We divven't bother with any of that.'

'Why?'

''Cos there isn't nowt ah wanted to be reminded of.' The kettle began to whistle. 'Hurry up and get that tab smoked,' the boy's mother told him.

'Why?'

'Ah'm telling ye to.'

'Why?'

The woman pointed at the smoked-glass door. ''Cos ah want him to take ye. That's why.'

'Well, ah'm not stopping with that auld gadgie. Ye'll have to take wor to Audrey's.'

'Ye kna she cannet have ye at the minute. It's just for a bit, man Sonny Gee. Ye kna ah always come back for ye. So ha'way and give him a good impression. Ye'll like it here.'

'Ah like that fire,' the boy mused. Leaning forward, he pointed the tip of his cigarette at the pair of black boots on the hearthstone. 'Are them to be hoyed in the fire?'

'Divven't talk daft.'

The boy studied the boots for a long time. The leather, though old and worn, was carefully polished. Nails were visible where the sole had been cobbled. The laces were fraying in more than one place. Sonny Gee reached out to touch them.

'Leave them alone,' his mother said.

Standing up, Sonny Gee walked across the room. An old portable black and white television set stood on a sideboard. The boy turned it on. It did not work. He pushed the switch a number of times. 'Nee way ah'm stopping here,' he said, coming back to the settee and slumping into it. 'The telly doesn't even work.'

In the kitchen, crockery could be heard chiming as it was placed clumsily on a tray. 'Ha'way, hoy that tab away noo!' the woman hissed, and then reached out to grab the cigarette. The boy evaded her skilfully, teasingly blowing out a cloud of smoke in her face. 'Ye kna what?' she said. 'Sometimes ah cannet wait to get shot o' ye, ye little bugger!'

The woman took one last drag on her cigarette which brought the red tip right to the filter, then she flicked it on to the fire. With a shrug, Sonny Gee threw his cigarette at the fire. It hit the wall above the fireplace and bounced back on to the hearthrug. A thin layer of ash settled softly on the gnarled leather of the boots. Quickly the woman rose and placed the cigarette end on the fire. The filters of the cigarettes curled at the edges, then writhed under a blue flame. Within a few seconds they had both been utterly obliterated. Just then the smoked-glass door opened. 'Who is he?' the boy asked.

'Just somebody,' the woman replied.

'Will he give us money? Audrey sometimes gives wor money.'

'Shut up, man.'

The tea things bounced on the tray as the old man backed into the room. He placed them noisily on the table, his breathing laboured. 'What's the matter with him, like?' Sonny Gee asked. 'His hands are all knackt.' His mother did not reply. The old man began to pour the tea, stirring in milk and sugar, he spilt them both liberally over the table. With a knife he cut open a packet of Lincoln biscuits, and taking out four, put them on a plate. When he picked up two of the mugs, the woman half rose.

'Ah divven't need nee help, me,' he growled and she sat back down.

The old man brought the mugs unsteadily over to the settee; the woman took them. Then he handed her the plate of biscuits.

'Ah divven't want that,' the boy said, staring at the surface of his tea. The woman tried to quieten him. 'Na,' he said, 'ah'm not drinking that with all them biddy-bits.'

She glanced up apologetically at the old man. 'He's not used to proper tea. Loose leaf. The real stuff. We just have the bags.'

'There is none,' replied the old man, simply.

'It doesn't matter,' the woman said.

The old man seemed to think deeply for a few moments. 'Ah'll pop next door. Elsie's got minerals and that. For when her grandbairns come.'

There was an awkward pause. 'Divven't bother,' she said.

The old man shuffled back into the kitchen. There was the sound of another door being opened, and then a draught stole into the sitting room from outside, worrying the fire. It was growing dark in the room now. Night drew in at the window overlooking the table, and the light from the fire was weakening. The black boots cast an even darker shadow across the hearthstone. 'Yus need petrol in there, man,' said Sonny Gee, pointing at the fire. 'To stop it gannin' oot. Hoy in a aerosol. That's what ye dee. It gans whoosh!' Laughing, the boy fluttered his hands in the flare of an explosion. The woman was silent. The boy looked about. 'Ah'm not stopping here,' he decided. 'Not even with a fire. When ye gan ah'm coming with ye. Ah'll just follow ye.'

A strange look had come into the woman's blank eyes. 'Ah kna,' she said with a sudden energy. 'Let's play a game.'

The boy turned to her suspiciously. 'What game?'

'Bet ah win.'

Puzzled, the boy took up the challenge. 'Bet ye divven't.'

'Bet ah dee.'

'Bet ye divven't.'

'Ha'way, let's play it then.' His mother spoke with forced enthusiasm. 'Hide and seek. Ah'll hide.'

'Na,' decided the boy after a moment's thought.

The woman stood up desperately. 'Winner gets a fiver.'

The boy jerked his head. 'Straight up?'

'Aye, count to ten.' She paused. 'Make it twenty. If it's for a fiver, it's got to be proper.'

'But what aboot him, that auld gadgie mista?'

'He's playing an' all.'

22

'Na, he's not.'

The woman nodded vigorously. 'Why d'ye think he's gone ootside then, ye daft bugger? Come on then. Dee it proper. Count to twenty.'

'One . . . two . . . three . . .' began the boy doggedly. He fell forward, burying his face in his lap. His hands cradled his skull. 'Four . . . five . . . six . . .' He paused. 'Mam? Does it have to be twenty?' There was no reply. 'Seven . . . eight . . . nine . . . ten . . . Mam? Ah divven't kna how to get there. Ah divven't kna up to twenty . . .' But there was still no reply. The boy's fingers writhed through his hair like elvers caught in a net. 'How d'yus dee twenty?' He fell silent, his lips moving as though they were counting.

Unseen to him, a stooped shape had materialised on the other side of the smoked-glass door. 'Mary,' began the old man suddenly from the kitchen. 'Ah want ye to gan. Ah've been in the yard thinking, and ah've decided that ah divven't want to see ye. Not ye. Not the bairn. Ah cannet forget what ye've done. So ah want yus to gan. To gan and to not come back.' There was a pause. 'Ah'm gonnae step back into the yard. When ah come back, ye'll be gone.'

In the sitting room, the clock continued to tick, but nothing else was moving. The fire crackled less frequently, its light diminishing in ever decreasing circles as the darkness advanced through the room, swallowing first the sideboard, then the table, and then the backs of the armchair and settee. On the hearthstone, the scuffs and the scars of long usage disappeared from the boots, leaving its leather smooth, featureless.

'Found ye,' said the boy, finally looking up when the old man eventually came back into the room.

'Eh?' the old man replied, bewildered.

'Found ye,' repeated the boy, staring up at the silhouette of the old man. 'Why d'yus dee that? Give yersel' up so easy? Ye were playing, weren't ye? Ah mean ah could hear ye.'

'Where is she?' The old man scanned the shadows of the room.

'Ah've caught ye,' said the boy. 'Even if ye weren't playing proper, ah've caught ye.'

With an uncomprehending shake of his head, the old man walked across the room, his slippered steps shuffling through the darkness. There was a click, and the room was flooded with bright light. The old man and the boy stared at each other through eyes blinking under the scalding dazzle of the electric bulb. 'Yer mam, where is she?'

Sonny Gee shrugged. 'How dee ah kna? But ah've found ye. So ye've got to help us find her.'

In the pitiless light, the wrinkles and deep lines of the old man's face were starkly emphasised. There was a bitterness to his features. The huge hand, still hovering at the switch, seemed misshapen to the point of deformity. At the same time, the flawlessness of the boy's skin, the clear, untainted blue of his eyes was also shown clearly. 'Ha'way, gadgie mista. Ye've got to help us. It's a proper game. Ye win a fiver. Ah'll split it with ye if yus help wor.'

They continued to stare at each other for a while, then the old man broke off the glance. He went over to the boots, and stooping painfully, picked them up. He took them over to the table, sat down on a chair and began to put them on. It was a laborious task. The boy watched him closely. First, he kicked the slippers off, then stepping into the boots, writhed his feet inside. Leaning down, he began to lace them with clumsy hands. When this had been finally accomplished, he yanked forcefully at the laces, tying the boots as tightly as he could. Breathless, he hoisted himself on to his feet and went through the passage door. He came back wearing a long coat and a flat cap. He held a walking stick. 'Get yer coat,' he said.

'Ah haven't got a one.'

'Ha'way then.'

'Are ye helping wor?' asked the boy, uncertainly.

'Ha'way.'

Sonny Gee followed him to the front door. 'Are ye gonnae help wor find her?' he added.

The old man stepped outside. 'Aye,' said the boy. 'Mebbes, she's ootside. But shouldn't we look inside first?'

Outside, the old man walked with a surprising vigour. With the collar of his coat up against the cold and his flat cap pulled low, he moved purposefully through the cold evening. Although he leant heavily on his stick, he was now an imposing figure. It was as though the boots gave him a power that he lacked while inside. The boy followed a few yards behind, his eyes roving. In the biting wind, the washing lines tugged uneasily, drumming out a brittle percussion from the metal poles.

'She won't have come that far,' said Sonny Gee as he stopped at the lone lamp-post deep in the cut. The old man carried on, turning a sharp corner. The sound of his boots scrunching on the cinders still rang out firmly. 'Me mam,' the boy called. 'She won't have come that far, auld gadgie mista.' Shivering in the chill, Sonny Gee waited miserably. Then he called out again. 'Just 'cos ye gave yersel' away, ye've still got to help wor. Ye've got to help wor find her. Even if ye're not playing, ye've still got to help wor.' The clatter of his voice echoed down the wooden fences of the cut. He could no longer hear the boots. He waited a little longer, but the old man did not come back. The boy kicked the fallen wheelie bin and then began to run. The old man was waiting for him at the mouth of the cut. 'She's hiding,' Sonny Gee said, coming up to him.

The old man stared at him, then shook his head. 'Aye, and she doesn't want to be found.'

'Are ye a divvy or summink? Course she doesn't want to be found. Ye gave yersel' away like a proper divvy but she won't. Not for a fiver. She'll be back inside. Ah telt yus we should have looked there . . .'

'Where d'ye live?' the old man interrupted him.

'She won't . . .'

'Where d'yus live?'

The boy shrugged. 'Bedsit.'

'Where?'

'Bensham.'

'Wheraboots in Bensham?'

'Near Old Parsonage Road.'

'Ha'way then.'

The old man took him to the bus stop. 'This'll take ye back there,' he said. 'Ah'll stick ye on it. Then ye get off when ye get hyem.'

They waited in silence. The boy hugged himself aggressively against the cold. A bus juddered into view, but it wasn't theirs. A stream of passengers got off, and the old man edged away into the shadows behind the brick-built shelter. When the passengers had dispersed, he came back. 'Ah'm not gannin' back there,' said the boy suddenly. 'To that bedsit, ah'm not gannin' back.' He narrowed his eyes in thought. 'Ah'm gannin' somewhere else.'

The old man shrugged slightly. 'Ah'm putting ye on that Bensham bus, boy.'

'There's a hoose for the birds. Ah'll live there. That's where ah'll gan.'

'Gan where ye like.'

A bus turned the corner on which the church stood, its headlights illuminating the red brick briefly. The old man scrabbled in the pocket of his coat, finally managing to bring out some coins. He held a fist out to the boy and then opened it. 'Yus'll have to take a fifty-pence bit. That'll get ye there. A half to Bensham. There's one.'

Gingerly, the boy reached out, but then stopped, suddenly fascinated. 'What happened to yer hand, gadgie mista?'

'Just take the money,' the old man snapped.

The bus drew to a halt. Once more the old man stepped

back into the shadows. 'Get on,' he urged the boy. Sonny Gee looked doubtfully back down the road to the mouth of the cut. For a moment he seemed about to gnaw at his bottom lip, but suddenly he bristled with defiance, jutted his chin out and climbed jauntily on board.

'Where ye gannin', bonny lad?' the driver asked.

'Bensham,' replied the boy. 'Old Parsonage Road.'

'Where's yer mam, lad?'

'Where's yours, gadgie, sitting in the dustbin eating bread and shit?'

'Hey . . .'

Unwillingly, the old man came out from the shadows. The cap was pulled even lower over his features. 'It's areet, his mam's waiting for him at the other side.'

'Is that ye, Joe?' the driver called down.

Walking away, the old man did not reply. Stopping, he heard the bus pull away behind him and without turning listened until he could no longer hear it. Then he carried on. 'Who was the bairn?' a voice suddenly asked.

The old man pulled up. A woman holding two full carrier bags came up behind him. 'Areet, Joe,' she said.

'Now then, Peggy,' he replied, grudgingly.

Peggy was a huge woman. Her body was almost entirely round, as was her head. Even her cheeks and chin were almost perfect spheres. It caused her a great deal of effort to set the bags down on the pavement. 'Who was that bonny lad?'

Joe shook his head. 'How dee ah kna?'

'Weren't ye with him?'

The old man paused for the briefest of moments before replying. 'Na.'

The woman tutted. 'Can ye believe it? A bairn that age left to himself. They get up to all sorts, ye kna.'

'Do they?' replied the old man, setting off back down the road.

The woman nodded her puffy face. Her eyes narrowed.

Picking up her bags, she waddled after him. 'Why aye, Joe. It's them that dee all the crimes. Ah was reading aboot it. It's the young bairns what dee them all. Rat boys, that's what they call them. They want taking away somewhere. That's what they want. Taking away somewhere. Them rat boys.'

'Aye, well,' replied Joe.

'Mind ye, it's not always the smallest ones. Ah'm sick o' them teenagers hanging aboot in the cut. They've hoyed someone's bin doon there, y'kna. And they dee drugs. Elsie foond a needle. The pollis dee nowt. They just let them ride that motorbike up and doon the cottages an' all.' Joe quickened his step. Catching a pebble, his boots rasped over a flagstone. 'Are ye sure ye divven't kna him?' Peggy called after him, but the old man did not look back. 'That little bonny lad. Ah could have sworn yus were putting him on that bus.' There was still no reply. 'Where ye off to in such a rush, mind? Where ye gannin' all muffled up, and yer cap awer half yer face? Ye've still got yer reading glasses on an' all, ye rude auld get!'

Joe did not turn down the cut but carried on to the church. The church door was heavy, and it took him a number of attempts before he managed to open it. This difficulty seemed to angrily baffle him. He walked up the hard floor of the aisle, the tap of his stick and the clump of his boots echoing in the hushed emptiness of the large building. It was dark, except for a stand of candles in front of a holy picture. Coming to the picture, the old man reached out to take a candle from the box. Fumbling, he stuck it in one of the little holders. Above him, three faces looked down from the framed picture. It was the Holy Family: Joseph, Mary and the baby Jesus. The depiction of the infant was strikingly lifelike. After Joe had lit his candle, he began fiddling with the money in his pocket. He had brought out a handful when the coins spilt between his fingers. There was a clatter as they hit the ground. With a heavy sigh, the old man looked down. Some of the coins were still spinning, some had come to rest and others were rolling away. For a while he watched them helplessly, then slowly he began to stoop.

When he had eventually retrieved all the coins, Joe looked up at the picture. His gaze remained on the baby for a while, before he closed his eyes. Lips moving as though in prayer, he stayed like that for a long time, swaying slightly as he stood, but when he opened his eyes again, they were weary and pained. A pinched look narrowed his features. 'Na,' he whispered bitterly. 'It's nee good. Nee good.'

Outside, the wind had risen. A gust caught the old man off balance and he stumbled. His coat flapped as he walked down the ash track of the cut. A sudden noise in front made him pull up. He stood motionless for a while, then pulling his body as upright as he could and gripping his stick tighter, he pushed onwards. The wind streamed into his eyes which were steely, determined. But when he reached the lamp-post, there was no sign of anyone. Only a cat. The cat greeted him, rubbing itself against his legs. Standing under the lamp-post, the old man stared at the animal. The cat followed him for a few yards, nimbly picking its way through a trail of broken glass, then disappeared like a wraith through a hole in the wooden fence.

By the time Joe returned home, the fire had gone out. He turned on the portable television set which stood on the sideboard beside the clock, and fiddled awkwardly with the aerial, but no picture formed, so he turned it off again. He sank heavily on to a chair by the table, and leaning down, began to untie his laces. Having tugged his feet free and put them back in the slippers, he placed the boots on the hearthstone. Without taking off his hat and coat, he lowered himself wearily into the armchair. As he sat there, his gnarled hands rested on his chest, rising and falling with the tide of his breathing, an ebb and flow which gradually slowed.

Some time had passed when a sudden roaring noise jolted him. The roaring was followed by strident shouting. Pulling himself up, the old man went over to the wall and switched off the light. He crept to the bedroom through one of the doors leading from the passage, and carefully lifted a corner of the net curtain just in time to see a motorbike roar past. Two youths were riding on it, their faces hidden by slash masks. The bike was followed by a cluster of teenage boys and girls, who were passing a bottle between themselves. A scream filled the air as one of the boys leapt on a girl's back. Piercing laughter burst from the others.

Joe waited until the group had passed on up the path before he dropped the net curtain and slowly shuffled back into the sitting room. Without switching on the light, he sat in the armchair. A little later the motorbike raged past again, its engine blaring. An ear-splitting shouting greeted it from the teenagers on foot. The roar of the motorbike faded into the distance. Tensely the old man waited for it to flare again, but it did not. The teenagers moved off too, their passing marked by a swing and slam of every gate of the row of cottages, and, finally, the shattering of glass as the bottle was tossed away. Then there was quiet. The old man relaxed in the armchair. Carefully he took off his glasses and manoeuvred them into his cardigan pocket. In the darkness, he pursed his lips. A little while later, a single soft note sounded. Repeating the note, he then whistled a snatch of melody. The whites of his eyes showed thoughtfully in the gloom as he continued to whistle the same tune. The whistling grew a little louder before it stopped abruptly, and shaking his head, Joe fell back into silence. He took off his cap and coat, and then laid his cardigan over the back of the armchair. Then he was still.

The old man must have drifted off into sleep, because the next thing he knew he was being woken by a hammering on his door. He tried to rise, but his joints had stiffened and he fell back in the chair. Listening, his eyes darted in the darkness. The knocking sounded again. Picking himself up painfully, he went through to the bedroom again, and with even greater care, lifted the net curtain. But he could see nobody. He was in the passage when the knocking rang out a third time. Picking up his stick and holding its handle foremost like a cudgel, the old man slowly approached the front door. His breathing grew shallow. He reached the door at which the fist knocked a fourth time, even more insistently now. He stood there waiting but there was no more knocking. Puzzled, he lingered at the door listening. On the other side was a soft sound like a small animal shivering in the cold.

He reached an unsteady hand out to slide open the bolt. With a rattle, he freed the chain. Then he opened the door.

The coldness of the air hit him, and he swayed uncertainly for a moment, flinching under the needles of a sharp rain. 'Ah'm not frightened of yous lot,' he called defiantly. There was no reply. His lips trembled as he looked out. He gazed up and then down the way. Nothing. His hand was back on the door to close it when a movement at his feet caught his eye. He glanced down to see a shape hunched on his doorstep. The shape was shivering. It moved, and all at once the face of a child was looking up at him. A pair of eyes, blue even in the poor light of the terrace's single street lamp, peered keenly through a shock of red hair. 'Areet, gadgie mista, got a tab?'

3

The old man woke in the small hours of the morning. For a long time he lay in the chill darkness of his bedroom, staring at the ceiling.

It was still dark when he eventually got up. Coming through into the sitting room, he found Sonny Gee fast asleep on the settee. The boy had kicked his blankets aside and was wrapped tightly in the old man's cardigan that had been left on the back of the armchair. Gazing at the cardigan bemusedly, the old man sat on a chair at the table and waited for the dawn. Sonny Gee slept soundlessly as the clock ticked in the dark room. The pulse of time slowed and nothing seemed to thin the blue-black light, pooled heavy as deep water at the window.

The night felt as thick as ever when a blackbird began to sing. It sang alone for a long time, but eventually its voice was joined by others. At last, morning broke, and all along the guttering of the retired miners' terrace, the sparrows started to stir. The sun rose. Streaming into the room the beams lengthened until they reached the settee and began to move over its worn upholstery. Joe sat there watching the sunlight travel slowly up the boy. Every so often he narrowed his eyes with thought.

Despite the sunlight, it was still cold in the room, and a few times the boy twitched in his sleep, trying to pull the cardigan more closely round himself. Moving quietly, Joe gathered up the ashes from the grate and then laid a new fire. Unable to control his movements, he scattered the ashes on the carpet of the sitting room and over the worn linoleum of the kitchen floor as he carried them out to the yard. Several coals fell from the shovelful he brought back from the coalhouse. In his attempts to light the fire he littered the hearthrug with snapped match heads and charred paper.

When the fire was eventually lit, the old man lowered himself into his armchair. The boy still did not stir. His sleeping face was framed by his thick red hair, a look of utter innocence softening his features.

Joe had been sitting there for some time when a bright knocking rang through the house. He did not move. A voice called through the lifted letter box. 'It's me.' There was a pause. 'Ah kna yus're in, so divven't pretend ye're not.' Clicking his tongue with annoyance, Joe watched Sonny Gee toss fitfully on the setttee. 'Ha'way, let wor in.' The knocking rang out deafeningly, and in a spurt of anger, the old man heaved himself to his feet. For a moment he stood there, looking down at the rug and then at the boy. 'Mr O'Brien!'

Joe went down the passage. He reached the door. 'It's areet this morning,' he whispered tetchily. 'Ah've lit the fire meself.'

There was a sound of scratching, low down on the outside of the door. 'Ha'way,' called the voice again.

'Ah divven't need ye today,' snapped the old man irritatedly. 'The fire's already lit. Gan on to Elsie's next door.'

'Ee, ye kna ah cannet dee that.' The scratching grew frantic. 'And Rusty wants to say hello, an' all.'

Joe blinked angrily. 'Will ye not be told? Ah divven't want ye or that mangy dog. And keep yer voice doon.'

There was a laugh. 'He's not mangy, and ah won't be told. Anyway, ye're on me list. Ah have to monitor yus closely.'

The old man wrenched the door open and stepped outside. A teenage girl was standing there, dressed in a very baggy pink tracksuit. A white dog with rusty spots on its glossy coat stood at her heel. 'Go away,' Joe snarled.

The girl fingered the short dreadlocks of her recently dyed blonde hair. 'Like me hair?' she asked, laughingly. 'Me mate did it for wor. Ah babysat for her the other night, so she dyed it and put in the dreads.'

The old man grunted. 'And ye're still friends with her?'

'Why aye, it's purely belter, divven't ye think?'

'Ye look as if yus've just spent the night in a hedgeback.' The old man shook his head. 'Anyway, yus've seen us. Done yer monitoring. Ye can get off noo.' He opened the door and was about to go back inside when the dog slipped in before him. 'Hey, get oot,' Joe ordered angrily. The dog scampered down the passage and by the time the old man had reached it, the girl had also come in. 'Have ye no idea of privacy?' he snapped.

'Ah just want to see that ye're areet, man Mr O'Brien.'

'Just because ah'm old it doesn't mean ah'm totally useless, y'kna.' Blocking the way, Joe stared at the girl for a while, his stooped body rising angrily. 'Ah'm just aboot sick of . . .'

'Who's that?' asked Gemma, pointing at the face of the boy which appeared momentarily as the door to the sitting room opened.

Before Joe could turn, the door had closed and Sonny Gee had disappeared. 'What's it got to dee with ye?' he demanded. 'Here, take yer dog and sling yer hook.' With a snort, he shunted the animal to Gemma.

'Wasn't that Sonny Gee?' she asked.

Joe's eyes flashed irately. 'It's none o' your business, girl.'

'Ah look after him sometimes, but what's he deeing here?'

'Do ah poke me neb into your business, lass? Do ah? Yus're supposed to be a home help, so help me by pushing off.'

'Ye kna ah've got to dee yer fire and breakfast, man Mr O'Brien. It's me job.'

Joe inhaled deeply and was about to speak when he suddenly sighed. Grudgingly he let Gemma into the sitting room. The boy was kneeling on the settee. As soon as he saw the old man come in, he dropped down and, wrapping himself back in the cardigan, pretended to still be sleeping. 'Aye, well, ye can see the fire's lit so off yus gan,' Joe said to Gemma. 'And ye can tell them that ye went in to see the auld useless gadgie, and that he can be left alone withoot yus banging us in a home for another day longer.'

Gemma grew serious. 'Ah'm only here to help.'

'Ah can ask, y'kna. When ah need help. Ah can ask for it. And until ah dee ask for it . . .'

'Ha'way, man Mr O'Brien,' said Gemma, interrupting him gently. 'Look at this place.' Walking over the room, she prodded a piece of the dropped coal with a toe, rolling it through some of the charred paper. Crossing over to the hearth, she stooped to pick up a broken match, holding it up between finger and thumb. 'What were yus trying to dee, burn the place doon or light the fire?' She pointed the broken match at the black boots. 'Them boots is the only thing ye take any care of, and they're that auld . . .'

'There's nowt the matter with them boots.'

'They're dropping to bits, man Mr O'Brien. Ah wouldn't mind but ah'm blue in the face with telling ye that ah can get ye a pair just as good as these.'

'And ah'm blue in the face with telling yus that ye cannet get quality like that nooadays.'

'But they're practically new. Someone give them to Arthur, and they divven't fit him.'

'Ah'm not having nee cast-offs.'

Sighing good-naturedly, Gemma took off her tracksuit top, revealing a T-shirt and an advanced pregnancy. 'Aye, divven't listen to me then, Mr O'Brien. Ah mean, ah'm only here to help.'

'Ah divven't kna aboot me not being able to manage,' said Joe. 'Ye look as if ye're gonnae gan into labour any minute.'

Moving over to the table, she hung the tracksuit top over the back of the chair. 'Ah want to work as late as ah can, me, so that ah can have longer with the bairn before ah have to gan back to work.' The girl's features hardened with determination. 'Ah divven't want to be one o' them mams that cannet manage. Or divven't care. Ah want to be different.' She seemed to drift into a reverie. 'Ah want to be there for me little babby.'

The old man smiled bitterly to himself. 'It all comes to the same in the end.'

'What d'ye mean, Mr O'Brien?'

He did not reply.

Gemma shook her head and gently placed her hands on her bump. 'This one's gonnae be different. This one'll want for nowt.'

'Except a father.'

Gemma sighed sadly. 'He's got a one.'

Joe narrowed his eyes cruelly. 'Where is he then?'

She shook her head. 'Ee, but ye can be a nasty man, Mr O'Brien.' Reaching out a hand, she stroked the dog pensively for a while. Brightening, she pulled herself to her full height, the bump of the new life within her emphasised. 'Anyway, ah've got me dog here to help. Ye wouldn't believe what he can dee. He's more like a person. Ah swear doon he is.' She laughed to herself. Then sobering, wandered over to the fire. Catching the eye of the boy on the settee, who immediately began snoring exaggeratedly, she smiled. Then tutted. 'Ye cannet have it like that, Mr O'Brien.'

'Like what?' Joe replied tetchily.

'Ye'll need a fireguard.'

'Listen, lass, ah've lived with fires all me life, ah divven't need to start with guards and what have ye noo.'

Gemma only half concealed her smile. 'But with the bairn. Ah mean, if Sonny Gee's gonnae be stopping here, ye'll need a guard.'

On the settee, Sonny Gee stopped snoring.

'He's not stopping here,' said the old man. He blinked and then looked Gemma in the eye. 'Divven't . . . divven't tell neebody aboot him. If it gets round, ah kna it'll have been ye, Gemma lass.'

The girl screwed up her face thoughtfully. 'Why d'ye want to keep such a bonny lad secret?'

He shrugged. 'Ah'll dee what ah want to dee. Anyway, he's not stopping here. Ah had him for the night, and that's all. He's gannin' right back to where he came from.'

'But he's yer grandbairn.' There was a long pause in which the last spoken word seemed to resonate. 'He is, isn't he?' repeated Gemma. 'Yer grandbairn?'

Joe spoke softly. 'Who told ye that?'

'Neebody.'

'Audrey's been gossiping again, has she?'

'He stays with us sometimes. Sonny Gee does.' She blinked. 'He is, isn't he? He's yer grandbairn.'

Joe swatted the air and clenched his jaw. 'Ah've got nee grandbairns, me.'

Gemma smiled. 'Why, look at him. And look at yersel'. Ah mebbes haven't got many GCSEs but ah can still count two peas in a pod. He's the spit o' ye, man Mr O'Brien. He's your Mary's bairn, isn't he?'

Joe stared at her, his eyes suddenly exhausted, fault-lined with broken veins. 'Ah've telt ye. Ah've got nee grandbairns. He's nowt to us,' the old man said wearily. 'Just nowt.' He looked down to the settee at that moment, and met the boy's eye. For a few moments they held each other's glance, then fell away simultaneously.

The glass of the kitchen door danced as the old man closed it firmly behind himself. 'Ah'm putting the kettle on noo if that's areet with ye,' he called caustically.

'Areet, bonny lad,' said Gemma to the boy.

'Areet, bonny lass,' Sonny Gee shot back.

'What's this, still in bed?' she asked him. He shrugged in reply. 'Say hello to me dog, Sonny Gee,' she said brightly. The dog scampered round the front of the settee.

'Is yer dog called Sonny Gee an' all?'

'Na, he's called Rusty. Ye kna him, man. D'yus like him?'

Suspicion knitted the boy's brow. 'Why, d'yus want shot of him?'

'Na, but yus can stroke him if ye like.'

'What, and get me hand bit off?'

'Ye kna Rusty doesn't bite neebody. Ye usually like him.'

'Your boyfriend's in jail,' said the boy.

'Aye,' replied Gemma, quietly.

Sonny Gee's eyes widened. 'Did he really kill that gadgie?'

Gemma's eyes flashed. 'It was a accident. He didn't mean to dee it. He wouldn't hurt a fly.'

'He hurt that gadgie.'

'It was a accident.'

The boy paused thoughtfully. 'Ah want to kill someone, me. Ah want to burn him. That Macca.'

Turning from the boy, Gemma began cleaning up the mess on the floor. She moved with the awkward grace of advanced pregnancy. Coming to the blankets, she picked them up. They were wet.

'Have ye swallowed a football?' Sonny Gee demanded, interrupting her before she had time to speak.

'Na.'

He pointed at the girl's bump. 'What is it in there then, a balloon?'

'Na.'

'A geet big blown-up rubber johnny?'

'It's a babby, man Sonny Gee. Ah'm gonnae have a babby.'

The boy laughed. 'Ye preggers then?'

'Aye,' nodded Gemma. 'Ah'm preggers.' She smiled softly, gesturing at the sodden blankets. 'Did ye have an accident in the neet, pet?'

'Na,' he replied.

'Ah'll tell ye what, ah'll take the blankets and bring them back washed.'

Looking at the blankets through the corner of his eye, Sonny Gee ran an anxious finger over his bottom lip, exposing his teeth. 'How d'yus gan and get preggers then? D'ye lie doon somewhere in the nuddy with yer big lad? D'ye pull yer knickers doon in the nettle patch and sting yer bare bum?'

'Ye still here?' called Joe from the kitchen. 'Or am ah the only one ye have to pester on the row? There's a whole row of fires for yer to light. And some of them really do need help so divven't let me stop ye.'

'Am ah coming to stay with ye now, Gemma lass?' Sonny Gee asked.

'Ee na,' said Gemma. She patted her stomach. 'After the babby, ye can come. Ah tell ye what, ye can help wor with it.' She suddenly straightened up. 'Ee, it's just kicked us,' she exclaimed, stopping suddenly. 'The babby's just kicked wor.'

'Ah cannet stand babbies, me. They stink o' shite and cry all the time.'

Gemma smiled. 'But ye're nowt much more than a babby yersel'.'

'Frigg off,' began Sonny Gee angrily. 'Ah had that lad on Old Parsonage . . .'

'Ha'way, divven't gan deein' a one of yer radgie specials noo,' coaxed the girl.

'They dee yer heed in, divven't they?' he asked proudly.

'Aye,' laughed Gemma. 'So divven't dee it.'

The boy gestured over at the kitchen. 'Ah could easy dee his heed in.'

Leaning over, Gemma began tickling him. '*Ah'll* dee your heed in, bonny lad,' she said. Struggling playfully on the settee, they both dissolved into a laughter that only stopped when they became aware of the old man standing over them.

'Ye want to be more careful in your condition,' he said acidly.

They stared up at him, then he went back into the kitchen. Gemma turned to look at the clock on the sideboard. 'Ee aye, ah better be getting next door. Elsie'll be wondering where ah am.' She put her tracksuit top back on. 'We'll have to get a special sheet to put under yus at neet, Sonny Gee. Ye kna, like the one ye have when ye stop at mine? Ah'll bring it awer.'

'Ah'm not stopping here,' said the boy.

'Where ye gannin' then, bonny lad?' asked Gemma.

Sonny Gee shrugged. There was a shout of pain from the kitchen. 'That flamin' teapot's nee use,' they heard Joe say angrily.

'Are ye sure it's the teapot?' Gemma called. She winked at the boy. There was no reply. 'Ah'll tell ye what then, Mr O'Brien. Ah'll come back later, when ah've done the row.'

'Divven't bother,' Joe shouted.

'To dee breakfast.'

Joe tutted with irritation. 'Ah can make me own porridge.'

'And what aboot the bairn? Bairns divven't eat porridge.'

'What's it got to dee with ye?'

'Ah'll pop in at Ronny's. He's got them variety packs. Not that he's got any grandbairns. Eats them himself. But ah kna for a fact he's not so keen on the Coco Pops.' Gemma knelt down by the settee. 'What's yer favourite, bonny lad?'

'Eh?' Sonny Gee replied.

'What cereal d'ye like on a morning?'

The boy shook his head. 'What yus gannin' on aboot?'

Gemma straightened up. 'Oh aye, ah remember. Ye won't take a bowl, will ye?'

'Ah just have a packet o' crisps, me,' said Sonny Gee.

'Well, ah'll bring ye a few, eh.' She turned to the kitchen door again. 'Ah'll bring him some variety packs from Ronny.'

'What's he want them for? He's only stopping here for another five minutes,' said Joe, coming into the sitting room.

Gemma waved aside his question. 'Ronny won't mind.' She stopped to pick up the blankets, winking at Sonny Gee.

The girl had made it to the passage door before Joe called

out to her. 'Where d'yus think ye're gannin' with them blankets?'

She looked down at the rolled-up blankets. 'Oh, ah'm deein' a few things for Elsie down the laundrette, ah'll just hoy these in an' all.'

'No ye won't.'

'It's nee bother, Mr O'Brien.'

'Well, it's a bother to me.'

'Ah'll get them back to ye today. Ah'll bring them with the bairn's breakfast.'

'Hey, man lass.' Joe's voice rose angrily as he shuffled across the room. 'Will ye listen to wor? Ah can manage me own washing thank ye very much. Ye're supposed to light wor fires, not run wor flaming lives.' Reaching Gemma, he grabbed the blankets. His face twisted with incomprehension. 'They're all wet. What's gannin' on? Why are they all wet?'

Gemma looked down at the boy, and then up at the old man. 'Ee, ah'm sorry, Mr O'Brien, it was the dog. He's slavered all awer them. Must have smelt a cat or summink. Ye kna that stray cat that hangs aboot the cut.'

'Divven't talk codswallop.'

'Well, ah'll just hoy them in with the other things. Ah'll bring them back when they're done.'

'Ye will not.' For a moment they pulled the blankets back and forth, Joe's gnarled, massive hands clawed at them.

Letting go of the blankets, Gemma looked down at the hands. 'Ah wish ye'd gan back to the doctor's to get them seen to again, Mr O'Brien.'

Joe threw the blankets down angrily. 'They're areet, man.'

'Have yus not heard back aboot the money yet? Ee, ah've half a mind to gan doon to London mesel' to sort them politicians oot. It's shocking the way they're making yus all wait for yer compensation. It's just wrang. It's purely wrang . . .'

'For the last time, will ye mind yer own business?'

When Gemma had gone, neither the old man nor the boy moved for a long time. Then Joe turned to Sonny Gee. He came over and pushing past the boy, felt the settee. His face puckered rancorously. 'Ye've wet it reet through an' all.' With a sigh he picked up the blankets. 'Ah'll have to sluice them in the sink,' he said expressionlessly. 'And the cushions. Then they can dry in the yard.' His face darkened. 'If they divven't ah'll have to light another fire tonight. And bang gans another load o' coal.' He pursed his lips. 'Ah'll get ye summink to eat before ye gan.'

The boy's face flickered uncertainly. 'Am ah not staying here, like?'

'No ye're not.'

'Why?'

'What d'ye mean, why?'

'Why am ah not staying here?'

''Cos ye're not.'

'Belter,' the boy said. ''Cos ah divven't want to stay here. It's friggin' shite here.' There was a pause. 'Neeone else'll have wor,' Sonny Gee boasted. 'Ah dee all their heeds in.'

'Gan to different places a lot, do ye?' Joe asked.

'Aye,' said the boy, simply. 'Ah can dee your heed in an' all.'

Joe stared at Sonny Gee for a while and then turned from him. When he had filled the sink with water and put in the blankets, he reached into the little fridge and began to bring out its contents. A tub of margarine, a bottle of milk, a few eggs in a bowl and some rashers of bacon wrapped in greaseproof paper. The match he lit had snapped, and cradling the flame, he held it awkwardly over the hissing gas at the hob. After a few moments the margarine began to bubble in the frying pan. With a look of intense concentration, Joe separated the rashers of bacon, placing all three in the pan. There was a hiss of fat. The old man cursed. 'What are ye deein'?' he asked, turning to see the boy watching him. 'Gan and sit at the table.'

'Why?'

Fumbling with a fork, Joe was having difficulty in turning the rashers. 'What d'ye mean, why?' he said, preoccupied.

'Why dee ah have to gan and sit at the table?'

The fat spat again, and the old man reached out to lower the gas. 'Eh? Just dee it.' Taking an egg from the bowl, he broke it. It slopped out on to the floor, splashing over the linoleum. Clenching his teeth, Joe stared down helplessly at the spillage for a few moments, then broke another egg and continued cooking.

The plates danced on the tray as he brought it through to the sitting room. 'Take yours then,' said Joe. The boy reached for the tray. 'Not the whole tray, man. Just yours.'

'What ye gannin' on aboot?' Sonny Gee replied.

'Take yours.' Shaking his head peevishly, Joe stabbed one of the plates with a thick thumb, an action that caused him to wince with pain. 'That one. Take it. Take your plate.' Uneasily, the boy picked up the plate indicated. The old man sat in the armchair, his own plate on his lap. He sawed at his food awkwardly with knife and fork then pronged each bit with the fork. He ate slowly, and the plate kept sliding over his legs. 'Ye not hungry?' Joe asked the boy, when he had finished.

'Aye,' replied the boy. 'Gis a packet o' crisps. Them Monster Munches. Pickled-onion flavour.'

'That's nee good. Get a proper breakfast eaten.' Joe rose and brought a bag of sugar and put it on the table. Then he went back into the kitchen. 'Ah'm brewing up,' he called. 'D'yus want a cup? It's not made with them bags, mind.' There was no reply. 'No? Suit yersel' then.'

When the old man came back in with the tea, he noticed that the table was covered in white granules. Puzzled, he glanced over at Sonny Gee. The boy's lips were smeared with sugar. Joe followed the child's guilty glance to the fire grate. The empty bag was bouncing on the flames. 'Have ye eaten the sugar?' he asked, staggered. Over the thick aroma of fried bacon came the cloying smell of burning sugar. 'Ye've eaten the sugar and then hoyed the bag on the fireback.' The boy did not reply. The old man came over to the settee. 'And there's yer plate of bacon and egg untouched.' The old man was completely perplexed.

The boy jumped up. 'Ye stupid auld get,' he shouted. 'At least ah haven't got monster hands like ye.' He vaulted the settee, and ran to the table. 'Ah saw a video with ye in it,' he said. 'The monster snapped a gadgie in two. There was blood all awer.' He jutted his chin out and looked challengingly over at Joe. 'Ye were the monster, weren't ye, mista gadgie mista monster mista.'

Bending down, the old man picked up the plate. 'Why didn't ye eat what ah give ye?' he asked in puzzlement.

''Cos it's shite,' the boy replied.

Joe sighed with disbelief. 'Ye're an animal. Nowt but an animal.'

'Ah'm not stopping here with ye, monster hands.'

'Aye,' said Joe, quietly. 'Ye're not stopping here.' Picking up the cardigan, he put it on.

Dragging out two chairs from under the table, the old man placed them in the yard. He brought the blankets from the sink and laid them over the backs of the chairs. Heavy drops of water began to drip from the blankets and drum against the concrete of the yard.

'Ha'way,' said Joe when he had put on his boots, his coat and his cap, and picked up his walking stick.

He led the boy to the cut. The sun shone and the distant sky was a brilliant blue, flawless but for the scars of jet smoke. The air was fresh with gathering spring, and the beech hedge enclosing the row of old colliery cottages was a vibrant green. Joe undid the buttons on his coat.

The old man and the boy reached the bus stop. When the right service came, Joe boarded it, ushering Sonny Gee on in front of him. The bus turned the corner on which the church stood, and as it passed the open space of grassland and newly planted saplings of the old Watergate Colliery, the song of a skylark entered it through an open window. At the bottom of the hill, the vehicle passed through the shadow of the Dunston Rocket tower block, then crossed and recrossed the waters of the River Team.

Eventually the bus came to a stop beside a parade of shops, and the old man rose. 'Ah divven't live here,' said Sonny Gee.

'Ha'way,' replied Joe.

They walked down the parade of shops. Half of the premises were shuttered with heavy, corrugated-metal sheets. The only businesses open were the housing office, a credit union, a chemist and a Londis supermarket, whose front was covered with the bannered slogan: 'Open and up for it!' As they passed the closed-up units, Sonny Gee rattled the shutters. 'Divven't dee that,' said Joe. The boy looked at him, and then rattled another shutter. The old man did not respond, so the boy stopped for a moment to kick at the next shutter. Joe came over. 'Ye're a canny clever lad, ye,' said the old man, with a bitter irony.

'Where we gannin'?' the boy demanded.

They walked on. Threading a way between empty houses and empty areas still strewn with the rubble of the demolished housing, they passed a doctor's surgery. A group of people were standing outside the surgery, smoking. The boy stopped. 'Gis a tab,' he said to a man with an arm in a sling. 'Or ah'll break yer other arm for ye.'

'Ha'way,' growled Joe.

They came to a block of flats. Joe began climbing the stairs, but Sonny Gee lagged behind. After two flights, the old man paused for breath. His eyes narrowed angrily at the sudden shortness of his breath. Below him the slow steps of the child could be heard. 'Why yus taking me here?' Sonny Gee asked, reaching him at last. 'Audrey won't have wor. This is Audrey's place. But ah cannet stay there this time.' Struggling with his breath, the old man did not reply. 'What's the matter with ye?' the boy asked.

'Nowt,' spat out Joe, eventually.

'And yer hands are knackt an' all.'

The old man paused. 'Nivver ye mind. Ha'way up them stairs.'

'Ah'm telling ye, gadgie mista, that Audrey wifie cannet have wor . . .'

At the top, they walked along the walkway to the last door. Below them stretched Gateshead in all directions. Beyond the buildings, the River Team could be seen running through green derelict industrial sites, its silvery course glimmering where it guts into the Tyne. The gentle crown of Lobley Hill rose in the distance. After a brief hesitation, Joe rang a bell. A long drawn-out tune could be heard playing inside the flat. The door was opened smartly. 'Audrey . . .' began the old man before he realised that a little girl was standing there.

'She's on the toilet,' the child informed him. Her hair was long. She wore a serious look, and a pair of glasses tied round the back of her head with a rubber band.

'Is that the door, Terri-Leigh?' a voice called from within.

'Uhuh, Nana.'

'Who is it then, Terri?'

Terri-Leigh studied Joe closely. 'Who are ye, mista?'

'Terri-Leigh?' the voice called again. 'Divven't let him in if it's that bloody TV licence gadgie again. Tell him ah'm oot. Been called out to an emergency. Tell him we got rid of the telly.'

Terri-Leigh looked back dubiously at the immense television set which was clearly visible from the door, blaring at high volume. Then she skipped out past Joe, and stretching up on her tiptoes, looked down over the parapet of the walkway. 'There's nee telly van,' she called back into the flat.

'Find oot who he is then,' replied the voice. 'And how

many times do ah have to tell ye? Divven't tell folks ah'm on the netty, tell them ah'm powdering me nose.'

'Ye're not from the council, are yus?' The old man shook his head. 'Ye collecting for the catalogues?' He shook it again. The girl sighed heavily. 'Have ye come to take wor sofa away again?'

Joe shuffled awkwardly. Leaning behind, he pushed the boy forward. 'Ah've brought him, that's all.'

'Hello, Sonny Gee,' Terri-Leigh said. 'Ee, have ye come for yer holidays again?'

The old man had descended the stairs and was halfway across the car park when he heard the shouting. He stopped. A toddler wrestling with a huge unopened packet of crisps stared at him, pointing up at the flats that loomed above them. 'Audrey's shouting on ye,' said the toddler's elder sister, taking the packet of crisps and opening them. Joe stared at the brother and sister.

'Joe O'Brien, get yersel' up here now!' the voice called down, echoing loudly in the enclosed area.

Holding out the now opened packet of crisps, the toddler mumbled something. Joe could not make out what he said. 'He's asking if yus want a one,' the sister interpreted. 'A one of his crisps.'

'No. Ta,' replied Joe, confusedly.

Climbing his way back up to the flat, this time the old man had to rest for twice as long. His breathing was tight, and its wheezing echoed raspingly in the cold concrete spaces of the stairs. 'Ee, isn't that lift working yet?' Audrey asked, meeting the old man at her door.

Audrey was a woman pushing back the boundaries of late middle age. She was dressed in a voluminous pink towelling robe. Her nails were also coloured luminous pink. As were her plastic earrings that swung every time she spoke.

'Ah can manage a few stairs,' Joe growled in reply.

'Good morning to ye an' all,' she said, opening her robe slightly to pull it more firmly round her ample figure.

The flat was dominated by the blaring television. In the kitchen area of the open-plan room there was a breakfast bar and a tall pile of coloured towels stacked on top of a fridge. The walls were covered in framed pictures of children. 'Terri-Leigh,' said Audrey. 'Stick the kettle on, pet.'

'Ah'm not stopping,' said Joe.

'But ah haven't seen ye for ages, man,' said Audrey.

'Ah'm not stopping.'

'Ha'way, Joe. Have a cuppa. At least take your coat off.'

The old man walked a few paces towards the television set. Sonny Gee was already sitting on a large leather sofa with Terri-Leigh, his eyes following the pictures on the large screen. 'See him?' Sonny Gee was telling her. 'That gadgie mista? His telly doesn't even work.'

Terri-Leigh gasped. 'Nivver.'

'And he lights fires in his own bedsit.'

'Ye'll have a drop of tea then, Joe,' said Audrey.

'Ah've told ye, man Audrey, ah divven't want owt.'

'The kettle'll not be long.' Audrey went over to the breakfast bar. The old man followed her. 'What ye deeing here then, Joe?'

Joe nodded over at the sofa. 'Ye kna, man Audrey.'

'Kna what?'

Joe spoke in a quiet, but tense voice. 'Divven't flash them cow eyes at me. It must have been ye that told her to come to me. She wouldn't have the nerve without it.'

Audrey shrugged. 'What ye gannin' on aboot?'

'She dropped him on us, didn't she? Then did a runner. Nee matter now, but. He's here now.'

'What d'ye mean?'

Joe glanced round at the pictures of children then pointed at Sonny Gee. 'Ah thought ye'd take him, like.'

48

The earrings swung as Audrey shook her head. 'Did ye now?'

'Aye.'

'Well, think again.'

'Eh?'

Audrey sighed. 'Ah cannet, man. Not at the minute. In a couple of weeks mebbes. But ah'm full up with bairns. They're coming oot o' the windows, man. And the social's watching wor like a hawk.' Audrey called over to the girl on the sofa. 'Terri, where is everybody?'

Terri-Leigh stood up on the sofa and cleared her throat thoughtfully. She began as though reciting a poem she had learnt by heart: 'Elliot and Caitlin are at the swings. Hannah-Jade and Dolly are at Clare Macarten's. Jak's on a quadbike. So's Linzi and Skye. And Brosnan an' all.' Terri-Leigh paused for breath. 'Oh aye, Keegan's with Elliot and Caitlin.'

'Which one?' shot back Audrey.

'*She*-gan,' the girl replied.

The kettle boiled and Audrey poured the water into the teapot. 'So where's *He*-gan then?'

Terri-Leigh shrugged. 'But ah've just remembered. Britney's here an' all. Aunty Leeanne dropped her off last night.'

Audrey glanced over to the fridge. 'Did ye put her towel oot for wor?' Terri-Leigh nodded. 'Good lass.' Audrey turned back to Joe. 'So ah cannet manage him at the minute. Ye see how it is. Normally ah would love to, but with all me grandbairns here and the social . . .'

'Audrey, man,' Joe interrupted. 'Ah divven't want the whole story. If ye cannet have him, then send him back to his mam.' Audrey stared at the old man. 'Well, if it's like that,' said the old man after a pause. 'Ah'll just take him meself. Where does he live?'

'Bensham. Clareville Place. Number nine ah think. It's a bedsit. Just off Old Parsonage Road. But . . .'

'Ah'll find it.'

'Have a cup of char first.' Pouring out two mugs of tea, Audrey placed them on the breakfast bar. 'There ye gan, Joe.' She glanced significantly at him. 'Yus've nivver seen where they live, have ye?'

'Audrey man . . .'

'The bedsits. Yus've nivver seen them, have ye?' She paused briefly. A harshness crept into her voice. 'Mebbes if ye saw where that bonny lad's been stopping then ye'd get a little bit conscience stirring under that auld miner's hide of yours.' She broke off. Then turned to the sofa. 'Terri, ye didn't tell wor where little Keegan is.'

'Ah've telt ye, Nana,'

'No. The lad. *He*-gan.' Audrey glanced over at the towels again. Her eyes narrowed suspiciously. 'He's with Toni, isn't he? Little Keegan's with yer cousin Toni-Leigh, isn't he? Isn't he?' Reluctantly, Terri-Leigh nodded. 'If she's taken him through that car wash again. She has, hasn't she? Hell's teeth. The last time they came back like a pair o' drooned rats. Ha'way, take her towel. Ah want her in.' Audrey spoke sharply. 'Terri-Leigh, gan and stick Toni-Leigh's towel out.'

Getting up, Terri-Leigh went over to the fridge and flipped through the towels. 'Is Toni's the Celtic one?'

'Ye kna it is, man,' replied Audrey. 'Hold on a second, lass.' Audrey pursed her lips thoughtfully. 'Put oot the towel and then gan doon to the garage for her. Take Sonny Gee with ye an' all. Nee buts, the telly's not gonnae run away.' Audrey turned to Joe. 'Ah divven't kna what ah'd dee withoot them towels. It's the only way ah can keep track o' them.' She turned to consider the pile. 'Each bairn's got a one, ye see. When they come and stay, ah put it out on the fridge. When they're oot playing, and ah want them in, ah stick their towel awer the parapet on the walkway. Like a flag, y'kna.'

When the children had gone, Audrey took the two mugs of tea, and set them on a coffee table in front of the sofa. Turning down the volume of the television, she sat down. 'Now we can have a talk. 'Cos we need to talk, ye and me.' She spoke softly. Reluctantly, Joe came over and, gripping the arm of the sofa, gingerly lowered himself. Audrey watched him sympathetically. 'How are the hands, Joseph?'

He shook his head.

'Any word aboot when yus get yer compensation?'

'Ah'm not here for small talk, man Audrey.' There was a silence. Audrey reached out to her mug and drank from it. As she sipped she looked at the old man through the corner of her eye. Bringing out a purse from the deep pocket of her bathrobe, she clicked it open and took out a cigarette. 'He's a bonny lad,' she said at last.

'What's that got to dee with owt?'

'What d'ye mean?'

'Ah divven't want to get involved, man Audrey.'

'Yus divven't want to get involved? Ye're his granda, man Joe.'

'And that's another thing. Why'd yus gan roond telling everyone aboot it? If ah want to wash me own dirty laundry in public ah'll dee it for mesel'.'

'Hold yer horses,' said Audrey. 'Ah've nivver telt neebody nowt.'

'So who was it that told Gemma then?'

'People aren't daft, y'kna. They can work things oot for themselves. Just 'cos ye seem to have forgotten that Mary's yer daughter, doesn't mean everybody else has.' Audrey lit her cigarette and, drawing on it, expelled the smoke in great clouds from her mouth and nose. 'Oh, divven't get us wrong, ah kna about what your Mary's done to ye in the past, Joe, and ah'm not trying to say she hasn't done yer wrang but . . .'

'What d'ye kna aboot what she's done?' The old man sighed. A look of utter exhaustion greyed him. 'Ah've tried to forgive her, man Audrey. What she did. God knas how ah've tried. But ah just cannet put it behind wor.'

Audrey sighed. 'Look, man Joe, ah divven't kna the ins and

oots of what happened, but what ah dee kna is that it's got nowt to dee with him. The bonny lad. Ah mean, it was before he was even born, wasn't it? So what's it got to dee with him?' There was a silence. As she smoked, Audrey looked thoughtfully at the pictures on the wall. 'Ah love bairns, me,' she whispered. 'Oh, ah kna what ye think of me. And the way ah lead me life. But see for me, when it comes doon to it, ah divven't care what anyone thinks. All ah kna is that bairns come first. The Joe O'Brien ah once knew used to have a heart.'

'Oh, spare us, for pity's sake,' said the old man, beginning to rise.

Audrey rested a hand on his arm to restrain him gently. 'Ye cannet blame Sonny Gee for the past. He's yer grandbairn.' Audrey shook her head. 'Ah mean, he's your flesh and blood. Ye must think aboot him sometimes.'

The old man shook his head. 'Ah didn't even kna he existed until last neet.' Joe paused for a moment. 'He's nowt to us.'

'Nowt?'

'Nowt.'

Audrey paused. 'It's funny that, like.'

'What is?'

'Him being nowt to ye.'

'What's funny aboot that?'

'He might be nowt to ye, but ye are all he has.'

The old man stared at Audrey. 'What about his mam?'

'She's in a bad way, man. It's not her. Deep doon, she's areet. It's just the drugs. She cannet get off the drugs. And the men she takes up with. That Macca she's with now, he's the worst of the lot.' Audrey broke off. 'He uses Sonny Gee, ye kna.'

'Uses?'

'For his drugs,' said Audrey. The old man gaped blankly at her. 'They all dee it,' Audrey continued. 'Them drug dealers. Neebody bothers searching a bairn. And if they dee, what they gonnae do? Ye cannet prosecute a bairn. So they get them to carry them.'

Joe shook his head, disparagingly. 'Ye've been watching too much telly, man Audrey.'

A sadness softened Audrey's voice. 'Ah wish ah had. But it's the way things are nowadays. That's the only reason Macca doesn't make Mary send him away permanent. He uses him to carry his drugs.'

'If ye kna this,' said Joe, 'why divven't ye gan to the pollis?' Audrey laughed.

'Have ah said summink funny, like, man Audrey?'

Audrey continued to laugh for a few moments and then broke off abruptly. She sighed. 'Ye divven't gan to the pollis aboot Macca. If ye did, it would be the last thing ye did. He knas that. Everybody knas that. So he does what he likes, and we let him. Ee, but ye've been living up in Lobley Hill too long in yer nice pretty little cottage.'

'We've got wor own toe rags,' said Joe.

'Most bairns gan to the airport for a holiday. The bonny lad gans there to pick up a package. It breaks yer heart. Thank God it's only tac at the minute.'

'Tac?'

'Cannabis. Aye, he only deals tac at the moment. But what happens if he starts dealing in summink stronger?' Audrey broke off. She looked Joe coolly in the eye. 'Unless summink's done, ah'd be surprised if that bairn of yours lived to be ten.'

Abruptly, Joe thrust Audrey aside and pulled himself up. He walked across the room to the door. A harshness crabbed his features. 'Ah divven't want to kna. He's nowt to us. That's how it is. How it's got to be. He's just nowt.'

'He's got neeone else,' Audrey cried. 'Just ye. Think aboot it. Yus're everything to him.'

The old man stopped. It seemed for a moment that he was going to reply. His mouth opened, but then closed again. 'Just off Old Parsonage Road, ye say?'

Joe was just about to leave when Terri-Leigh burst in, followed by another girl, very similar to her except for her hair which was cut short. She even wore glasses tied by an identical rubber band. This second girl was pulling a bag-on-wheels from which a toddler's head protruded. With a shriek, Audrey ran over and scooped the toddler out. He was covered in mud. Audrey swore under her breath. 'Yus've had him in that River Team again, haven't ye, eh? Haven't ye?'

Terri-Leigh nodded. 'They were playing baby Moses.'

'God help wor, ah'll swing for ye, so ah will. Ye kna the rules. Ye divven't gan oot o' sight of yer towel.'

Toni-Leigh stared back. 'But ah wasn't.'

'Divven't ye lie to me, madam. The towel's hanging up from that parapet and the river's miles away.' Audrey shook her head disapprovingly. 'What did ye use for a basket this time?'

'A bread crate.'

Audrey juggled the little boy from shoulder to shoulder as she pulled on her cigarette. 'One o' these days this babby'll get taken by the current and flushed on to the Tyne. Ah can see it noo, we'll end up having to fish for him with a rod off Tynemouth pier. Are ye listening to me, young lassie? Ah won't have ye turning yer cousin into a fish.'

'But ah wasn't,' explained Toni-Leigh, breaking the silence that followed her grandmother's tirade.

'Eh?' demanded the exasperated Audrey.

'Ah wasn't oot o' sight of the towels.'

'Divven't try and back oot of it, yus'll only make it worse for yersel'. And ye were given that Celtic towel special, 'cos Hannah-Jade had the Toon Army one.' Audrey paused, and looked round the room. 'Where's Sonny Gee gone?'

'He's outside,' said Toni. 'And ah wasn't.'

'Wasn't what?'

'That towel. Ah could see it all the time.'

'But ye were doon at the river, ye said so yerself.'

'Aye.'

'So what ye got then, lass, a pair o' hawk's eyes? That river's reet the far side o' the parade and in the auld rope works.'

Toni-Leigh shook her head. 'Na,' she said. 'Ah've got this.' The short-haired girl reached into a pocket and brought out a telescope. It was an old nautical piece with the aura of an expensive heirloom.

Audrey was staggered. 'And where the hell d'yus get this from?'

Toni shrugged. 'Won it.'

'Won it?'

'In a game of hopscotch. Ah beat Alana Cooper twenty-five to twenty-four. So ah won it.'

'And where did Alana Cooper get it? She's a seven years auld schoolgirl not a friggin' antiques dealer. Ah won't have ye involved in nothing dodgy, Toni-Leigh. Where did Alana Cooper get that telescope?'

'She swapped it.'

'Swapped it?'

'Aye; for a hairband.'

'A hairband?'

'And a one o' them My Little Ponies. Except withoot the mane. That's why it got thrown in. It's all baldy but . . .'

'And who did she swap it with?'

'Charlotte Armstrong.'

'Charlotte Armstrong?'

'She got it from her Uncle Ginga.'

Audrey crossed her arm sternly. 'Did she indeed?'

'Aye; he didn't want it nee more.'

'Didn't want it?'

'Aye; he said that he'd lived half his life at sea with nowt but horrorizons, and the other half of it a mile under the groond with a shovel in his hand and a lamp on his heed like a one of them seven dwarfs. So between the devil and the deep blue sea, he said that there was nowt in the whole wide world worth seeing that ye couldn't see with yer own pair o' eyes.'

Audrey shook her head. 'Neemore. Neemore. Ah divven't kna where ye get it from lass, ah swear doon ah divven't. Gambling awer a game o' hopscotch. Ye'll either end up a Saint Dismus or a Dives; but ah divven't kna which. Anyway, ye'll take it straight back to Ginga. Straight back. D'ye hear?' Audrey paused to stare meditatively at her cigarette. 'Where'd Mr O'Brien go?'

'He's gone,' said Terri–Leigh. 'He left when we came in. Ah said hello, but he just blanked wor.'

As the old man walked back through the houses and past the doctor's surgery, outside of which a different group of smokers now stood huddled together, he seemed to be lost in thought. Then the parade of shops came into view, and he spotted Sonny Gee. Slowly he approached him. The boy was nonchalantly kicking a football of kebab and fish and chip papers against a metal shutter. But by the time Joe reached him, the football had disintegrated, and the child sat on the kerb disconsolately. 'Ah told ye,' he said when the old man stopped, pointing up at the flats.

'Eh?' said Joe, turning to see the green of the towel which still hung from the parapet like a flag.

'Told ye she wouldn't have us an' all. Neebody wants wor.'

'Where we gannin'?' the boy demanded.

'Ye'll see,' returned the old man.

They did not speak as the bus took them across Gateshead. The sun slid behind a cloud, and when it began to emerge again, great fingers of light fell like an open hand over the borough. For a while the immense beams continued to fan down. They pointed out the shrinking housing estates and burgeoning birch thickets of the former industrial workshops; they pointed out the old colliery lands above which skylarks rise like never-ending shaft lifts; and they pointed out the little River Team whose straightened channels dream of a meandering past of water mills and crystalline trout pools.

They got off the bus on Old Parsonage Road. Suspicion darted over the boy's features. 'Where we gannin'?' he demanded.

'Will someone be in?' Joe asked.

Sonny Gee did not reply. He looked at the old man, his eyes narrowing. 'Ah'll run off,' he said.

But the old man had laid a hand on the boy's arm. 'And ah'll grab ye,' he replied. The child looked at the hand and then up at Joe's face. For a moment he seemed to be searching for something there, then the old man began to walk, and as though cowed, the boy followed. 'And ah'm taking ye to the door,' added Joe, 'just so that there's no mistake this time.'

They walked along Old Parsonage Road. It was busy. Rabbinical scholars wandered up and down the pavements in pairs, along with a steady stream of women, both Jew and Gentile, who propelled pushchairs while pulling two or three older offspring behind them. Traffic bounced by, pulsing with the loud beat of stereos; every so often a car pulled up at the pavement and ejected a driver who ran out to pick up a newspaper or lottery ticket. On the bench outside the betting shop, a group of men sat hunched silently over the horse pages of a paper as though they were poring over the mysteries of the universe. As they walked, the boy hung his head, casting mistrustful glances at Joe's hands.

When they reached the end of Old Parsonage Road, Joe stopped. 'Where is it from here?' he asked.

'Neeone'll be in,' said Sonny Gee quickly.

'Is there not someone there what looks after ye when she's oot?'

The boy looked puzzled. 'Na.'

The old man paused for a moment, looking up and then down the road uncertainly. 'Show us the way from here then,' he said at last.

'Ah've told ye, gadgie mista. There's not gonnae be neeone there.'

Turning off Old Parsonage Road, Sonny Gee led Joe through a complicated maze of back alleys and carless streets. 'What d'yus take me for?' Joe said, stopping after about a quarter of an hour. 'This isn't the way.' He lifted his stick to tap the roots of an alder tree growing from a backyard wall. 'We've come past here already.'

Sonny Gee looked down. 'Ah've forgotten how to get there.'

'Divven't give us that, man.' There was a pause. 'Well, if ye won't take wor there, then we'll just gan back on Old Parsonage Road and ask. It's Clareville Place, isn't it?'

The old man set off. The boy followed him for a few yards, and then stopped. 'Gadgie mista,' he called. 'Ah'm not gannin' back there.'

Joe turned to him. 'What yus gannin' on aboot? It's where ye live, isn't it?'

Sonny Gee did not reply for a few moments, then he shook his head. 'Na. Ah live at the bird flats, me.'

Joe walked back to where the boy stood. 'The bird flats?'

The boy's face flickered dreamily. 'Aye, that's where ah'm gannin'.'

'What yus on aboot, bird flats? Ah thought Audrey said it was Clareville Place. Number nine?'

'Na, we've moved.'

The old man shook his head. A bitterness flickered on his face and then died, leaving him expressionless. 'Ye'd say owt but yer prayers, ye. Come on, ah'm taking ye hyem.'

At last they came to a street which was blocked off at one end with huge boulders to deter joyriders. It was strangely quiet, the hum of the town heard only softly like the roar of a distant crowd. They threaded a way between the boulders. It was Clareville Place. The terrace of huge houses was hidden from the trafficless street by unkempt gardens choked with thick groping tendrils and dark-leaved trees. Finding a faded number 9 on a pair of old sandstone gateposts, Joe passed between them. Slowly, the old man picked a way through the garden, walking down the long, intermittent path, which was paved with broken slabs of concrete, and negotiating the branches and unchecked growth of foliage. He passed a child's slide which lay forlornly on its side in the rank scrub, its bright colours already smothered in the dank green of ivy. The bustle of Old Parsonage Road seemed miles away. Nothing of it could be heard here.

It was a huge building. The front, north-facing and greened with moss, was dark and dingy as a neglected sepulchre. Rearing up from the overgrown garden, it was like an immense Victorian mausoleum. A run-down, crumbling mausoleum, holding the remains of those too long gone to be remembered by the living. Joe shivered involuntarily. The cemetery silence was broken by the alarm call of a blackbird.

'Which one?' he asked, nodding at the unlabelled bells which studded the wall beside the door.

The boy shrugged. 'None o' them work.' The old man stared at the bells blankly for a while. Rust stained the green stonework beneath them like dried blood. He was about to knock when the door was caught by a breeze and opened an inch. It was not locked. The boy squeezed in first. 'Ye can gan noo,' he said. There was a pleading tone in his voice. 'Ah'll just gan in meself. Ye get off, gadgie mista.'

'Na. Ah'm not having ye landing on me doorstep again. Nee chance. Ah'm handing ye over to someone.' The old man stepped over the threshold into the hall.

There was no carpet, only a few coloured shreds visible on nails which peppered the floorboards. Once a respectable residence, the house had been divided and subdivided into ever smaller units until whole families lived in the single rooms. 'What one's yours?' Joe's voice echoed slightly in the hollowed-out hall.

'Told ye,' replied the boy. 'Ah divven't live here nee more . . .' Sonny Gee's words died as he followed the old man across the hall. There was no door on the first bedsit. Peering inside, the old man could see that everything had been ripped out. Even the wallpaper had been shredded. Rats could be heard scurrying behind the chipped skirting boards. 'Neeone stops in that one,' the boy said. 'There was a bust. The pollises came.' The old man stumbled over a warped floorboard as he walked to the other door leading off from the hall. He knocked at it. There was no reply. He leant forward and felt the touch of a delicate fabric on his face. It was a spider's web. Looking up, he saw that the web stretched all the way down from the ceiling. Its silken strands were grimed with dust. Brushing the fibres from his face, he knocked again. 'See,' Sonny Gee said. 'Ah telt yus. Neeone's in. Why divven't ye just gan?'

A fly could be heard up the stairs. Having just woken up

from the winter, it droned its sleepy way down towards them. For a few moments it buzzed between them, and they watched it as though mesmerised. It flew perilously close to the strands of web Joe had brought down, then, all at once, found itself trapped. Buzzing frantically, it tried to tear itself free. From nowhere, a spider appeared. It paused for an instant, raising a leg as though to pluck one of the silken strings. Then it moved at sickening speed. There was a struggle, ended by the hypodermic of the spider's fangs.

'Who are ye?' a voice rang out clearly in the hall. The old man turned to see that a face was watching them suspiciously from the narrowly opened door. A fetid stench came through the gap. 'Ah said who the frigg are ye?'

The face was drained of all moisture, its features seemed to have shrunk on the bone. The old man flinched involuntarily. Trained on him suspiciously, the eyes seemed huge in the wizened face. 'The bairn,' Joe faltered.

'Eh?'

'Ah've brought him back.'

There was a pause. 'What yus gannin' on aboot?'

'The bairn's here.' Joe thrust Sonny Gee forward.

The huge eyes scrutinised the boy. 'What do ah want with him?'

'He lives here, doesn't he?'

'No. Ah'm Sean Macarten. He lives upstairs, doesn't he?'

'Ah nivver said it was here,' said the boy immediately.

Joe stared down at him, and then up at Sean. 'Well, ah'm sorry for disturbing ye,' he said uncertainly.

The old man and the boy had already mounted the first decade or so of stairs when Sean called out to them from his door. 'Got any spare change, mista?' he solicited. 'A fiver'd be belter . . . ah need a fiver for me next wrap . . . ha'way, man, gis a fiver . . . ah'll take him for ye, ah'll take him for ye for a fiver . . .' The buzz of the voice grew increasingly desperate as it followed them up the stairs. 'Thems up there divven't want him . . . but ah'll take him . . . ah tell ye what, ah'll have him for a fiver . . . cannet say fairer than that, can ah? For a fiver he can stay here long as he wants and ah'll not send him away . . .'

On the first floor Joe looked over at three doors facing them. A quiet, hopeless weeping could be heard from behind one of them. Sonny Gee shook his head, and they began mounting the stairs again. The higher they went, the more dishevelled things grew. The banister listed like a broken fence, and then stopped, leaving no guard over the increasing drop to the hall below. Resting for a moment, the old man leant against the wall, bringing down a lump of plaster. It fell through the stairwell, landing on the bottom with a distant sough. The stairs narrowed and grew steeper so that each step was an effort for the old man. The thud of his boots rang out slowly over his toiling breath. At last they reached the top. At the far end of this floor was another flight of about three or four stairs and a small landing terminating with a door. The boy stared at this door and then turned to Joe. His face was stricken with terror. 'Divven't make wor gan in there, gadgie mista. Divven't make us gan in there.'

The old man was puzzled. 'But where else is there for yus to gan?' he asked.

'Anywhere,' Sonny Gee said eagerly. Across the features of his face, a dreamy look contended with the fear. 'Ah'll gan to the bird flats. Ah'll be areet there. With the birds.'

Joe shook his head and walked up these last few stairs. A metal bucket with a mop stood on the little landing; and a wardrobe door stood propped against the wall. Negotiating these obstacles, the old man knocked at the door. In fright the boy dropped to a squatting position. 'Ah've brought him back,' the old man called out. A fit of coughing erupted from the other side of the door. Joe waited for it to subside. 'Ah said ah've brought him back.' He swallowed. 'Mary. Come out here and take yer bairn. Ah've brought yer lad back. Mary . . .'

The door was flung open. 'Well, what the fuck did yus want to gan and dee that for?'

In the silence that followed Joe stared at the man confronting him.

He was thickset. His hair, cropped brutally short, emphasised the bluntness of his head which a towering forehead dominated. The ears, nose and mouth seemed so strangely small as almost to be residual. Tattoos, faded to an indeterminate blue, could be seen spiralling round his bull-neck like the weals left by a hanging rope. In his fixed, unblinking gaze was something of the restless inscrutability of a strangulated man. Suddenly, the figure withdrew into the room. The old man looked back at the boy, whose body was tensed for flight. Then, steeling himself, Joe pushed his way inside.

It was an attic room and the ceiling sloped severely. Stalactites of mould hung down, and the walls glistened with smears of damp. The rough wooden floorboards were full of splinters; the cracked tiny single window was covered with newspaper. From the highest point of the ceiling, hanging over the bed like a head in a noose, dangled a shadeless bulb. 'Having a good neb aboot, auld fella?' the man demanded.

Joe turned to the figure who was now sprawled on the bed which stood in the middle of the room. 'Ah've brought the bairn.'

Finishing a cigarette, the man stubbed it out in the ashtray resting on his wide chest. 'Fuck off oot o' it, ye stupid auld bastard,' he said, and reaching out for a remote control, pointed it at the television, the only recent item in the whole room. The volume of the television quickly grew as he continued to aim the remote. There was a banging from the ceiling below. Ignoring this, he continued to raise the volume until it had reached its maximum. The banging intensified, heard above the blaring television only as a pulsating vibration. Shots were being fired on the screen, someone died with a lingering scream. Suddenly, the figure jumped from the bed.

The ashtray was sent flying, scattering its contents all over the floor. Falling to his knees the man pounded the floorboards with two huge fists. 'Any time ye,' he screamed. 'Any fucking time ye want ah'll come doon there and slash ye.' Getting up he bounded over to the door and threw it open. 'Ah'll come doon there and cut yer friggin' balls off,' he yelled down the stairs. The banging desisted. With a look of triumph, the figure padded back into the room and threw himself on the bed.

The television fell silent abruptly. Joe put down the plug which he had pulled from the socket on the wall. 'Ye must be Macca,' he said. For a few moments Macca stared at him open-mouthed. Then he quickly heaved himself into a sitting position. Standing up, he approached the old man menacingly. 'Ah've brought the bairn,' said Joe. 'He's ootside. The bairn what lives here.'

Macca continued to approach. The floorboards creaked under his weight. 'Ah divven't like people bursting in on wor,' he said quietly. 'In fact, neeone's ever been divvy enough to dee it.' He smiled savagely. 'Ye're lucky ah've just scored some tac, because if ah hadn't ah'd throw ye doon the stairs, heed first. After ah'd crushed it, that is.' Suddenly, he clapped his hands an inch from the old man's face. There was a great crash as his powerful hands collided, but the old man did not blink.

'He's outside,' said Joe. 'Yer bairn.'

'He's nee friggin' bairn o' mine,' countered Macca.

'Aye, well, ah've brought him back.'

'Well, what the fuck d'yus gan and dee that for? Ah've only just got rid o' the friggin' cunt.' Macca seemed to be studying the old man. His eyes were heavily drugged. 'D'ye want to score some tac?' he asked. 'Ha'way, ah'll roll ye a one. Only a fiver, mind.'

Macca went over to the window and, reaching up, pulled out a brick above it. He scooped a hand into the cavity and brought out a small brown object covered in shrink-wrap. 'Course, if ye want summink a bit stronger, ah could see aboot getting hold of it. Ah'm thinking aboot branching oot as it happens.'

Joe stared at the brown object. 'That's illegal.'

Macca's laughter filled the room. 'Be a divvel. It's only a fiver.'

'Is this where he lives then?' the old man asked uncertainly, looking at a cot pushed up against a wall.

Macca turned to Joe. ''Cos ah'm spaced, ah'll dee ye a favour; fuck off oot o' it, while ye can still walk.'

The old man tried to clear his throat. 'Ah asked ye if this is where he lives.'

Macca stepped over to Joe. 'Who the frigg are yus, any road?'

'Ah'm . . .' the old man seemed to think for a moment. 'Ah'm Mary's father.'

There was a pause. 'Well, stone me, ye've risen from the grave.'

'What d'ye mean by that?'

'The bitch telt me ye were deed.'

'Aye, well, ah've brought the bairn,' said Joe, retreating a few steps to the door.

'But ah divven't need him for a couple of weeks yet.'

The old man stopped. 'Where is she?' Macca had begun to roll a joint. 'Ah said where's Mary?'

'Oot.'

'Ah'll wait for her to come back then.' Joe walked over to the window. He stood there, leaning on his stick, the point of which was placed between his two heavy boots. Just then there was a rattle from the landing as the mop was knocked against the metal bucket. The old man looked over to see Sonny Gee emerge at the door.

When Macca had finished rolling his joint, he looked up. His eyes widened and narrowed erratically. 'Ye still here?'

'Ah'll stop until Mary gets back.'

'Ye're beginning to dee me heed in, ye. Ye're as bad as that lad.' Macca fiddled with the joint like a craftsman. A discoloured, thickly coated tongue flicked out to stick the paper down. 'Ha'way, auld fella. Ye can have this for a fiver.'

The boy spoke quietly. 'He's cheating ye, gadgie mista.'

Macca looked up. 'The friggin' bastard's back,' he growled.

Sonny Gee stood his ground. 'Aye. He wants one joint for a fiver, but yus can get a whole wrap for that doon Old Parsonage Road.'

Macca took a pace over to the door, his forehead lowering. 'Ye friggin' little bastard. Ah thought ye'd frigged off to that Audrey's or somewhere.' The boy did not reply. 'Hey, ah'm talking to ye.' Macca laughed. 'Neeone want ye again? Ah heard even yer dad didn't want ye.' Sonny Gee looked down. Reaching up to the window, Macca replaced the block of cannabis in the hole and put back the brick. 'How is yer dad, bonny lad?' Still looking down, the boy's knuckles whitened as he clenched his fists. 'The last thing ah heard he was eating from a bin. What's the matter, bonny lad, didn't ye kna yer dad's a dosser?'

'He isn't.' The reply was hissed.

Macca smiled. 'Ah saw him yesterday, stinking o' piss and puke. He was drinking from a toilet and eating a dogshite sandwich.'

Before Macca had time to protect himself, the boy had darted across the room and thrown himself head first at him. Winded temporarily, Macca doubled up. The joint fell to the ground.

A fierce hatred burned in the boy's eyes: 'It's not my dad. It's yours. He eats crap. Liar, liar, yer cock's on fire,' Sonny Gee chanted. 'Yer dada's in the dustbin eating bread and shite.'

'Ah'm gonnae dee ye,' Macca said quietly as he straightened up and caught his breath. 'This time ah'm gonnae dee ye good and proper.'

Evading a powerful but clumsy grab, the boy jumped on to

the bed. 'It's ye what eats dogshite, and it's ye what lives in a toilet!' he screamed.

As Macca lunged on to the bed, it collapsed beneath his weight. He fell heavily. Sonny Gee darted in at him quickly and kicked him three times in the head before jumping free. Stunned, Macca turned over. He bellowed as he groped his way off the collapsed bed. Rolling on to the floor, Macca stared at the boy, and for a moment only his hand moved, tugging at his neck as though trying to loosen a rope. Then he was on his feet again. The floorboards reverberated as he charged. The boy tried to dodge him, but there was nowhere left for him to go, and finally he was cornered behind the cot. 'That's right,' Macca laughed, approaching menacingly, 'hide behind yer cell. 'Cos ah'm gonnae stitch ye up, and then stick ye in solitary confinement until ye gan mentals.'

With a musteline body swerve, the boy just managed to escape across the room, but Macca rushed after him. The heavy man was about to take him when he suddenly found his path checked. Joe had stepped out in front of him, and the two of them clashed. The old man staggered with the impact. Macca looked at him bemusedly. 'Are ye taking the piss or what?' The old man did not reply. 'Ah mean, ah could break yer neck with one chop.'

'Could ye?' replied Joe, regaining his balance. Gripping his walking stick, he raised it.

Macca was utterly baffled. 'Course ah could,' he said, taking a step towards him.

The old man held his ground. 'Ye sure aboot that?'

'Why aye.'

'Well, have a gan then.' There was a pause. Macca watched him closely. Just then, Sonny Gee slowly began to approach Macca. 'Get oot,' said the old man softly. The boy did not respond. 'Ah told ye to gan!' Joe's shout reverberated about the room. The boy stared at him bewilderedly and then ran to the door.

Macca and Joe continued to gaze at each other. Suddenly Macca grunted, and going back over to the bed, he lifted it back on to its legs. It sagged heavily as he dropped himself on to it. The springs groaned. 'Ah'm gonnae find oot where ye live,' Macca said slowly. 'And then, ah'm gonnae pay yus a visit.' Fumbling for matches, he lit the huge joint. The old man watched him. 'Ah've told ye, piss off. Ye can leave that little bastard to me, he'll come back, he always does, there's fuck all for him to gan, and when he does come back, ah'll settle him. And ah'll settle with ye an' all, one o' these days.' Still the old man would not move. 'Will ye fuck off oot of it?'

Joe seemed calm. 'The thing is,' he said, 'ah didn't bring him back. The bairn. Ah only dropped in to pick up his things.'

'Things?' Macca laughed. He scrutinised Joe for a few moments then gestured at a wardrobe. 'Help yersel'.'

The old man walked across the room. The door to the wardrobe was hanging off its hinge. He pulled it aside and it fell off, crashing to the ground. Joe peered inside the wardrobe; there was nothing there but a few shapeless, crumpled, frayed, unidentifiable garments. On the floor of the wardrobe was a washed-out, pilled, little orange fleece. Stooping heavily, the old man picked it up. He turned to where Sonny Gee was standing at the door, but he was not there any more. The child's running footsteps could be heard bounding down the stairs. Then there was silence. 'Aye,' laughed Macca. 'She keeps a canny good house, your lass.' The old man gazed at the fleece for a few more moments and then dropped it back in the wardrobe. He walked across the room. 'Divven't take him too far, mind,' said Macca, his voice suddenly serious. 'Ah'll be wanting him soon. There's a little bit business he needs to see to.'

Joe left the room, and slowly descended the stairs. The weeping on the first floor had stopped, replaced by a breathless sighing. As he came down the last flight of stairs, he saw the boy sitting on the doorstep to the bedsits. The old man paused to stare at him for a while and then carried on. 'Ha'way,' he said, coming up behind Sonny Gee.

Sonny Gee stood up. 'Am ah gannin' with ye, gadgie mista? Are ye having wor?'

5

The old man walked down the path, his walking stick tapping against the broken concrete slabs. He stopped at the forlorn little slide abandoned in the rank herbage, and turned. 'Ha'way,' he repeated. The boy waited until Joe had reached the end of the garden, and then getting up, ran to him.

'Where we gannin'?' Sonny Gee asked as he followed the old man back down Old Parsonage Road. They waited at the bus stop. The service came quickly and they climbed on board. The boy studied the old man's face carefully. 'Where am ah . . .' he began, but broke off. There was a look of admiration in his eye. 'Ye're geet hard, ye,' he said.

Joe turned to him. 'Divven't talk daft,' he snapped.

The boy clenched his jaw. 'Where am ah gannin' now?' he demanded.

The bus laboured as it began the long climb up Lobley Hill. It passed the forest park of the old Watergate Colliery and the old man stared through the window at the saplings growing on its rising mounds where the coal spoils had once been heaped. Turning at the church corner, the bus slowed for its stop. 'Am ah stopping at yours?' the boy asked as they walked to the cut. 'In that small hoose. Am ah stopping at yours? If ah dee, can ah light the fire?'

Coming out of the cut, they walked down the row of cottages. In the light breeze, washing fluttered on the lines, white sheets and towels frayed at the edges through long usage and an old shirt that filled and bounced flimsily like an ailing ghost.

Joe stopped at his front gate, and gazed down at the cottage.

A bulging black bin liner had been left at his door. He knotted his brow and walked down the path. With irritation, he picked up the bin liner. Inside was a selection of children's clothes. 'What the flaming heck?' he said in annoyance.

He went inside the house and dropped the bin liner on the table. Panting with the exertion of lugging the clothes, he stared through the window into the yard and waited for his breathing to ease. Then suddenly he strode through to the kitchen and yanking open the back door angrily, went out. Two carrier bags had been left there. The old man rummaged inside the bags. There were games, jigsaw puzzles, comics and a red cowboy hat. 'That Gemma, ah'll swing for her,' he hissed to himself, bringing the bags into the house. 'They'll all know now.'

When Joe came through to the sitting room, the boy was sitting on the settee. 'Am ah staying with ye then, gadgie mista?'

Joe stared at him without replying. 'It's way past dinner time,' he said. 'Ah divven't bother much with it meself, but ah'll get ye summink. And this time yus'll eat it properly.'

'So ah am stopping here then?'

In the kitchen, the old man opened his cupboard. There were three slices of bread left, and a tin of baked beans. His fingers slid painfully over the shiny surface of the can as he struggled to open it. He was able to light the gas hob on the third match. As he cooked the food, his eye was caught by the shining patch on the linoleum, where he had dropped the egg earlier in the day. The beans began to boil. He had forgotten to toast the bread. He hesitated for a moment, and then, putting the slices of bread on a plate, and covering them with the beans, he brought it through to the sitting room. 'Sit at the table. And drink that an' all,' he said, placing a mug of water beside the plate. Getting up, Sonny Gee came to the table. 'Well, sit doon then, get it while it's hot.' The boy continued to stand at the table. 'Ha'way, lad,'

'How can ah?' replied the boy.

'What d'ye mean?'

'Them chairs, they're ootside.'

Joe blinked tetchily. His voice was harsh. 'Well, gan and bring a one in then.'

Bringing a chair back in, the boy sat down, and then stared blankly at the plate. 'It's beans on bread,' said the old man irritably. 'Have ye nivver seen that before?' Sonny Gee reached a hand out. 'Na,' snapped Joe. 'Use the cutlery provided.' After a few moments, once again the child reached a hand out. Joe looked narrowly at him. 'Divven't ye even kna how to eat beans on toast?'

'Course ah dee,' the boy retorted.

'Well, let's see ye then.'

'But it's not beans on toast. It's beans on bread. Ye said so yerself.'

The clock ticked as time passed. The food cooled. 'Ye're not gannin' anywhere until ye eat what's been put in front of you.' The old man stood above the boy, watching him.

'It's cold,' Sonny Gee said at last.

'It wasn't when ye got it.'

'But it is now.'

Joe frowned. 'So? Some folks eat beans cold.'

The boy shook his head. 'They divven't.'

'Yes they dee.'

'Divven't.'

'They dee.'

'How d'ye kna, gadgie mista?'

'Don't call us that.'

Sonny Gee turned his huge blue eyes on the old man. 'What dee ah call ye then?' There was a pause. 'Am ah stopping here then?' said the boy.

'Ye're gannin' neewhere until ye've eaten yer dinner.'

'Ah divven't want to stop here any road, me,' Sonny Gee mumbled. 'It's shite . . .'

72

'Will ye just shut up?'

The silence lengthened between them. Neither of them moved. The boy stared belligerently at the plate in front of him. The old man stared without focus at the window. After a while, Joe eased himself into a sitting position on the arm of his armchair, and stooping down, began to take off his boots. He gazed at them, his eyes narrowing as they studied the leather.

'Cooey!' A loud voice shattered the heavy silence. Coming through an opened letter box, the woman's voice reverberated down the passage. 'It's me!' A loud rapping of knuckle on wood followed.

'Gadgie mista,' said the boy when the old man made no sign of moving. 'There's somebody come.' Joe kept still. 'Didn't yus hear? There's a wifie hammering at yer door, gadgie mista.' With a terse gesture, the old man quietened him, then crept across the room.

'Joe!' shouted the voice at the door.

'It's that Audrey wifie,' Sonny Gee said.

'Shut up,' Joe hissed.

'She's at your door, man,'

'Ah kna she is.'

'Well, why divven't ye let her in?'

'Because ah divven't want to.'

Opening the door, the old man stared down the passage. A pair of eyes could be seen peering through the letter box. They moved from side to side as they scrutinised the darkened passage. Slipping back into the sitting room, the old man closed the door.

'Ah kna ye're in there!' yelled Audrey.

There was another volley against the door. Joe waited in the silence that followed, but there was no more knocking. He came back to the table. 'Ye divven't like people, ye, do yus?' Sonny Gee asked. The old man did not reply. A minute passed, then a scrambling could be heard from the backyard. Joe went to the window. Audrey was straddling the low wall that separated the old man's yard from his next-door neighbour. She was dressed in a short imitation-leather skirt and matching jacket, zipped low to reveal a deep cleavage. Her legs kicked out stiffly as she tried to hoist them over the wall; her hair, dyed with peroxide, full-bodied and piled high under the duress of spray, shook as a single mass. Swaying uncertainly for a few moments as though riding a bucking pony, she then disappeared from view. When Joe opened the back door, she was picking herself up from the ground.

'Ye've laddered me stockings,' she said accusingly.

'Me?' returned the old man.

'Aye.' She lifted a hand to pat her hair gingerly. 'And ye've knackt me Dusty Springfield cut. If ye'd been like any other normal person ye would have let us through the front door so ah didn't have to bother Elsie to let us through hers.'

'And if ye'd been like any other normal person then ye would have gone away when neebody answered, and not bother folk who divven't want to be bothered.'

'But ah knew ye were in.'

'How did ye?'

'Because ah saw yer walking stick in the hall.' There was a pause. 'Ye gonnae ask wor in then, Joe?' The old man shook his head. Audrey's high heels clattered over the yard as she went to the window. Peering in, she smiled. 'Ah thought ye were taking him back to the bedsit?' she asked. Joe did not reply. Coming over to the blankets draped over the single chair, Audrey picked them up. 'These are nee good. Ha'way, let us in. Ah've got some proper bedding for ye oot the front.'

'Bedding?'

'Why aye.'

'What ye gannin' on aboot bedding for?'

'Gemma popped roond. Did ye get that stuff she left? Ah thought ye might need some fresh bedding an' all. Ah've got a special sheet . . .' she lowered her voice. 'For any little accidents. Ye kna, the right bedding . . .'

'What yus gannin' on aboot bedding for?'

'For the bairn, man. Since he'll be staying with ye.'

Joe narrowed his eyes. 'He's not staying.'

'But he's in there, ah can see him.' Audrey rapped the window and waved. 'Areet, bonny lad,' she called. She came over to the old man. 'Ah knew ye wouldn't be able to leave him there.'

'It doesn't mean he's staying here.'

'Where else can he gan?'

The old man shrugged.

Audrey smiled. 'Ah knew once ye'd seen that bedsit, ye wouldn't be able to leave him there. So ye've got a conscience in there somewhere, after all.'

'Will ye listen. It doesn't mean he's stopping here.'

Suddenly, from over the tall wall at the bottom of the yard, a bell sounded, after a few moments a child's voice could be heard. The voice was joined by others, until the sound of children playing soared over the wall. Audrey and Joe looked over. 'Ah love to hear the bairns at playtime,' Audrey said. 'And Holy Family's a lovely school.' They listened for a while to the children, the notes of their play rising and falling like music.

'A few days, man Audrey. Ye've got a few days to get things sorted.'

'Me?'

Joe nodded solemnly. 'He can stay here for a couple of days, but that's all. After that, he's away. Ah'll look after him for a few days, but then ah've washed me hands of him.'

Nodding, Audrey smiled. 'Ha'way then, let's get that bedding. And ah'm clamming for a cup o' tea.' She stopped as she passed the old man, leant up and kissed him on the cheek. 'Thanks,' she said.

'Three days,' grimaced Joe, swiping Audrey away.

'Them bedsits,' said Audrey. 'They're nee place for a bairn. Specially not for yer grandbairn.'

'Three days,' repeated Joe.

When they went into the sitting room, the boy was on the settee. His plate was empty; his hands and face were smeared with tomato sauce from the beans. 'Ee, what's being gannin' on here, Sonny Gee lad?' Audrey asked.

'Did ye use yer hands?' the old man asked, quietly.

'Are ye still not eating proper, bonny lad?' Audrey asked. She turned to Joe. 'Sonny Gee's got a little problem with eating, haven't ye?'

'Have ah fuck,' responded the boy.

'Hey, ye,' said Joe.

'Oh, it doesn't matter,' said Audrey. 'We'll soon get him cleaned up.' Before the old man could tell him off, she whisked him through to the kitchen. 'Have ye got a flannel, Joe? A tea towel?' Looking about quickly, Audrey brought out a handkerchief from her ample cleavage. She held it under the tap.

'Mings,' said Sonny Gee.

'A bit of perfume, that's all, bonny lad. Ladies have to smell of perfume.'

'Some lady, ye,' called the old man gruffly. 'And bring him in here, ah want to talk to him aboot his dinner.'

'What's happened to that cup o' tea?' Audrey asked as she swept Sonny Gee back into the sitting room. 'Ee, look at all them,' she declared, pouncing on the carrier bags. She brought out the games and puzzles. 'Ee, look, the Lone Ranger.' Scooping up the cowboy hat she placed it on the boy's head. Sonny Gee swiped it off. Audrey opened up the black bin liner. 'People are good, aren't they?' The old man did not reply. 'Ah mean, giving him all these things.'

Joe shook his head. 'Ah've nee room for anything here, they'll have to gan back.'

Audrey delved into the bin liner, bringing out the children's clothes and putting them on the table. 'We'll soon find yus summink in here, bonny lad. But ha'way ootside first and give us a hand with the bedding.' They came back into the room staggering under the weight of two huge boxes. 'Ah had to get a taxi here, y'kna,' Audrey said. 'And it was a bugger getting them boxes doon that cut. Ah had to plead with the driver to get him to help wor. Still, it'll be worth it to see him all settled. Ah've even looked oot a towel for him awer at our place for when he comes for his tea an' that . . .'

'Audrey man.' Joe's voice reverberated about the room. Audrey waited for him to speak, but he said nothing more. Going over to the armchair, he lowered himself into it and sat there staring blankly at the cold grate, filled with the ashes of the morning's fire.

'Now then, bonny lad,' began Audrey again, sorting through the clothes. 'What ye gonnae wear today?'

'Am ah stopping here?' replied Sonny Gee.

'Aye.'

'But he doesn't want wor here,' he said, pointing at the old man.

'He does,' answered Audrey. 'Divven't ye, Joe?'

Joe did not reply.

'See,' said the boy, triumphantly.

'He does, pet.'

'He doesn't, 'cos he doesn't like wor. He doesn't like ye either.'

Audrey laughed. 'Aye, he can be like a bear with a sore heed,' she dropped her voice. 'But he's harmless really. He wouldn't hurt a fly.'

The boy shook his head vehemently. 'Aye, he would. He was gonnae have a battle with Macca, but Macca chickened oot. Macca was flapped of him.' Sonny Gee rolled his eyes with appreciation. 'Macca chickened oot.'

'Will ye stop with that nonsense,' said Joe tersely.

Audrey delved in the bags. 'So what ye gonnae wear then, bonny lad?'

'This,' he replied.

77

'Eh?'

'Me strip.'

'But it's dirty, pet. Ye've had it on all day. Ha'way, let's put summink else on. Look at all these lovely clothes here.' Audrey held up a sweatshirt, but Sonny Gee looked away. She brought it to him and he pushed it away. Kneeling in front of him, she lowered her voice. 'Ah was talking to Gemma. Ye like her, divven't ye?'

'She's got a bun in the oven.'

Audrey smiled. 'Aye, there's another one on the way. But ye like Gemma, divven't ye, Sonny Gee?' Sonny Gee nodded. 'Well Gemma told us all aboot yer little accident.' She waited a moment for the information to sink in. 'So let's pop yus oot o' yer little strip and get summink clean on.'

The boy watched her as she dipped her hand back into the bag and brought out a top. Coming back to him, she took hold of his shirt. Then, when she began to pull it up, he knocked her hand away. 'Ee,' gasped Audrey.

Joe stirred in his seat. 'What d'yus dee that for?' he demanded.

'It's areet,' replied Audrey, 'ah caught him with a nail.' She tutted at herself. 'Ah divven't kna for how long ah've been meaning to get a emmery board on it.' She looked down at the large, pink, false nail. Her earrings bounced as she winked at the boy. 'Ah'll be more careful, hinny,' But once again, as soon as she began lifting his shirt, the boy knocked her hand away, with even more force this time. 'But bonny lad, divven't ye want a nice new top?'

'Na,' he shot back. 'Ah divven't want owt, me.'

Audrey narrowed her eyes in confusion. 'Come on, bonny lad,' she said softly.

'Fuck off, big titties!'

'Hey, ye,' called Joe, getting up.

Sonny Gee took a step towards him. 'And ye, gadgie mista.' The old man and the boy stood there in confrontation, and despite the difference in age and the texture of their skin, the same determination shaped their jaws. In those few moments of squaring up, Audrey had come between them and taken hold of the boy's shirt. 'There's nowt to be frightened of, pet. Here, look, ah've another lovely little Toon Army top for yus to wear. This one's newer an' all.' Before the boy could swat her away, she had lifted the shirt up and was pulling it over his head. Sonny Gee writhed for a few moments like a netted fish, but then as the shirt was lifted off, he stopped struggling. He looked down at his navel. A sash of livid scars hung across his stomach. 'Ee, pet,' whispered Audrey. 'What's been gannin' on there?' Lifting his arms to cover the scars, the boy shrugged. Reaching out for the top Audrey held, he put it on. 'Has someone been stubbing oot tabs on ye or summink?' she asked.

Ignoring the question, the boy went over to the rest of the clothes and began rifling through. With a look at Joe, Audrey followed Sonny Gee. 'Ah'm glad we got ye oot o' there, bonny lad. It looks like it was just in time.'

The boy looked at her. 'Ah divven't want to gan back there again, Audrey. Macca . . . he . . . he . . .' Sonny Gee bowed his head. 'It's friggin' shite there.' The boy's voice was quiet. Audrey reached out to him, and stroked his head. 'Can ah not stop with ye?' he asked.

'There's nee room at the minute, pet,'

The boy lifted his head, and looked at Joe. 'Will he let wor stop here? That gadgie mista? Will he let wor stop here for a bit?'

Audrey looked over at Joe too. 'Ah divven't kna, pet, ah divven't kna.'

The old man did not move for a while, then shuffled to the table where he sat with his back to them.

Sitting him on the settee, Audrey began peeling off the boy's socks. 'What's this?' she asked, feeling a lump in the empty sock. Upending it, a lighter fell out. With an anxious glance over her shoulder at the old man, Audrey snatched up the lighter. She shook her head sternly at the boy.

'Ah was looking after it for me mam,' he said.

'Aye, well. Let's leave it there.' Reaching up, she placed the lighter on the mantelpiece beside the miner's lamp. 'Ha'way, put these lovely clean socks on now. There's a nice pair of troosers and some flashy trainers as well. Then we'll get that bedding sorted.' She turned to Joe. 'Is he on the settee again toneet?' The old man made no answer. 'Is the bairn sleeping on here again?'

'Na,' said Joe tetchily. 'Since the queen's not coming for her supper tonight, ah thought he could have the master bedroom with the en suite bathroom.' Audrey laughed as she made up the settee, fitting an oil sheet under the rest of the bedding. 'Divven't be bothering too much with that,' he called over. 'A shake-me-doon'll dee. It's just for a few days, y'kna.'

'Might as well have it nice,' she said, folding the last corner of the sheet around the lip of a duvet. She patted the makeshift bed. 'Ee, ye'll be snug as a bug in a rug.' Picking up the cowboy hat, she put it on the boy's head. Once more Sonny Gee knocked it off. 'Divven't ye like the hat, bonny lad?' Audrey asked. 'Ah thought all bairns loved a cooboy hat.'

Sonny Gee glanced at the hat through the corner of his eye. 'Thems is for puffs,' he said.

'Well, ah've got to be gannin',' she said. 'They'll be wanting their teas soon.' She came over to Joe, and lowered her voice: 'Ye did a good thing,' she said, 'taking the bonny lad in.' As Audrey left, the door was slammed behind her.

The old man slowly lowered himself into the armchair. 'Are ye really not scared of Macca?' Sonny Gee asked him from the settee.

The old man tutted in irritation.

The boy's eyes widened slightly as he studied Joe. 'But yer hands are knackt, and sometimes yus cannet even breathe.'

Sonny Gee exhaled in wonder. 'Straight up? Are yus not flapped of him?'

'Why should ah be scared o' him?' Joe replied tersely.

There was a long pause. When he spoke, Sonny Gee's voice was less sure of itself than usual. 'Am ah stopping here with ye then?'

'Look,' replied the old man quietly, 'ye just sit there and shut up.'

'Why?'

''Cos ah have to work oot what to dee with ye, that's why.'

'So am ah stopping with ye?'

The old man sighed. 'Just for a few days.'

The hours of the afternoon passed in silence except for the constant ticking of the clock, but even that seemed to merge into the general stillness. The quiet weighed as heavy as the boots that stood on the hearthstone. At the end of the school day, the voices of the children drifted over the wall again, and for a while the room seemed to take on some life, but after a little time the children drifted home and the hush descended once more. Sitting in the armchair, the old man fell into a shallow sleep from which he woke fitfully a number of times before succumbing to a deeper slumber. Once, he seemed to wake abruptly, and pursing his lips, whistled two or three notes, but when Sonny Gee looked over, Joe had fallen back into his slumbers. He continued to whistle hesitantly for a while in his sleep, but gradually the music of the notes faded and were lost in the tuneless rhythms of breathing. The boy watched him sleeping for a while and then got up. Stealthily he stepped over to the mantelpiece, and reaching up, took the lighter Audrey had left there. Sitting back down, he flicked it a number of times, staring closely at the flame, and having fed its fire on imaginary places, watched the conflagration that would have ensued. 'Macca,' he whispered to himself, as a hand mimed an explosion of fire. 'Macca.' A grim look came into his face, and for a long time he sat there motionlessly, apparently lost in thought. At last he moved, and hiding the lighter down his sock, bent forward to stroke its hidden shape.

Some time later Sonny Gee picked up the cowboy hat and idly pulled at the white braid which ran along its brim as he looked about the room. He tried the hat on a number of times, eventually leaving it on his head. Then he fell to watching the old man closely. He stared at him, as though mesmerised. Getting up, he crept over to the armchair and slowly reached out to the hands which rested on Joe's chest. He was just about to touch one of the fingers when the old man suddenly stirred. The boy started in shock and backed away. He studied Joe closely, but the old man did not stir again. On his tiptoes, Sonny Gee stole through to the kitchen.

He searched through the fridge first, and bringing out a half-full bottle of milk, gulped it down. Realising that he had almost emptied it, he filled it at the tap and put it back in the fridge. Then he opened the margarine tub and poked it with an exploratory finger, gingerly tasting what he had scooped out. Hoisting himself on top of the Formica surface, he walked along it to the cupboard. He opened the door, grabbed the packet of Lincoln biscuits from inside and began cramming them into his mouth. When there were only a couple left, he climbed down from the surface and put the remaining biscuits down the sock with the lighter. After a few moments' thought he threw the empty biscuit packet on top of the cupboard. It landed on the edge, teetered for a few seconds and then came down, scattering crumbs. Sonny Gee picked it up again, this time stuffing it at the back of the little fridge. He went over to the cooker and grabbed the box of matches. Holding them up to his ear, he rattled them appreciatively, and taking a few out, put them with the crumbled biscuits down his sock. At that instant there was a sudden roar from outside the front of the cottage. Instinctively, the boy shrank to a squat, his legs poised to spring.

Anxiously he waited for the old man to wake and find him

in the kitchen, but he didn't stir, and straightening up, Sonny Gee crept into the sitting room. The roar screamed out once more and Joe mumbled in his sleep. His knotted hands grasped at the air for a few moments, and the boy watched them anxiously, but they fell inert again. Sonny Gee tiptoed past him stealthily.

A motorbike was just throttling past when the boy opened the front door. Two figures rode by on it, their faces hidden in slash masks so that only the whites of their eyes showed. The bike disappeared up the cut, the din of its engine magnified by the wooden fences. Sonny Gee ran after it.

He had reached the lamp-post when he heard the screaming bike heading back down towards him. It grew louder and louder, bellowing like a cow in a knacker's yard as it turned the corners in the twisting cut. Then it burst round the last corner, and the boy was only just able to fling himself behind the discarded wheelie bin as the machine screeched past. The gravel of the path was sprayed into his face.

Sonny Gee bolted out of the cut. The motorbike was scrambling between the washing posts, its riders ducking the lines and the few things which still hung there, its wheels churning up the grass.

The boy sprinted down the row of cottages, stopping at the old man's. He climbed on to the gate. The stench of petrol fumes and the shriek of the engine filled the air as the bike circled under the washing lines. Then the pillion rider grabbed at a sheet. The wheels beneath him skidded dangerously, and the bike went on, the sheet flying out from behind, until the youth let it go and it fell softly to the ground. 'Yous are shit,' shouted Sonny Gee as the two youths bounced past him. The bike turned, shaking convulsively as it ripped towards the boy again. The front wheel lifted up as it approached. Sonny Gee leant back and spat. The phlegm hit the youth driving the motorbike in the eye, and as he groped to pull off the mask, the machine careered out of control. Mounting a hump in the grass, the pillion rider was thrown clean off, while the motorbike crumpled to the ground. 'Yus're shite, yous,' shouted Sonny Gee, laughing. 'Ye'd shit yersel's on a merry-gan-roond doon Metroland.'

Slowly the riders got up. Picking up the bike, they wheeled it over to where Sonny Gee stood. The pillion rider was small, but squat. He still wore his mask. His companion was tall and lanky, his complexion pitted. 'What are ye laughing at, ye little prick?' the shorter one called through his mask.

'It's ye that's the prick,' replied Sonny Gee, swinging on the gate.

'What d'yus say?' the small one demanded threateningly.

'Ye've even got a rubber johnny on,' Sonny Gee said, pointing at the slash mask.

The pillion rider pulled off his mask, revealing a baby face, soured by an ugly leer. Sonny Gee leant down and took out a biscuit from his sock. Continuing to swing on the gate, he munched nonchalantly on the biscuit as the two approached. 'Yous two aren't having a one o' these,' he challenged, waving the biscuit in the air.

The tall teenager pointed at Sonny Gee's cowboy hat. 'Look at him, thinks he's Woody from *Toy Story*.'

'Better than being a friggin' Rugrat,' answered the boy, looking directly into the eyes of the small youth, whose sparse blond hair reinforced his resemblance to a six-month-old baby. 'And ye,' he said, turning to his taller companion, 'ye shag Teletubbies.'

The tall one bridled. 'Well, ye . . . ye . . .' he faltered, struggling for a riposte.

But the boy got there first: 'Where d'ye get that bike from, chaver, a Airfix model kit?'

The driver of the motorbike grunted and stepped forward, but his friend stopped him. 'Ah kna ye, divven't ah?' the pillion rider asked. There was a pause. 'Ye live in Bensham, divven't ye?'

Swinging on the gate, Sonny Gee stared at them. 'Ah'm not scared of ye two.'

'Aye, ah kna ye,' said the pillion rider.

'Ha'way, Jimmy, sort the little munchkin,' said the tall one, his voice cracking up a few notes in anger.

'Ooo, Jimmy,' Sonny Gee minced mockingly. 'Let's sort the little munchkin.' He looked up at the tall one. 'What's the matter, arsehole, not hard enough to take me on yersel'?'

Jimmy spluttered with laughter. 'Aye, ah kna ye areet,' he said. He turned to his friend. 'It's Sonny Gee, man Mally. Ye kna. The mad lad.'

'Sonny Gee,' repeated Mally, thoughtfully.

'That's me name, divven't wear it oot, arsehole,' retorted the boy.

'Ye cheeky scruff,' Mally spat.

'Frigg off!' hissed the boy. 'It's ye what's the scruff.'

Mally took another step towards him, but once again Jimmy restrained him. 'He's Macca's mule, man,' he said.

'Mule?' Mally asked.

'Aye.'

'Carries his gear, man. Shifts his tackle for him. Carries his tac, man.' Jimmy shook his head in exasperation at the slowness of the tall one. Then turned to the boy. 'How ye deeing, mule?'

Swinging on the gate, Sonny Gee paused uncertainly. 'It's yous that's the mule.'

'Na; it's ye,' said Mally, and then brayed like a donkey. 'Macca's mule, Macca's mule!' he jeered.

Sonny Gee spat once more. The phlegm sailed through the air and splatted Mally between the eyes.

'Ha'way then,' Sonny Gee challenged Mally who had swept past Jimmy. 'If ye think yus're hard enough. Ah had that lad doon Old Parsonage Road, ah could have ye.' Jumping off the gate, Sonny Gee went over to Mally and stamped on his foot, following it with a kick at his shins.

Mally yelped. 'Ah'm gonnae dee ye,' he said, advancing menacingly.

'Ha'way, man, he's only a munchkin,' laughed Jimmy.

'Better than being a dwarf,' Sonny Gee said, pointing at Jimmy. 'What happened to ye then, d'yus come back shrunk from the laundrette or what?'

Jimmy's baby face leered horribly. Mally tried to clamp a hand over his mouth, but it was too late, and the laugh escaped him. Jimmy stared him into silence, then turned to Sonny Gee. 'How auld are ye?'

'Put it this way,' said Sonny Gee. 'Ah've got more chance of being served a pint in the Wheatsheaf on Old Parsonage Road than ye have. Ah swear doon, ye look like that doll in the *Evil Dead II* video.'

Jimmy shook his head. 'Put it this way an' all, if ye weren't Macca's mule then ye wouldn't be aroond for another Christmas.' His face darkened even further. 'Ye might not be aroond then anyway, if what a little birdy telt wor is straight up.'

Sonny Gee's face was suddenly innocent as curiosity filled his features. His voice was small. 'How d'yus mean, like; a little birdy?'

'A little birdy what telt wor a certain Macca's gonnae expand his market. Gan big. A little birdy what telt wor he's gonnae start dealing in summink a little stronger. What d'yus think o' that, mule boy?'

'Ah'm nee mule!' Sonny Gee ran at Jimmy, but his friend grabbed him and, hoisting him up on to the gate, pinioned his arms. 'What ye deeing roond here anyway?' Jimmy asked when Sonny Gee had stopped struggling. 'Ye're a lang way from hyem. Yus live in them bedsits, divven't ye?'

'Ah divven't.'

'In Bensham.'

'Ah divven't.'

'With Macca and yer mam.'

86

'Ah divven't. Ah divven't live with thems.'

'Who do ye live with then?'

Sonny Gee hesitated for a moment. A strange look came into his eye. 'Me dad.'

Jimmy snorted. 'What, are ye in jail an' all?'

'Na. Told ye. Ah live with me dad.'

Jimmy and his friend laughed mockingly. 'Where is he then?'

'Here,' replied Sonny Gee, turning to point at the row of cottages behind him.

'Yer dad lives here, in a one o' them?' Sonny Gee nodded. 'With a one o' them auld grave dodgers?'

'Me dad's not a grave dodger.'

'The auld gadgies what live in there couldn't even get two numbers up on the lottery, let alone stick it up your slapper of a mam.'

The boy was not listening. 'He's geet hard an' all. Me dad. Geet hard. Harder than ye.' He paused, then spoke more quietly. 'He's harder than Macca.'

Mally looked at Jimmy. 'What's he gannin' on aboot?'

'And there's birds an' all,' Sonny Gee added, dreamily. 'We live there together, with the birds.'

'Birds?' said Jimmy. 'The only friggin' bird roond here is a cuckoo. And that's ye, 'cos yus're a divvy, man. A divvy.' Jimmy thrust his head right in front of the boy. 'A friggin' divvy, and so's yer dad!' Reaching over, he knocked the boy's cowboy hat off.

Sonny Gee writhed free of Mally's grip and jumped down from the gate. Picking up the cowboy hat, he put it back on, tucking the string under his chin. He looked at Jimmy. 'Gis a gan on yer bike then.'

Jimmy and Mally exchanged glances, their eyes glinting maliciously. 'Are ye sure, bonny lad?'

'Course ah am,' the boy spat back, defiantly.

'Ye might fall off, but,' said Mally with mock concern, starting the engine up.

'Ah'll take him,' said Jimmy, pushing Mally out of the way and taking the bike.

'Jimmy man, it's my bike, but,' Mally moaned.

'Ah said, ah'll take him,' repeated Jimmy. He climbed on the bike and revved it. 'Hop on, mule,' he called.

Sonny Gee jumped on the back seat. 'How fast does it gan?'

'Fast enough,' cried Jimmy as the bike shot off, its front wheel rearing in the air.

The motorbike thundered up the cut. As it came back down, Jimmy swerved close to one of the fences. Sonny Gee's trousers were ripped as they grazed against the wood. On the open ground, Jimmy drove round and round, dragging the back wheel in skidding circles.

'Call that fast?' Sonny Gee asked, when they came to a halt where Mally stood at the old man's gate.

'Think ye can gan any faster, like?' Jimmy demanded.

'Course ah dee,' replied the boy, witheringly.

'Ha'way then,' Jimmy said, jumping off.

The bike fell to the ground. Without a sound, Sonny Gee picked himself and the bike up. 'Hurt yersel'?' Mally asked, pointing at the blood that could be seen soaking through the material of the boy's trousers. The boy looked down, and at that moment Mally flicked off his cowboy hat. Sonny Gee tried to catch it, but Mally got there first. With a flick of his wrist the teenager sent the hat flying through the air.

'Are ye getting on this bike or what?' demanded Jimmy.

The boy looked at his hat and then at the bike. 'Course ah am,' he said. Sonny Gee tried to get on the bike, but it was too big for him to balance so he pushed it over to the gate.

Jimmy held the bike steady for him as he climbed on to it using the gate as a booster. 'Bet ye cannet gan nee faster through that cut than what ah did,' he challenged, kick-starting the engine.

'Course ah could.' The boy revved up the bike. It shot forward a few yards. Stopping, Sonny Gee put a hand out and leant against the little wall in front of the old man's front garden. Revving once more, he was just about to set off again when a shout suddenly caught his attention.

'What the heck d'ye think ye're deeing?' a voice demanded angrily. Sonny Gee looked over to see the old man standing at the open door. He came down the path. 'Get doon from there before ye break yer neck.' Reaching the boy, he pulled him from the bike. The old man turned to the teenagers. 'Jimmy Walsh, ah might have known.' He shook his head. 'What ye trying to dee, kill the bairn?'

'Didn't dee nowt,' Jimmy replied.

The bike fell down. 'Yus'll knacker it, man,' Mally said, dashing over.

'Have ye got a licence for that thing?' Joe demanded.

'Divven't need it,' Jimmy returned. 'It's a off-the-road vehicle.'

'Ah'll bloody well off-the-road ye in a minute,' said the old man angrily. 'Ah'm sick o' ye lot flying up and doon the shop on that bike. Ye'll kill someone one of these days.' The old man shook his head. 'Where d'ye get the money to keep this thing gannin'?' he asked.

'What's that got to dee with ye?' Jimmy shot back.

'Lads like ye, ye're not working, are ye? What are yus, fifteen, sixteen?' Joe narrowed his eyes. 'Where's the money coming from?'

'His stepdad,' said Jimmy.

'Let him dee his own talking.' The old man turned to Mally. 'Is that reet, does yer stepdad give yus the money?' Mally nodded. The old man stepped over to the bike, knocking Mally aside with his body. Mally staggered with the force and fell. Hiding the pain that rocketed through his body, Joe levered up the bike. 'Tell this stepdad of yours to come doon,' he said. Joe wheeled the bike through the gate and took it down the little path.

'Can ah have it, gadgie mista?' asked Sonny Gee, his eyes flashing.

'Ye cannet dee that,' spluttered Jimmy. 'That's private property.'

'Oh aye, Jimmy Walsh, and since when did ye begin to respect other folks' property?'

Mally stared imploringly at his friend. His face crumpled. 'Jimmy man, the grave dodger's twocking me bike.'

'Divven't cry, man lass,' said Jimmy contemptuously.

'Ah'm not taking it,' said Joe calmly.

'But me stepdad'll kill wor if ah divven't bring it back tonight. He wants to take it up the auld colliery with his mates.'

'Well then, tell him to come here and get it.'

Calmly the old man leant the bike against the wall of the cottage and then walked back up the path to the gate. As he shut it, he came face to face with Jimmy who had stepped forward.

'Ah want that bike,' Jimmy said.

'Ah've told ye,' said Joe quietly. 'Ah'll give it to his stepdad, when and if he comes to see wor.'

Jimmy opened the gate. 'He's not scared o' ye, Rugrat,' called out Sonny Gee.

'Ye get in that hoose,' the old man said to the boy without taking his eye off Jimmy.

'He's not flapped of anyone,' Sonny Gee boasted.

'Ah said get back in that house!' Joe's shout reverberated against the fronts of the terrace. As Sonny Gee reluctantly retreated through the open door, faces began to appear at windows, one or two doors opened tentatively. The old man turned to face the youths. 'Ah kna ye, Jimmy Walsh,' he said.

'Ye friggin' well give us back that motorbike,' Jimmy replied.

The old man shook his head. 'Ye think ye're hard, ye, but ye're not, ye're nowt. Ah've hoiked oot bigger pieces of coal than ye and thrown them awer me shoulder.'

'Ye're a friggin' mental radgie,' said Jimmy, but he backed away through the gate as the old man approached.

'It's time summink was done aboot ye, Jimmy Walsh.'

'And ye,' seethed Jimmy. 'Ah bet ye've got a meat cleaver or summink stashed doon yer drawers.'

Mally laughed, but it was a nervous titter and soon petered out. 'Aye, ye want putting in a home,' he said.

Joe shook his head. 'Shut up, ye. Ah'm talking to the organ-grinder, not his monkey. Ha'way, Walsh, ye're a big man when ye're on that bike, but not so big now, eh?' He glared at Mally. 'Now ye. Ah want to make sure that this stepdad of yours knas exactly what ye dee with the money he's stupid enough to give ye.'

'Yus've got claws for hands, ye,' said Jimmy. 'Ye're a friggin' monster from the deep.' Puffing out his cheeks, he pretended to roar. The old man stepped forward. Jimmy no longer backed away. They stared deeply into each other's eyes. 'And neeone calls me a friggin' organ,' added Jimmy in a quiet, sinister voice.

'Thick as well as a menace,' replied the old man.

'Ye're asking for it,' whispered Jimmy, advancing himself now. 'Ye're asking for it.'

The old man glanced around quickly. From each cottage he could see a terrified face frozen at the window, or a figure standing anxiously at the open door. 'Na. It's ye that's been asking for it. Ye dee nowt but ruin our lives here. And it's got to stop.'

They remained motionless, warily watching each other. Then suddenly they moved, both at the same time. There was a click, and a blade sprang out.

'Fuckin' hell,' Mally gasped. Holding the knife at his side, Jimmy stared pointedly at it and then at Joe, deadly determination narrowing his eyes to slits. 'Jimmy man,' said Mally, retreating towards the cut. 'Leave it. Leave it, Jimmy man. Ah'll send me stepdad doon.'

Jimmy and Joe continued to stare at each other. As they stood head to head the stoop of the old man's body appeared to straighten and a vigorous strength coursed through him so that he towered above Jimmy. The youth wavered and then slowly backed off, keeping the knife visible to the old man. 'Ah'm gonnae get ye,' called Jimmy. 'Divven't worry aboot that. Ah'm gonnae get ye.' The faces of the elderly watchers stared at him fearfully. 'All o' yous grave dodgers, ah'm gonnae get all o' yous!' he yelled.

'Me stepdad'll be roond to ye,' Mally shrieked, his voice wobbling.

'And ye, ye little cunt,' added Jimmy, pointing at the boy who was peering through the net curtain at the window. 'Wait till Macca gans into his new line o' business. YE STUPID LITTLE MULE. YE STUPID LITTLE FUCKIN' MULE!'

The old man watched the two teenagers disappear into the cut, then picked up the cowboy hat and walked back down the path. With a huge effort, he manoeuvred the bike through the door, hoisting it over the threshold. He wheeled it down the passage, across the sitting room and then through the kitchen and out on to the yard. When he came back inside, he stood there breathless, a vacant look in his eyes. Then, as though drained, he sank wearily into the armchair.

'Ye did him,' said the boy from the settee after the old man had been sitting in his armchair for some time. 'Yus're geet hard, ye.' Sonny Gee laughed. 'Ye should have seen his face when ye took his bike.' Sonny Gee imitated Jimmy's surprise. 'Ye made him dee a runner. Ah bet ye could have anyone on Old Parsonage Road, nee bother.' The boy smiled. 'It was purely belter, even when he pulled the weapon ye didn't . . .'

'Look,' interrupted the old man tersely, 'ah did what ah had to. There's nowt clever aboot that.'

'That beanpole an' all, ye should have seen him when . . .'

'Shut up,' he said, tossing him the cowboy hat.

Sonny Gee put the hat on immediately. Then, puzzled, he stared at Joe. 'But ye're hard as . . .'

'That's it. Finish. Ah divven't want to talk about it.' He paused, then looked the boy in the eye. 'Being hard's nowt, man lad,' he said bitterly. 'And if ye think it is then ye're on to a hiding for nothing. Ah did a job all me life what was only for hard men. And ye kna what? Ah was stupid. Ah was just plain stupid.' A heavy silence fell between them. The old man seemed bewildered by his own outburst. After a while, the boy took off his hat, and began picking at the white braid.

'Lucky ah'm stopping here with ye, mind,' began the boy, quietly. 'Ah'll weigh in with yus when that puff's stepdad comes.' There was a pause. Sonny Gee seemed to shiver. 'And ye can help me, if he comes back. If . . .' he swallowed hard. 'Then if Macca or anybody comes, ye'll weigh in for me.' Neither of them spoke for a long time. 'Gadgie mista,' said Sonny Gee at last, speaking in a small voice, 'ah'm glad ah'm staying here. Ye can come with wor for a burn on that bike later eh? But ah'd better drive. Ah divven't kna whether yus'll be able to steer with them hands o' yours.'

The afternoon lengthened into evening. The light changed at the window. Part of the white braid came away from the brim of the cowboy hat, and the boy tossed it on the cold grate. Neighbours knocked at the door, calling quietly through the letter box, but the old man did not get up for them. 'How, gadgie mista,' said Sonny Gee at last. 'Is that telly not working yet?'

There was no reply. Then, after a long time, Joe turned to look at the old portable set that stood on the sideboard. 'It doesn't work,' he said. Eventually the boy got up and crossed the room. He went into the kitchen. 'Leave that bike alone,'

Joe ordered. Sonny Gee wandered back into the sitting room. He crossed to the passage door.

'And where d'ye think ye're gannin'?' demanded the old man.

Sonny Gee shrugged. 'Ah always gan ootside on a night, me.'

'Aye, well, ye divven't when yus're here. Sit down.' The boy opened the passage door. 'Ah told ye to sit down.'

'But ah want to gan out and play. It's deeing me heed in, stopping in all the time.'

'And look what happened to yus the last time ye went oot.'

Sonny Gee held up his hands in appeal. 'So? Thems are nowt. Neewhere near as hard as the chavers on Old Parsonage Road.'

The old man tutted irritably. 'This isn't Old Parsonage Road. Not yet anyway. Thank God.'

The boy came back across the room. 'Who's God?'

'Eh?'

'Who's this God, gadgie?'

'What ye gannin' on aboot now?' Joe asked perplexedly.

'It was ye what said it. Ah divven't kna what it is. God. Audrey gans on aboot him an' all. Others dee an' all.'

The old man stared at the boy. His lips trembled slightly as he thought. 'Hasn't neeone never told ye aboot God?'

Sonny Gee shook his head. 'Is he just a swear word? Has he moved from Gatesheed? When ah asked me mam, that's what she said. Said he wasn't here any more. And ah kna for a fact he doesn't stop in Bensham, 'cos ah've nivver seen him on Old Parsonage Road.'

Joe closed his eyes for a moment. He half raised himself from the armchair, and then fell back, shaking his head weakly. Sonny Gee crossed back to the door. 'Ah thought ah told ye to sit down.'

'Ah want to gan oot.'

'Ye can't.'

'Why not?'

Joe seethed angrily. 'Just be told, won't ye?'

'Why?'

'Because ah have to have ye here for a few days and in that time ah won't have ye getting into nee trouble like ye did the moment me back was turned.'

'You were sleeping, man,' laughed the boy.

'Ye're not gannin' oot and that's the end of it!'

'Aye, ah am gannin' oot and that's the start of it!'

Joe sighed heavily. His eyes narrowed thoughtfully. 'It'll be dark soon, mind,' he said quietly.

'So?'

The old man stared at his gnarled hands which rested on his chest. 'Areet then, off yus gan, but keep a lookoot.'

'Who for, the ponce's stepdad, or that God?'

'Na,' said Joe, significantly. 'Spring-heeled Jack.'

'Eh?'

The boy stared in puzzlement. The old man shook his head. 'If ye gan oot, mind, he'll get ye. Spring-heeled Jack. So be careful.'

Wide-eyed, Sonny Gee moved back to the settee and sat down. 'Who's him?'

Looking over, Joe fixed his glance on the boy. 'Lives doon the cut. If ye gan there when ye're told not to, he'll grab ye.'

'Grab ye?'

'Aye.'

'Ah'm not scared of him.'

'Ye would be.'

'Ah could have him easy, me.'

'Ye wouldn't see him, man lad.'

Sonny Gee grew utterly still. 'Why not?'

'He hides. Waiting for lads to come by. Keeps hid in the darkest corner. Then when they're looking for him, he jumps up behind them. He's got springs on his feet, so he bounces out, gets a hold of ye and then bounces away again.'

There was a pause. 'Where to? When he jumps off. Where does he take ye to?'

The old man lifted his hands mysteriously, then shook his head. 'Neebody knows.'

'Why not? Why doesn't neebody kna where that Spring Jack gadgie takes ye?'

'Because neebody's ever come back. Once ye hear them springs, it's all awer.'

The ticking of the clock filled the room. 'Ah'll just not gan doon the cut then,' the boy said at last, but his tone was unsure.

'Oh no,' said Joe, seeming to think. 'That's only where he lives. He gans aboot the spot pretty freely.' Abruptly he pulled himself from the armchair and walked over to the window. 'That's where he lives,' he said, his back turned to Sonny Gee. 'In the cut by the lamp-post. But he comes out and roams all aroond here. Especially at night.'

When Sonny Gee spoke again his voice was tremulous. 'How d'ye kna, gadgie mista? Is he even harder than ye?'

'Ah kna him.' Joe continued to stare out of the window. 'Ah've often seen him. In fact, look, there he gans noo.'

'Where?' demanded the boy, getting up and moving over beside the old man.

'He's gone. Ye missed him.'

Together they stared out on to the yard. Then suddenly, the boy began to shake. Growing pale, he went back over to the settee, perching right on the edge. 'Are ye his mate?' he asked, terror contorting his face.

'Aye,' said the old man with a sudden savagery. 'So dee as ah say. It's aboot your bedtime noo, ah reckon. So ha'way, gan to bed.'

'What's he look like then?' asked Sonny Gee softly.

The old man shrugged. 'Head like a frying pan. Sausage for a nose. Fried eggs for eyes. And a rasher of bacon for a mouth. And d'yus see them boots on the hearth?' The boy nodded.

'He's got a pair just like them, but aboot ten times the size. With geet springs on the soles. So if ah were ye, ah'd get into bed. 'Cos that's the only place ye're safe when Spring-heeled Jack's aboot.'

6

The next morning, Sonny Gee woke early. He sat upright with a jolt. A loud twittering noise was coming from the yard. The boy's eyes darted as he listened closely. 'Ah'm not scared o' ye,' he called out. There was no reply. Getting up, he edged round the table and crept to the window. Furtively, he peered out. Just at that moment something blurred into his line of vision. Ducking, he closed his eyes. When he opened them and lifted his head once more, there was nothing to be seen. 'Ah'm not scared o' neeone, me,' he said, but a little uncertainly now.

For a while he stayed there, looking through the window. His attention was just beginning to wander when something flashed over the tall wall at the bottom of the yard. The boy gasped. It was a bird. He stared open-mouthed as the house martin flew, weaving and bobbing through the air with great agility. Then, straightening suddenly, it came towards the window. It seemed bound to collide with the glass. Sonny Gee threw up his hands in horror. Only at the very last instant did the bird suddenly lift and sweep up into the eaves above the window.

Rushing outside, delight filled the boy's face. He stared up at the eaves just as the chirruping house martin streaked back overhead. Suddenly, the whole air seemed to be filled with house martins and Sonny Gee gazed at them down the row of cottages. Streaming from over the tall wall, the birds were flying above the yards, playing, sailing and bulleting into the eaves. The boy stood there mesmerised. He did not move, his eyes widening as the birds continued to gather. Then he brought his gaze back to the yard. A house martin had perched on the handlebars of the motorbike which stood propped against the wall of the cottage. Cocking its head, it watched him.

At that moment a sudden noise from the back door broke Sonny Gee's trance. Turning, he saw that the old man was standing there. The bird took flight. His face still beaming, the boy pointed at the flying bird. 'Look,' his wonder managed to whisper at last.

Joe glanced up. 'They're back, are they?'

The awe did not dim in Sonny Gee's blue eyes; he lifted both arms and gestured along the row of cottages. 'Look.'

'Filthy creatures. They mess all doon the wall.'

'Thems,' said the boy, his face beaming, 'thems is mint.'

The old man glared at him. 'Ah want a word with ye. Ha'way inside.'

'But . . .'

'Now. Ah'll fix porridge for breakfast, and yus'll eat it properly.'

'But the birds,' the boy replied.

'In now.'

With a final look at the chattering house martins, the boy sighed and followed Joe inside.

The old man was waiting for him in the kitchen. The tone of his voice was icy. 'Ah'll have to make the porridge with water, there's nee milk.' The bottle of milk stood on the Formica surface behind Joe. Sonny Gee looked at it. 'And if anyone comes roond, there's nowt to offer them with their tea.' Beside the bottle was the empty packet of Lincoln biscuits. There was a pause. 'Kna anything aboot this? That was nigh on a full packet o' biscuits there.' The boy shrugged. A heavy pause weighed itself between them. 'Ha'way, lad. What d'yus kna aboot them biscuits and the milk?'

The boy looked about the kitchen. 'Mebbes that gadgie took them.'

'What gadgie?'

'Oh aye, ah've just remembered,' said Sonny Gee with sudden conviction. 'Last night ah heard him. Ah got up and there he was, noshing them biscuits doon.'

'Who?'

'Ah telt him not to. Ah telt him ye'd dee him if ye caught him but . . .'

'Who?' repeated Joe in confusion.

'The frying-pan fella.'

'What yus gannin' on aboot?'

'Your mate, gadgie mista. Springy Jack lad.'

'Eh?' Bewilderment buzzed about Joe's head like a wasp; he swatted at it irritably.

'It was him what scoffed them biscuits and swilled yer milk. Ah telt ye, ah saw him dee it. A geet big gadgie he was. Jumping aboot in a pair o' boots ten times bigger than yours . . .'

'Divven't talk drivel . . .'

'Ah'm not. It was him. Last neet. He woke wor up. He couldn't stop eating. Just like that mentals gadgie from the *Silencer Lambs* video.'

'For pity's sake, shut up!' The loudness of Joe's voice was startling in the small space of the kitchen. With a snort of frustration the old man reached up to the cupboard and brought out the box of porridge oats.

'When's that Gemma lass coming?' Sonny Gee asked obdurately. Scattering the flakes of oats into a pan, Joe did not reply. 'Ah said when the frigg's that Gemma lass coming by?'

'Hey ye, ah won't have that.'

'Ah'm not stopping here. Ah'll gan with . . .'

The old man turned on the boy. 'Ah've told ye, ah won't have nee language.'

'But ah didn't say owt,' Sonny Gee said innocently. 'Ah only said frigg.'

'That's what ah mean.'

'That's not language.'

'Well, ah won't have it.'

Sonny Gee looked over challengingly. 'Well, ah will have it.'

'Look,' snapped the old man, 'if you're gonnae be here for a few days then let's get a few things sorted oot. For a start ah won't have nee language. D'yus understand that? Do ye?' Joe took up the matches. In his anger he struck at one energetically. The flaring head flew off. 'Now look what ye made me dee!' he growled. 'With yer bloody stupid lies!'

The boy looked down with an unnatural submissiveness. 'Are ye gonnae start now?' he asked, abjectly.

There was no reply. When the old man had managed to light the gas and was stirring the porridge he spoke: 'What d'ye mean, start?'

Still Sonny Gee did not look up. His voice was cowed. 'Yus gonnae start battering wor?'

Joe stopped stirring the porridge for a moment. He glanced over at the boy. 'Ha'way, get washed and ready,' he said.

'Are yus gonnae batter wor then?' the boy asked suspiciously.

'We haven't got all day, ye kna.'

Sonny Gee continued to study Joe. 'D'ye promise ye're not gonnae batter wor?'

'Look, we're having breakfast now.'

Shrugging, Sonny Gee relaxed. 'Ah just have crisps, me.'

'Nivver mind that. Get washed and ready. After breakfast we're gannin' out.'

'Where to?'

'School. Mebbes ah cannet put nee morals into ye, but if ye're gonnae be staying here for a few days then yus're gonnae gan to school. Besides, ah'm not gonnae have yus in the hoose all day.'

'Ah'm not gannin' to nee school.'

Sending the boy into the bathroom, the old man went back

to the porridge. When it was ready, he ladled it out and brought the bowls through to the sitting room. Going over to the window, he stared through it, his face glowering at the flying house martins. A few moments later Sonny Gee came back into the sitting room. 'Ah thought ah told ye to wash,' Joe said, tersely. 'Come here.' He waited for the boy to approach him. 'Ye're still filthy. Nee water's been near ye. Get into that kitchen.'

'Ah divven't want nee wash.'

'Well, ah do.'

'Well, neeone's stopping ye.'

'Cut oot that cheek, lad. It's ye that has to get washed.'

'Why do ah have to get washed?'

''Cos ye divven't want to be dirty all day.'

Sonny Gee shrugged. 'Ah divven't mind being dirty.'

'Well, ah do.'

'Well, ye're not.'

'Dee as ah say.'

'When's that Gemma lass coming?'

'We're gonnae be oot and away before she gets here so divven't think ye can get out of it that way.'

When Joe had filled the sink, Sonny Gee peered over it. 'What d'ye want wor to dee in there, gan for a swim?'

The old man shook his head. 'The sooner ye get to school the better. Ye're deeing me heed in.'

'Ah telt yus ah would,' beamed the boy. 'And ah've telt ye ah'm not ganning to school neither.'

'Put yer hands in,' the old man began. 'Ah said put yer hands in.' Reluctantly, the boy dipped his hands into the sink. 'Properly. Reet, noo get a lather.' Sonny Gee looked at him blankly. 'There it is.' Joe told him. 'On the draining board.' The boy did not move. 'The soap. Get that cake of soap.'

'Cake?'

'Aye, the cake of soap.'

Sonny Gee reached out to the soap and tentatively picked it up. 'Funny-looking cake, but, gadgie mista.'

'Use it for a lather then. Ha'way, put it in the water.'

'In the water?'

'Aye.'

'What yus deeing hoying a cake in the water?'

Joe sighed. 'Just dee as ah say, will ye.' Leaning over, he knocked the boy's hand so he dropped the soap. It plopped into the water. 'Reet. Now pick it up.'

Plunging his hands in, the boy found the bar of soap. He brought it out of the water, but it slipped from his fingers. He tried to catch hold of it again, but it kept sliding free. 'What's the matter,' burst the old man, irritatedly, 'haven't ye nivver had a wash before?' In the silence that followed, the boy turned from Joe's harsh face and looked out through the little window on to the yard. His eyes widened as he watched a house martin. 'Ye cannet eat properly, ye cannet wash, ye cannet tell the truth; is there owt ye can dee?'

The bird disappeared from view as it went up to the eaves. 'Do thems stop here?' Sonny Gee asked, softly.

'Eh?'

'Thems? The birds?'

Joe followed the direction of the boy's gaze. He saw the house martin plunging over the tall wall. 'Not for long they divven't,' he said. 'Ah take the broom handle to their nest.' There was a splash as the old man plunged his hands into the sink. 'Forget aboot them birds and get washed. Ah'll not tell ye again.'

Sonny Gee looked at Joe. Under the water the boy felt the rough skin of the old man's hands brush against his own. Using both hands, the old man was able to shovel up the soap. As he lifted his gnarled hands out of the sink, the water streamed from them. He held them there, raised, staring at them as the droplets scouring the surface slowed to a drip.

'Do thems hurt?' the boy asked softly. 'Yer hands, gadgie mista, are thems sore?'

The old man closed his eyes. Neither of them spoke for a while. The moisture glistened on the old hands, each callus and ugly knot shining under the light from the window. 'Just get washed,' he said in a small voice. He seemed to be studying the water in the sink. 'Rub the soap against yer hands. That's it. Rub the hands together, then sluice them off.' He paused as the boy followed his instructions. 'Now dee the same with yer face.' When the water hit his cheeks, Sonny Gee flinched. Closing his eyes, he threw up the water, showering the floor. 'Careful,' barked the old man. The boy washed away the soap and placed the bar on the draining board. 'Ha'way, we divven't want to be late for school.'

'Ah'm not gannin' to nee school.'

'Divven't tell wor,' put in the old man. 'Neeone on Old Parsonage Road gans, so ye're not gonnae either.'

Showering more water on his face, the boy looked at Joe wide-eyed. 'How d'ye kna?'

'And divven't shake like a dog,' the old man said, handing him a tea towel.

'Are ye really gonnae keep that bike, gadgie mista?' Sonny Gee asked as Joe went through to the sitting room.

The boy stared through the window, but the house martins had gone. Raising himself up on to the ledge above the sink, Sonny Gee gazed down the backyards. As quickly as they had arrived, the birds had disappeared. Without their light-hearted twittering, the silence felt dismal. With a sigh, he lowered himself back to the ground. Seeing the soap, he picked it up. His eyes narrowed as he held it to his nose. Slowly, he brought it to his lips.

'What the hell yus deein'?' demanded the old man, coming back into the kitchen to find Sonny Gee spitting repeatedly into the sink. Joe looked at the soap which had been tossed on to the window ledge. There were teeth marks in it. Shaking his head, the old man watched the boy wiping convulsively at his mouth. Finding an old apple in the cupboard, he handed it to the boy. 'It'll take the taste away,' he told him, guiding him to the plastic carrier bag hanging on the door handle. 'Take a bite,' he said. 'And then spit it oot. That's it. And again. That's it.' When the boy had finished the apple, Joe gave him a glass of water. 'Swill it aboot and then spit. That's it. Aye. That's it.' He took the empty glass. 'Why d'ye dee it?' he asked at last.

'Ye said it was a cake,' Sonny Gee said, miserably.

'Aye, a cake of soap. Ye divven't eat soap.' The old man turned and went into the sitting room. 'Ha'way,' he said. 'Let's get wor breakfast before anything else gans wrong.'

'Ah'm not hungry,' said the boy, staring down at the bowl of porridge before him on the table.

'Not this again,' said Joe, wearily.

'Ah'll just have a packet of crisps, me.'

'Crisps? That's not a proper breakfast.'

Sonny Gee pursed his lips nonchalantly. 'It's what ah have.'

'Not when ye're here, ye divven't. Ha'way, eat that porridge. Ye need building up. Ye're skinny as a rake.'

'No ah'm not. Anyway, ye are . . .'

'Look, ah'm not bandying words with ye. Just get that food doon ye.'

As Joe ate, the boy continued to stare down at his porridge. 'Ah'm nee skinny ribs, me. Ah had this lad on Old Parsonage Road. He was eleven, but ah had him. Knocked him doon . . .'

'If ye divven't eat, mind, ye'll not grow,' Joe interrupted him.

Sonny Gee stared at him in bewilderment. 'What d'ye mean?'

'It's what happens,' explained the old man as he chewed on a mouthful of porridge. 'If ye divven't eat, ye'll stay the same size as what ye are now.' Joe glanced furtively at the boy. 'How would that gan doon on Old Parsonage Road then?' he asked archly. 'In ten, twenty years' time, ye showing up there and still the same size as ye are now.' Through the corner of his eye the old man watched the boy leaning down to smell the porridge. 'That eleven-year-auld lad, he'd be three times yer size. He'd knock yus into the middle of next week. They'd all wait for ye to walk past, just so they could take a kick at the little lad what nivver grew.' Sonny Gee took a handful of porridge and ate it. 'That's it,' said Joe. 'But ye use yer spoon.' He waved his own spoon in the air.

Tentatively, the boy picked up his own cutlery. Scooping up some of the porridge, he brought it over to his mouth, but before he reached it, the glutinous food slipped from the angled spoon. He tried again with the same result. The spoon bounced against the bowl as he flung it down. He scooped some up in a hand. The old man stirred with irritation, but checked himself. 'What's the matter with ye, gadgie mista?' Sonny Gee asked, the porridge flecking over his top lip.

'Nowt,' said Joe, brightly. 'Eat with yer hands by all means. It's just that, well, ye divven't get much of the goodness that way.'

'What d'ye mean?' the boy demanded, suspiciously.

'Ye mean ye divven't kna?'

'Kna what?'

'That if ye eat with yer hands then ye divven't get much of the goodness.'

'So?'

'Oh, nothing. Ye just won't grow as much, that's all.' The old man paused to finish his own breakfast. 'Put it this way, lad. If ye eat with yer hands, ye'll grow a bit bigger than ye are noo, but that eleven-year-auld'll still be waiting for ye doon Old Parsonage Road.'

The boy narrowed his eyes, mistrustfully. 'How de ye kna aboot it?'

Joe shrugged. 'Ah'm auld. Ye see it all when yus're auld.'

Sonny Gee did not speak as he took up the spoon again.

The metal of the cutlery scraped noisily against the bottom of the bowl. He flinched when the spoon knocked against his teeth. 'Ye eat the porridge, not the spoon,' said the old man.

'Why, isn't there nee goodness in it?'

When the bowl was empty Joe nodded. 'Ye'll have to gan and get yer face washed again, but,' he said.

'Why?' asked the boy, screwing up a face that was thick with porridge.

''Cos ye cannet gan to school looking as though ye've grown a beard.'

'Ah'm not gannin' to school, me.'

The school stood beside the church, and was made out of the same red bricks. It was early when the old man and boy arrived there, and the gates were locked. 'Is that it?' Sonny Gee asked. Nodding, Joe led the boy into the church grounds, a rough-grassed, lime tree-filled area. He stopped at a bench and sat down, his body leaning forward slightly, its weight propped against the walking stick which rested between the thick toes of the black boots. Surreptitiously, Sonny Gee approached the school gate and surveyed the buildings on the other side. 'Hey, gadgie mista,' he called. 'Ah telt ye, didn't ah? Neebody gans to school.'

'Divven't be stupid, it hasn't opened up yet,' Joe responded.

A particularly tall lime tree grew above the bench on which Joe sat. Sonny Gee walked towards it. Leaning against its trunk, he stared out, looking around, casting furtive glances at the school. The leaves of the lime tree were not fully out yet, and picking up a fallen twig, Sonny Gee explored the stickiness of the buds, probing the construction of each one. 'Why's it all sticky?' he mused.

Joe did not reply.

After they had been waiting there a while, a few people, mainly pensioners, entered the church. The old man watched them through the corner of his eye. 'Funny-looking school-kids, them,' Sonny Gee said. 'And they're gannin' in the wrang place.'

'They're not gannin' to school. They're gannin' to eight o'clock.'

'Eh?'

'Mass lad, eight o'clock Mass.'

The boy took a step towards the bench. 'What's that?'

Joe stared at the boy and then at the tall red-brick church. He sighed. 'It's to dee with that God that yus kna nowt aboot,' he said.

Movements could be seen inside the school building as the teachers began to arrive, entering from the car park at the other side. But still the gates in front of the old man and boy remained locked. People began to file out from the church; Joe watched them go and then stared abstractedly at the ground. Sonny Gee tried to pull another twig down from the lowest branch of the tree, but couldn't reach it. Slowly, he circled the trunk, pressing his hand against the rough surface. 'Why's it green on this side?' he asked, when he had been round the girth of the tree twice. 'It broon there, like, but green on this side. Why?'

'It's moss,' replied the old man, looking up for a moment.

'Moss?'

'Aye. The moss grows on the north side.'

The boy pressed both hands against the mossed surface of the bark, and then, leaning forward, rested his face against it. 'Why?'

''Cos the sun doesn't get to it.'

'Why?'

Joe sighed. 'That's just the way it is. The sun only ever shines on one side of things.'

'Why?'

But the old man was looking at the ground again.

'Gadgie mista,' put in the boy, 'why does the sun only ever

shine on one side of things? Why? Why cannet the sun shine everywhere?' When Joe still did not reply, Sonny Gee slowly rounded the tree again. 'It's not fair,' he said softly. 'That sun's stupid. It should shine everywhere. It's not fair.' The boy continued to study the trunk of the tree, every so often glancing up at the sun mistrustfully. Then, lifting out the tail of his T-shirt, he began rubbing at the green, trying to scour the bark clean.

'I thought that was you, Joe,' someone called a little later. Startled, the old man looked up. Instantly, Sonny Gee darted behind the trunk. 'I saw you sitting there when I came across to say Mass.'

'Hello, Father,' Joe said, heavily.

'Haven't seen you for a while.'

'No, well . . .'

'I keep meaning to come and see you.' There was a pause. The priest was a young man. He wore jeans and a sweater. 'And who's the bonny lad?' he asked.

Joe hesitated for a few moments. 'He's stopping with me for a few days, Father.'

The priest smiled at Sonny Gee who had just peered round the side of the trunk. The boy stared back for a while suspiciously. Then cautiously came over. 'Nice to meet you, young man.'

'Have ye just come from there?' the boy asked, pointing at the church. The priest nodded. The boy blinked thoughtfully. 'Are ye God?'

The priest laughed.

'Divven't talk stupid,' said Joe, irately.

'Well, d'yus kna him?'

There was a pause. 'Do you mind if I join you for a few minutes, Joe?' the priest asked, pointing at the space on the bench. The old man shook his head. Sitting down, the priest took out a packet of cigarettes. Lighting one, he smoked it contentedly for a few moments. He wore a silver ring on his middle finger and when the sun came out it glinted. All three of them watched this gleam until the sun disappeared behind a cloud.

'It's stupid,' said the boy thoughtfully. 'That sun.' Then he looked at the priest. 'Gis a tab, God gadgie,' he said.

'Reet, that's it,' thundered Joe. He swept his stick belligerently over his head. 'Ah'm sick of ye.'

'Ye said yus wouldn't,' replied Sonny Gee. 'Ah asked ye, and ye said yus wouldn't batter wor.'

Joe laid the stick over his knees. 'Ah'm not gonnae hit ye,' he said. 'Ah'm just sick to the back teeth of yer back-answering and cheek.' The old man saw the tail of Sonny Gee's T-shirt; it was stained green from the moss. 'And what have ye been deein' to yer jersey?' he asked. 'It's covered in mess.'

The boy glanced down at the thick stain. 'Wasn't me,' he shrugged.

'Wasn't ye?' demanded Joe. 'What d'ye mean it wasn't ye?'

'It was the sun what did it.'

The old man closed his eyes. 'It's just one lie after another with ye. Gan awer and stand by them gates. Gan on, now! And divven't shift until ah come.'

The boy looked over at the school doubtfully. He was about to speak when he suddenly stopped himself. With a shrug, he began to walk over to the gates. Joe and the priest watched his slow progress. The old man narrowed his eyes. 'He's me grandbairn, Father.'

'I didn't know you had one.'

There was a bitterness in Joe's voice. 'Neither did ah.' He sighed. 'He's me Mary's lad. Ah'm looking after him for a few days.'

'I see.' The priest glanced at Joe.

The old man felt the glance, and shifted uncomfortably on the bench. 'Still haven't given the tabs up then, Father Michael?'

'Oh, I gave them up long ago,' laughed the priest, 'it's them that won't give me up.'

Sonny Gee was climbing up on to the school gates. 'Get doon,' the old man bellowed. The boy sprang down. There was a pause between the two men.

'Did you see Mary?' the priest began again, delicately. 'When she brought the boy round, did you see her?'

'Aye, for the first time for six, almost seven years.'

'Did you talk to her?'

Joe breathed out softly. 'She didn't come to see me. Turns up oot of the blue and drops her bairn on wor. That's all.' He gestured over at the boy. 'He's a reet handful.'

'You can tell,' said the priest, thoughtfully.

'What d'ye mean, Father?'

'Tell that he's your grandson. Just by looking at him. He's a younger version of yourself, Joseph.'

The old man watched Sonny Gee closely for a while. Then the boy started climbing back up the gates. 'Get doon!' Joe shouted. He turned to the young priest. 'See what ah mean. A real handful.'

'How is Mary?'

'Ah'd rather not talk aboot her, Father.'

'Getting on for seven years is a long time not to speak to someone, specially when that someone's your own daughter, Joe.'

Joe seemed to study his stick. 'Ye kna how it is, man Father,' he said quietly. 'Ah've telt yus all aboot it in confession. Nowt's changed. It's nee use. Ah cannet forgive her for what she did. For what she did to her mam.'

The priest nodded his head. 'It was a cruel blow all right.'

'Cruel?' As the old man turned to the one beside him, his eyes were tortured. The pained expression flared for a little longer, then died, leaving Joe's gaze empty, lifeless. 'This isn't the first bairn she's dropped off on us, ye kna. There was another one. Na. This isn't the first.'

'You've never mentioned anything about it before.'

'What was the point?' Joe broke off for a moment. When he spoke again it was softly. 'It was before your time here. Years agan now.' He paused, the recollection was painful, and his eyes were patterned with broken veins like the cracks on a drought-ridden piece of earth. 'It was just after she left hyem for the first time. She came back pregnant.' The word seemed to hover heavily in the air for a while with the smoke from the priest's cigarette. Slowly it disintegrated, along with the smoke which drifted past the lime tree trunk. 'Joan took her in of course, despite what folk said, and we had the two of them with us for a . . .' Suddenly, Joe stopped. He looked at the man beside him on the bench, and coughed with embarrassment. 'Why, ah'll shut up noo.'

The priest flicked the ash from his cigarette and inhaled deeply. 'Why?'

'It's ancient history.'

The priest shook his head. 'Ha'way, man Joe, you cannot bottle it all up. You've got to get it out. I know what you old pitmen are like. Hard as rock, and stony as shale. But everybody's got to talk.'

The old man turned to the priest. 'Ah cannet forgive her. Ah just cannet.' He bowed his head. 'Ah'm ashamed of meself. But ah cannet dee otherwise.'

There was a pause. The boy rattled the gates. 'We're none of us perfect,' said the priest. 'We all need forgiveness. Healing. That's what it's all about. If we didn't need any help then we wouldn't be human. You know the Bible as well as me. Nobody sends for the doctor when they're feeling well.'

A distant look dimmed Joe's eyes. 'He was a lovely little babby,' he began, quietly. 'Lovely little nature. It did yer heart good to see him. Honest, it was a real tonic just to be with him. We both got attached. Joan more than me, but . . . but ah still did an' all. Ah loved him. Then one day his mam just disappeared. Took him away with her. We nivver saw him again. He'll be grown up by now. Eighteen years old. Wherever he is. That little babby'll be a man.'

'I didn't know,' said the priest after he had waited for Joe to continue. 'Is there no way of finding out where he is? Of getting in touch?'

The old man stared over at Sonny Gee, who was beginning to scale the gates again. 'No,' he said. 'What's passed is passed.' With a heave, he levered himself to his feet. 'We forgave her even that, Father,' he added, distantly. 'Even that. It was what she did to Joan that broke it.' He took a few steps towards the gates, and then stopped. 'Ah cannet understand owt, me. It's like God's tooken everything away.'

'Still,' said the priest, dropping his cigarette and grinding it under his heel, 'He's given you something back now.'

Joe turned. His face was contorted with angry outrage. 'Eh?'

'The bonny lad there,' replied the priest gently.

'Is that some kind of a joke?'

'I've never been more serious. The bonny lad. That's your gift from God.'

The old man shook his head. 'Well, if he is, then ah divven't want it. He can keep His present.'

The priest looked at him levelly. 'Well, that's up to you. Only you can't say He's taken everything away from you any more.' The old man did not reply. 'Will I see you at Mass again one of these days, Joe?' the priest called, after Joe had walked about ten yards.

'Na,' responded the old man sadly. 'Na.'

Joe walked on.

'What you going to do then?' the priest called.

The old man stopped once more. 'What d'yus mean?'

'With your gift, the bonny lad there? What you going to do with him?'

Joe seemed to consider this for some time, then he started walking again. His voice was mechanical. 'He's only staying with wor for a few days. Ah'm gonnae put him at the school. Keep him out me hair . . .'

'Before you wash your hands of him?'

The old man nodded grimly. 'Aye, that's reet.' Then he turned to the priest. 'Father, will ye start him at the school?'

'It's not up to me, Joe.'

'But ah thought it was a Catholic school?'

'Yes, but you'll have to see one of the teachers.'

'Ah'll dee that then.'

'I mean, I can have a word with them about it, if you like . . .'

'There's nee need, Father. Ah divven't want anything complicated. The bairn just needs to be there a few days.'

The priest watched Joe move slowly to the school gates on which the boy had climbed again. The old man reached them and lifted his stick to tap the boy's legs. Joe spoke, but the priest could not hear the words. There was an angry exchange between the old man and the child, after which the boy jumped down. Sighing, the priest headed back to the church.

The old man and the boy stood in silence for a long time, staring at the school, their noses pressed against the metal bars of the gates. At last the caretaker came over. 'Areet, Joe,' he said.

The old man nodded. 'Areet, Tom.'

The caretaker winked at the boy. 'Areet, Sonny Gee.'

Joe bridled. 'Kna each other, do ye?'

The caretaker smiled. 'He's stopping with ye, isn't he?'

'Who are ye?' the boy demanded.

'Me? Ah used to work with yer granda,' said the caretaker as he opened the gates. They swung open, creaking heavily.

Sonny Gee stared at Tom. 'Who's me granda?' he asked.

Puzzled, the caretaker looked at Joe. 'They need oil,' put in the old man quickly. 'The hinges. They're crying oot for oil.' He shook his head. 'Not like ye to neglect yer tools, man Tom.'

When the caretaker had gone, Sonny Gee reached out to the gate. 'Divven't even think aboot it,' Joe warned him.

'Who's me granda?' the boy shot back.

There was no reply.

The children began to arrive. Their shouts filled the air as they crowded into the yard. 'Ha'way,' said the old man.

'Na,' replied the boy.

'What d'ye mean?'

'Ah'm not gannin',' the boy said. 'Neebody gans to school. Only divvies. Or swots.'

Shaking his head, Joe carried on through the gates. More and more children were arriving. Sonny Gee had retreated from the gates back through the church grounds to the large lime tree.

'Can I help you?' A teacher was moving across the yard to the old man.

'They sound happy enough,' the old man said, indicating a laughing group of children.

The teacher did not seem to hear him. 'Can I help you?'

'Ah just live awer there,' began Joe. 'Yon side of that.' Raising his stick, he pointed out the wall.

'Do you want something?'

'Aye.'

The teacher waited for a few moments, more children arrived. 'Well?' she said, a querulous tone creeping into her voice.

'It's a canny enough school this one, isn't it?'

The teacher broke off, to call an instruction over at a boy. The old man turned to look. 'I'm sorry, you can't stay here,' she said.

'Eh?'

'You can't stay here.'

Puzzled, Joe looked levelly at the teacher, a young woman in her mid-twenties. 'What d'ye mean, lass?'

'I mean it's school policy. We have to challenge any strangers we find on or about the premises.'

'Strangers?'

The woman crossed her arms. 'I'm just doing my job. I've no doubt that there's nothing suspicious about your presence but the policy states that if we encounter any strangers we must challenge them.'

'What are ye gannin' on aboot strangers for?'

'If we see a stranger we must . . .'

The old man interrupted her. 'What do yus mean, strangers? Ah've lived on the hill all me life.' The teacher tried to speak, but he silenced her by stiffly turning his body about to describe the arc of the school buildings. 'Ah built that school. With me own hands. After a shift of ten or twelve long hours underground holding a drill and swinging a pick.' He jerked his head to the church behind. 'And that church an' all. Ah can tell ye what bricks ah laid and what ones ah didn't.' His breathing grew shallow as his agitation increased. 'Before any o' this was built, ah sat in a shack that was both school and church, shivering in winter.' His eyes widened with increasing bewilderment. 'There's been an O'Brien on this hill for as long as there was coal beneath it. We were here before the famine brought the rest of Ireland to Britain.' His head shook, flecks of foam beaded his top lip. 'So how can ah be a stranger? How can anyone be a stranger when they're more part of a place than the trees or the birds?' There was a silence, filled by the laughter of children. Joe sighed heavily. 'Oh, what's the point?' he added despondently.

'I'm only doing my job,' the teacher said at last.

'Aye,' replied the old man, tonelessly. 'Aye. Anyway,' he began again, wearily, 'there's a bairn ah want ye to meet. He's a bit shy so he mebbes won't come right over. And ah cannet pretend he's not difficult, but if he causes yus any trouble just come and get me. Ah'll sort him oot for ye.'

'Hold on, what are you talking about?'

'There's a bairn,' Joe turned. 'There he is,' he said, lifting the stick once more to point. Sonny Gee could be seen under the lime tree, his hands grasped defensively round the trunk behind him, his eyes downcast as the children streamed past him through the gates. A game of cricket had started up around him, but he did not lift his head. 'It'll only be for a few days. A week at the outside.'

'Oh,' said the teacher. 'You want to enrol somebody.'

'Ah divven't kna aboot any enrolling . . .'

'Well, what do you mean then?'

'It'll just be for a few days.'

'What school does he attend now?' The old man blinked. 'Is he in education?' The teacher looked over at the boy.

'Look,' replied Joe, 'ah keep on telling ye, it's only for a few days. He's over there. Ah'll tell him to come over, and if there's any problem ah'll come to the school straight away and sort him oot. Ye could even call wor from here and ah'd hear.'

The teacher shook her head, and pursed her lips. 'Ye want a child to start attending this school?'

'Ye ask Father Michael, he knas wor.'

'Father Michael?'

The old man narrowed his eyes. 'He knas who ah am.'

'That's not the issue here.'

'What is then?'

'You can't just walk into a school, leave a child and expect him to start.'

'Why not?'

'Because it doesn't work that way. I mean, are you his legal guardian?'

'Ah'm looking after him.'

'You know his parents, do you?'

'He's staying with me for a bit.'

'Well, who are you?'

The old man swallowed hard. 'Ah'm his grandfather.'

'I see. Well, you'll have to have an appointment to which you must bring all the correct documentation.'

The old man's eyes flashed. 'Ah'm sending a lad to school, not buying a hoose.'

'Birth certificate, baptismal certificate and all the appropriate paperwork forwarded from his last school. And even then we'd have to see his legal guardian.' The teacher paused for a moment. 'We'll have to see his mam.'

'His mam?'

'Or his dad,' she added uncertainly.

'Even just for a few days?' There was a note of desperation in the old man's voice, and as the young woman nodded, he looked away from her.

'How old is he?'

Glancing about for a few moments, Joe watched the children play. 'Ah see how it is,' he said softly and then turned.

He walked back across the yard and out through the gates. When he reached the boy, Sonny Gee studied his face. 'Ah knew them's wouldn't want wor,' he said, proudly. 'None of them dee.'

Joe did not reply. When they had gone a short way one of the little cricketers struck the ball so that it raced away, running between the old man and the boy, coming to rest just in front of them. They stopped. Joe looked at the ball and then at the boy. 'Ha'way,' he said, 'throw it back for them.'

The boy bent down and picked up the ball. One of the fielders stopped about ten yards away and smiled. Sonny Gee stared back at him, puzzled. A smile hovered over his own features for a moment, and then faded. He lifted his arms and hurled the ball further away. Bemused, the fielder ran away to get it. 'That's nee four,' he shrieked back to the batsman. 'That's nee four.'

They walked down the cut. Joe stopped abruptly at the lamp-post. 'What d'yus want to gan and dee that for?' he asked.

'What?'

'Hoying them little lads' cricket ball away.'

'Ah just did.'

'Yus'll nivver make any friends like that.'

Sonny Gee shrugged. 'Divven't want nee friends, me.'

'Yes ye do,' replied the old man with annoyance.

'Ah divven't.'

'Ye dee.'

'Ah divven't.'

'Aye ye dee. Everybody needs friends.'

The boy blinked. 'Well ye haven't got none neither, gadgie mista.' He looked closely at the old man. 'Apart from that Springy Jack chaver.'

They were nearing the garden gate when a woman shouted after them. She was round and her cheeks puffed out as she came up the row from her own cottage to meet them. Joe put his head down and quickened his pace. 'Joe, Joe!' she cried.

'Hurry up,' Joe hissed at Sonny Gee, but before he could turn his key in the lock, the woman had reached them.

'Ah've been shouting of ye,' she said, breathlessly.

Joe turned the key and opened the door. 'Ah didn't hear ye, Peggy.'

'Didn't hear? Ah was shouting meself blue,' said Peggy, opening the gate and rolling down the little path like a ball. 'Hello, bonny lad. Who are you?'

'Kevin Keegan,' replied the boy. 'An' which Teletubby are ye, auld wifie?'

'Eh?' said Peggy, she turned to the old man. 'Ah knew it. The other night. Ye lied to me. Ah thought Catholics weren't supposed to lie. And ah was calling on ye. Ah kna who he is an' all, and that's another thing ah thought Catholics weren't supposed to dee. He's your Mary's, isn't he?'

Ushering the boy into the house, Joe turned to block

Peggy's way. 'Ah divven't hear so well in me left lug,' he said.

'But ah was coming from the other side.'

The old man shrugged. 'Aye, well, me right one's not so chipper either, but.'

'Ye were ignoring us, man Joseph O'Brien.'

'Ah wasn't.'

'Course ye were. Ah bet they could hear us the other side of Gatesheed.'

'Well, they usually can, Peggy man.'

'And what's that supposed to mean?'

Joe sighed. 'Look, Peggy, ah'm busy right now.'

'Ah kna who he is. He's the same one what was at the bus stop the other day, isn't he? He's the same one ye said what wasn't with ye.' A smile carved out a curve on Peggy's fat, rubicund face. 'Ha'way, let's have a look at him.' Joe began to close the door. 'Let's see the bonny lad. Let's see yer grandbairn.'

'Frigg off, auld wifie Teletubby!' shouted Sonny Gee.

The door closed with a crashing slam.

'Ee!' she gasped. 'He shut the door in me face. He shut it reet in me face. He's always been a moody beggar, but this caps the lot.' There was a pause. When she spoke again, it was loud enough to be heard both inside and outside. 'Mind ye, now ah've seen him ah kna for sure. What Ethel said Gemma said. Ah kna for a fact. He's a chip off the auld block, him,' she yelled bickeringly at the door. 'Reet doon to the lack o' bloody manners. D'ye hear, ye mean divvel? Ye friggin' left footer.' Her voice rose to a shout. 'Nee wonder your Mary turned oot the way she did, with ye as a father. Nee wonder she's spawned a line o' bastards. Anybody would have gone bad with the likes o' ye. Ye miserable get. Yus're like a geet bloody Eeyore, the way ye gan aboot the place. Ye've nee more heart than a seam o' coal. And yer grandbairn; why, he's the pot model o' ye. He's the spit o' ye and just as bloody ignorant.'

Inside the house, the old man and the boy stood in the passage without moving. Sonny Gee stared at Joe, suspicion narrowing his eyes. 'Gadgie mista, who's yer grandbairn?' he asked after a while.

7

Delving into the bin liner brought by Audrey, Joe pulled out a pair of trousers and a sweatshirt. He laid them over the back of the settee. 'That should be enough for a few days,' the old man said. 'The rest of that lot can gan straight back. And yus divven't want them toys.' Without looking at the boy, he held a hand out. 'Pass us that hat, they might as well have that an' all.' Sonny Gee was standing at the window; he did not reply. 'Ha'way, look sharpish. Give us that hat.' The boy raised a hand to lightly touch the red cowboy hat he was wearing. 'Are ye deaf, lad?'

'Na, but ye are.'

'What d'ye mean by that?'

'That's what ye told that Peggy wifie.'

Joe looked down at the objects on the table. 'Put them out in the back, will ye?'

One after another the boy lugged the things outside. When he came back, the old man was sitting at the table. 'Ah told ye, sling the hat in one of them bags. Divven't say ye want to keep it?' The boy shrugged. 'Well, ah suppose it won't dee nee harm. They can have it back when yus've gone. Divven't knacker it any more, but; ah see yus've already pulled off part of the frill.'

The boy moved over to the settee and crashed down as though exhausted.

'What's the matter with ye, like?' Joe asked.

'Ah'm knackered.'

Joe snorted. 'Ye haven't done nowt.' Placing a newspaper on the carpet, the old man began to polish the boots. He worked meticulously, and despite the odd jar of pain in his hands, he brushed and rebrushed every inch of the cracked leather until it shone. With satisfaction he lifted each boot up in turn and studied it. Sonny Gee watched him. 'Why did yus say that to Peggy?' Joe asked some time later. 'Ye were rude, man lad.'

'So were ye.'

Joe paused awkwardly. 'Aye, but ah didn't use language.'

'Neither did ah.'

'Ah've told ye, that's language.'

'What's language?'

'That word ye used.'

'What word?'

'Ye kna very well, lad.'

The boy shrugged. 'But ah didn't say fuck.'

'Ah kna what ye're deein',' the old man said, shaking his head. 'Divven't think ah divven't kna what ye're deeing.'

'Ah'm gannin' to sleep,' said Sonny Gee wearily. 'That's what ah'm deeing.' He pulled the brim of the cowboy hat low over his face.

The old man glowered at the boy. 'It's the middle of the day.'

'So?' replied the boy.

'So stir yer stumps, man. We're away oot noo.'

'Eh?' The boy looked at Joe. 'But ah'm knackered.'

'Nivver mind that. And divven't think ye've got oot o' it. Ah won't have language.'

'It wasn't nee language.'

'Ye've an answer for everything, ye.'

'Well, divven't ye?' shot back the boy, lifting the hat off his head.

'See?'

'See?' parroted the boy.

'Yus'll just rile folks, gannin' on like that, lad. Ye're in with yer bit of cheek before anyone can say Jack Robinson.'

'Is that his name then?'

'Eh?'

'That Spring man. Is his real name called Jack Robinson?'

They gazed at each other for a few more moments. 'Ye always have to have the last word,' said Joe.

'Ah divven't.'

'Aye, ye dee.'

Sonny Gee shook his head vibrantly. 'It's not me what gets in the last word. It's ye.'

'Divven't talk daft.'

'Ah'm not.'

'Ye are.'

There was a pause. The old man levered himself to his feet. 'Ha'way,' he said.

The boy sighed wearily. 'Where we gannin' noo?'

'Ah'm not having ye lying there all day.'

'But ah'm knackered.'

'Ye've done nowt.'

'Ah went to that school.'

'That's nowt, man.'

'And ah got washed. And carried all that tackle aboot an' all.'

'Dear me, if ye think that's hard work. What d'yus dee at yer mam's?'

'Nowt. Not in the day.' With an almighty effort, the boy pulled himself to his feet. But he only managed to make it to his knees. With a dramatic yawn, he fell neatly across the hearthrug. 'Ah telt ye, gadgie mista, ah'm knackered.'

'Get up.'

'Ah'm gannin' to sleep.'

'Get up.'

Sonny Gee closed his eyes, and pretended to snore. For a while Joe stared at the boy in puzzlement. Then his eyes narrowed. 'Pity he's asleep,' he mused loudly. 'He won't be able to get his present now.'

The boy pretended to stir. 'Eh?' he asked.

'Ah thought ye were asleep.'

'Ye woke wor up.' There was a pause. 'How d'yus mean, present?'

'Doesn't matter, since ye're so tired.'

Sitting up, the boy yawned. 'What was that aboot a present, gadgie mista?'

'Ah thought ye were knackt oot.'

Sonny Gee stretched extravagantly. 'Feel better for them forty winks.'

'No, no, no,' remonstrated Joe. 'Ye stay and have yer kip.'

'Ah'm areet noo,' said the boy, standing.

Joe nodded. 'Ha'way then.'

Sonny Gee followed Joe down the passage. 'Why ye gonnae buy wor a present when ah purely dee yer heed in?'

'Because ah'm not having ye chewing on all day. Just because they won't have ye in school, doesn't mean ye have to sit on yer hands all day.' Joe moved to the kitchen, then he stopped in the doorway. 'Just sit there for a bit, will ye, and then we'll gan.'

Turning from the boy, the old man went to the cupboard and opened the door. Taking out the contents, a tin of pork sausages in baked beans, a tin of soup, a few slices of bread, a box of porridge oats and a salt cellar, he laid them quietly down on the surface, then turned his head warily to check the door to the sitting room before bringing out the last thing. It was a tea caddy. Taking out his glasses from the pocket of his cardigan, he put them on, then, with one eye hovering watchfully at the door, he opened the caddy. Carefully upending it, a wad of notes fell free, some coins spilling out loudly. Joe froze as the coins jangled noisily over the surface. Hiding the notes behind his back, he crept over to the door. But the boy was sitting on the settee, fidgeting with the brim of his hat. Going back to the cupboard, Joe carefully peeled one of the notes from his small store, then, after deliberation, took a second one. Softly he began to whistle. The whistling grew louder. He had just repacked the contents of the cupboard when he turned to see Sonny Gee watching him. Their eyes met. 'What ye deeing there?' Joe demanded. The boy did not reply. 'Ah said what ye deeing there? What did ye see?'

'Ah didn't see nowt,' answered the boy, bewildered by the severity of the old man's inquisition.

'Are ye sure aboot that?' Joe barked, stuffing the notes in a pocket.

'What yus gannin' on aboot, gadgie mista?'

Surreptitiously Joe felt the two notes he had put in his pocket. 'Are ye sure, yus didn't see nowt?'

Sonny Gee shook his head. 'Ah cannet whistle, me. Ah'd love to. It's mint.'

'Ha'way then,' the old man said. 'We're gannin' oot.' When the old man came back from the passage he was carrying the walking stick and wearing his coat and flat cap. He pulled his heavy boots on.

'Where d'yus get thems from?' the boy asked.

There was no reply. Together they walked down the passage. 'Take that daft hat off,' said Joe, pointing at the boy's cowboy hat.

'Why should ah?'

'Ye look like a donkey on the sands at South Shields.'

'So do ye.'

'Don't talk daft. Do ye even kna what a donkey is?'

'Aye, ah dee.'

Joe looked levelly at the boy. 'Come on then. What is a one? What's a donkey?' The boy did not reply. The old man snorted. 'Told ye.'

Sonny Gee shrugged. 'Ye didn't.'

'Ah cannet believe ye,' replied Joe. 'Ye're so stubborn. Ye just won't be told. Ye might not kna what a donkey is, but ye could teach a mule a few tricks.'

The boy blinked. He glowered at the old man for a few seconds, then began shouting. 'Ah'm nee mule, me,' he yelled. 'Ah'm nee mule!'

In sullen silence they walked down the cut. The boy stared about anxiously as they passed the lamp-post. 'Is he at school then? Springsy Jack?'

'Aye,' replied Joe. 'But he'll be back this afternoon.'

The bus took them down Lobley Hill and then across the Team Valley Trading Estate. Here the roads are wide, and countless Transit vans shift busily between light industrial units like beetles. Where once the little River Team meandered across water meadows under the shifting dazzles of the sun, it is now imprisoned in culverts and between steep concrete banks. In days gone by, the colliers cultivated this land, supplementing their meagre income by fattening pigs and geese and growing vegetables.

Coming out of the valley, the bus climbed Windmills Hill where the cherry trees grow. The boughs of the trees lifted and fell in the breeze like the sails of the mills which gave the hill its name. With each little gust, cherry blossom as white as flour scattered on top of the bus.

When they stopped on Old Parsonage Road, Sonny Gee turned a puzzled eye on the old man. But Joe shook his head tersely, and the bus pulled off once more. 'Where we gannin'?' he asked. 'The airport?'

'Divven't talk daft; what do we want to gan to the airport for?'

The service terminated at Gateshead Central Interchange. The old man and the boy got off with the rest of the passengers, and walked along a pedestrianised street lined with charity shops, estate agents, housing offices and a green-grocer's. They passed a Tesco supermarket and then the windowless warehouse of the Jobcentre outside of which stood a group of smokers huddled round their cigarettes. A faster flow of people came up the stairs from the Metro Underground, but Joe did not quicken their speed. 'Where we gannin'?' demanded Sonny Gee. The boy stopped for a moment to watch a girl roller skate by. 'Ha'way, pet,' he called. 'Give wor a lift.' Tutting, the old man carried on. Above them loomed the empty multi-storey car park, whose sheer concrete sides rise above the skyline of central Gateshead like sea cliffs. 'Where we gannin'?' The sudden roar of buses turning at the terminal continually pulsed out over the scene, like the restless heaving of waves seething themselves on to a shore. Following the old man, Sonny Gee came to the square.

A small figure sat alone on one of the many benches there. He was surrounded by pigeons. The boy watched as more and more birds arrived, landing heavily, inelegantly, perching on the bench around the small figure. They flew in from roosts on the roofs and the endless ledges of the multi-storey car park, until the small figure was scarcely visible beneath their fast-flapping wings. Sonny Gee watched, his mouth wide open.

The figure stood up, and for a moment his arms showed. He raised them high, the palms of his hands full of seed. But quickly he vanished beneath the prod of beak and feather of the scavenging birds. Just then the alarm of a shop rang out and the flock took fright. A woman ran through the square, closely pursued by two security officers, but the boy was mesmerised by the pigeons. Sonny Gee stared up as they lifted, his head tilting back to follow as they rose higher and higher. The feeder was nowhere to be seen, as though he too had wings and was wheeling with the flock over Gateshead's centre. It was only when the boy's eyes lowered to the square once more that he found the little man. He had sat back down on his bench. Unaccompanied, solitary, he seemed somehow even smaller without the pigeons, a lonely figure with a crumpled bag of seed.

The shouts of the security officers echoed loudly against the concrete sides of the square, followed by a single, forlorn cry from the woman as she was apprehended. A little while later, the two security guards passed back through the square, one of them holding the woman captive, the other gripping the small booty of her theft: a packet of disposable Pampers. 'Mista, tell wor summink,' said the boy.

The small man raised a hand as a pigeon fluttered down from a litter bin. It landed on the hand. Both man and pigeon looked over at Sonny Gee. 'What shall ah tell yus, bonny lad?'

The boy pointed at the bird. 'Do thems talk?'

There was a pause. The man stroked the bird, his broken-nailed, nicotine-stained finger delicately caressing the pigeon's gleaming green crop. The bird cooed softly. 'Ye try him,' the man offered. Cautiously, the boy approached. Stretching out a finger, he too stroked the bird. Again it crooned its pleasure. 'See?' asked the man.

Sonny Gee sat down on the bench beside him. 'Na,' he said, 'ah divven't mean that. Ah mean proper speak. Like . . . like a gadgie.'

The man smiled thoughtfully. 'Ah divven't kna aboot that.'

Another bird landed at the man's feet, then a second. The birds cooed. Disappointment clouded the boy's face. He shook his head. 'Ah want them to talk. Ah want them to talk.'

'What are ye deein'?' The boy looked up to see Joe standing over him. 'What are ye deein' bothering that gentleman?'

'It's areet,' said the man. 'Ah divven't mind the bairn.'

'Well, ah dee, get up now.'

As he stood up, Sonny Gee had to duck the incoming pigeons. The old man strode over the square; the boy followed. 'Ah wasn't bothering him,' he called.

'Ye were, ah could see ye with me own eyes.'

'Ah wasn't bothering him.'

Sonny Gee reached Joe who had stopped for him. 'What were yus doing then?' the old man asked.

'Talking.'

'Aye, well, that's bothering him.'

The pair of them looked across the square. The diminutive figure was once more submerged under the gathering flock of pigeons.

For a few moments the boy continued to stare over the square at the pigeons, then he looked up at the old man. 'Where we gannin', gadgie mista?'

'Ha'way,' sighed Joe, setting off again.

They passed under the gilded balls of a pawn shop, went by the bright window of a Cash Generator and passed the open door of a vertical tanning shop called Tanfastic. Its advertising read: *Stand as you tan. New tubes just in. Tan up to four times faster. £5 worth of free beauty make-over vouchers.* They reached the entrance to the indoor market. 'Belter,' said the boy.

'Kna the market, do yus?'

'Course ah dee. Ah want to gan to the pet shop. It's mint.'

They pushed through the heavy doors, just on the other side of which a market researcher stood, pen poised over a clipboard like the spring of a trap. 'Got a few minutes, pet?' she asked a man who had entered the market just behind Joe and Sonny Gee.

'That's the best offer ah've had all day,' replied the man.

Sonny Gee stopped to stare at the market researcher. 'Are ye a prozzy?'

'Ha'way, ye!' snapped the old man.

'Can ah just ask yus if ye can remember seeing any o' these products?' the woman asked, flipping open a series of pictures.

The young man looked at the pictures of alcoholic drinks. 'If ah dee then they cannet have been doing their job properly.'

'Ah want to gan to the pet shop,' said Sonny Gee, falling in with Joe.

'Ye just divven't kna how to behave ye, do ye?'

'That pet shop's belter, gadgie mista. Ah'm gannin' there now.'

'Ye're coming with me first.'

'Na, ah'm not. Ah'm gannin' to that pet shop.'

'Yus won't get yer present.'

The boy's face flashed with sudden excitement. 'What's me present gonnae be?'

'Ye behave yerself and then ye'll see.'

Under a low ceiling, they walked down the aisles, tightly packed with stalls offering everything from kitchenware to clothes, from second-hand electrical goods to a paperback exchange, and from greetings cards to tarot card readings. The hands of the buyers and sellers moved over the stock with the dexterity of conjurors. The further they walked into the market, the more pervasive grew the smell of fried food. The chatter of human voices grew louder too. At last they reached the café. Unbuttoning his coat, the old man put it over a chair. He took off his cap. 'Sit down then, lad, it's dinner time.'

'Ah'm not hungry, me.'

'There'll be nee present then.'

On the table stood two vinegar bottles, one was full of vinegar, the other sugar. Reaching out, Joe pointedly pulled the sugar over to his side. The boy sat down. Immediately he had stretched a hand to the little metal foil ashtray. 'Put it back,' Joe told him.

The boy stared at him in confusion. 'But them two tab ends are only half smoked.'

'Ah said put it back.'

The boy threw the tray across the table, scattering the cigarette ends. 'Ah'm gannin' to that pet shop, me,' he said. As he rose, he knocked the side of the table so that the stick which had been balancing on the corner clattered to the ground. The noise seemed to check them both.

'It's dinner time,' said Joe quietly after a while.

'Ah divven't care.'

'It's dinner time. Ye need to eat.'

'Ah divven't.'

The old man raised his eyes to the ceiling. A profound

weariness swept over him. 'Areet then,' he sighed. 'Ah'm not gonnae argue with ye any more. Ah'm not gonnae battle. If ye divven't want to eat, divven't bother. It's nee skin off my nose.'

'Have ah done yer heed in?' asked the boy, but there was no boast in his tone.

'Aye,' replied Joe quietly.

Sonny Gee reached out to pick up the vinegar bottle, but after playing with it a moment, he put it back. A look of worry seemed to cloud his blue eyes. 'Am ah still getting me present, gadgie mista?' The old man did not answer. The voices of the other customers seemed to cluster together. 'Is it me birthday?' The tone of the boy's voice was so strange that it caused Joe to look over at him. 'Ah hope it is,' he continued in the same unfamiliar tone. 'Ah've nivver had a birthday, me.' The child's eyes flickered dreamily. 'Ah'll have some dinner,' he said softly. 'Ah'll eat owt if ah can have a birthday present.'

The old man stared at him in bemusement.

'Please, gadgie mista, make it me birthday.'

The old man continued to stare for a while, then roughly pulled himself to his feet. 'Ah'll gan and get wor dinner,' he said gruffly. At the counter he put on his glasses and consulted the large menu fixed to a grease-splattered wall, his lips moving as he read it. 'One soup and a roll,' he said after some time. 'And one ham butty.' In the mirror fixed on the wall over the huge tea urn, Joe could see the reflection of the boy. He gazed at him, his eyes narrowing. Sonny Gee was looking around the café, his glance roving quickly from table to table. A fork was dropped by someone right at the other side of the café, and instantly the boy turned to where the noise had come from.

'Ah'll bring them over,' said the teenage girl in stained white overalls who was serving the old man. 'Ye divven't need to wait. Ah'll carry them awer.'

With a jolt Joe came round to himself and slowly returned

to the table. A few moments later the girl brought the tray over. She waved a spoon questioningly. Through the corner of his eye, the boy peered nervously at it. 'The soup's for me,' Joe said.

The old man had been eating for some time when he noticed that Sonny Gee had not touched his sandwich. 'It's areet, man,' he said. 'Ye can use yer hands.' But still the boy did not start to eat. 'Gan on. That's why ah got yus a butty.'

Sonny Gee was staring dubiously at the sandwich. 'Is it chips?'

'See for yerself.'

Sonny Gee bent his whole body over the sandwich and lifted a corner of the bread. 'Funny-looking chips, them.'

'It's not chips.'

The boy's face turned lopsided with incomprehension. 'What is it then?'

Joe took another mouthful of soup, and then waved his spoon at the boy's plate. 'It's ham, man.'

'Ham?'

'Divven't say yus've nivver had a ham sandwich?'

The boy tutted. 'Course ah have,' he said, but he prodded the bread uncertainly. Taking a bite, he chewed mistrustfully. 'Gadgie mista,' he whispered, having swallowed the mouthful with an effort. 'They've had ye.'

The old man took a bite from his roll. 'What ye gannin' on aboot?'

Sonny Gee looked furtively at the counter where the girl was shovelling chips from the fryer on to a plate. 'They've put grass in there.' He pointed at the sandwich, and took another bite. He crunched loudly. 'Ah think there's a dock leaf an' all.'

'It's salad.'

'Eh?'

'Salad.'

'What's that?'

'Ye divven't kna what salad is?'

'Course ah dee,' boasted the boy. 'Na, ah divven't,' he admitted a few seconds later.

Joe sighed. 'It grows in the groond,' he said.

'In the groond?' said the boy. Understanding dawned on him. 'Like tac,' he said, nodding. 'They raided the bedsits down from us. The pollis found them all empty. Inside was growing all the tac. Under geet big lamps. They tried to pin it on Macca but . . .' Abruptly the boy broke off. He stared over at the man. 'When ah'm not staying at yours any more,' he said, quietly, 'where am ah gannin'?'

Joe took another bite from his roll, then began eating the soup again. 'Ha'way,' he said. 'Get that sandwich eaten. It's full of goodness.'

'Can we gan to the pet shop now?' demanded Sonny Gee.

'Later. We'll finish wor dinner and then we've yer schooling to see to.'

'Ah'm not gannin' to nee school. Ah'm gannin' to the pet shop.'

The old man led him through the market, stopping at a stationery stall. On the table before them was a small selection of notebooks, pens, pencils, tin pencil cases. Wads of paper stood stacked between bottles of ink on a shelf. A mug of tea balanced on a stool was the only sign of a proprietor. The old man peered closely at the notebooks, adjusting his glasses with stiff fingers. He looked at each one on display before making his selection. It was a small, red hard-backed A5 book. 'What d'ye think o' that one?' he said to Sonny Gee. The boy shrugged, and turned again in the direction of the pet shop which could just be seen between two other stalls. 'It's not very big,' continued Joe, 'but ye won't know many words yet, do ye?'

'Ah kna two. Pet and shop.'

'That's three,' answered the old man, a gnarled forefinger resting on the smooth red of the little notebook's cover. 'Anyway, by the time ye get to know more words ye'll be back at your auld school. This'll dee for now. It's only for a few days.'

'Then where am ah gannin'?' Sonny Gee asked.

'What about a pencil?' the old man replied. 'D'yus want a pen or a pencil?'

Sonny Gee sighed and looked back at the pet shop. 'Divven't bother, ye can get them free.'

'Free?'

'Aye. Argos, Index or the bookies.'

Joe knotted his eyebrows so that the glasses lifted slightly. 'Ah'll get yus a pencil an' all.' He began to root through the pencils, which were all held together by a rubber band.

'Ha'way, it'll be shut if ye divven't get a move on. The gadgie what owns it gans to the café for his dinner. Takes ages to eat it.'

'The pet shop can wait.'

The boy turned a desperate, voracious face on the old man. 'Na, it cannet. They've got scorpions there. Ginormous centipedes. Geet big lizards . . .' Sonny Gee's voice faltered with amazement. 'It's just . . . it's just . . . the bestest place in the world!'

'Aye, well, think about what pencil ye might want,' said Joe, frowning. 'There's a Toon Army one in there, or a Beamish Museum one.'

The boy was not listening. 'They're all just there. In the pet shop. Ye can gan in and just see them. Ye just gan in and see everything.'

'Beamish Museum,' mused Joe, studying the pencil. He glanced closely at the little ink drawing on the wood. 'Heritage museum. A pit village of yesterday.'

'Aye,' said Sonny Gee enthusiastically. 'It's purely belter in that pet shop. Ye look at them and thems look back at ye. All with geet big eyes.'

The old man shook his head. 'Who in their right mind wants to remember them days?'

135

'And sometimes ye think there's nowt there, but it's watching ye all the time.'

'It was blood, sweat and toil, and noo people gan there for a day oot.'

'Like what ye think was a stick or summink wasn't. It was a insect. Or a snake.'

At that moment their eyes met in mutual incomprehension. 'What ye gannin' on aboot now?' the old man asked.

'What are *ye* gannin' on aboot?' the boy replied.

'Which pencil d'yus want? There's a Toon Army one or a Beamish one?'

'Ah divven't give a toss aboot nee pencil, gadgie mista, ah want to gan to the pet shop.'

The old man looked at the wares on the stall. He pointed at the bundle of pencils. 'Take one from there,' he said quietly. 'And any more from ye and we're gannin' straight home.'

Fear widened the boy's eyes. 'But what aboot me present and the pet shop?'

'There will be nee present and nee pet shop if ye divven't behave.'

'And what aboot if *ye* divven't behave?' Sonny Gee burst out. He was about to add more, but he stopped himself by physically clamping a hand over his own mouth. He reached out for the pencils, and without looking, selected one.

'That's reet,' nodded Joe. 'Ye'll want that one with a rubber on the end. So, we'll have that pencil, and that notebook.' The old man handed the notebook and pencil to the boy. 'Ah wonder where the owner is?' he said, craning to see behind a curtain. Taking the things from Joe, Sonny Gee began to walk off. 'And where d'ye think ye're gannin'?' the old man asked.

'The pet shop,' replied the boy.

'Ah haven't paid for them yet.'

'Ah kna,' the child smiled widely. 'Ha'way.'

'Ye come back here this instant,' Joe hissed. 'Shop?' he called loudly. 'Anyone in the shop?'

A few moments later the curtain twitched, and a woman emerged, yawning. 'Ee, ah must have dozed off,' she said. She reached out to touch the mug of tea. 'It's stone cold,' she said with a shiver.

'We'll take these please,' the old man said. Turning to the boy, he gestured him forward. With a long-suffering sigh, Sonny Gee handed the pencil and notebook to the woman.

'Thanks, sonny boy,' the woman said, yawning again.

'It's Sonny Gee,' the boy said, petulantly.

'Ee, that's an unusual name,' the stallholder remarked. 'Is it from a film?'

'A racehorse more like,' quipped Joe. 'Or a donkey on South Shields front. Aye, he's got the hat to gan with it an' all.'

The boy narrowed his eyes. 'Better than being called gadgie mista,' he spat back.

'Aye,' said Joe, fumbling his money out. 'Ah suppose it is, just aboot. But then neeone calls us that. Except ye.'

'Are ye gonnae carry them, Sonny Jim?' asked the stallholder.

'Ah telt ye, it's Sonny Gee,' said the boy, taking the notebook and the pencil. 'Not Sonny Jim. Sonny Gee.'

'Behave yerself, ye,' warned Joe, 'and give wor them things. Ye'll only lose them.'

They walked through the market in silence. When they reached the pet shop, the boy broke and ran over to it; walking more slowly, Joe followed him inside.

The steamy heat hit them immediately. It was the close, humid air of a rainforest. Tanks and cages lined endless metal stacks; ferns and other greenery grew from huge earthenware pots. From somewhere deep within the shop came the cry of a jungle creature. The cry was taken up by countless other voices until a deafening din reverberated round the shop. Slowly it died down. Sonny Gee stared widely about him; for a few moments, his excitement seemed to overwhelm him and he did not move. Then, coming round, he dashed to the nearest tank, and falling to his knees, peered within. For a long time the boy remained motionless with the old man standing at a distance watching him. Slowly Joe approached. 'Divven't make a sound,' said the boy without looking up. 'They have to think ye're not there.'

'Eh?' replied Joe.

'Shh,' shot back the boy.

The old man came up behind him. 'There's nowt there, man,' he said.

'Ye've got to be quiet, man,' Sonny Gee murmured stridently. Joe gazed at the boy as he peered into the tank. 'They have to think ye're not here,' he breathed. 'They'll only come oot when they think neeone's aboot.'

The old man bent down, but as he was stooping his stick dropped. It clattered on the ground. There was another screech from deep within the shop. 'Now ye've done it,' snapped the boy. 'Ah telt yus to be quiet, man gadgie mista.'

The old man lowered himself painfully to pick up his stick. His face twitched with a sharp burst of agony. 'Divven't call us that,' he said softly.

There was a pause. 'What do ah call ye then?'

Just at that moment there was a screech from a stack high above them, and then something swept overhead. Instinctively they both ducked. 'What was that?' the old man asked.

Sonny Gee was trembling with excitement. 'It was a bird,' he said. 'A geet big bird.'

Joe stared after it, but the bird had flown further into the shop.

'Can ah help ye?' a voice suddenly boomed from some-where.

'That's him what owns it,' said Sonny Gee. 'But divven't worry. He's areet. He lets yus stay for ages just watching.'

'Welcome to Ronny's Exotica Petotica,' continued the loud and confident voice. 'We've got a wide range of exotic pets, ranging from the microscopic to the twenty-foot lang.' A flush of pride further beefed the voice. 'We're Gatesheed's premier stockist o' unusual hoose companions, as we call them in the trade nowadays.' The voice was growing louder, as its owner approached them. Suddenly, there was a rustling from in among a thick growth of ferns. 'Put it this way,' said the voice, from somewhere in the ferns, 'if it came off the ark then it'll be here somewhere.'

'Areet then, Ronny,' said Joe.

'Areet?' said the voice uncertainly, the rustling of foliage ceasing momentarily. 'Is that ye, Joe?'

'Aye.'

Sonny Gee looked up at the old man. 'D'ye kna him, like?' he asked disbelievingly.

'Ronny? Why aye. He lives at the end of the terrace.'

'Your terrace?'

'Aye.'

The tall ferns began to shimmer and shake.

'The pet shop gadgie lives on your auld terrace?' The boy's face screwed up with incredulity.

Suddenly, a hand appeared among the fan of ferns and parted them. A figure slowly emerged, head first so that a beaming, red-cheeked, cherubic face, framed by a pith helmet, materialised among the fronds. Then the rest of the body breasted itself free of the foliage. It was dressed in a full safari outfit. A pot-belly overhung a belt considerably; chunky calves bulged in fawn socks; and a huge ponytail dangled through a special hole made in the pith helmet. 'Joe O'Brien, ah presume?' the figure said with a grin.

'Areet, Ronny,' replied the old man. 'How's it gannin'?'

'Canny; yersel'?'

'Canny.'

Ronny nodded at Sonny Gee. 'Areet, bonny lad, ride 'em cooboy! Ah like yer hat.' He turned to Joe. 'Ah thought it was him,' he said. 'He's often mooching about the shop, so when they telt wor aboot the bairn staying with ye ah . . .' Ronny wilted under the old man's glare.

The boy's eyes expanded dreamily. 'Ah love this place, me.'

'Anyway,' said Ronny, shifting his feet. 'Have yus seen a African grey? It's a parrot, y'kna? Grey-coloured.' There was a squawk from behind a stack and once again something swept overhead. 'That's him,' said Ronny.

'Belter!' exclaimed the boy, setting off in the direction the parrot had flown.

'Careful,' the old man called.

'He's areet,' said Ronny.

'Well, ye've got this place looking grand,' remarked Joe. 'Just like a real jungle in here, isn't it? Bit hot, but.' He undid the buttons of his coat.

'Jungles are, man Joe lad, jungles are. This place is a concept, more than just a shop.'

'Aye, ah like yer plants.' The old man pointed at the pots of ferns.

Ronny nodded. 'Ah got them in a job lot from a fella ah kna on Woodside Gardens. Call him Big Al Three-Bellies. Had that mobile shop what sold shrubs and woody ferns. Jurassic Bark, he called it. Strictly speaking, they divven't have these exact ones in Africa. But the hoi polloi divven't kna that. They're from a garden centre in Middlesbrough originally, ah think.'

'Cannet yus dee summink aboot the heat?'

Ronny shook his head. 'That's what ah'm telling ye, man Joe. It's a concept.' Ronny took off his hat, carefully pulling free the ponytail. The rest of his head was completely bald. Beads of sweat clustered all over his brow. 'Take Iceland. Ye divven't want Iceland hot. Ye kna, when people walk into Iceland they expect it to be cold. So they'd expect an Exotica Petotica to be hot.'

'Iceland?'

'It's that shop. Y'kna, food. Frozen food.' Ronny deflated a little. 'It doesn't matter.' Then he rallied. 'Ye're not getting the full concept here, man Joseph.' Reaching into a pocket of his safari shorts, Ronny brought out a little remote control. Aiming over towards the counter, he pressed it. There was a click, followed by a hiss, and then music began to play.

'Born free,' a singer crooned, 'as free as the wind blows, as free as the grass grows . . .'

'Aye,' smiled Ronny, his eyes narrowing to appreciative slits. 'That hits the spot.'

For a while they listened to the music as they followed Sonny Gee down the shelving.

'Ah cannet see it nee more. That bird,' the boy called.

'We'll find him,' replied Ronny indulgently.

'How's trade then?' asked the old man. Ronny did not reply. 'Doing areet, are ye then, Ronny?'

'Aye, aye,' replied Ronny airily, wafting a hand. 'Born free!' he sang, in time with the tape. There was a loud chirp of birds. 'Thems is me lovebirds. Ah love me lovebirds, me. Ha'way, come and have a look at them.' He beamed widely. 'See this?' he said, indicating the shop with a wide sweep of his arms. 'Beats working undergroond in a pit, this.'

'That wouldn't be hard,' said Joe. He turned to Ronny. 'So is it them what's the most popular? Them lovebirds. What ye sell the most of, y'kna.'

Moving on from the lovebirds, Ronny drew Joe over to another cage with reinforced wiring. His voice dropped with awe. 'Ah bet ye won't have seen a one o' them before? They're ferocious them, y'kna. Ah tell ye what, in the wild we wouldn't get this close. Careful. Divven't reach doon to it. It'll have yer hand off as quick as look at it.'

'It looks deed to me.'

'Divven't be fooled.'

'Ah cannet see nee bird,' Sonny Gee called out.

'We'll find him,' replied Ronny.

Joe looked levelly at the other man. 'Yus aren't deeing very well, are ye, man Ronny?'

A haunted look came over Ronny's face, and the overweight, middle-aged man in the safari suit seemed to deflate. 'Hamsters,' he mumbled.

'Ye what?'

'Hamsters,' repeated Ronny, despairingly. He looked disconsolately about the shop. 'The whole place is underscored by frigging hamsters.' He paused, shaking his head. 'Ah've got the widest bloody range of strange pets in Tyne and Wear, y'kna, and all people want is hamsters.' Ronny fell silent for a while. Meditatively, he pulled gently on his ponytail. 'What kind of people prefer a hamster to me wide range of carnivorous fish?' He sighed. 'See, if ah won the lottery, kna what ah'd do? Ah'd buy a big place. Bout the size of the whole market . . .' His eyes widened as the idea grew within him. 'About the size o' the whole o' Gateshead, and ah'd make it like a natural environment, y'kna, what me exotic ones require, like. A rainforest, a river an' that, and ah'd fill it with the weirdest animals there are. And ah'd nivver sell a one. Ah'd let them all live in freedom. See, if ah won the lottery ah'd buy the whole Team Valley, dig up all the roads and units an' that, and ah'd turn it into . . .'

'Ye're a dreamer, that's what ye are,' said Joe, shaking his head sadly. 'Ye always were, even when ye worked doon the pit with wor.'

'Ye may say ah'm a dreamer,' sang Ronny with feeling, 'but ah'm not the only one. Ah hope some day ye'll join wor, and the world will live as one.'

'But ye are the only one, man Ronny. Who else in Gatesheed dresses up like Daktari, animal doctor?'

'Ye kna summink, but,' said Ronny, narrowing his eyes. 'Ye're summink of a one-off yersel', man Joe. But it's what makes the world gan roond. A bit colour.' He paused to meditate. 'Ah'm just deeing what John Lennon and Elvis Presley did, in me own way.'

'What?' asked the old man sceptically. 'Ye mean if they'd been from Gateshead they'd have opened a pet shop what neeone buys from?'

Ronny sighed. 'Gis a chance, man Joe,' he begged helplessly.

'Ye were deeing areet before ye got all them strange animals in what neebody wants. And changing the name of the shop. What was the matter with Ronny's Pets?' The old man glanced at his friend severely. He relented slightly. 'Sorry, marrer,' he said. 'Ah've one or two things on me mind at the minute.'

'The bonny lad,' replied Ronny, nodding his head. 'Cannet be easy having a grandbairn coming oot o' neewhere.'

'Divven't dee that,' called out the old man as Sonny Gee began delving through some dusty boxes underneath a shelf.

'Let him be,' mused Ronny.

'Born free,' mused the singer on the stereo system again.

'Free as the wind blows,' echoed Ronny. 'It's on a loop,' he added.

'Doesn't it play anything else?' asked the old man.

'Oh aye. "The Lion Sleeps Tonight". But that's on another tape. D'yus want wor to put that on?'

'No, ye're all right.'

There was a pause. The boy was noisily rifling through the boxes. 'Ye kna Big Al?' began Ronny again, somewhat darkly. Lowering his voice, he looked about suspiciously. 'He knas someone what's just moved into a new line of business. Fur. Hamster fur. Takes stacks o' them just to make a little jacket, like. But with the amount of them ah get through in a year ah could easy be a supplier.' He broke off to flick his ear, the lobe of which was missing. 'See that?' he asked. 'That was a hamster. Bit it off in a second.' Ronny sighed. 'Still, they're only creatures trying to make their own way, like the rest of us, ah suppose. Ah read somewhere that they actually hate human contact. Takes them twenty minutes to recover from the stress of being stroked.'

The old man stared at Ronny, shaking his head. 'Ye need a holiday, man Ronny.'

For a few moments they both watched the boy as he continued to search under the shelving. 'That bird won't be there,' said Joe testily.

'How d'ye kna?' Sonny Gee shot back.

'Got your looks,' mused Ronny.

The old man snorted acerbically. 'Been talking to Audrey, have ye? Or was it Gemma?'

'Gemma came doon for some breakfast cereals the other morning. But she didn't say who they were for. Ah put them doon to her cravings. Being up the stick an' that. Actually, it was auld Walter what telt wor.'

'What, jug-eared Wally from number five? He knas an' all? But he doesn't even kna what day of the week it is.'

Ronny nodded. 'Everybody does, man.' There was a pause. 'We all kna he's come to live with ye.'

'Well, yous all kna more than ah dee then.'

'Ha'way, Joe, ah've seen him meself, man.'

'He hasn't come to live with wor. He's only staying for a few days.'

'How long's he been there for now, like?'

There was a brief pause. 'A few days,' said the old man.

'So what ye gonnae do with him?'

Joe sighed. 'Ah divven't kna.'

'Born free,' crooned the tape.

'Will ye turn that off?' Joe demanded.

With a puzzled shrug, Ronny pointed the little remote control at a speaker. Steadily the music increased its volume until it reached distortion pitch. Then there was a final, ear-shattering hiss, and the sound died. 'The system's a bit dodgy,' admitted Ronny sheepishly. 'Big Al put it in for wor. He keeps on saying he's gonnae fix it.'

Just then, a figure could be seen coming into the shop. The top of a head was quickly concealed by the ferns. 'Welcome to Ronny's Exotica Petotica,' began Ronny, smoothing down the creases in his safari suit, a childlike enthusiasm brimming in his words. 'We've got a wide range of exotic pets from the microscopic to the twenty-foot lang. Let yer imagination swim through wor miniature Amazon. We're Gatesheed's prem-ier . . .'

'Hello, Ronny,' said the little girl who was standing in front of him.

'. . . stockist of small, furry rodents,' Ronny finished lamely, before wearily adding, 'Areet, Shereen. Not at school again the day?'

'Ah've come for some more bedding for me . . .'

'Just a minute, pet,' said Ronny, sighing as he bent beneath the counter to bring up a polythene bag of hamster bedding.

'. . . hamster,' finished Shereen.

When Shereen had gone, Ronny stared at the door miserably for a while. Then, leaning heavily against the cash register, he turned to Joe. 'Ah met Audrey in the café this morning.'

'Ah'm not talking aboot it any more.' The old man looked testily in the direction of the boy. 'Get up from there.'

'She was telling wor aboot the bedsit,' said Ronny. 'Y'kna, where he's been living with his mam.' Ronny paused, and looked away embarrassedly. 'Ah kna ye two had a falling-oot, man Joe.'

'Is that what ye'd call it?'

'Divven't worry, man. Ah'm not prying. Ah'll ah'm saying is that, why ah divven't think ye can send the bairn back there. To that bedsit.'

'Divven't ye?'

'Na. Ah'm not digging up the past, but ah divven't think

your Mary's up to caring for a bairn. Not at the minute. Not while she's all mixed up with drugs and that Macca gadgie. Between ye and me, that Macca's a bad lot. Big Al keeps his ear pretty close to the groond and ye should hear what he says about him.' Ronny dropped his voice to a whisper. 'Gannin' into heroin supplying, so Big Al says.' Ronny stared unblinkingly at the old man.

'This Big Al seems to kna just aboot everything,' said Joe drily.

'Aye,' nodded Ronny. 'He does. Put it this way, in a place like Gatesheed where pot-bellies come in sizes, it takes someone special to get the name Big.' Ronny broke off to laugh. 'Ah'm saving that for me comedy routine,' he said.

'Oh aye,' said Joe pointedly. 'Being a comedian. That's another dream o' yours, isn't it? Ah'd forgotten that one.'

'What ah'm trying to say is that ah divven't think we can send him back there.'

A bitter smile played over Joe's lips. 'So what d'ye suggest *we* dee, like?'

Ronny shrugged. 'All ah kna is that we cannet send him back there. Audrey cannet have him at the minute. Neither can Gemma. Anyway, we want summink long-term. And ye cannet have him. Not long-term, like.'

'Why not, expecting us to pop me clogs?'

Ronny smiled sadly. 'Ye've said so yersel'. Ye divven't even want him for a few days.'

'Well, would ye?'

'Aye,' Ronny nodded. His eyes gleamed. 'That's summink ah've nivver done. Mebbes ah would like it. Aye. Ah think ah've always fancied being a dad, me.'

'Being a dad? Ye divven't kna what yus're talking aboot.'

The abrupt severity of the old man's voice stunned them both into silence. 'Aye well,' began Ronny again after a while. 'The most important thing is to keep him away from Macca. Even being in care is better than being anywhere near Macca.'

'Care?' Joe spoke softly, but quickly.

'Aye,' nodded Ronny. Taking hold of his ponytail in one hand, he gently pulled at it, while the palm of his other hand explored the slap of his bald head. 'The thing is, if ye could get a good family . . .'

'A good family?'

'To foster. Or adopt even. If ye get a good family, then it's smashing.' He mused thoughtfully. 'Nee disrespect to your Mary, but if we could get a good family for him then it would be the best thing all roond.'

Joe blinked thoughtfully. 'Aye, that's what he needs.'

'The thing is, but,' said Ronny, 'if ye get a bad family, it can be messy. When all's said and done a good family isn't easy to find. And the homes they stay in, well, they dee their best, but from what ah've heard, they're proper shocking.'

But the old man wasn't listening. 'Adoption,' he said to himself. 'Find a good family. Adoption. Ah hadn't thought of that. Adoption.' He rolled the word about in his mouth.

'Where's the bairn gone?' Ronny said.

As Ronny and Joe had been talking, the boy had stolen up and then down the aisles of the shop, searching for the bird. Suddenly, he had stopped and, hearing a scrabbling on the stack high above his head, looked up. There, perched on an upturned tank, was the African grey parrot. 'What-ye-look-ing-at?' the parrot suddenly squawked.

The boy's eyes widened. He gazed at the bird breathlessly. 'D'ye talk?' he asked. As though in a trance, Sonny Gee watched the bird cleaning its feathers. 'D'ye talk?' the boy breathed once more.

'Where's-fat-boy?' the bird demanded, cocking its head at Sonny Gee.

'Ye dee talk!' the child marvelled. 'Ah knew it.' He tiptoed closer to the stack, lifting his head right back as he stared up. The bird stopped cleaning itself for a moment and glanced down. 'Ah knew it,' Sonny Gee whispered. 'They all telt wor ah was a divvy. But ah knew it. Ah knew birds could talk.'

There was a flurry of feathers as the parrot flew up. It landed lower down on the stacks, perching only a yard or so from the boy's rapt face. 'Ye're belter!' Sonny Gee breathed intently. 'Ye're . . .' He broke off to stare at the bird in utter wonder. After a few seconds he began once more, his voice barely a murmur. 'Will ye tell wor summink, mista bird?'

'You-ate-all-the pies,' the parrot interrupted him with a screech.

Sonny Gee shook his head. 'Not that,' he said.

'He's-fat-he's-roond-he-boonces-on-the-groond,' yelled the parrot.

Sonny Gee laughed. 'Ah divven't want to kna that.'

'Where's-fat-boy?'

'Not that. Ah want to kna . . .'

'What-are-ye-looking-at?'

The enthusiasm flickered for a moment on the boy's face. 'Listen, ah want to ask ye a question . . .'

'He's-fat-he's-roond-he-boonces . . .'

'Na,' Sonny Gee said, agitatedly. 'Listen to wor . . .'

'You-ate-all-the-pies-you-fat-bastard-you-fat-bastard-you-ate-all-the-pies.'

Sonny Gee shook his head bewilderedly. 'What yus gannin' on aboot that for, man? Ah want ye to tell wor who . . . ah want ye to tell wor where . . .' The boy broke off, agony dimming his eyes. 'Ye kna what ah want to ask, divven't ye, gadgie bird?' The bird flew up noisily. 'Ha'way, ye kna what ah want to kna aboot. So tell wor. Tell wor. Tell wor!'

A feather came fluttering down as the African grey perched back at the top of the stack. 'Who-ate-all-the-pies?'

The boy caught the feather and examined it for a while. Slowly his fist closed over it and he bowed his head. 'Ye cannet talk, can ye?' he mumbled. 'Not proper, like. Not really. Not like a gadgie.'

'You–fat–bastard . . .'

'It's nee good,' Sonny Gee said. 'Mebbes thems are reet. Mebbes ah am a divvy. Mebbes they cannet talk proper.' With a dreadful shriek, the parrot flew away into the shop, disappearing round the corner of a stack. The boy's stricken face followed its progress. 'What am ah gonnae dee?' he asked himself. 'How am ah gonnae kna? How am ah ever gonnae find oot where me dad is?' His hands fell weakly at his side, the feather spiralled to the floor. With a sigh, Sonny Gee closed his eyes.

'Hello, bonny lad,' said Ronny, coming up behind the boy at that moment. 'So this is where ye got yersel'.'

'Not causing trouble, are ye?' Joe asked.

'Ee, lad, are ye areet?' Ronny asked, gently.

'Aye,' replied the boy, belligerently, his eyes still screwed tight. 'Ah saw yer bird.'

'It talks, ye kna,' said Ronny brightly.

'It's stupid.'

'Aye,' admitted Ronny. 'Ah must admit, he doesn't make much sense.' The large man reddened. A hand rested uncomfortably on his belly. 'Ah got him when ah was worried aboot me weight. Thought he might help wor to lose it, y'kna. If he kept on gannin' on aboot being fat an' that, ah thought he might goad wor away from the pantry. So ah taught him a few sentences to shock wor into slimmin'.' Ronny paused wistfully. 'Didn't dee nee good. In fact, it did me heed in that much, ah just ended up eating more. Any road, as Big Al says, ye're only as fat as ye feel.' Ronny prodded himself. The overweight man turned to the boy. 'Yus're looking all red, man.' Ronny bent down, so his face was on a level with the child's. 'Ye sure ye're areet? Ye look upset. Ye haven't been crying, have ye?'

Sonny Gee opened his eyes. 'Fuck off!' he spat.

'Hey, ye,' called Joe.

'Hey, ye,' the boy replied. 'Where is it then?' he demanded. 'Me present what ye said ah could have, well, ah want it now.'

'There'll be nee present with language like that,' the old man returned. 'Ah've nivver known the like of ye . . .'

The boy charged off up the aisle. A few yards down he stopped, and plunging to his knees, began pulling boxes out from underneath the metal shelves. 'It's in here,' he called. 'What ah want. It's in here.'

'What d'ye think ye're deeing?' Joe demanded, coming over.

'It's here. Ah've saw it here before. What ah want. What ah want for me birthday present.'

'Ah telt ye,' snapped Joe. 'Ye're not getting a present.'

'Ha'way,' put in Ronny, edging between the two antagonists. 'If it's yer birthday, ye've got to have a present.'

'It's not his birthday,' said the old man angrily. 'Who told ye that?'

Ronny shrugged uncomfortably. 'With him getting a present an' that, ah just thought . . .'

'Well, divven't think, Ronny,' replied the old man. 'And there's nee way he's gonnae get owt now.'

Ronny shifted from foot to foot. The boy stopped rifling through the boxes and folded his arms obdurately. 'Anyway,' began Ronny in a lighter tone, 'mebbes it is the bairn's birthday. Or near enough. Mebbes ye'll have to get him summink, Joe. Mebbes yus'll have to get him a birthday present. Hey, Sonny Gee, when's your birthday?'

'Today,' replied the boy, pettishly.

'It is not,' said Joe.

'Ha'way, lad, when is it really?' Ronny asked.

'Ah just want me present, it's in here. Ah kna it is.'

'But when's yer birthday?'

The boy shrugged and stared down at the boxes.

'Ha'way, bonny lad,' said Ronny. 'Everybody knas when their birthday is.'

'Just leave him, Ronny,' put in Joe. 'If he doesn't have the manners he was born with . . .'

At that moment the boy pulled a box out from under the stack. He stared at it for a long time before rising to his feet. 'What ye got there?' asked Ronny.

The old man bristled. 'Will ye keep oot o' this. It doesn't matter what it is, it's gannin' straight back under the shelf again.'

Sonny Gee held the object close to his chest, cradling it lovingly. He walked over to Ronny and showed him what he had chosen. 'Ye've got good taste, ah'll give that to ye, Sonny Gee,' said Ronny. 'Ha'way, bonny lad. Say sorry and then mebbes he'll give ye it as a present.'

'Ah've told ye,' snapped Joe. 'Anyway, he's already got his present.'

'Ah knew it was there somewhere,' said Sonny Gee to Ronny. 'Ah've seen it before, me. Ah've always wanted it. Ah nivver thought ah'd have it for mesel'. Ah thought ye'd sold it.'

'Well, ye can put it back,' yelled the old man.

'Steady on, man Joe,' soothed Ronny.

Sonny Gee turned to Joe. 'Ye said yus were gonnae give wor a present.' He spoke slowly, deliberately. 'And this is what ah want.'

The old man nodded. 'Aye, ah did, but that was before ye pulled that stunt. Anyway, ye've already got yer present.'

'Already got it?' The boy twitched with puzzlement. 'Ah haven't got nee present.'

'It's canny good this, but,' put in Ronny, holding up the boy's box. 'As spider-starter kits gan, it's the best there is.'

'A spider-starter kit?' asked Joe.

The boy nodded. 'It's what ah've always wanted, me.'

Joe brought out the red notebook and pencil. 'But yus've got these,' he said, simply.

Sonny Gee stared at the pencil and book. 'But what dee ah want with them?' His voice was quiet with disbelief.

'Tell ye what,' said Ronny, who was following the conversation uneasily. 'Get the spider kit, for his birthday.'

Sonny Gee was staring fixedly at Joe. 'Ye said ah could have a present.'

'The pencil, the book,' said Joe. 'Them was yer present.'

'Present?' The boy's face was contorted with disgust. 'Some present that . . .'

'Will ye shut up,' the old man suddenly shouted. 'Ah'm sick of ye twining on. Be told. For once. Just be told!'

'But . . .' began Ronny.

'And ye!' snarled Joe.

'Ha'way, Joe,' said Ronny.

Sonny Gee snatched the box back from Ronny. 'Ah'm having it any road, gadgie mista. Even if ah have to twoc it.'

At that instant there was a loud parrot squawk from somewhere in the shop. A few moments later the bird flew over. 'So that's where ye are,' Ronny said.

'Fat-boy-fat-boy!' shrieked the African grey, turning round in mid-air.

'Careful,' warned Ronny. The bird shot away, the tips of its wings brushing against the tanks and cages as it careered down the aisle. 'Slow down. Ye'll knock doon one of the spider tanks.'

'You-ate-all-the-pies-you-fat . . .'

Ronny waved his arms. 'Calm doon, man bird man.'

The parrot swooped away, narrowly missing the stacks. 'He's-fat-he's-roond-he-boonces-on-the-groond!'

'WATCH OOT!' begged Ronny, chasing after it. The parrot perched on the edge of a cage and watched Ronny quizzically as he approached. 'Here,' he coaxed, stalking the bird. 'Good bird. Here.' When he was within arm's reach, Ronny paused craftily for a moment, feigning disinterest, then suddenly reached out. Despite its flapping struggle, he grabbed the bird, but the movement unbalanced him and he began to topple. After a few seconds clutching desperately at the air, Ronny fell to the ground, his shoulder thudding heavily against the stack as he went. The stack tottered and then fell, coming to rest against the stack on the other side of the aisle. A brief silence followed, broken by a soft metallic glissando and then a crash. A tank had slid down the slope of the fallen stack and hit the floor. 'Oh no,' whispered Ronny. 'Please God, no.'

The parrot fluttered down to perch on Ronny's pot-belly. 'Ye-ate-all-the-pies,' it chanted, staring over the mound of Ronny's pot at the fallen tank. Something long and slow slithered free from the wreckage. 'Ye-fat-bastard,' the parrot finished.

Ronny lay there for a few moments more. He met the parrot eye to eye. 'It hasn't, has it?' he asked.

'He's-fat-he's-roond . . .' hazarded the bird sheepishly.

'Oh God,' gasped Ronny.

The parrot hopped over to where the remote control had spilt from Ronny's pocket. It pecked at it. There was a click, followed by a hiss.

'Born free,' began the singer on the tape.

'That means that the monster's oot again.' Letting out a yelp, Ronny leapt to his feet. He sprinted to the counter and snatched up a phone. 'Hello, Bill? Emergency,' he breathed urgently into the receiver. 'Aye . . . that's reet. It's oot again.' With a surprising show of energy, Ronny crashed down the receiver, and dashing over to the door, locked it. 'Bog window, bog window,' he repeated to himself as he ran back to the counter and went through into the back room. He reappeared a few seconds later. 'Lucky ah didn't have a curry last neet, otherwise that window would have been well and truly open. Now at least we kna that it's on the premises somewhere.'

The old man and the boy stared after him. 'What's gannin' on?' Sonny Gee demanded.

'Is there a fire or summink?' Joe asked.

'Ah'm pretty impressed with ye two, mind,' said Ronny, skidding to a halt. He craned about, his eyes darting from corner to corner. Joe gave him a puzzled look, mirrored by Sonny Gee. Ronny emitted a low whistle. 'Ah'll give it to yous two, ye're both taking it pretty calmly. Most folks climb the walls.'

'Climb the walls?' said Joe.

'Aye, when this happens.'

'What's happened, like?'

Ronny pulled an embarrassed face. The chimes of a tannoy rang out. 'Attention please,' the announcer began.

'They'll shut wor doon this time for sure,' moaned Ronny. 'They almost did last time it happened.'

'Will all customers look out for an escaped python,' the announcer continued.

'Python?' the old man asked.

'Python!' smiled the boy.

'Python,' nodded Ronny abjectly. He stepped over to the thicket of ferns and with a trembling hand parted them.

'Ye're joking,' said Joe.

'Straight up?' whispered the boy.

'Friggin' hell,' finished Ronny.

'Wor auld friend the monster,' continued the announcer, 'is twenty-foot lang and weighs in at . . . at . . .'

Ronny shook his head. 'That bloody parrot, if ah've told it once, ah've told it a thoosand times: Divven't fly near the reptiles.'

The announcer laughed. 'Put it this way, yus'd kna it, if yus saw it, 'cos it's a canny chunky bugger.'

'Is it in there?' Joe asked, nodding at the ferns.

'Probably,' replied Ronny. 'It likes a bit cover. Summink like its natural habitat.'

'Where d'ye think you're gannin'?' demanded Joe as Sonny Gee strode over to where Ronny stood at the foliage.

'Ah want to see it,' the boy replied, breathlessly. 'Ah want to see the monster.'

'Ye will not,' snapped the old man. 'And ye're not having that spider-starter kit neither.'

'Here gans,' gulped Ronny.

'Born free,' yodelled the tape.

'Gadgie mista,' snarled Sonny Gee, 'ah want to see the monster.'

'Well, ye're not gonnae.'

The ferns shimmered as Ronny edged nervously into them. 'Here, monster,' he whispered. 'Here, monster.'

'Gan-on-fat-boy, gan-on-fat-boy!' shrieked the African grey, skimming overhead.

'How, Ronny,' called the boy, picking up the spider-starter kit box and pushing through the ferns after the corpulent pet shop proprietor. 'Can ah come and stop here? Can ah, can ah come and stop with the monster and all them spiders? Ah divven't want to stop with that auld gadgie monster nee more; ah want to stop with ye and the monster.'

'Divven't worry, but,' continued the announcer, 'Exotica Petotica have assured wor that it's very fond of children.'

'*Please* let wor stay here, Ronny,' cried the boy, disappearing as the ferns closed in behind him. 'Ah love it here, me.'

'Free as the wind blows . . . free as the grass grows . . . '

8

Spring waxed over the gentle hills of Gateshead. The hawthorn trees flowered, their hedges of white blossom drifting like slow smoke down the sloping fields of Whickham Thorns to the vast shopping malls of the Metro Centre. On the spoil heaps of the old colliery lands, meadows bloomed, their cowslips nodding beneath the endless song of skylarks. And all along the length of the row of retired pitman cottages the house martins began to build their nests.

Early one morning, the boy stood in the yard, watching the house martins as they came and went, disappearing and reappearing from over the high wall to the school and church, carrying mud in their beaks, their chattering filling the air. 'Hello, bonny lad,' a voice called from one of the yards. Sonny Gee did not look away from the house martins. 'Ye still here? Ah'd have thought he'd packed yus off by noo.' It was Peggy.

There were two birds building a nest under the eaves of the old man's cottage, and the boy gazed at them, following their twisting, arrowing movements. 'There's two of them,' he called back down to Peggy. At that instant one of the birds flew over Sonny Gee's head. He spun round to watch it slip up to the nest. 'That un's got more white on its back; and its wings is more bluer.' Disappearing, the bird reappeared a few moments later, its head bobbing at the hole. Carefully it added its beakful of mud to the growing cup of the structure. 'They only dee a bit,' said Sonny Gee.

'Eh?' returned Peggy.

'Ah've been watching them. Them birds. They only build a bit each day.'

'What yus gannin' on aboot?'

'The rest of the time they just play.'

'Play?'

'It's the way they dee it.' The boy pointed down the row of eaves to Peggy's cottage. 'See for yersel'. They're deeing it for ye an' all.'

'Deeing what?'

The boy shrugged. 'Ah divven't kna.'

Beneath the nest, propped against the wall, stood the motorbike. It was covered in the white droppings of the birds. 'Ye're always stood oot there in the yard,' Peggy said. 'Is that what ye're deeing there? Looking up at them daft birds?'

'Thems isn't daft,' whispered Sonny Gee, gazing up at the nest.

'Hey, ah'm talking to ye. Haven't ye been taught nee manners? It's rude not to look at someone when they're talking to ye.' More droppings landed on the motorbike as the house martin flew from the nest and twittered over the wall to the church. 'How lang yus been here noo? More than a fortnight. Getting on for three weeks.'

Sonny Gee sprang lithely from one foot to the other as he followed the progress of the looping house martin.

'Ah'd have thought he'd have had yus away by now.'

Without looking at her, the boy flicked the Vs.

'Ye cheeky little bugger,' she spluttered. 'Ah'll come doon there and give ye what for in a minute.'

Just then both house martins flashed over the tall wall into the old man's yard. The two birds met in mid-air to transfer mud between their beaks. They rolled through the air together, dropping for a brief instant, before separating to regain altitude. The boy watched them dreamily. Pursing his lips, he tried to whistle in imitation of their chittering, but only a soft rasp came out.

Standing on tiptoes, Peggy craned her neck to see the yard in which Sonny Gee stood. 'Ah see ye've still got that motorbike. It's all covered in mess an' all. Ah cannet believe they've left it there so long. Well, it'll all come to a head.'

'So what?' called Sonny Gee. 'We're not scared.'

Peggy shook her head. 'Ye're just like yer granda ye. Pig-headed. Neeone can tell ye nowt. He's been like that since he was nee bigger than ye are noo . . .'

'And ye're bigger than everyone noo.'

'Eh? Ye cheeky young . . .'

Once again the boy flicked the Vs.

Peggy narrowed her eyes. 'He doesn't want ye, y'kna. That time ah saw yus at the bus stop he pretended he wasn't with ye. Cannet wait to get shot o' yus. Send ye back to wherever it is yus're from. It's Bensham, isn't it?'

Sonny Gee stared back up at the nest. The birds flew around him, he watched in delight. 'See noo?' he breathed softly. 'They're just playing noo.'

Peggy shook her head. 'And ah wouldn't get too attached to them if ah were ye, 'cos that auld miserable cuss of yer granda doesn't let them finish their nest. He always takes the broom handle to them. In fact, ah'm surprised he hasn't done it yet.'

The boy clenched his fists until the knuckles whitened. 'Fuck off, ye friggin' jelly-baby wifie!' He ran to the wall and was just about to vault it when the back door opened and the old man came out.

'What's gannin' on here?' Joe demanded. Sonny Gee stared back at him without replying. 'Who were ye shouting at?' The boy gestured down the yards. Joe looked. 'Oh,' he grunted. 'Areet, Peggy?'

'Divven't ye areet me,' she replied, hands on her hips.

'Suit yersel'.'

'Ye bitch . . .' spluttered the boy.

Joe glowered at him. 'In ye gan and lay the breakfast table,' he snapped.

With one last scowl down the yards, Sonny Gee went inside.

'Shouldn't he be at school instead of cheeking folk?' Peggy asked. Without replying, the old man walked to the window and looked up at the eaves. 'Hey, bugger lugs! Ah'm talking to ye.'

Joe studied the nest for a while, before turning to Peggy. 'Was that ye, Peggy?'

'He should be at school. He's been with yus for getting on three weeks.'

The old man was about to reply when he checked himself. 'Messy buggers,' he said, pointing up at the birds. 'They've got that lad's bike all messed up. Still, if his stepdad cannet be bothered to come and get it.'

'They're just gonnae break in and take that bike,' said Peggy.

Joe shrugged. 'Let them, ah'll be waiting for them.'

'Ee, ye still think yus're twenty-one, ye dee, Joseph O'Brien. Ye shouldn't have stuck yer neb in with them teenagers.'

'Ye mean ye wish them stupid little boys was still riding that bike up and doon the cottages?'

'Ye've stirred a swarm of hornets there.'

Joe was still looking up at the growing nest. 'Ah'll give them this much. The hoose martins. They nivver give up. Every year they build their nest here and every year ah knock it doon. Doesn't seem to stop them.' Joe stared up at the nest and then down at Peggy. 'What did ye say to upset him?' he asked.

'Who?'

'The bairn.'

Peggy laughed harshly. 'Ah cannet believe it.'

'What ye gannin' on aboot?'

'Ah nivver thought ah'd live to see the day. Ye sticking up for someone else.'

The old man frowned. 'Ah asked ye what ye said to upset him.'

'Nowt. Ah didn't say nowt. Anyway, ah wish yus'd get shot

of him. Ah cannet stand him hanging aboot the spot. Ah lost a towel from me washing line the other day. Ye haven't seen it, have ye?'

Joe turned to Peggy. 'Ye should be ashamed o' yersel' ye, Peggy lass. Upsetting a bairn that age.'

'Divven't come that with me,' replied Peggy acidly, shuffling against her wall so that the top half of her body hung down over the edge. 'Ye of all people, Joseph O'Brien.'

'Ha'way, Peggy, if yus've got summink to say then divven't hold back.'

Peggy snorted. 'Ye divven't want him here any more than ah dee.' Peggy paused. 'And he's yer own flesh and blood an' all.' The old man did not reply. 'Turning away yer own flesh and blood. Mind ye, yus've already done that once.'

Joe narrowed his eyes. 'What d'ye mean by that, like?'

'Ye kna.'

'Na, ah divven't. That's why ah'm asking ye.'

'Put it this way, your Mary couldn't wait to get away fast enough. And her with a bairn an' all.' Peggy stared archly at Joe. 'But then ah suppose that had nowt to dee with ye, did it, Joe?'

The old man stared down the yards at Peggy for a few moments and then turned. 'Ye divven't kna what ye're talking aboot,' he said, walking across the yard to the back door.

'Anyway,' called Peggy, 'ah'm only asking, 'cos there's a law, isn't there? Divven't social services have to kna, what with your hands an' that . . .'

But the old man had gone back into the house. Peggy stayed there for a while, gazing down the yards, her face hardening.

Coming into the sitting room, Joe found the boy sitting on the window sill staring out on to the yard. The old man looked over to see the wing of a bird brushing the windowpane as it flew up under the eaves. 'What's it deeing?' asked Sonny Gee without turning.

The old man blinked. 'Ah won't have ye giving cheek to an adult.'

'She started it . . .'

'And ye carried it on. Ah won't have it. D'ye hear me?' But the boy was staring through the window as though mesmerised. The old man paused. 'Ye love them birds, divven't ye?'

'They keep coming and gannin'. With bits of mud in their mouths. And putting it on the wall. What they deein'?'

'What they dee every year,' shrugged Joe, going through to the kitchen.

'What's that?'

'Building a hoose. Now get down from there.'

'What do they build a hoose for?'

'To hold their eggs.'

'Eggs?'

'Get doon from there.'

'What eggs?'

'What we have for yer breakfast, but left in the shell.'

'Why?'

'Why what?'

'Why do they have eggs then?'

'Get doon!' The old man appeared for a moment in the doorway. 'And have yus laid the table like ah telt ye?'

'When ye tell us aboot eggs ah will.' The boy's face was taut with curiosity. 'Why do they have eggs?'

''Cos that's where babbies come from.'

Sonny Gee seemed stunned. 'Babbies come from eggs? Straight up?'

'Aye. Birds do. For birds, eggs are their bairns. It's new life, y'kna. A fresh start.' The old man paused for a moment. 'That's why Ronny gave yus that Easter egg.'

'Was that a egg?'

'Just a chocolate one. They're to remind wor aboot the time of year. Spring, y'kna. When everything begins again. What's dead an' that, well, it comes to life again now.' Joe broke off.

'Well, that's what they say,' he added quietly to himself. 'In church an' that.'

The boy's mouth was open with awe. 'And all that's in a bird's egg?'

Joe shrugged. 'Get doon from that window sill before ah pull ye doon, and lay the table like yus've been telt.'

When he had laid the table, Sonny Gee came through to the kitchen. 'Can ah gan oot on to the yard?'

'But ye've only just come in.'

'Ah want to watch the hoose martins.'

The old man shook his head. 'Yer breakfast's ready.'

They sat at the table. Sonny Gee ate the two rashers of bacon first. Then he began picking at his egg. 'Eat it properly,' said Joe tersely, as the boy prodded the yolk gingerly. 'Ye kna how to.'

'Can ah eat it?' he asked.

'Course ye can.'

'But ye said it was new life.'

The old man glanced at the boy. 'Only the wild birds, man. Not chickens. Only the birds that ye see flying aboot.'

The boy cut a piece from the fried egg. 'Like the hoose martins, ye wouldn't eat a hoose martin's egg. 'Cos it's new life, eh?'

'Aye, ye would eat it, if yus were starving.'

Sonny Gee thought about this. 'Na,' he decided at last, 'ah wouldn't. Not if ah died, ah wouldn't.' After this, the boy ate hungrily, without pausing to speak again. The old man watched him for a while and then fell into a reverie.

'Gan and fetch yer book,' Joe told him when Sonny Gee had finished his breakfast.

'What aboot the pots?'

'We'll have to dee yer lesson first.' Joe moved the dishes to clear a space. 'The pots can wait. Ah've a lot to dee today.'

'What yus deein', like?' The boy's face crumpled with

suspicion. As he walked over to the sideboard he shot furtive glances at the old man. 'Am ah gannin' away the day?'

The old man looked at him. 'Na, not the day.' There was a pause. 'But yus're not staying here for ever. Ye kna ye cannet.'

The boy folded his arms and jutted his chin out bullishly. 'Ah divven't want to stop here anyway.'

'Aye, aye,' said the old man wearily. 'Ye divven't need to gan through the whole routine.'

'Ah'll gan anywhere, me,' continued Sonny Gee. 'Audrey's, Gemma's. Me mam'll be back for wor soon, and if she's still with that Macca then ah'll gan and live in Ronny's shop . . .' The boy broke off. He glanced uncertainly at Joe. 'When am ah gannin' then?'

'Soon,' replied Joe. 'Not today. But soon.'

'Ah'll kill Macca and live with me mam.'

The old man sighed. 'Ah might be able to tell yus toneet. Where ye're gannin' next. Ah might be able to tell ye toneet.'

'Why not now?' There was no reply. Opening the sideboard door, Sonny Gee reached inside. 'Do we have to dee work noo?'

'Aye. We dee it every day.'

'Even if ah gan somewhere else?'

'Aye.'

'Why? Neebody else ever tries to learn wor but ye.'

'Ah divven't care. Ye'll always need learning.'

Sonny Gee peered into the sideboard. 'Ah'll tell ye what,' he said. 'If that Springy Jack gadgie ever tries to get wor, ah'll hide in here.'

'Will ye?'

The boy fell to his knees and pushed his head right inside. 'Aye, it's big enough.' His voice echoed slightly in the enclosed space.

'Ah thought ye weren't scared of him?'

'Ah'm not,' replied Sonny Gee quickly, he withdrew his head and looked over at Joe. 'Ah'm not scared of neeone, me.

That's why ah'd gan in here. Not 'cos ah was flappin' or owt. Na.' The boy eased his head back within the sideboard. ''Cos d'yus kna why ah'd hide in here?'

'Look, just get yer notebook and pencil and let's make a start. Ah've told ye, ah've a lot to dee the day.'

'Ah'd hide in there so that ah could spring oot on *him*. Then ah'd get him. 'Cos *he'd* be shitting himself, wouldn't he? And when he was flappin', ah'd settle him.' Scrambling, the boy's shoulders disappeared inside. 'Canny good spot,' he called.

'Ah won't tell ye again.' The old man looked over. 'Hey, what d'yus think ye're deeing in there? Get oot now and bring yer tackle.'

The boy emerged with the notebook in his mouth. He panted like a dog. 'Ah'm Rusty, me,' he said. 'Ah'm Gemma's dog.'

'Divven't be stupid.'

'He's a belter dog, but. D'ye see him this morning when he pissed on Peggy's gate?'

'That's enough. Sit doon.'

Sonny Gee came over and laid the notebook in front of the old man. 'Ah cannet find the pencil.'

'It's where it always is, man lad.'

'It's not.'

'Divven't make wor have to get up.' With a heavy sigh, the boy went back over to the sideboard and reached inside again. 'Ah'd still hide in there,' he mumbled to himself. Sitting down, Sonny Gee flicked the pencil over the table. 'It's nee good,' he said.

'What d'ye mean?'

'That pencil, it doesn't work.'

'Divven't talk stupid.' The old man sighed. 'Will ye not give up complaining aboot that pencil? It's every day the same.'

'Ah hate it, me.'

'Ye chose it.'

'But it's pink.'

'Well, ye should have looked more closely.'

'It's got a one o' them Barbie doll pictures or summink on it, man.'

'Aye, well, it'll teach yus to keep yer mind on the job. Ye were too full o' that spider business. And that flamin' snake.'

Sonny Gee's face shone eagerly. 'Ah'm still having summink though, aren't ah? Ye promised. Summink from Ronny's shop. Aren't ah though?'

After a few moments, Joe nodded slowly. 'Summink. If yus dee yer work. Not a spider, mind. And definitely not a python. Summink more sensible.'

'Ye promise?'

'Ah promise.' A look of uneasiness flickered in the old man's eyes. 'But only when yus've learnt yer alphabet.'

'It could live in the sideboard cupboard. And ah could stop with it there . . .'

'Ha'way,' interrupted Joe. 'Let's get ye learning summink. By heck, lad, if it was left to ye, ye'd dee nowt. Now, where were we?'

'Glasses,' said the boy. 'Yus'll need yer glasses.' He got up. 'D'yus want us to put them on for ye?'

Joe stared at him for a while. 'Ye can put a thing off, lad, but it's always there waiting for ye. It's best to dee a thing quickly instead of flimflammying aboot with losing pencils and that.'

The boy stared at Joe. 'Flimflammying?'

'Aye.'

'Ah just want to help ye,' said the boy.

'Eh?'

'It hurts ye when yus put yer glasses on. Ah've seen.'

The old man's lips trembled angrily. 'Divven't ye start gannin' like that Gemma lass,' he snapped. 'Ah'm not a cripple, y'kna.'

The boy's eyes widened innocently. 'Ah nivver said ye were.'

'When ah need for yer help, ah'll ask for it.' The old man

snorted irritably. 'It's me that's looking after ye, not the other way roond. So remember that, lad. Eh? Just ye remember that.'

'Ah'm only helping.'

'Aye, well, divven't.'

Joe took out his glasses from the cardigan pocket and stiffly placed them on his face. Then he flicked slowly through the notebook with a gnarled finger. On each page a large single letter had been written, the rest of the page was littered with smaller, spidery imitations of varying approximation. The old man licked the pencil and then on a new page began to trace a letter.

'How's the hands the day?' Sonny Gee asked, watching him.

'Divven't be cheeky.'

'Ah'm not. Ah'm just asking. And is that condensation still not come?'

'Condensation?'

'From the gadgies in London. For knackering yer hands.'

'Compensation, ye mean? That's got nowt to dee with ye.' Joe finished the letter. 'Ha'way, stop looking out that window. Them birds can dee withoot ye for a few minutes.' Joe handed the book and pencil over to Sonny Gee. 'That's a letter M. M,' he repeated the letter lingeringly. 'Loads o' words begin with M . . .'

'Ming,' shot out the boy.

'Proper words, ah mean.'

'What d'ye mean, proper?'

'Well, words that ye'd use.'

'But ah dee use it. When ah smell a fart, ah say it mings.'

'Areet, areet,' said Joe. 'It's any excuse to be rude, isn't it?'

'Microwave chips,' said the boy. 'Mississippi mud pies. Ah twocked a packet o' them once from the Londis shop. They were lush.'

'Ah divven't want to kna.'

'Metro Centre. Monster.'

'Ah wish ye'd forget aboot that python.'

'It'd fit in that sideboard cupboard nee problem, ye wouldn't have to see it, and then when ah went away ah'd just take it with wor . . .'

'Concentrate, lad. We're looking for words with a M sound.'

'Flimflammying.'

'Ah said proper words.'

'It was ye what said it.'

'A body needs the patience o' Job to teach ye.'

'Well, divven't bother then.'

There was a long pause. 'Ha'way,' said Joe, scrutinising Sonny Gee, 'yus're usually good at this.'

The boy began to speak, but stopped himself. He tried again. Then a third time. 'Mule,' he was able to say at last.

Grunting, Joe nodded. 'That's a good one. Where d'ye hear that?' The boy shrugged uneasily. 'Right, we'll do mule. Except ye haven't learnt the U yet. And we're not gonnae get to that one for a while yet.' The old man nibbled the end of the pencil. 'Is there nee other words what we've done all the letters to?' Falling into deep thought, his eyes wandered across the room. They came to rest on the boots on the hearthstone, and then slowly raised themselves to the mantelpiece. Joe gazed at the lamp. He pursed his lips thoughtfully. The few notes of a tune whistled free. 'Mine,' he said, softly to himself.

'The pencil?' asked the boy. 'Why then, keep it if it's yours. Ah've telt ye ah divven't want it, but ye have it if ye like Barbie so much. Ah'll get a Toon Army one instead.'

'Not that kind of mine. Mine. *Mine.*'

'Mine?'

'Aye. As in the place undergroond. Ha'way, pass wor the book.' Concentration puckered the old man's face as he wrote out the word. 'All we need is to dee the letter N at the same time then ye'll know the whole word.'

Sonny Gee watched the slow, painful process of Joe's writing intently. 'Ah thought ye just said proper words.'

'What ye chuntering on aboot now?'

'Ah divven't kna what a one is.'

Joe put down the pencil. 'Ye divven't kna what a mine is?' The boy shook his head. The old man's face creased with incomprehension. 'How can ye be a Geordie and not kna what a mine is?' Sonny Gee shrugged. Joe stared at him. He sighed. 'But ye wouldn't, would ye; there hasn't been nee mines in Gatesheed for years.' He narrowed his eyes. 'A mine's summink deep under the groond. Men used to gan doon there to work. They were called miners. They dug coal . . .'

'Ye mean pit?'

The old man broke off and nodded. 'Why aye, it's the same thing. Ye call a miner a pitman.'

'Ye were a one of thems, weren't ye, gadgie mista?'

'How d'ye kna, like?'

'Ronny telt wor. Said ye were the best cutter . . .'

'Well, ye divven't want to be listening to him all the time.'

'He told wor aboot how deep doon it was an' that. The pit. It was like as far as it is on the bus to the Team Valley, but undergroond.'

'Ronny tell ye that an' all, did he?'

'Aye. He telt wor all aboot it.'

'Did he?'

'He said it was geet dark. And stank like shite . . .'

'Hey . . .'

'That's what Ronny telt wor.' Curiosity burned on the child's face. 'How did yus see if it was geet dark?'

The old man shrugged. 'We had wor lamps.'

'Eh?'

'On wor helmets. We wore wor lamps on wor helmets.'

'What happens if ye didn't have nee helmets?'

Joe knitted his brows in thought. 'Pass wor that from the mantelpiece.' He pointed over at the miner's lamp.

'The ormanent?' said the boy, picking it up.

'Gis it here.' The old man took the lamp and studied it for a long time. The boy watched Joe's face. 'They had these before.' His eyes narrowed. 'Aye. It was geet dark.'

'Ronny said that the dust was a reet bugger.'

Joe leant forward slightly and peered at the boy. 'What else did he tell ye, like?'

'Ah asked him aboot Springer-heel Jack.'

'Eh?'

'Ah asked where he came from. And he telt wor he was brought up from the pit with the coal. He was asleep doon there and ye woke him with a drill. He was dug up and brought here.'

'Ronny told ye that?'

The boy nodded his head. 'He'd been asleep for a million years, and ye woke him up.'

'He's nee more sense than he was born with, that one.'

Sonny Gee paused, his eyes shone as they gazed at Joe. 'Doon that pit, what was it like?'

There was a silence. 'We dug for coal,' said the old man at last. 'Dug it oot of the rock.'

'Is that how yus knackt them then? Yer hands.'

Joe did not answer for a while. 'Aye,' he said, simply. 'That's how ah knackt me hands.'

'How?'

For a while, the old man gazed thoughtfully at his hands. Then he shook his head. 'Ah kna what yus're up to, lad. Ye're just trying to put off wor lesson. Well, it won't wash. Come on, put this back on the mantelpiece.'

Reluctantly the boy took the lamp and placed it above the fire. 'Did yus wear them big black boots doon the pit mine?'

Taking up the pencil again, the old man licked the tip once more, and began to etch another letter on the page. Then he wrote a word. 'Now ye,' he said, handing the book and pencil over to Sonny Gee. The boy licked the pencil, then leaning low over the table so that his forehead nearly touched the page, he began to write. Joe watched him. 'Ye learn fast, ye,' he said. 'Ye're doing well.'

'Am ah?'

'Aye. That ye are, lad.'

When Sonny Gee had finished writing the word he handed the book over to the old man. 'That's good,' Joe said softly. 'That's really good. Ah think mebbes we can dee another word. Mebbes even that one ye thought of. Ah divven't want to hold ye back.'

'Which one?'

'Ye said mule, didn't ye?' There was no reply from the boy. 'Ha'way, ah'll write it oot for ye.'

As Joe wrote the new word, the boy reached out to the stack of dirty dishes. 'Why d'ye always lick that pencil?' The old man did not answer. 'What's a flimflammying?' Playing uneasily with the cutlery, Sonny Gee sent a greasy spoon flying. It landed on the page. 'Will ye learn wor how to whistle like what ye dee?'

'Careful, man,' barked Joe. Watching the slow creation of the letters, Sonny Gee's face flickered with anxiety. He reached out for the mug of tea, and surreptitiously dragged it over. Pretending to reach for something, he knocked it over. The page browned with tea. 'Ye young fool,' shouted the old man. 'What ye want to dee that for? Just when ye were getting on so well.' Lifting the notebook out of the puddle, Joe rubbed it with the cuff of his cardigan.

'Ah divven't want to write that word,' said the boy through tightly clenched teeth. ''Cos ah divven't . . . 'cos ah divven't . . . 'cos ah'm nee mule, me.'

Joe looked him in the eye. 'Ah nivver said ye were a one. Ha'way, man lad, take a hold of yerself, neebody'll have yus if ye pull stunts like that.'

There was a pause. The clock suddenly seemed to tick more loudly. 'What d'ye mean?' Sonny Gee asked, quietly.

When the old man spoke again, his voice was softer. 'Ye want people to think well of ye. Nice people. So that they'd want yus.'

'Why?' returned the boy suspiciously.

'Ye just dee. Ah mean, if . . .' Joe broke off. The old man looked away, uncomfortable under the scrutiny of the child. 'Ah'll tell yus aboot it later.'

'Tell us now.'

A couple of times, Joe began an explanation, but neither time could he find the words. 'Not now. Ah'll tell yus aboot it later. Ah promise. Ha'way, put the notebook on the mantelpiece to dry. Ah'll light the fire tonight.' The old man paused. 'Reet, what's next?' He stared at the boy thoughtfully. 'Aye,' he said to himself after a while. 'That'll need deein'.' Going over to the sideboard, Joe delved inside. He brought out a pair of scissors. 'Take a chair into the yard,' he said.

'Hey, gadgie mista,' said the boy as he picked up a chair from the table. He gestured at the sideboard. 'Did ye find that doon the pits an' all?'

A grass mower could be heard in the distance as the old man followed Sonny Gee out into the yard. 'Sit doon then,' Joe told the boy who was standing in front of his chair. Sonny Gee sat down. 'And keep yer head still.'

'What ye gonnae dee, like?' demanded Sonny Gee, edgily viewing the scissors.

'Yer hair, man. It's awer long.'

'So?'

'Ah want it looking respectable.'

'What's that, like?'

'Keep still.'

'Ah divven't want it looking like nee bull.'

'Eh?'

'Ye said ye were gonnae cut it like a bull.'

'Ah said *respectable*.'

'Same difference. There's that bull on a cartoon what get's killed. Ah divven't want nee . . .'

'Oh for pity's sake!'

The boy flinched at the first snip. 'Na,' he said.

'Why, like looking like a lass, do ye?' A smile hovered on the old man's face for an instant.

'Ah'm nee lass, me,' replied the boy.

'Well, what ye scared of?'

'Ah'm not scared of owt, me.'

'Let wor cut yer hair then.' Joe's tongue protruded from between his lips as he stared fixedly at the unruly mass of red hair. 'Just like cutting privet, ah suppose,' he mused, holding the scissors in two hands as though they were a tiny pair of hedge shears. A house martin flew into the eaves. 'If ye look up like that again, lad, ye'll end up losing a nose.'

'Would ah? Is that what ye did to that Jack Springs? Did ye cut his hair? When ye woke him up? Is that why he's got a banger for his hooter?'

'Aye,' replied Joe, snipping the scissors loudly.

There was a sharp intake of breath. 'Did ye?'

The old man did not reply as he continued to concentrate on the hair.

'Can ah have them when ye're finished?' asked Sonny Gee.

'What?'

'Them scissors. Ah want them.'

'Why?'

'So if that Jack chaver jumps oot on wor ah'll cut his sausage hooter off too.'

Joe sighed. 'Ah'm sick o' ye gannin' on aboot him. Ah thought ah explained that to ye the other day. When ye were scared . . .'

'Ah wasn't scared, me,' put in the boy, aggressively.

'Areet, areet. But just remember, it's like ah said, he'll nivver come for ye.' The old man's voice was gentle. 'Not when ah'm here.'

'Ah'll jump oot on him from the sideboard.' The boy closed his eyes for a moment. When he opened them there was real fear there. 'But what am ah gonnae dee when ah'm not staying here nee longer? What happens if he follows wor then? What happens when ah've gone and he jumps oot . . .' The boy arched his back and turned an agonised face on the old man.

'What's got into ye this morning?' asked Joe. The boy slumped back in his chair. The old man leant down closer. 'Is it that Peggy what's upset ye?'

'Ah divven't care aboot Teletubby wifie, me.'

'What did she say?'

The boy jutted out his chin. 'Gadgie mista,' he said, 'ah've thought of another word.'

'Eh?'

'With the M sound.'

'What is it?'

'Macca.'

A silence lengthened between them.

'Gadgie mista?' began the boy again, his tone challenging. 'Ah'm not scared of him neither.'

'Aren't ye?' Joe's voice was quiet.

'Na.' Sonny Gee blinked. ''Cos ah'm gonnae kill him.'

The scissors clicked noisily as, slowly, tufts of hair wafted to the ground. 'Keep still,' whispered the old man.

'Ouch!' yelped the boy.

'*Keep still.*'

'But ye nipped wor, man.'

'Aye, well, ye moved.'

'Ah didn't.'

'And these scissors are blunt.' The old man carried on for a bit longer, then, stepping back, viewed the boy's head. 'What ye have to remember, lad, is what me own granda used to say. The difference between a good haircut and a bad one is a fortnight.'

There was a long silence, filled only by the click of the

scissors and, from further away, the moan of the grass mower. 'What's a fortnight?' Sonny Gee asked at last.

'Two weeks,'

'What's a granda?'

The scissors stopped. Only the mower could be heard for a while. Then even that stopped. The gentle purling of the twittering house martins was the only sound of the day. 'Divven't move,' ordered Joe, walking to the back door. He came back from the kitchen carrying a pudding bowl. 'Now stick that on yer heed.'

The boy took the bowl and stared confusedly at it. 'That's a granda?'

The old man sighed. 'No. That gans on yer heed. And ah cut roond it.'

The old man clipped slowly round the rim of the bowl. 'Gadgie mista,' said Sonny Gee after a while, 'do ye knock doon them hoose martins' nest?'

'Aye,' Joe replied.

'Divven't,' said the boy.

Coming round the front of Sonny Gee, the old man adjusted the bowl which had tilted forward over the boy's eyes. 'They're dirty, man. The hoose martins. Just vermin really. Look at that bike already. They'll have the whole wall soiled if ah leave them.'

Their eyes met. 'Divven't,' repeated Sonny Gee.

'We'll see. We'll see.' Standing behind him once more, Joe continued to cut the hair. 'Who told ye aboot that, like?'

'Big mooth Peggy.'

'Hey, ye.'

'That's what ye call her.'

From over the wall, the sound of children's voices could be heard as they swept into the yard for playtime. 'Did she tell ye anything else?' asked Joe.

The boy nodded. 'Aye.'

'Keep still, or yus'll send that bowl flying.' An uneasiness crept into the old man's voice. 'What did she tell ye, like?'

'She said yus didn't want wor.'

The scissors stopped. The bowl was lifted off the boy's head. The grass mower started up again, but the children's voices were louder.

'Divven't ye, like; divven't yus want wor?'

'It's not that, man,' replied Joe uncomfortably. 'These cottages are for pensioners. Ye're a young bairn. Ye need . . .'

'Neebody nivver wants me,' said Sonny Gee. 'And ah divven't care.'

The old man studied the haircut. For an instant he rested his knotted fingers on the boy's head. 'That's better,' he said, gently.

When Joe had put the bowl and scissors away, he came back. Sonny Gee had not moved from the chair. 'Ha'way,' said the old man. 'Get that hair swept up. Y'kna where the brush is. Ye can put the sweepings in wor compost bag.'

'Are we gannin' doon to the allotments?'

'Na; ah'm busy the day.'

'Why, what ye deein'?'

'Nivver ye mind.'

'And why yus gannin' oot toneet?'

'Ah'll tell yus later.'

The old man went into the cottage. Standing at the window, he watched the boy move slowly to the coalhouse. Sonny Gee brought out the brush; it was almost twice his height. Grappling with the handle of the brush, the boy began to sweep, from time to time pausing to stare up dreamily at the house martins' nest.

A soft whistling played from the old man's lips as he fell into a reverie watching his grandson. The tune was slow, melancholy; the mournful air of a sad song. And as he whistled, Joe was utterly absorbed. A sudden knock at the door roused him. He went down the passage to the front door, irritation hovering over his features. 'Who is it?' he called tersely.

'Joe?' a man replied.

Joe opened the door. 'Father Michael.'

The priest was standing on the doorstep. 'I've been threatening a visit for some time,' the priest said with a smile. 'You haven't got such a thing as a cup of tea, have you?'

The priest followed Joe into the kitchen. He stood on the threshold of the open back door and looked out at the boy. 'How are you then, bonny lad?'

'Areet,' the boy replied, stopping his sweeping for a moment. He pointed up at the nest. 'D'ye have a one o' these, God gadgie?' he asked.

'Hey,' warned the old man.

'It's all right,' laughed the priest, stepping into the yard.

'It's a nest,' said Sonny Gee.

For a while they stood there together looking up at the eaves; in the kitchen the old man could be seen bent over the tea things. Still staring at the nest, the priest took out a cigarette and placed it in his mouth. There was a click of a flint and he looked down to see Sonny Gee holding a lighter up for him. 'Thanks,' he said. Inhaling, he looked down at the lighter. 'Where d'ye get that from, Sonny Gee?'

The boy cast a furtive glance at the kitchen and dropped his voice. 'It's for Macca,' he said.

'It's Macca's? Who's Macca?'

'Na.' The boy shook his head vehemently. 'It's for Macca.'

'Come through, Father,' called Joe.

Sonny Gee bent down and placed the lighter in a sock. 'It's for Macca,' he repeated to himself as he continued to sweep the yard.

'How are the hands today, Joe?' Father Michael asked, watching the boy.

'Ah manage.'

'Still no word about compensation?'

The old man finished preparing the tea things before he spoke. 'He's no religion, y'kna, Father,' he said, pointing through to the yard. 'The bairn. Doesn't even know who Jesus is.'

The priest nodded. 'When you dropped him off at the special children's service the other day, he mentioned something about a Spring-heeled Jack?'

Joe sighed. 'Ah told him that to keep him in the hoose. Y'kna, an auld story to scare him into doing as he's told. Ah was telt the same thing.' The old man paused. 'The thing is, ever since ah've told him, he pesters me aboot him. That's the way with him. Ye tell him summink, and he wants to kna more until he gets to the bottom of it.'

'He's a bright lad. I was saying how May is the month of Mary. You know, I was trying to explain about Our Lady to the little ones. Well, our bonny lad had his own story to match. He knew a Virgin Tracy. Used to live near him apparently. She too had a baby without having a lad, or at least that's what she told her stepdad when he went looking for the culprit.' The priest finished with a laugh. 'It was good of you to let him come to the service. I'm glad you brought him, Joe.'

Joe stared at the gas flame for a few moments. 'Ah wasn't gonnae let my difficulties stand in his way. Ah want him to, y'kna, meet God for himself. Then he can decide.'

'You should have come in yourself. We miss you. The parish misses you.'

'Oh,' said Joe with a dismissive wave, 'they can dee very well withoot me.'

Putting down his brush, Sonny Gee came to the back door. The kettle was boiling in the kitchen. 'Y'kna this Jesus gadgie, what ye're always gannin' on aboot?' the boy asked the priest.

'Hey, show some respect,' said Joe, sharply.

'It's all right,' laughed the priest.

'Aye, well, just stay ootside for a bit, lad,' the old man told him. 'Ah want to have a word with Father Michael.'

'Just a minute, Joe,' said Father Michael, turning to the boy. 'What about this Jesus gadgie?'

'Well, y'kna when he was killed and that? Ah've been thinking aboot it. Why do yus call it Good Friday?'

'What do you mean, bonny lad?'

Sonny Gee shrugged as he turned to walk across the yard. 'With the size of them nails gannin' in him, ah'd call it *Bad* Friday, me.'

Joe was sitting at the table when Father Michael came into the sitting room. 'He's a character, Joe.'

'Is he?'

'I wonder where he gets it from?' A smirk played about the priest's lips. Then he grew serious. 'Have ye thought any more about what you're going to do?'

'Ah'm glad yus've come, Father, 'cos that's what ah want to talk to ye aboot.' The priest looked away discreetly as the old man struggled to pour the tea. Underneath both mugs, puddles gathered. 'What d'ye know about adoption an' that, Father?' The priest blew on the surface of the tea, before taking a sip. 'Sorry, did yus want sugar?'

'No, it's fine as it is, Joe.' He swallowed the scalding tea, gingerly cooling it in his mouth a little first. 'That's just what I needed,' he said appreciatively. A weighty look came into the young man's eyes. 'It's not easy. Adoption. Not easy.'

'But what d'ye think of it?'

'Well, in the right situation, it can be a great thing.'

'And does it take long?'

'I'm not an expert in these matters, but I think it can take quite a long time sometimes.'

'And where do they go as they're waiting?'

'The child?' Joe nodded. Lifting his mug unsteadily to his lips, he kept his eyes on the priest as he drank. 'They can get fostered,' said the priest. 'Or stay at a home.'

'A home?'

'The Church has some. Cuthbert Care, they're called. Used to be Catholic Care.'

Joe narrowed his eyes in thought. 'So he could go to a Catholic home, as he's waiting?'

'As I say, it can take a long time though. There's a family in the parish who've adopted.'

'In our parish?'

The priest nodded. 'In Holy Family. But it took them a long time to complete the process. By what they said, it can be quite harrowing. When they began . . .'

'So he could even get adopted by someone from Holy Family?'

The priest looked closely at Joe. 'It takes a long time, Joe. His mother would have to agree. Then there's the whole lengthy process. I wouldn't raise any hopes.'

'Aye, Father, but it's possible?'

'Of course it's possible.'

'And there's Catholic homes, ye say. Are they in the parish an' all?'

'No. But there's a local authority one. It's Sunnygarth House.'

Joe looked puzzled. 'But they call that the naughty boys' place.'

'I think you'll find things have changed.'

There was a pause. The old man got up and went through to the kitchen. He brought back a packet of Lincoln biscuits. 'Ah've just got these in,' he said. Still standing, he tried for a while to open them, but his fingers could find no grip on the shiny packaging.

Without a word, the priest reached out to open them. 'He was living with his mother, wasn't he?' he asked, offering Joe a biscuit.

The old man declined the biscuit. His lips curled slightly. 'She's nee good for him.'

'You care about him, don't you?'

179

'We fight like cat and dog, man Father.' There was a pause. 'He cannet stay here for much longer. He needs a strong hand. He needs a good influence.' Joe narrowed his eyes. 'At first ah thought he was a lost cause, but he's still young. He's not a bad lad.'

'I heard he's a good help down at the allotments.'

'There's moments when ah look at him and ah . . .' The old man smiled to himself, then grew serious again. 'If someone got him who could be a good influence. Someone to teach him right and wrong. If only a good family would take him. That's why ah've been smartening him up. Cutting his hair. Stopping him using language. He doesn't wet the bed every neet now.' Joe sighed. 'Ah've been thinking aboot it. This adoption business is his best bet. Ah was gonnae look into it tonight. Now ye say there's a Catholic one, it'll be even better.'

Biting into a biscuit, the priest looked through the window. Sonny Gee could be seen, standing under the eaves, staring up. Around his feet were scattered the wisps of his shorn red hair. 'Well, you've certainly cut his hair for him.'

'D'yus think it's too short?'

'No disrespect, Joe, but I don't think I'll be coming to you for my next haircut.'

The two men laughed briefly. As they gazed outside, a house martin landed on the ground and flew up once more to its nest, a sprig of the hair in its beak. The priest turned back to the old man. 'There's something I need to talk to *you* about, Joe.'

'Oh aye?'

'It's about the last conversation we had. Can you remember what we talked about?'

Joe paused thoughtfully. 'Ah told ye aboot the first one. Aboot me auldest grandson.'

The priest nodded. 'Ah've found out about him, Joe.' There was a long pause. Father Michael anxiously scanned the old man's face, but there was no perceptible reaction. 'I know you didn't want to find out about him, but . . .' The priest broke off. 'Look, I've found out. I thought I should tell you about it.'

Joe's lips trembled slightly. 'The babby?'

Father Michael half smiled. 'He's no baby now.'

'No, course not.'

The clock ticked, resonating in the silent room. The letter box clicked as something fell through it, landing on the doormat. The old man shuffled to the passage door. He brought back a flyer leaflet. 'They fire anything through yer door these days,' Joe said, placing the leaflet on the sideboard. 'Offering us loans now. Loans? Where would anyone on this terrace get the money to pay them back? Yet they keep on posting them. The council even puts them in their free magazine.' Joe came back over to the table. After watching the boy through the window for a few moments, he lowered himself back on to his chair. 'What did yus find oot, Father Michael?' he asked quietly.

'It's not good news. I don't have to tell you, if you don't want to know.'

'Don't want to know?'

'After all this time; you might think it's better not to know. To let sleeping dogs lie. Like you said, the other day.'

Joe twitched tersely. 'Ha'way, man Father. Ah'm nee bairn. If ye kna summink then ah want to kna.'

The priest watched him from the corner of his eye for a while, before speaking. 'It was by chance really. I've a friend who's the chaplain at Castington, and I double up with him there sometimes, cover for him when he's on holiday.'

'Castington? So he's moved away?'

'Castington Young Offenders Institute.'

'Ah divven't follow, Father.'

'I went in with my friend the other day. Part of his job is to visit the new prisoners, and if they're Catholic, to see if they want to attend Mass or anything like that.' Joe's face was creased with puzzlement. The priest hesitated for a moment, then began again, more certainly. 'There's no easy way to say this. He was there. Your grandson. He'd just been transferred from another institution. It was his being down on the list as O'Brien that made me wonder. Your Mary's definitely his mother. I looked at his records. Checked it all. Perhaps I shouldn't have done that, but I think you've got a right to know.'

'He's in jail?'

'Yes.'

Nothing was said for a long time. Joe cleared his throat. 'Do ah know him, Father? Ah mean, before he went to jail. Did he live in the area? Would ah have known him?'

'He's known as Sewell. That's because he was brought up by his grandfather . . .'

'His grandfather?'

'Paternal grandfather. Somebody called Sewell. William Sewell.'

Stupefied, the old man shook his head. 'Not Billy Sewell from oot Chopwell way? One of Ginga's mates?' He broke off. 'Aye; his lad'd be aboot the age.'

The priest shook his head. 'It's a terrible thing.'

Joe exhaled softly. 'Ah kna him.' He paused. 'Ah kna the bairn.'

The priest waited for the old man to continue, but he had lapsed into thought. 'As I've said,' Father Michael began once more, 'on the official records, he's down as O'Brien. And Mary's his mother. His father's Gary Sewell. One of the staff knew him, this Gary Sewell, been in and out of the system all his life apparently.'

'Tell me,' said Joe abruptly. 'What did he do; me grandbairn, ah mean; what did he do?'

Father Michael sighed. 'Joe, do you remember that trouble down at the Quayside a while ago? Two young lads held up a newsagent's? The newsagent had a heart attack?' The old man nodded. 'Well, that was him.'

'Oh aye. Ah remember.' The clock ticked. The sound of sweeping which they had heard throughout their conversation had stopped. A sudden gust of wind played with the back door, half closing and then opening it again. When the old man broke the silence at last there was a sad smile on his mouth. 'Funny that, the babby being brought up by Billy Sewell. Ah used to see them together from time to time, ah nivver dreamt . . . ah nivver thought . . .' Joe faltered. 'It's just as well Joan's slipped away. This would have destroyed her. Finding oot now, that all that time the babby was so near. Ah mean, we could have helped in his upbringing. Ah mean, we might have got to kna him.' The smile had evaporated from Joe's face. He turned his grief-stricken eyes on the young man. 'What else can happen to me noo, Father? What else?' The old man sipped some of his tea. Putting down the mug, he seemed to see the puddle he'd spilt for the first time. He stared at it for a long time, before looking back up. 'It's all gone wrang, Father Michael. Ah'm a cripple, and ah've lost me wife, me daughter, and now me grandson's a murderer.'

'What about the bonny lad?' The two men stared out the window, but the boy was nowhere to be seen. 'You've still got him.'

'Ah've lost everything.'

'But found him.'

'No,' replied Joe. 'Ah haven't. Ah want the best for him. But ah cannet give it to him.'

'Why not?'

'Because what he needs, ah haven't got.'

The priest cleared his throat. 'Mebbes all he needs is a bit of love.'

Joe smiled briefly, sadly. 'But mebbes that's just what ah haven't got in me heart to give him.'

At that moment there was the sound of something scuffling

against the wall of the cottage. The guttering could be heard creaking. Getting up, Joe went through to the kitchen. Throwing open the back door, he stepped out into the yard. Father Michael came up behind him, and followed the old man's gaze up to the eaves. Sonny Gee was clinging to the gutter, hanging just under the roof. 'What ye deeing now?' Joe demanded angrily. 'Get doon this minute.'

'There's eggs,' the boy called excitedly. 'Gadgie mista, God gadgie! There's eggs! And y'kna me hair what yus've just cut? Them eggs are wrapped up in it. Ye cannet knock it doon now. Not now. Not now there's eggs there wrapped in me hair!'

9

The wind rose. It coursed down the cut, boiled over the school wall, hurling itself headlong at the cottages with the rage of a tidal wave. With the coming of the evening, it grew even stronger, until all along the terrace there was the moan of its restless sifting through the eaves. Nothing was still; everything shifted and tugged maddeningly, unsettled by the growing gale. 'Divven't gan oot,' said the boy from the settee.

'Ah've got to,' the old man replied.

'Well, cannet ah come with ye?'

'No. Ye cannet. Ye're in bed.'

The boy yanked back the blanket from his body, and pulled himself up into a sitting position on the settee. 'No ah'm not. Look.'

'Lie down.'

'Where ye gannin'?'

The old man pulled the laces on his boots tight and then tied them. 'Ah told ye, ah'll tell ye when ah get back.'

'But ye've been oot all day. We couldn't even gan doon the allotments . . .'

'Ah thought ye liked being with Ronny?'

'Ah dee.' The boy folded his arms. 'Ha'way, gadgie mista. Ah'll come with ye. Ye won't even kna ah'm there. Ah'll walk behind ye on me tiptoes.'

The old man shook his head. 'Ah won't be late. And put that blanket back on. Yus're supposed to be asleep by now.'

'All this stopping in's geet boring. It's deein' me heed in.'

Joe glowered over at him. 'It's horse work with ye, isn't it? Ye cannet come with me and that's all there is aboot it.'

'Well, ah'm not stopping in. Ah'll just gan oot on me tod.'

Going through the passage door, Joe came back with his coat and cap on. He was holding his walking stick. 'Ye're forgetting someone, aren't ye?' The boy shook his head. 'If ye gan oot, man lad, what aboot Spring-heeled Jack?'

The boy sighed. 'Well, tomorrow ah'm gannin', ah'm not stopping here.'

'Oh aye, and where would ye gan to?'

Sonny Gee shrugged. 'Stacks of places. Ah could gan to Beacon Lough.'

'Beacon Lough?'

'Aye, ah kna where it is.' The boy paused for a moment. 'Ah could gan to Ireland.'

The old man glanced quizzically at the boy. 'Ireland? How ye gonnae get there, like?'

'Just will.'

'Costs money, that.'

'So?'

'Where ye gonnae get that from, like?'

'Ah can get money anywhere, me.'

'Oh aye, how?'

'Ah'll gan and work doon the pit.'

'The pit?'

'Aye, Ronny'll come with wor.'

'Where yus gonnae find a pit roond here, ye daft ha'p'orth.'

'Well, ah'll just dig me own, ye daft ha'p'orth.' The boy stared pleadingly at Joe. Then his bottom lip began to throb petulantly. 'In Bensham ye can get money anywhere . . .'

'This isn't Bensham.'

'Ah could get it from here an' all.'

The old man's voice was soft. 'What d'ye mean?'

'Twoc it, couldn't ah?'

'Are ye talking aboot stealing?'

Sonny Gee shrugged. 'Easy-peasy get money, me. Shops. Hooses. Anywhere.'

Joe sighed. 'Up to yer auld tricks again, are ye? Ah thought ye were better than that. Ah honestly did.'

There was a long pause. Sonny Gee's eyes widened. 'Ah kna where money is, me.'

The old man involuntarily looked over at the kitchen where the tea caddy stood hidden. His voice was quiet. 'What d'yus mean by that, like?' There was no answer. 'Ha'way, lad. What d'ye mean by that? Where is this money ye're gannin' on aboot?'

Sonny Gee suddenly shook his head imploringly. 'Ah promise ah won't twoc nowt if ye let wor gan with ye.'

'Ye said ye knew where money is. What did ye mean?'

The boy rubbed his eyes with the heel of his hand. 'Please let wor come with ye.'

Joe continued to stare at the boy, then shook his head. 'Yus're staying in,' he said. 'How many more times do ah have to say? Now, ye've the fire on.' The stick rose as he pointed it at the brightly burning fire. 'So remember . . .'

'Treat it with . . . summink,' put in the boy.

'Respect. And that means . . .'

'Divven't gan near it unless ye are there.' Sonny Gee droned the words as though well rehearsed.

The old man came over. 'And there's another thing ah want ye to promise. Divven't gan ootside.'

The boy stared at him. 'Ah telt ye. Ah'll stay in toneet. But tomorrow ah'm gannin'. Ah'm sick of this hole. It's shite.'

'Language.'

'Ye didn't even get wor that present ye promised us. Just got wor a crappy pink pencil.' Sonny Gee looked away from Joe. 'Mebbes ah'll just have to twoc mesel' summink for me present an' all,' he mumbled. 'Aye, it's just fuckin' shite here. Ye're not allowed to dee owt. Ye cannet swear, ye cannet gan oot at neet, ye cannet . . .'

'Well, just gan then.' The old man's voice was quiet.

'Eh?'

'If ye cannet stand it so much then just gan.' Joe paused. Sonny Gee did not move. The old man shook his head sadly. 'Ye cannet gan, can ye? 'Cos there's not neewhere for ye to gan.'

'Ah could . . .'

'Shut up, man lad,' Joe suddenly called. 'Ah'm sick o' these performances of yours.' The old man's voice rose angrily. 'Ye divven't kna when ye're born. When ah was a lad we had nowt. D'ye hear me? Nowt.' The old man glowered at the boy. He shook his head in irritation. Swept on by the momentum of his annoyance, he continued, his voice growing louder and louder: 'Ah was a little bairn in the year of the strike. And let me tell ye that that was deein' withoot, good and proper. So stop giving us all this aboot a present. We didn't even have wor own clothes. We had to get parcels or gan aboot in rags. We nivver had owt to eat neither. Nor wor own bed. There was nowt in the hoose, nowt. Ah was ten year auld before ah knew what fresh bread was. So divven't give wor this; when ah was a bairn things were much worse. That was real deprivation, not like anything ye have nowadays. It was . . .'

'Bet ye had a birthday present.' The boy's voice was hushed, but it brought the old man to a stop.

'Eh?' the old man replied, panting slightly with the unexpected exertion of his tirade.

'Ah bet ye had a birthday present.'

'Aye,' nodded Joe sarcastically. 'Summink me auld man made for us while sitting on his arse worrying aboot how he was gonnae make the next handoot stretch to four mouths . . .'

'It was still a birthday present.'

The old man stared strangely at the boy, his eyes flickered. 'Ah remember it,' he said in an unusually soft voice. 'It was a little whistle, carved oot o' wood. Just wood he'd cut from a tree.' Joe closed his eyes thoughtfully for a few moments. 'When ye blew it, it gave oot a two-toned whistle.'

'See? Telt yus ye had a present.'

Confusion hovered over Joe's features. 'Why have ah remembered that?' he asked quietly. He sighed. 'Must be getting auld. Haven't thought of that whistle for seventy-odd years and now . . .' He tailed off. His body stooped slightly as he continued to stand there deep in abstraction. 'He carved it sitting at the closed colliery gates. Sat there day after day, carving it for wor. Must have taken ages. But he did it.' Joe's face filled with wrinkles at the hint of a smile. 'Me dad. He used to say it was a present from Winston Churchill. Since it was him that wouldn't let the miners work. Him what wanted to break wor. A present from Winston Churchill. But ah knew it was from me dad. Ah must have been . . . aboot your age.' The old man broke off. 'Hey, lad,' he said with a strange brightness after an interval, 'when is yer birthday?' The boy did not reply. ''Cos ah was thinking mebbes ah could get ye summink then, eh? Not just for ye learning yer letters, but a proper present. For yer birthday. Ah mean . . . ha'way, lad, when's yer birthday?'

But the boy had turned his face away.

Joe continued to stare at him for a while. His body stooped further, and as his breathing slowed, his brow grew more and more troubled. Then suddenly he shuddered, and straightened himself. 'Well, ah better be gannin'. Remember, divven't open the door. Not for anyone.'

'D'ye think ah'm a divvy, like?' spluttered Sonny Gee without turning to look up. 'D'yus think ah'd let ye-kna-who spring oot on wor and drag us off doon the pit?'

The old man nodded. 'Aye. Good then.' He paused at the passage door. 'Divven't get too frightened, but, lad. He nivver comes in the hoose.'

'Ah thought ye said he gans all awer the spot.' The old man pulled his coat collar up. The boy stood up. 'Why cannet ah come with ye? Ah'd be good. Ah wouldn't use nee language

189

or nowt.' Sonny Gee broke off for an instant. 'Is it because ah'm nowt to ye that yus won't let wor come?'

'What ye on aboot?'

'That's what ye said. That ah was nowt to ye.'

Joe's lips trembled in bewilderment. 'Ha'way,' he said at last, 'it's way past yer bedtime. Just gan to sleep like any other lad o' your age.'

'Neebody gans to bed this early on Old Parsonage Road,' Sonny Gee shot back.

'Ah divven't kna how many times ah have to tell ye . . .'

'Ye're not on Old Parsonage Road now!' the two of them finished together.

'Cannet ah come with ye?' Sonny Gee began again.

The old man exhaled wearily. 'Ah've told yus once. Ah'm not gannin' through that again. And that's flat.'

'Why is it flat?'

'Just lie doon!'

Reluctantly, the boy lay back down. Joe came over. 'Yus're all untucked now,' he said. He hovered at the settee. Cautiously, he reached out to the blanket and tried to tuck it in under Sonny Gee, but he withdrew his hands in a sudden spasm. The boy looked up at him with appealing eyes. The old man struggled to tuck him in again. But he could not. 'Yus'll just have to tuck yersel' in,' said Joe awkwardly, moving back to the door. He hesitated there for a few moments more, before opening it. An instant later the front door could be heard slamming, as it was caught by the wind and wrenched out of the old man's grip.

Left alone, the boy did not move. He gazed at the fire which had been banked up for him. It crackled and spat, uneasy in the wind howling down the chimney. Sonny Gee picked up his cowboy hat from under the settee and put it on, then leaning down, he felt the blanket where the old man had touched it. He stared at that piece of the blanket for a long time, before lying back with a sigh, his hand still resting where Joe's had been.

The old man had only walked ten yards when he stopped to look back at his cottage. The trail of smoke, just visible in the gathering gloom of evening, was being blown back over the roof almost horizontally. Joe could feel the power of the wind tugging at him as he stood there and he had to shift his feet to keep balance. Appalled by his own frailty, he walked on to the cut.

Coming out of the cut, he passed the church. Walking past a hairdresser's, he crossed the busy road at the pedestrian bridge by Di Biasio's fish and chip shop. Pausing on the bridge, he looked out over the roofs of Lobley Hill and beyond. From where he stood he could see all the gentle hills of Gateshead. At this hour the graciously undulating land was pinpricked with the first street lamps. Here and there could be seen the darker, unlit tracts of waste grounds and old colliery lands that beautify the borough. Joe stared out over it all, his body propped against the parapet to shore himself against the gusting wind. Two or three people crossed over, glancing at him as they went by. 'Ye areet, mista?' one of them asked. 'Aye, aye,' replied Joe tersely.

Moving at last, the old man struggled down the steps on the other side.

As Joe walked through the streets of the estate, he watched the children playing in the wind. The twilight air was full of their shouts. The pavements were strewn with cut grass and daisies, blown from the open areas mown earlier in the day. The wind chased bits of litter into corners from which they fluttered and struggled in vain to escape, the empty crisp packets floundering like beached flatfish. Approaching a corner, Joe could see the shapes of a teenage gathering. Involuntarily he stopped. Even from where he stood he could hear their voices rising sporadically, like smashing glass. With his hand gripping the handle of the walking stick more tightly he began to move again.

At first they did not appear to notice him. As he passed through them, in the corner of his eye he could see empty bottles of Lambrella standing on the low wall behind the group. Then he felt a face turn on him. 'Ee, it's him,' one of the group said. 'Isn't that the auld gadgie what's got Mally's motorbike?'

'Na,' someone else answered.

'Ye sure?'

'Why aye. He's a pure pyscho him what's got it. That gadgie there's a pure grave dodger.'

Joe had walked past them a few yards, but paused and for a moment seemed to be about to turn. But he bit his lip and passed on; as he did so, his nostrils filled with the acrid stench from the joint of tac the teenagers were passing round.

'It is him,' someone said when the old man was out of earshot. 'Ha'way, we better tell Jimmy.'

About twenty yards on, Joe heard wild shouts flaring up behind him among the teenagers. A dog in a nearby house took up the noise, and soon it was passed along the close in a chain so that each house the old man passed throbbed with barking. The estate seemed to reverberate with the sound of dogs. Only slowly did the barking fade. Crossing the old coke works, Joe walked by the wreck of a car, dumped there by joyriders. Three children stood on the bonnet with their arms outstretched, trying to lean into the wind. As he passed them one of them unbalanced and fell to the ground.

At last he came to a cul-de-sac down which two little girls were part swaggering, part tottering in their mother's high-heeled shoes. The sleeves of the adult blouses they wore flapped in the wind. Joe watched as one of them tripped in a pothole, her friend grabbing her before she could fall. 'Is this Sunnygarth?' he asked one of them.

The little girl just laughed, and bustled off with her friend.

They stopped at about a distance of twenty yards to stare at Joe. 'Aye,' they called together.

Sunnygarth was two houses knocked into one at the bottom of the cul-de-sac. No one answered the old man's first knock. Nor his second. And he had already turned from the door, when he heard it open behind him. A harassed face scanned him. 'Not another one?' the woman at the door said.

The old man cleared his throat.

'Just a minute,' said the woman, disappearing back into the house.

Joe stood on the doorstep waiting. At the other end of the cul-de-sac the two little girls continued circling. Not long later the woman came back. 'I'm sorry about that,' she said. 'We're just in the middle of a crisis.'

Stepping through a hall, the old man followed the woman into a small room. 'Can I leave you there for a moment?' the woman said before disappearing again. 'I won't be a moment.'

There was a coffee table in the centre of the small room. On the table stood a vase with an arrangement of dried grasses spearing from it. Joe stood there, gazing at the vase. Cigarette ash was scattered all over the table around the base of the vase. The door opened, and a man looked into the room. 'Are you being seen to?' he asked. Suddenly, there was a burst of shouting from a room above. Joe looked up at the ceiling. 'Na! Just fuck off, man!' exploded the shouting.

'Fireworks tonight!' laughed the man, disappearing.

A few minutes later there was a flurry of feet on the stairs, and the woman came into the room. 'Look, if you've come to complain about what happened this morning then all I can say is that the matter's been turned over to the police.'

'Complain?' asked the old man, puzzled.

'It's been all day. You can't believe the amount of people we've had coming by to complain.' The woman paused. 'Please, sit down,' she said.

Narrowing his eyes, Joe eased himself into an armchair,

while the woman watched him with weary eyes. 'It's blowing a gale oot there,' he said at last.

Together they listened to the wind. 'It just makes them worse,' she said. 'The wind upsets them. Gets them high as kites. There's always trouble when it's windy. It gets to them. Same with animals, apparently.'

'Who?' asked the old man uncertainly.

The woman shrugged. 'The kids.'

Joe looked about the room. 'Still, ye've got it nice in here,' he remarked, nodding his head at the vase of grasses. 'It's nice for them. Like a real home.'

'What have you come to complain about then?'

'Ah haven't come for that,' said the old man uncertainly. 'Ah've come . . . well, ah came at this time because ah thought they'd all be in bed. So ah could have a chat with one of the staff.'

There was a thudding on the ceiling above them. Shouting burst out, followed by the high-pitched scream of a girl. 'Now he's set her off,' the woman said. She closed her eyes in desperation. 'We'll have our work cut out now.'

'Set who off?'

'Look, I'm sorry, I'll have to go and see.'

A chilling scream was followed by a stream of abuse, every word of which was audible to Joe in the small room. An abrupt, eerie silence followed. Then a low whine began, hardly separable from the disturbances of the wind, but it grew to a steady, persistent, drill-like sound until, to Joe, it somehow sounded less human than the moans of the wind. The old man screwed up his face in confusion as he stared rigidly up at the ceiling. The woman could be heard above him, her words a continual soothing patter which gradually seemed to diminish the whine. Joe was just beginning to look about the room again when the door was thrust open. The old man turned to see a boy standing there. 'Hello,' the old man said after a few moments.

The boy continued to stare at him. He seemed about ten, perhaps eleven years of age, although his face appeared ravaged by an early attack of acne. His hair was shaved drastically short. A haunted look made his eyes shift ceaselessly. There was something stunted about him like a birch tree that germinated too high on a mountain. 'Who the fuck are ye?' the boy demanded. But before Joe had a chance to answer, he had crossed the room and sat down. For a few moments the boy sat there utterly motionless, then his eyes began to dart again, and his fingers played uneasily with a cushion. His hands were tiny, like those of a pixie. And the fingernails were long and sharp. 'Ye come to complain an' all?' he demanded.

'Na.'

'Have ye got any tabs?'

'Na.'

'Any money?'

Abruptly springing to his feet, the boy went over to the table. Rattling the vase with his tiny fingers, he upended it. Along with the plumes of grass, a number of cigarette ends fell out. The boy chose the biggest one and lit it. 'If she comes in, say it's yours.' Inhaling deeply on the cigarette end, the boy watched Joe intently. The boy's face contorted with aggression. 'She's a friggin' lesbo, her, ye kna.' The old man knitted his eyebrows. 'She thinks ah'm staying in the neet. Well, she can shove it up her cunt.' Taking one last drag, the boy flicked the end of the cigarette. It landed on the arm of Joe's chair. The old man leant over and picked it up; when he looked up again, the boy had gone. He sat there bewildered. Slowly, the cigarette burned to its filter and then died.

'Look, I'm really really sorry,' said the woman, coming back into the room later, 'but one of our residents has absconded. I'll have to see you tomorrow. Was it really important?'

The old man rose. 'Ah just wanted to ask a few questions.'

'Go on then, if you can be quick.'

Joe's forehead ruffled with thought. 'When they're adopted . . .'

he began, but broke off. 'Do they get . . .' Again, he broke off. His eye rested on the dead cigarette end he had placed on the table. 'The young boy ye've got here,' he said, more fluently now, 'how long has he been here?'

Exhaustion came over the features of the woman. 'Shaved hair?' Joe nodded. 'He's been here since he was nine.'

The old man started. 'What? About a year or so?'

'Year or so?' The woman shook her head. 'Longer than that. He's fourteen now.'

'Fourteen?' Bewilderment contorted Joe's features.

She nodded. 'It's him you want to complain about, isn't it? I know he looks young, but he's fourteen.'

The old man walked across the room. 'Ah didn't kna they stopped here so long before being adopted an' that.'

'Not many are adopted. Most of them are in the system until they're sixteen.'

'Ah nivver knew that.' Joe looked about the room. 'And they just stop in a place like this?' he asked. 'If they divven't get adopted, would a lad just stop in a home like this?'

Nodding, the woman walked him to the door. 'Is there anything else you want?'

The old man shook his head. 'Na,' he said. 'There's nothing.'

Joe stumbled outside. Night had fallen and he wandered aimlessly through the estate. After a long time, he came to a metal bench outside a little group of shops, and sitting down, perched on its hard edge. Slowly, he crumpled into it and the cold of the metal seeped into him. The wind tore through him. The litter, harrowed by gusts, gathered at his feet.

Spring-heeled Jack was on the roof, Sonny Gee could hear him. He was grappling for a hold on the tiles. His claw-like fingers scrabbled and tapped, but even when the wind knocked him off balance and he rolled over the edge, Spring-heeled Jack immediately bounced back. The boy lay there on the settee listening with every fibre of his being to the intruder on the cottage roof. Eyes wide, blanket tucked right under his chin, Sonny Gee pictured him. The cruel face, featureless but for a sausage nose; the lifeless wisps of cobweb hair; the huge boots with springs attached. Every creak and moan of the wind showed the progress of the grey sprite trying to get in.

The wind relented for a few seconds, then all of a sudden, an even more powerful gust shook the windowpanes. Sonny Gee jumped, and then quickly pulled the blanket over his head to escape the frying-pan head staring in at him from outside. He was half smothered under the blanket, but still he did not move, until in the sound of his own heartbeat he heard Spring-heeled Jack's taloned fingers drumming on the wall. Unable to stand it, he threw off the blanket and sat up, blinking. It was then that he heard the rattling of the front door. 'Get lost, ye,' he said, but his voice wavered. 'Ah'm not scared of ye, ah had that lad doon Old Parsonage Road. Ah . . .' But once again, the giant was trying to get in at the front door, and Sonny Gee fell silent. With the rattling of the door, he was certain that he could hear the sound of springs coiling and uncoiling expectantly. The sweat on his brow ran cold.

Heart beating sickeningly, his head pounding with terror, the little boy stood up. He crept across the room and opened the passage door. Falling on to his hands and knees he went into the old man's bedroom. Silently, he slithered over to the window and began to lift a corner of the net curtain. But before he could see through, there was a third clatter at the door, and the whole cottage seemed to vibrate under its impact. 'Ye'll not get us,' Sonny Gee said with a sudden surge of courage. 'Not me, ye'll nivver get me.'

Back in the sitting room, the fire was still burning, although it had begun to wane. Sonny Gee went over to the television and flicked the switch. He fiddled with it desperately, but the set stayed dead. Pulling the cowboy hat firmly on his head and wrapping himself with a blanket, the boy looked about. His gaze came to rest on the sideboard. Slowly, he approached it and opened the door. It was then that he heard the voice.

Sonny Gee froze. The voice was in the yard at the back door. 'Ah'm not opening that one neither,' he called, but his words were no more than a whisper. He peered over to the glass of the kitchen door. 'See, if ye come near me,' he began, 'then ye kna what ah'll dee? Ah'll get ye good and proper. D'ye hear, Spinger Spaniel Jack? If ye come near me, ah'll settle ye.' Sonny Gee stooped to take something from his sock. It was the lighter. He clicked the flame into life. 'If ye come near me, ah swear down, ah'll burn yus to a Rice Krispie.'

'Ha'way, bonny lad, let wor in,' the voice suddenly called out. Shivering, Sonny Gee stared through the glass. The blood had drained from his cheeks. 'Ah kna ye're in there,' the voice continued, echoing in the kitchen. 'And ah kna auld psycho meat cleaver's gone oot.'

Terrified, Sonny Gee crouched low at the open sideboard door. 'Ah'm not scared o' . . .' he whimpered softly, but broke off, and then, as though losing all strength in his legs, sank to the ground. He tried to get up, but he could not. Like a cornered, defeated animal, he stared up through glass-like eyes.

There was a hammering at the back door. The voice was suddenly hard and cruel. 'Ah kna yus're in there all on yer own an' all. So ha'way and open the door for wor.'

The boy raised the lighter flame in front of his face, and shutting his eyes, cowered, chewing nervously on the chin cord of the cowboy hat. The door shuddered as it was kicked. A screw from the lock shot out. Then there was a strange stillness. The silence lasted a few seconds before being shattered by the scream of splintering wood. At that instant Sonny Gee jumped to his feet, and with an agile wriggle, crawled into the sideboard cupboard, pulling the door shut behind himself.

In the kitchen a foot had smashed its way through the back door. 'Oh, mule,' Jimmy sang out, coming into the sitting room. 'Where are ye?' He paused. 'Reet,' he whispered to his companion. 'Ye gan into the bathroom. That's where the pills'll be. Ah'll look for his pension an' that. They always have money stashed away somewhere.'

'Why divven't we just take the bike, it's stood oot there?' asked Mally nervously.

'Are ye mental? It's open hoose here. Anyway, what aboot the mule?'

'We can come back for him any time, man Jimmy.'

'What's the matter, ye shitting yersel' or summink?' Jimmy leered. Moving about the room, he began to look under the table. 'Aye,' he whispered, 'if ah were ye, ah'd keep me head doon an' all, bonny lad. 'Cos when ah find yus, ye'll wish ye'd nivver been born.'

Mally strode nervously across the room. 'Is it through here then, Jimmy, the bathroom?'

'Ah thought ye'd cased the joint?'

'That was Peggy's ah went into.'

'Well, this'll be the same, man. All of these is the same.'

Mally stumbled down the passage and into the bathroom. In the sitting room could be heard a clattering, followed by the smashing of glass as the medicine-cabinet door was wrenched off its hinges. 'Bingo,' Mally said, coming back into the sitting room, rattling a few jars of pills.

Jimmy snatched them from him. 'Bingo big time,' he said. 'Auld mentals meat cleaver must be in a bad way if he's having all of these. Nee wonder his hands is like a geet pair o' claws.'

'Where's the mule then?'

'Divven't kna.'

'Are yus sure he does live here?'

'Well, he said he did, didn't he?'

'Aye, but . . .'

'And it was ye what saw him hanging aboot here again the other day.'

'Well, mebbes he's gone oot an' all then.'

Jimmy shook his head. 'Na, auld meat–cleaver claws was by hisself. The others saw him.'

'They couldn't be certain it was him, mind. Mebbes we shouldn't hang aboot.'

'Ye're getting worse than yer stepdad, ye,' laughed Jimmy. 'Friggin' yellow-belly. He wouldn't even come and get yer bike for ye.'

Mally shook his head. 'Couldn't trust his temper. Might lose it with meat cleaver. He's on probation . . .'

'Bollocks, he's a puff.'

'What happens if meat cleaver comes in?'

'Look. The auldie's oot and the mule's in here somewhere.' Jimmy looked about for a little longer, then turned back to his companion. 'Ha'way, divven't stand aboot like a lemon. Let's see what else there is. Ye do the bedroom. And remember to look everywhere. Them grave dodgers put their money in the stupidest places.'

The other youth laughed. 'Aye. Remember that auld biddy up on Beacon Lough? She kept hers . . .'

'Get moving for frigg's sake, man.' Going through into the kitchen, Jimmy opened a drawer; the cutlery bounced on the linoleum floor as he upended it. Bending down, he picked up the scissors. 'Handy,' he said to himself. The old man's meagre stores were thrust out of the cupboard. Tins hit the ground, the box of porridge oats tumbled down, and the salt cellar, having rolled along the Formica surface, came to a rest on the edge, its contents pouring over the side. It did not take Jimmy long before he found the tea caddy. 'Belter,' he cried.

'Foond him?' asked his friend, coming through.

'Na.'

'What ye got then?'

'Dosh, man.'

There was a wobble of excitement in Mally's words. 'Straight up?'

'Hold on to yer horses. There's only aboot forty quid.'

Holding up the notes, he fluttered them under his friend's nose.

'Gis half.'

'What ye foond, like?'

'Nowt yet. Gis half.'

'Find summink yersel'.' Jimmy stared challengingly at the other teenager, who stepped back.

'Ha'way, Jimmy man. We've got to find Macca's mule. He wants him, y'kna. We told him we'd find him.'

'Divven't wet yersel', man.'

'Ah think he'll be at Audrey's. She takes in all the bairns. Why divven't we tell Macca that's where he is?'

'Oh aye, and what happens if he isn't? D'ye kna what Macca does to them what lets him doon?'

There was an uneasy silence. 'How much is he giving wor to find him, like?'

'And divven't ye worry aboot that,' Jimmy snapped. 'If he's not here noo, ah suppose we can always come back for him.' He grinned. 'Meanwhile, let's help worselves to a bit of fringe benefits. Have ye looked under the bed?'

With a slight, nervous shake of his head, the tall youth went back through to the bedroom.

Jimmy moved into the sitting room. There was a loud scratching as he ran the scissors against the grain of the table. 'How d'yus spell tosser?' he called.

His accomplice poked his head round the passage door. 'Depends,' he said.

'On what?'

'What kind of tosser it is.'

'Well, smart-arse, what kind is it if ah want to say: Fuck off, ye auld tosser?'

Mally considered this for a while. 'One S,' he said. The scissors scratched away. He looked about anxiously, hovering at the door. 'So isn't he here then? Ha'way, let's just snatch the bike and get missing. Ah've looked everywhere in the bedroom. And there's not nowt to twoc neither. Not even a porno mag.'

'Them grave dodgers divven't care aboot that kind o' thing.' Jimmy leant back to look over his handiwork on the table. 'Ah could have done art, me.' He smiled. 'Ah want him to get the message, me. Ah want him to kna ye divven't mess with Jimmy.'

The pillows from the settee and the armchair were tossed aside as the two youths continued to search. The miner's lamp was lifted from the mantelpiece and dropped; its glass smashing on impact with the hearthstone. One by one, the drawers in the sideboard cupboard were taken out, their objects scattered. 'Is he a Jehovah Witness or what?' the tall youth sneered as he sifted through the contents. He held up a pair of rosary beads, draped round a crucifix.

'All this useless shite,' moaned Jimmy, flicking at the television switch. 'It's deeing me heed in. That telly's not nee good neither. Ye divven't break into a hoose for forty quid and a few jars o' sweeties.'

'Where's Macca's mule, but?'

Jimmy flared angrily, flourishing the scissors under the other teenager's nose. 'Will ye shut up aboot that an' all.'

'He won't be very happy if we cannet find him. Specially not after ye telt him we'd collar him nee bother.'

'And ah'll tell ye summink in a minute an' all, if yus divven't fuckin' stop crying like a girl. Now let's get this opened.' Reaching out to open the sideboard cupboard door, Jimmy paused for a moment. 'He's not getting the stuff for a while yet. There's a bag coming from Amsterdam to the airport. He'll want him for then. We can wait a bit. Got a bit leeway, y'kna.'

'Ah heard there was nivver any leeway with Macca.'

'Macca's areet for a while yet.'

'How do ye kna, like?'

Jimmy snipped the blades of scissors together meaningfully.

'This is the big time now, lass. If ye divven't know these things, ye divven't get very far. Kna what ah mean?' Slowly, deliberately, the baby-faced youth lowered the scissors to his companion's groin.

'Aye, ah kna what yus mean,' the other responded, weakly.

Putting aside the scissors, again Jimmy stooped down and reached for the sideboard door. 'What was that?' he suddenly demanded, straightening up once more.

'What?'

'Shut up!' Jimmy hissed. Holding up his hand to keep his companion silent, his eyes darted about the room as he listened intently.

'Ah cannet hear nowt, me.'

'Ah thought ah heard someone.'

'Did ye?'

'Mebbes not.'

'What was it?'

'Ah fuckin' said mebbes not.' The air between them was fraught. They stared at each other for a few moments. 'It's just the wind, man.'

Caught by the wind, the broken back door opened and closed restlessly in the jamb.

'Mebbes he's not staying here now,' said the tall one, his voice beginning to chunter anxiously. 'Mebbes he's gone to live somewhere else.' He paused. 'Mebbes we'll not collar him. Mebbes we should just get off with the bike. Mebbes we'll have to tell Macca we cannet find him.'

A grin widened across Jimmy's face. 'Neebody lets Macca doon,' he said as he leant down to open the sideboard cupboard door. 'See if we divven't find him? Then it's ye what's the mule. Ah thought that'd flap ye. Now let's get this opened.' The door creaked as Jimmy began to open it.

Joe walked with his head down. One hand was on his cap to keep it from being ripped away by the wind; the other clutched the walking stick. Struggling in the teeth of the gale, he moved slowly, his body stooped severely. Frequently he had to pause to catch his breath. The gusts were increasing in their ferocity, and he knew after climbing only a few steps up that it would not be safe for him to use the pedestrian bridge which spanned the road. Retracing his steps, he moved to the kerb and stood there for a long time waiting for a break in the speeding traffic. Looking down, he noticed a dead ginger cat in the gutter, the imprint of a front wheel stamped across its limp body.

When at last he managed to start crossing the road, he found himself marooned in the middle on the central reservation. On either side of him two lanes of traffic screamed by like a river in spate. A bus, pressurised by a tight timetable, roared past, displacing a whirlpool of air. This sudden gust of wind unbalanced the old man. He clawed for a hold on the air and opening his fingers, the stick was thrown free. There was a resonant clatter as it hit the surface of the road, and a split second later, a loud crack. The wheel of a lorry had snapped the walking stick like a femur bone. A piece of it was hurled back on to the central reservation. Bending down stiffly, the old man picked it up. The stick had been snapped about two feet down from the handle, and the end was splintered. He gazed at the broken stick for a long time, his lips mumbling silently.

Looking up at last, he stared at the speeding vehicles with a wearied bewilderment. Then, shaking his head, he stepped off the central reservation. Cars screeched to a halt as Joe walked out in front of them. A driver leant out of his window. 'Watch what ye deeing, ye stupid auld idiot,' he shouted. But Joe did not seem to hear. 'Ye nearly got yerself killed.' The cars in the second lane skidded to a stop. The noise of their horns rose angrily, as, still buffeted by the wind, the old man reached the other side of the road.

'Ye want locking up in a home,' another irate motorist

shouted, before rolling up his window to roar recklessly along Whickham Highway.

The old man carried on. Reaching the church, he went up to the door.

Inside the church, Joe walked up the aisle, collapsing on to the pew beneath the picture of the Holy Family. The light of candles played over his face, casting his fitful shadow over the cold floor. The shadow included the crook of the broken stick which rested across his knee. 'Why?' he began, softly. The shadow changed shape as the stick was raised. 'Will ye just tell wor why?' The old man's voice echoed in the night-time building. The buffeting of the wind was muffled. Occasionally the glass of a window rattled. 'Why d'yus dee these things? Me? Ah divven't care aboot me. Ye've done yer worst to me, but the lad, he's only a bairn. Why cannet ye leave the lad alone?' Joe paused for a moment. 'Will ye not answer me? Will ye not . . .' His voice, having risen to a shout, broke off abruptly. The shadow held its position on the ground for a little while longer and then melted away into nothing as Joe stood up. He looked up at the picture imploringly, then turned and walked down the aisle.

Without the full length of the stick, his progress was even more painful. He stopped at the mouth of the cut, chest heaving. When he had recovered enough to move off again, he slipped from the road down into the lightless recesses of the cut. With one hand he propelled himself along the fence, heedless of the spells of the rough wood lacerating his skin, while with the other he brandished the stump of the stick. Every so often, glass tinkled at his feet, and metal scratched the cinders as he unwittingly kicked aside an empty can of lager. Tunnelled, the wind streamed into his face, raising the tears in his eyes. It lifted off his cap and hurled it away. He did not go back for it. The lamp-post in the middle of the cut carved the silhouette of a gibbet on the night. The old man looked up anxiously as he walked underneath, peering at the metal arm which seemed to be swinging dangerously in the storm, noisily creaking as though under a dead weight. At that moment there was a sudden crash and the old man froze, instinctively throwing his arms up in protection of his head.

For a few seconds he waited for the impact of the lamp-post hitting the ground, or its striking his own bent body with a glancing blow. A sense of unreality stretched the moment so that he felt he had been standing for a long time when he finally lifted his head. Blinking, he looked up to see that a wheelie bin had been lifted by the wind and thrown against the fence. It had landed a few paces from him. He stared numbly at the bin and then pressed on.

As he neared the cottage, a light could be seen spearing down the little garden path. The front door was wide open. The old man paused. His eyes widened with disbelief.

Stepping over the threshold, he walked down the passage. All the lights in the cottage were on. Passing the bathroom, he saw that it was utterly dishevelled. The bedroom door was open too, showing the chaos of a theft. But it was only when he walked into the sitting room that he realised the full extent of the violation. He looked for the boy, but there was no sign of him.

As Joe stood there, motionlessly surveying the destruction, something glinting on the hearth caught his eye. Mechanically, he went over to it, and stooping, picked up the broken miner's lamp. He held it in his hands as though studying it for a long time with a strange absorption. He did not notice the steady drip of his blood on to his boots and the hearthstone, nor realise that the glass of the broken lamp had cut a finger deeply.

Still dripping blood, he moved over to the glass door. He waited there for a while. Then with a deep breath he pushed it fully open.

He did not react when he saw the discarded tins and boxes, the upended drawer and the scattered knives and forks. Going over to the restlessly clashing back door, he tried to close it, and when he saw that it had been kicked in, he placed a heavy pan against it. Picking a way over the wreckage as though it was not there, he made for the tea caddy which stood on the hob of the cooker. The tea caddy did not rattle when he shook it. 'So,' he said quietly, his face ashen, 'he's taken it.' The lid of the tea caddy creaked as the old man's knotted fingers fretted with it. 'He waited until ah was gone. Then he took it.' A look of puzzlement deadened Joe's eyes. 'He told me he was going to but ah didn't believe him. Ah . . .' The old man continued to mumble inaudibly. Then he fell silent. A dark curtain seemed to fall over his face. He did not move for a whole minute until, suddenly, with all his strength, he hurled the tin against the wall. It ricocheted across the kitchen, coming to rest on the floor among the other objects, its lid dented with the impact. Apparently calm once more, the old man stooped to pick it up, and having put it back into the cupboard, he quietly closed the door.

With an almost tranquil air, Joe brought a chair from the sitting room and dragged it out into the yard, placing it against the wall. The wind tore at him, and as he stepped up on to the chair, his coat billowed. Holding the stick, he raised the handle up to the eaves. But broken, it would not reach them.

The legs wobbled precariously as the old man pressed up on his tiptoes. The chair creaked and juddered beneath him. Falling foward, his cheek grazed against the side of the house, but he did not seem to notice it, and a few moments later, he began to stretch up again. He was about to raise his shattered stick once more when he felt it being held. 'What the hell are ye deeing?' a voice suddenly shouted.

Joe looked down. 'Leave us alone, man Ronny,' he yelled.

'Eh?' Ronny said.

'Let go of me stick.'

'It's blowing a gale. Ye'll kill yerself.' The old man did not reply. 'Ye've been turned over, man,' Ronny explained desperately. 'Didn't ye kna?'

'Course ah kna.'

The two men gazed at each other. They had to shout over the wailing wind to be heard.

'What ye deein', man Joe?' Feeling the old man pulling against him, Ronny looked up at the eaves. 'Ye're nivver seeing to that nest now, are ye?'

'It wants doing.'

Ronny spluttered with disbelief. 'But ye've just been done over.' He waved an arm, pointing down the terrace. He tried to speak, but his words were torn away by a sudden gust. 'They came,' he screamed. 'Came down the backyards. Elsie heard something. They've smashed everything. Did Walter's and Peggy's over an' all.' But Joe was not listening. 'Don't ye even want to know about the bonny lad?' roared Ronny, the veins standing on his neck as he shrieked at the top of his voice.

'Na!' The old man's hissing vehemence ripping through the storm so surprised Ronny that he lost his grip, and Joe was able to pull the stick free. The wind tore at the old man as, swaying, he raised it above his head.

'Ye're gonnae kill yerself. What ye doing this for when the bonny lad . . .'

'Ah've told you. He's finished. Gone. Ah nivver want to hear a mention of him again.'

'What the fuck are ye gannin' on aboot?' yelled Ronny. 'Ye . . .' But his words were snatched by the gale.

'This is what the fuck ah'm gannin' on aboot!' shouted Joe, his voice a howl on the night as, with a swipe of his stick, he hit the air below the house martins' nest.

'Are ye oot of yer mind?'

'Aye,' Joe screamed. 'The minute ah took him. That was when ah was oot of me mind. Ah offered him me hand, and he bit it like the whelp that he is. But it's over with now. It's awer and done with.' Straining every muscle in his body, Joe reached up again to knock the nest. He missed. His boots slipped right to the edge of the chair and as they struggled for a grip, the chair wobbled on to two legs.

'Frigg me sideways,' cried Ronny, hurling himself at the chair to steady it. Joe's whole body heaved as the old man prepared to strike the birds' nest again. 'They haven't found him yet,' Ronny yelled. 'Ah've been flying up and doon. Everybody's out looking for the bonny lad. Ah called the police as soon as ah saw.'

'The pollis have got him, have they?' the old man shouted. 'Who?'

'There was forty pounds he took from me cupboard. All ah had. Ah took him in, and he robbed us. Ah was right. Ah knew ah shouldn't have let him stay with wor. Ah knew ah shouldn't have trusted him.'

'What the hell are ye gannin' on aboot?' bellowed Ronny, jumping up and down with increasing agitation, trying to grasp the broken walking stick. 'It wasn't him.'

But at that moment the old man called on all his remaining strength to stretch himself up and wield the stick. There was a shriek from the bird who flew from the nest just as it was knocked away. There was a sudden cessation of the wind as two tiny objects fell through the night to the yard beneath the eaves. In the strange stillness of the storm's momentary interval, the sound of the breaking eggs seemed like an explosion. Ronny looked down at them in disbelief. Then the wind began to whine again. And the birds flew about the old man's head, screaming their bereavement.

'Gadgie mista,' called the boy, appearing in the door.

'Sonny Gee, thank fuck for that,' said Ronny, running over and embracing the child. 'We didn't kna what had happened to ye.'

'Ah hid,' he shrugged.

Staggering dangerously, the old man stepped down on to the yard.

'What have ye done?' Sonny Gee shouted as he tried to see

past Ronny. Ronny let go of him. The boy pushed past him and pointed up at the eaves. 'What have ye done?' he demanded.

'They've took the bike back an' all,' cried Ronny, gesticulating at the empty wall where the bike had been propped. 'That clinches it then. It must have been that Jimmy Walsh and Mally.'

'Eh?' shouted Joe, his face creased with confusion.

'What robbed ye, man. They broke in. Who knas what would have happened if they'd found this little bonny lad?'

'Foond him?'

'When they heard me, they scarpered. Otherwise they would have found him. Still, ye're areet, eh, Sonny Gee. Ye must have had a good hiding place.'

The boy fell to his knees. Tears tore from him in explosive sobs as he felt the broken shells. He hid his head in his hands for a few moments and then looked up at Joe. From the light cast through the window and the open door, the old man could see, under the brim of the red cowboy hat, the tears running down Sonny Gee's face. Joe stared at the boy's face, crushed with anguish.

The birds continued to fly about the old man's head. Bewildered, he tried to knock them away with a wave of his broken stick, but they would not be deterred. Again and again they dived at him, their pitiful shrieks mingling with the raging wind, until at last they gave a final drawn-out keen and disappeared over the wall to the church.

10

After the night of the storms, fair weather set in over Gateshead. For two weeks the sun shone in an ever bluer sky, and at night bright stars twinkled above the urban glow. Spring sat on the cusp of early summer as the green fields of rye above the Watergate Colliery redevelopment slowly began to ripen.

'It's big,' said the old man.

'Aye,' whispered the boy, his voice hushed with awe. 'It's geet big.'

'And look at them legs.'

'Them legs is belter.'

'Them legs is canny long.'

'Geet hairy an' all.'

'Now remember what Ronny said . . .'

The boy repeated the words as though learnt by heart. 'Ah've got to keep that tank well secured, and the temperature reglated.'

'That's right.'

'What does reglated mean again?'

'Divven't worry aboot that at the minute.' Joe looked over at the window through which the sun was streaming. 'It's another scorcher oot there. Put it this way, if your little mate here got oot the day, he'd thrive.'

Sonny Gee's eyes shone excitedly. 'There's nee way he's getting oot. Ah'm not having Teletubby Peggy squashing him.'

'Nivver mind that.' Joe sat down. The boy continued to lean forward, head propped on hands, gazing into the tank which stood on the table. 'Isn't it aboot time ye came up with a name for it?'

'Ah divven't kna,' replied the boy. 'Ah keep thinking aboot it.'

'If it needs a name. Mebbes spiders divven't need names.'

Sonny Gee was adamant. 'Course they dee.' He paused to think. 'How aboot calling it Peggy?'

'Is it a lass?'

'Ah divven't kna, how d'yus tell?'

'Won't they tell yus doon at the Spider Society?'

'Aye, but ye've got to be ten before ye can join.'

'Ah thought Ronny was gonnae take it down there for ye. So they can check it awer for yus.'

'He is.'

'Getting a bit lazy in his auld age, Ronny. Ah'll get on to him aboot it again. He's been a bit doon in the dumps for a while.' The old man turned to the window, blinking in the strong sunlight. 'Have ye fed it yet today?' The boy shook his head knowledgeably. 'Well, divven't ye think ye should?'

'It's a Chilean Rose spider, man. Ye only feed them twice a week. That's when ye hoy the crickets in.'

'Aye, well, keep them things secure in the jar. Ah divven't want them hopping all awer the room again. Took wor all day to get them back in. Cannet ye get summink easier to feed it with, but?'

'It's the only thing they eat.' The boy sighed. 'Ah wish ah was ten. Then ah could join the Spider Society.' Sonny Gee paused. 'Will ah still be here when ah'm ten?' The old man did not reply, and Sonny Gee stared at him furtively for a while before looking away. The boy twisted his head from side to side in his scrutiny of the spider. 'If it is a lad then ah'll call it Springy Jack.'

The old man sighed heavily. 'It's time ye forgot aboot all that. Ah wish ah'd nivver telt ye. Anyway, ah thought Ronny was gonnae explain summink aboot it to ye. Aboot it being a story an' that?'

'Just Jack on its own then?' replied the boy. 'Or Spring-heel Spider?' The two caught each other's eye. 'Ah love it, me. Me spider. Thanks, gadgie mista.'

The old man looked away. 'Well, ye deserve a present.' He paused with embarrassment. 'And after them birds . . .'

'Ronny telt wor it was a accident.'

'Aye. It was an accident. We'll get ye summink for yer birthday an' all. If ye'd tell wor when it is . . .'

'Can ah take it oot again?' Sonny Gee asked. 'Ah'll make sure it doesn't gan under the settee, this time.'

Joe looked over at the clock on the sideboard. 'Na.'

'Oh, gan on.'

'Ah said na. We've work to do. Doon the allotment.'

'Belter!' cheered the boy, standing up. His face lit up. 'Are we gonnae start on it today then?'

'We're gonnae make a start.'

'Make a start?'

'Aye.'

'Why cannet we make a finish an' all?'

Joe shook his head. 'Summink like this takes time, lad. It doesn't happen all in a day.'

'Why not?'

The old man paused thoughtfully. 'That's the way of things, lad. Anything worthwhile takes more than a day.'

They went into the yard and Sonny Gee darted in front of Joe to pick up an empty sack from the coalhouse. Moving back through the house, the boy snatched his cowboy hat. 'Ye not hot in that?' the old man asked as he closed the front door behind them. 'It's boiling ootside.'

'Ye not hot in yours?' the boy asked, pointing at the old man's cloth cap.

'And ah'd better take the sack.'

As they walked down the row of houses, the doors opened

213

one by one. People came out with carrier bags full of kitchen scraps. Collecting them all, Sonny Gee dropped them in the sack. 'Tell wor when it's too heavy,' the old man said.

'Ah can carry twice this,' boasted the boy, swaggering importantly under the load.

'It's not full yet, mind.'

'Well, ah can carry three times that.'

'And how are yous two the day?' a woman in a housecoat asked.

'Areet thanks, Elsie,' replied Joe.

'Planted yer leeks oot yet?'

'We're doing it now,' said Sonny Gee excitedly. 'That's where we're gannin'. We're making a start.'

They walked on. 'Hows the pair o' yus the day?'

'Not so bad, Walter,' replied Joe.

'When ye're gonnae put yer leeks in?'

'That's where we're gannin',' said Sonny Gee, smiling. 'We're making a start.'

They hadn't gone much further when someone else called to them.

'Now then.'

Joe paused for a moment before answering the round woman standing at her gate, eyeing them suspiciously. 'Hello, Peggy.'

'Divven't come looking here for any compost. Ah've given my bag to Arthur.'

'That's areet,' said Sonny Gee. 'We want them leeks to grow, not poison them.'

'Ee,' said Peggy to the old man, 'he's the pot model of ye areet, reet doon to the foul mouth. The pot model.'

Walking on, they reached the cut. 'Ah'll take the sack now,' Joe said.

'Ah can manage,' replied the boy. They walked under the lamp-post. The wheelie bin had been lifted up by someone, and pushed in against the fence. Sonny Gee looked about furtively. 'Is he at school again today, auld Springer Spaniel Jack?' he asked.

By the time they reached the church, the child was struggling under the bulky weight of the sack.

'Ha'way, man lad, ah'll have it now.'

'When ah want help ah'll ask for it.'

'Suit yersel'.'

'Ah will.'

They crossed the Whickham Highway, having to dodge the cars speeding past. 'It's thirty mile an hour limit here, mind,' remarked the old man. Turning thoughtful for a moment, he looked at the boy. 'Ye've got to promise wor summink?'

'What?'

'Promise wor yus'll nivver cross it withoot me or Ronny.'

'Why are ye always making us promise things?'

''Cos there's always people stupid and selfish enough to put saving a minute on a journey above the life of a child; and some of them drive along Whickham Highway. The pollis divven't dee owt aboot it.'

The boy looked up at him, puzzled. 'Eh?'

'Look, we divven't want to lose ye,' Joe snapped.

'Who doesn't?'

'Ha'way, let's cross.'

They walked on to the Watergate Colliery land, passing through an avenue of saplings. But before they had gone very far, the old man turned down a lane. The lane was scattered with stones and deeply rutted where the rainwater coursed down it during downpours. Thick hawthorn trees lined its sides, making it a cool tunnel. The lane ran down through the open farmland that surrounds Lobley Hill, and as they walked, the call of a cuckoo reached them from somewhere in the distance, its cry sonorous, sleepy. From their field, cows shyly watched them pass, their huge eyes peering through the dense lattice of the hawthorn foliage. Lugging the sack over his back, Sonny Gee wobbled for a few steps before catching his balance. 'Ye'll dee yersel' an injury, mind, lad,' the old man remarked.

'What's a pot model?' returned the boy.

'Eh?' asked Joe, walking ahead.

'Ah said what's a pot model?' Sonny Gee had stopped walking.

'A pot what?'

The sack slipped from the boy's shoulders, and a few of the plastic bags of kitchen scraps fell out into the lane. Still Joe did not stop. 'Model,' called Sonny Gee. 'What's a pot model?'

'It's when something looks like summink else,' the old man told him when the boy had repacked the compost sack and reached where Joe stood waiting. 'That's what ye call a pot model.'

'Eh?' asked the boy.

Joe reached up to the branch of a hawthorn. Gingerly avoiding the thorns, he plucked two leaves, and held them out in the palm of his hand. 'Ye might say them two are pot models. Look, one's the same as the other.'

Grunting with effort, the boy put down the sack and studied the two leaves. 'No, they're not,' he said. 'That one's bigger. And that one doesn't have . . .'

'Ye shouldn't ask questions if ye divven't listen to the answer,' said the old man irritatedly.

'Why?'

Joe kicked the sack lightly. 'Look. Ye cannet manage the compost sack, can ye?'

'Course ah can,' replied the boy, heaving it up again. The old man walked on. Behind him, Sonny Gee surreptitiously dropped a few of the carrier bags, to lighten the load. But it was still too heavy for him. He stumbled on for another ten yards before the old man pulled the sack forcibly from him. But Sonny Gee would not let go. 'Ah can dee it easy, me.'

'No, ye cannet. Look back there. Yus've dropped half of it.' As Sonny Gee turned, Joe yanked at the sack, but still the boy

216

kept a grip and spinning round he began to pull back. 'Hey, divven't dee that, ye'll tear it.'

'It's not me, it's ye,' the boy shot back.

'Course it's ye.'

'It's ye.'

'And ye shouldn't have brought that cowboy hat. Ye're sweating cobs underneath.'

'No, ah'm not.' The two of them heaved against each other before reaching a deadlock. 'What's a cob?'

The old man's eyes twinkled slightly. 'A horse.'

'Eh?'

'A male swan.'

'Eh?'

'A round loaf o' bread. And mebbes even a spider.'

They both stopped pulling at the sack. 'What ye gannin' on aboot?'

Joe shrugged. 'Ye asked us what a cob was. Ah'm just telling ye.'

'A cob means all them things?'

'Why aye, lad. There's loads o' words that have more than one meaning.'

Sonny Gee screwed up his face in thought. 'No, there isn't.'

'Course there is. Pit and mine. Ye kna them.' The old man leant down to pick up a stick lying deep in a clump of white stitchwort on the bank above them. 'Then there's bark,' he said.

Sonny Gee looked about. 'Bark?'

Joe's gnarled fingers rubbed up and down the stick. 'Ye call this bark. It's like the tree's skin.'

'Gemma's hoond barks an' all,' put in the boy, imitating a dog.

'Aye and so do people.'

'Eh?'

'When they're angry and shouting at ye. Ye say they're barking at ye.'

'Aye,' said Sonny Gee dubiously, 'if they're barking mad.'

'Exactly,' exclaimed the old man crisply. 'That's another meaning. Words just nivver mean one thing.'

'Pot,' said the boy.

'Eh?'

'Some folks call tac pot; and then there's that pot model, and the pots what ah wash in your kitchen at hyem.'

'Ah've already telt ye not to talk aboot tac or whativver it is.' The old man's voice rang out angrily down the quiet lane. 'Ye've left all that tac rubbish behind ye now, lad. That's all back on Old Parsonage Road, and that's where it'll stay.'

'Ha'way, gadgie mista, divven't bark at wor.'

It began as a sparkle in Joe's eye, and was quickly passed on to the boy. A few seconds later the first chuckle broke out. The chuckle became a guffaw. For a long time the old man and the little boy laughed, and throwing their heads up, the sack shook between them. Only slowly did their laughter fade. 'Ye're a full-time job, ye, and nee mistake,' said the old man. 'There isn't nothing ye divven't want to kna.'

The cuckoo continued to call. In the distance a cow lowed.

Breaking the human silence, the boy spoke softly. 'Will it?' he asked.

'Eh?'

'Stay back on Old Parsonage Road? All the tac an' that. Will it stay there for good?' Sonny Gee gazed at Joe's hands. 'Am ah stopping here with ye, gadgie mista?'

Joe paused to scrutinise him. 'D'yus want to, like?'

Sonny Gee shrugged. 'Aye.'

They stared at one another for a while, and then looked away. 'Ha'way, lad,' said the old man. 'Give us the sack. We'd be there by now, if ye'd let me take it.'

'Ye wouldn't have been able to gan any faster.'

For a few moments more they both pulled at the sack. Then Joe stopped. 'We'll share it,' he said, quietly.

'What?'

'Ye carry half, and ah'll carry half. What d'ye think aboot that, lad?'

Sonny Gee nodded. 'Aye, areet.'

Spreading the ungainly shape of the sack between them, they moved at a snail's pace down the lane. Joe carried the stick in his spare hand. The sunlight fell in heavily shaded dapples on the track. The lane deepened, its verges full of Queen Anne's lace and foxgloves. A big bee bumbled by. 'That's the pot model of a bee,' said the boy.

'Na,' said the old man. 'That *is* a bee.'

They walked on a little further. 'Look,' began Joe, 'it would just be easier if . . .'

'Why am ah the pot model o' ye?' They both stopped walking at the same time. Slowly they put down the sack. 'That Peggy said ah was the pot model o' ye.'

'Aye, ah heard her.'

'Why?'

Joe looked up and then down the lane. He pointed at a grassy bank with the stick. 'Let's sit doon,' he said. 'Watch oot for nettles, mind.'

'Ah divven't care aboot nettles, me.'

'Ah thought ye wouldn't.'

Sonny Gee threw himself high up the bank, and roly-polied down. The old man sitting at the bottom stopped him from rolling on to the stones of the lane. 'Why?' asked the boy, sitting beside him.

'Why what?'

'Why did ye kna that ah wouldn't care aboot getting stunk by nee nettles?'

'Well,' said the old man, ''cos when ah was your age, ah didn't neither. And the word's stung, not stunk.'

'Not if yus got hoyed into them nettles roond the back of the empty hooses off Old Parsonage Road. Where all the dossers piss. Then ye'd say stunk . . .' Breaking off, Sonny Gee looked up at Joe with wonder. 'Were ye my age once, gadgie mista?'

'Course ah was. And ye, one of these days, ye'll be my age now.'

Astonishment widened the boy's blue eyes to saucers. 'Nee chance.'

'Ye will, man.'

'Straight up?'

'Why aye. Though what the world'll be like then doesn't bear thinking on.'

The boy shook his head in disbelief. 'But how?'

'Well, that's just the way it gans, y'kna.' The bee came back; flying past them, it entered the opening of a foxglove bell. 'Yus get born,' mused Joe. 'Yus live. Yus grow auld. And then . . .'

'And then?' The bee's hum could be heard reverberating from within the purple shell. The boy stared at it, his head held slightly on one side with the force of his curiosity. 'Is a pot model the same thing as a granda?' he asked at last.

The old man did not reply for a long time. When he spoke, his voice was quiet. 'Ah've told ye, a pot model is when summink is like summink else.'

The bee re-emerged, the black and gold wool of its body glistening with nectar. 'So why am ah like ye?'

'Ah suppose it's because some of the things ye dee, well, ah dee an' all.'

'Why? What do ah dee that ye dee?'

There was a long pause. 'Well, for a start, ah used to ask questions an' all . . .'

'Why did ye?' the boy interrupted him eagerly.

'Well, why do ye?'

Sonny Gee shrugged. ''Cos ah want to kna aboot things.'

'Well, ah did an' all.'

'Divven't ye want to kna owt nee more?'

The old man mused. 'Aye. Ah still dee.'

'What questions d'yus want to ask now?'

'Oh, this and that.'

The boy screwed his eyes up. 'Thems is funny questions.'

'Aye,' agreed Joe. 'And ah'm still looking for someone what knows the answers.'

Leaning down to a blade of grass, Sonny Gee cupped his hands round a ladybird. Bringing it under his chin, he stared at it. The ladybird crawled up and down his fingers. Reaching the tip of his thumb, it took flight. The two of them watched it meander down the shady lane. 'Gadgie mista, what's a granda?'

Joe sighed. He reached out and picked a dandelion which was plump with seed. 'Aye, well. Ah suppose it's time ah explained it all to ye. Time ye knew.' He faltered for a while before beginning. 'A granda is two generations before ye.'

'Eh?'

'A granda is a part of yer family. A granda is . . .' he broke off in confusion. 'A granda is yer mam or yer dad's dad. Aye, that's what a granda is.'

Sonny Gee had been watching the dandelion as Joe fidgeted with it. Now he looked up at the old man. 'Gadgie mista, are ye my granda?'

The old man slowly raised the dandelion to his face and, breathing in, he blew. For a few moments the air about them was filled with countless tiny seeds. 'Aye,' he said. 'Ah'm yer granda.' The seeds drifted over them both, lodging in the minute crevasses of their clothes and bodies. 'Here, now ye blow,' Joe said, picking another dandelion. The boy blew, and once again the clock spilt its hours all over them.

Sonny Gee picked up one of the tiny parachutes, studying it on the palm of his hand, before sending it off with a lusty blow.

'Aye, well,' said Joe. 'So now there's nee need for ye to call me that stupid name any more.'

'What stupid name?'

'Ye kna.'

'Ye mean, gadgie mista?'

'Aye. There'll be nee more gadgie mistas. 'Cos now yus kna what to call wor, divven't ye?'

The boy looked intently at him. 'Na.'

'Ye call us granda, lad, ye call us granda.'

There was a silence. A shrew ran from the cover of the Queen Anne's lace. Scurrying eagerly around the bank, it disappeared in the grass between the grandfather and his grandson, its little pelt sheened with the seeds of the dandelion clock. 'That's why ah'm always gannin' on to yus, Sonny Gee. Making ye promise things. It's because ah . . .' There was a pause. 'It's because ah want the best for ye.'

'Ah divven't want to gan anywhere else, me,' began Sonny Gee softly. 'Ah want to stop with ye. Can ah?'

Joe closed his eyes for a moment. 'We'll still be able to see each other,' he said in a measured voice. 'Even if yus have to gan away somewhere else . . .'

'Na,' said the boy firmly. 'Na. Ah want to stay here. Even if ye divven't let wor dee what ah want. Ah want to stay with ye.' Sonny Gee looked up at Joe. Yearning creased his young face. 'Why cannet ah stop with ye?'

'Aye,' mused the old man thoughtfully. 'Why cannet ye?'

Just at that moment there was a crunching of the stones higher up on the lane. A bell rang out, and a few moments later a bike appeared. 'Areet, Joe. Areet, bonny lad.'

'Areet, Arthur,' the two replied simultaneously.

'Got the leeks there?' cried Arthur as he rode past them on the bank. 'Ah'll beat ye at the showing this time. Just ye wait and see!'

'Get on with ye,' responded Joe.

'Nee chance,' responded Sonny Gee. 'We're making a start.'

The bike disappeared round a corner. For a while the tyres could still be heard on the rough surface of the lane, but then they faded. 'There's nee way Arthur's or neebody else's leeks are gonnae beat ours,' said Joe, raising himself up from the grass. 'And d'yus kna why not?'

'Why not?'

'Because ye and me are gonne use wor secret weapon that'll top the lot of them come the Gateshead Show.'

'What is it, wor secret weapon?' asked the boy, getting up too.

The old man lifted a finger and shook his head playfully. 'It's secret. Only ah kna. But today, so will ye.'

'Will ah?'

'Ye will.'

'Belter.'

The boy delved into the grass. He brought out the stick which Joe had picked up a few minutes ago, and held it out to the old man. 'That's an ashplant,' said the old man, taking it.

'That's a walking stick.'

Joe tested it. The wood was springy but strong. He walked a few paces with his weight on it. 'Aye, that's just the thing.'

'It's the pot model o' yer last one,' said Sonny Gee.

'Na,' replied the old man. 'It's better.'

Sonny Gee walked over to the sack. 'Well, now that ye've got yer stick back, ah'd better take the sack.' Picking it up, he hoisted it on to his shoulders.

'Areet, ye win. But just this time, mind.'

They walked on, Sonny Gee struggling under the unwieldy weight of the sack, Joe tapping the tip of his new stick against the stones. They arrived at the allotments and walked through the open gate down a dusty track. They passed doors of every conceivable style improvised in fences of corrugated-iron sheets, old property hoardings and wooden industrial pallettes. As they walked further into the allotments, animal sounds drifted over the fences. Foraging geese cackled, hens chuntered. From behind one door, a pig could be heard grunting eloquently.

Joe's allotment was right in the middle. The old man took

out a large key and managed to turn it in the huge padlock at the first attempt. Ushering the boy inside, he then slid a bolt across. 'Divven't want nee spying,' he said solemnly, before winking.

A neat path led through fertile beds to a cleverly constructed wooden hut raised on a balcony. Although everything was well tended and cared for, one or two weed colonies were beginning to establish themselves, especially in the places hardest to hoe.

'Reet, let's make a start.' As the spade bit cleanly through the soil, pain jolted the old man's face. Hiding it, he straightened up and beckoned the boy over. 'Now ye.' Sonny Gee took the spade, lifting it uncertainly. 'Just dee what ah was deeing,' Joe explained. The blade of the spade skated over the surface. 'Ha'way, lad, ah didn't dee that.' Joe took the spade back. Again he gripped it with the palms of his hands, his fingers resting inertly on the wood. There was a clean rasp as he dug into the gound; once more he concealed the agony it caused him. He knotted his eyebrows, as though puzzled by the pain. He turned to the boy. 'Ye've got to point the spade at the ground. Now ye have a go.' The boy tried again. 'No, man,' tutted Joe with growing irritation. 'Ye put yer fingers roond it, to get a better grip. Otherwise it'll keep slipping. Ye've got to . . .'

'Well, ye divven't,' Sonny Gee interrupted him.

'Aye, well, ah'm telling ye to. Forget about me,' the old man snapped.

'But ye said dee what ye're deeing.'

The old man flared. 'Aye, well, my fingers are knackered. Imagine yus're holding a cricket bat.' Joe calmed. 'Aye. That's more like it. Ye divven't need a full spit every time, but.'

'Ah'm not spitting.'

'Aye, lad,' nodded Joe approvingly at last. 'That's it.' Sonny Gee dug by himself for a little while. 'Reet,' said Joe, taking the spade off the boy. 'Ah'll dig with that one, and ye . . .' The old man disappeared round the back of the hut, coming back with a much smaller spade.

'Who's that for, like?' the boy asked.

'That's for ye. Ha'way, let's get cracking. We've a trench to dig.' Turning the spade speculatively in his hands, Sonny Gee did not move. 'Come on, lad,' urged Joe. 'It's got to be deep, mind, so there's plenty o' nourishment for them.'

'That's not fair.'

'Eh?'

'Why've ye given wor the broken one?'

'It's not broken.'

'Aye it is, look at it.'

'No it isn't.'

The boy came over to the old man, and put his spade alongside the full-sized one. 'Put it this way, mine's nee pot model o' yours.'

'Ye divven't have to say it all the time.'

'Say what?'

'Pot model.'

'Well, if ye had to dig with this one ye'd say it an' all.'

'Look, ah'm not giving ye my spade. If ye want to help, then use the one ah've given ye, or not at all.'

A strange sound floated into their ears. 'Ginga's goat,' Joe said. 'It'll have slipped its tether.'

'What's a tether?'

'Nivver mind,' replied Joe. 'But it won't be lang before ah get to the end of mine if ye divven't start working.'

'And what's nourishment?'

'Is there nee end to yer questions?'

'Na. What's nourishment?'

'It's sustenance. Food.' The old man paused to think. 'See these leeks? They need a lot of hard work and care. That's why ye've got to give them the compost. Right down deep. Then they'll grow nice and juicy for wor to pull them up. Ye get back what ye put in.'

'Pull them up?'

'Aye, when the time comes.'

'And when's that; when's that time coming, like?'

'Not for a canny while yet.'

They worked on in silence for a while, before the boy stopped. 'So we won't be pulling them up today then? The leeks.'

'Not the next day neither.'

Once more they set to work, only for Sonny Gee to stop again. 'What aboot the day after that?'

'NOT FOR MONTHS, MAN!' shouted the old man. 'Now nee more questions.'

The old man dug with his back to the boy so that he could allow the flashes of pain to show on his face without being noticed. As he worked, his breathing grew heavy and laboured. But although his body ached, he gave himself only the briefest of rests, forcing his joints and muscles to obey, until, chest heaving with exertion, he had to fight for each breath. The sudden failing of his body confused him. Turning abruptly, he went up the path, climbed up on to the balcony and went into the hut.

He stood in the hut leaning against a potting bench, waiting for his breathing to recover. When it had, he still did not move. Two welts were already raised on his palms; he studied them perplexedly as though the hands belonged to a different person. Only slowly did his legs begin to feel steady beneath him again.

'Ah've been sorting out a cup of tea,' the old man said, coming back down the path. Sonny Gee had swapped spades again, and was manfully struggling with the large one, working as quickly as he could. 'Gan easy, man lad,' the old man said.

'There's work to dee,' the boy replied.

'Aye, so give wor me spade back, so ah can dee it.'

'Ah want to get as much done as ah can.'

'Eh?'

'Ah'll dee it for wor,' said the boy. 'Ah'll dee everything. Ah'll dee the pulling up an' all. When the time comes. Gan and have yer rest.'

Joe stared at him for a few moments, then coming over to him, angrily grabbed the spade. 'Ah'll tell ye when ah need a rest, d'ye hear me? Now use yer own spade.' This time the old man worked facing the boy, concealing the pain that shot through him every time he raised and lowered the blade of the spade into the earth.

As they dug, a butterfly sauntered by, pausing for a moment at the old man's marigolds which grew here and there on the plot. The boy worked on, but the old man straightened to watch it. He waited for the boy to see it too, but Sonny Gee was too absorbed in his digging. When Joe returned to work, it was only with a wrench that he was able to bend down once more. Grunting with effort, he began to dig up the deeper, wetter earth. 'Divven't pile up what ye dig oot too near the trench,' he managed to point out to the boy. His words came out in jagged snatches as his lungs struggled for breath. 'Look, it keeps on falling back in . . . Set it back further, lad . . . Ye can dig as fast as ye like . . . but if it keeps on falling back in the trench . . . then ye might as well dee nowt . . . Aye, that's the way . . . But gan easy, man . . . Anyone would think . . . ye were digging for buried treasure.'

The sun beat down on them so that the soil, upended to the light of day, sparkled darkly, black as mined coal. The heat began to shimmer off the corrugated-iron fence. 'Ye're sweating spiders,' said the boy, breaking off to point at the old man's head. Still stooped over his spade, Joe looked up. Drips of perspiration coursed down his forehead and scoured down his nose. Having lifted a hand to his face, he lowered it, and holding it out, stared at the droplets of sweat there. The sun caught them, turning them into shining gems of different colours. As though mesmerised, Joe contemplated them, until, gradually drying, they had disappeared. His head was beginning to throb. 'D'yus want this?' Sonny Gee asked. He had taken off his cowboy hat and was holding it out to the old man. 'Ye can. Ah divven't want it for a bit. And it's belter for keeping the sun oot yer eyes. Better than that cap of yours.'

The old man turned to Sonny Gee. He could barely see him because of the rivulets of sweat that still filled his eyes like tears, stinging them remorselessly. The red of the hat seemed to swim in the heated air. 'Ah'm gonnae have to rest,' Joe said, the words sounding strange in his ears. There was a crisp rasp as the old man speared the spade into the ground. Dazed, and with one hand on the small of his back, he straightened up. A blackbird flew between them and disappeared into the thick fruit bushes which grew at the far end of the plot. Joe tottered over to the balcony and lowered himself down on to the bottom step. He stared blankly at his soil-encrusted boots. The blackbird began to sing.

'Do we just stick the leeks in the groond, like?' said the boy after a while.

The old man looked over. He narrowed his eyes as though trying to focus. 'We've a lot more digging to dee yet, lad.'

'Aye, but when we've finished. Do we just hoy them in the groond?'

'There's more to it than that.'

The boy nodded wisely. 'When we come to it, ah'll dee it for ye. Ah'll dee it geet well. Nee good just hoying them, but. Ye can just gan in the hut and have a cuppa.' Falling silent for a while, the boy worked on. 'And when the time comes for wor to pull them up again, ah'll dee the pulling,' Sonny Gee started once more.

The rhythm of the boy's digging filled the air, and Joe found himself beginning to nod off. He roused himself angrily, but a few moments later he was feeling tired again. He tried to stand, but couldn't. A little while later the old man looked over and saw that the boy was staring at him. 'When?' asked the boy.

'When what?'

'When do we pull them up?'

Joe closed his eyes. 'Not for ages. It's called the harvest.'

'When is it then? When is this harvest? When will the time come?'

'Not for a while.'

'Aye, but when?'

The boy's vehemence made Joe sit up. 'Well,' he began, puzzled by Sonny Gee's impassioned reaction, 'we'll probably start pulling up in autumn. Then all through the winter an' all.'

A lean look of hunger pinched the boy's features. 'When's autumn?' he demanded.

'Not for a while yet.'

'But when?'

The old man searched for the words. 'Autumn and winter are different seasons from now,' he began, bewilderedly. 'They . . .' Sighing, he broke off. 'What's all this about, man lad?'

Sonny Gee let his spade drop. He did not pick it up. He looked up at the old man. 'Ye'll need me to pull them up, won't ye?' he said in a small voice. 'Ye'll need me to pull them up again.' The boy paused for a moment, then gestured over all the earth he'd dug up. 'Ah've done all that. Ah can dee all the digging. And ah can hoy them leeks in and then pull them up again.' Picking up his little spade, he began digging wildly. 'See?' he begged. 'See?' He continued to speed up, attacking the earth as though digging for his very life. Pursing his lips together, the boy tried to whistle. He produced only an ugly, desperate rasping sound which syncopated the rough rhythm of his spade. 'And soon ah'll be able to whistle with yus an' all,' he pleaded. 'Soon ye'll have learnt wor how to whistle and then ah'll whistle for ye, so ye divven't need to and ye can just sit in . . .'

The old man hoisted himself to his feet. For the first few steps he feared that he was going to fall on his face, but he managed to steady himself. His strength seemed to be slowly returning. Reaching the boy, he gently took the spade from him. 'What's got into ye?'

The boy looked him in the eye. 'Ah'll have to stay with ye until them different seasons. Won't ah? Ye need me help. So ah'll have to stay with ye until when that time comes.' The boy faltered. ''Cos who'll help ye with the leeks? And who'll help yus pull them up when it's a different season? And who'll borrow ye their hat? And ah'll be able to dee even more if ye let us use the proper spade. And ah'll be good. Nee language. Ha'way . . . ha'way . . .' The boy fell silent, anguish contorting his face. Then the rest of his features grew expressionless, leaving only his eyes alive, their blue burning like the blue inner flames of a coal fire. 'Divven't send wor away. Not until the time comes. Let wor stay . . . Granda.'

Joe narrowed his eyes. The grandfather and his grandson stood there looking at each other, not even looking away when the blackbird bulleted back between them from the fruit bushes. Time passed, and still they did not move. The throbbing in the old man's head slowly faded. His eyesight cleared and the desperation in the boy's unblinking blue eyes dazzled him. 'Aye,' he whispered. 'Not until when the time comes.' He seemed to want to say more, but the words appeared to evade him, and smiling sadly, he led the boy to the hut. 'Let's have a sit, ye and me. Let's just sit worselves doon.'

'Canny morning for it, mind!' cried a voice from the other side of the allotment door some time later.

The old man and the boy were sitting in two deckchairs on the balcony of the hut. 'Now then, Ronny marrer,' Joe called back.

'Now then, Ronny marrer,' shouted the boy.

'Divven't be cheeky,' said Joe.

'Areet, Joe. Areet, me bonny lad.' Ronny replied. 'Can ah come in, or is it still all top secret roond here?'

The old man winked at the boy. 'We haven't got to the

secret bit yet. Ha'way in.' Joe nodded at Sonny Gee, who ran down the path to open the door. The old man watched the boy as he slid back the bolt.

Ronny was dressed slovenly in a pair of beach shorts and a Hawaiian shirt, a single button of which was fastened over his protruding belly. Stains were visible around the armpits. 'That's the trench, is it?' he asked, looking down at where they had been digging. 'And ye helping an' all, bonny lad? By ye've been busy, but.'

'We've been grafting. There's nee passengers on board here, laddy,' said Joe.

Ronny came over to the hut. 'Are ye areet, man Joe?' he asked.

'Eh?'

'Ye look done in, man.' Ronny stared narrowly at Joe. 'Not working too hard, are ye?' Joe glowered at him. 'Still,' put in Ronny, 'ye've got the bonny lad to look after ye.' Walking on to the first step, he scanned the upended tea chest which stood between the old man and boy. There was a pot of tea on it. 'Is there a cuppa gannin' begging, like?' Joe began to lever himself out of his deckchair. 'It's areet,' said Ronny. 'Ah'll get it.'

'Ah can manage,' growled Joe, gripping the side of the deckchair until the tendons stood out on his wrists. With a wrench he climbed to his feet and disappeared into the hut.

'How's that spider of yours the day, bonny lad?' Ronny asked.

'Belter ta, Ronny,' Sonny Gee replied.

Ronny smiled. 'Ah telt ye they made canny pets.'

'Aye, canny daft,' replied Joe, coming back on to the balcony with a stool. 'Ha'way, lad, let Ronny sit in the deckchair, man,' he told the boy. 'Ye sit on the cracket.'

Sonny Gee took the stool.

Ronny collapsed into the deckchair. 'Are ye sure ye're areet, man Joe? Ye look knackt.'

'Ah'll be a whole lot better if ye stop wittering on.' He gestured at the tea chest. 'That pot's freshly brewed.'

'Canny.' Ronny sat down. 'Ye want to take things easy, man Joe,' he hazarded. 'Specially on a day like this.' Taking out a begrimed rag from the pocket of his beach shorts, he wiped the sweat from his brow. 'Like being in the jungle this,' he mused. 'What ah want is to stand under a nice cool watering can full o' water.'

'Why, ye been grafting an' all?' Sonny Gee asked.

'Na,' returned Ronny. 'Ah'm just hot.' There was a pause as they looked at the leek trench. 'Ah'll be mother then,' said Ronny at last, pouring the tea.

'Mother?' Sonny Gee asked.

'Divven't even ask,' the old man said.

As they drank, the old man seemed to slowly revive, but his eyes remained sunken, the skull-like sockets still glistening with sweat. 'Durham's got a new star,' began Ronny. 'Young lad. Only seventeen. Two shy of his century against Surrey yesterday. Canny prospect.'

'Ye went to the cricket yesterday?' Joe asked. Once more the goat could be heard bleating. 'That one's slipped his tether again,' said the old man.

'Aye,' replied Ronny. 'Ginga's Billy. Been in nosing aboot Arthur's leek trench. It's on my patch noo.' Ronny's glance travelled round the plot. 'Ye keep it nice, but, divven't ye, Joe? Bit behind, aren't ye, mind? Ye haven't even got yer muck mulch oot awer there, ah see. Gonnae keep it piled there much longer?'

'Not at work today, Ronny?' the old man asked sharply.

A cloud passed over Ronny's face. 'Na,' he said.

'Cricket yesterday, nee work today. Won the lottery, or divven't ye need to earn yer living nee more?'

Ronny sighed. He took a drink from his mug. There was a long silence. 'Have ye seen the size of Gemma?' he began with a forced brightness. 'There's elephants that drop their bairns before they get to her size.' The attempt to lighten himself failed and Ronny sighed again.

'Ye a bit doon in the mooth there, Ronny lad?' asked the old man.

'Ah'm areet.'

'Come to think of it ye've been green aboot the gills for a while.'

'Aye,' put in Sonny Gee. 'Gemma said yus've been hanging aboot the café in the market like a wet weekend.'

'Divven't ye speak like that to yer elders,' said Joe. He paused, then turned to Ronny. 'That lass is always dipping her neb in other folks' business. What's it to her anyway?'

Ronny shrugged. 'She's been helping wor oot a bit.'

'She's been in all week. Gans there after she leaves ours,' said the boy.

'Ah won't tell ye again, man lad,' snapped Joe.

'That's areet, man Joe,' said Ronny with a weary shake of the head.

The old man turned to him. 'Is that true?'

Ronny nodded. 'She wants the money.'

Joe shook his head. 'Ah divven't kna why she bothers coming roond to us in the morning,' he said. 'All she does is sit on the settee and get her breath back. So ah cannet see what use she can be to ye. Ye said yersel' she's like a elephant.'

Ronny tried to smile. 'Well it is a jungle shop.'

'Divven't be stupid, man.'

'She can manage.'

'And what happens if that snake gets oot again?'

'Why? It's 'armless enough.'

'She's hardly in any condition to chase it, but.'

Ronny roared with a forced laughter. 'D'ye get it? What ah said aboot the snake?' His pot-belly wobbled as he continued to laugh and the single button came loose. 'Ah called the snake 'armless. 'Cos that's what it is, isn't it? It doesn't have nee arms.'

'Aye, well, divven't give up the day job,' said the old man. 'With jokes like that, somehow ah cannet see a career for yus in the clubs.'

'Why not?' Ronny shot back. 'That's one place where being fat and ugly is a definite bonus.' Ronny's laughter grew bitter. Cupping his hands together, he spoke through them as if they were a megaphone. 'Appearing on stage noo at a Fat Loser's Club near you: The-one-the-only-R-Slater. Or as he's known to his friends, Head First.' Mocking himself cruelly, Ronny rocked with laughter. 'Get it? Head first, because ah'm Ronny Slater. R Slater. Arse later.'

'Mind yersel',' said Joe tersely. 'There's a bairn aboot.' He shook his head. 'Get yerself back to the shop, man. Ye cannet leave that lass by herself. Not the state she's in.'

'Ah hope me spider gets preggers,' mused Sonny Gee, his face dreamy. 'It's mint. They have thoosands of babbies.'

'And that's another thing,' said the old man. 'Ye were supposed to take the bairn's pet with ye to the next meeting of the Spider Society.'

'Ah haven't been meself for a bit,' said Ronny heavily. Bending low over himself he rebuttoned his shirt. 'The membership was doon to just three at the last coont, and two of them were in arrears with their subs.' He sighed. 'Na. Ah haven't been for a bit.'

'That's not like ye.'

'Mebbes it's preggers already,' mused the boy.

Ronny turned to the boy. 'There's one way of finding oot aboot it all,' he said. 'There's another one o' them Chilean Roses in the shop. Ah'll bring it home, we'll stick it in the tank with yours and then we'll see.'

'How?' asked Joe and Sonny Gee together.

''Cos if they're both two males then they'll fight. If they're not then they'll mate, the female'll eat the other one and we'll

be left with one pregnant spider.' Ronny shrugged philosophi-
cally. 'And that pretty much sums up life for the rest o' wor an'
all.'

'What if they're both lasses?' asked the boy.

Ronny pulled thoughtfully on his ponytail. 'Ah divven't
kna. Nowt. At least we'll still kna.'

'But ah divven't want nee other spider to eat mine,' put in
Sonny Gee.

'It might be yours that's deeing the eating,' explained
Ronny.

'How could ah tell, but?'

'What's the difference? At the end of the day ye'd be left
with a pregnant spider.' Again Ronny paused. 'Eat. Get eaten.
Get left with a baby.'

'Ah divven't care. If me spider's a lad, ah divven't want him
getting eaten.' The boy sighed. 'Ah'll just have him withoot
the babbies.'

Ronny shrugged. 'Suit yerself.'

They all sat in silence for a while. 'Why cannet men have
babbies?' Sonny Gee suddenly asked.

''Cos they cannet,' replied Joe, tersely.

'Why?' demanded Sonny Gee.

''Cos they cannet get pregnant.'

'Mebbes Ronny is.'

'Ronny, pregnant?'

'Aye, look.' The boy pointed at Ronny's protruding
stomach. 'Mebbes there's a babby in there.'

'Na,' Ronny shook his head. 'That's just me pot.'

'Pot?' responded Sonny Gee.

'Ye belt up, boy.' The old man turned from Sonny Gee and
stared severely at Ronny. 'And ye, if that pet shop gans to pot
then ye'll only have yerself to blame.'

Sonny Gee shook his head. 'How can a shop be on pot?'

'Ah said divven't start that again,' said Joe.

'Aye, well,' sighed Ronny.

'Look. Oot with it,' demanded Joe. 'What is it with ye these days? Ye seem sick as a pike.'

'Do ah?'

'Why aren't ye at work?'

Ronny studied the mug of tea. When he spoke, his voice was hushed with despair. 'It's not gannin' that well, man Joe. All folk want is hamsters.'

'What's wrong with that? If they want hamsters, give them hamsters. As long as they pay ye for them.'

'It's not that. Ah can sell as many hamsters as the next pet shop.'

'What is it then?'

'Well, ah didn't gan into the trade just to deal in hamsters. Ah went in for the exotics.' Ronny paused, his eyes flickering dreamily. 'Thems is what gives wor me juice.'

'Eh?' asked the old man and the boy simultaneously.

'All them years working undergroond at the face. Then they close all the pits. With the bit redundancy payment, and the bit ah've managed to save, ah decide to give it a gan. Follow me dreams.'

Joe frowned. 'Ah thought ye opened a fish and chip shop with Ally Three-Bellies?'

'Ah mean after that. Exotica Petotica.' Stretching indolently, Ronny waved a hand dismissively in disparagement of his dreams. 'But neebody wants them.'

'Ah dee,' said Sonny Gee. 'Ah love that spider, me.'

Ronny pointed at the boy and smiled. 'Thanks, bonny lad. Thanks.'

A soft silence fell over them. Ronny sipped loudly from his mug of tea. 'So ye're just gonnae pack it in then?' demanded the old man.

'Ah divven't kna, man Joe.'

'And then what ye gonnae dee? Hang aboot the allotments all day?'

'Mebbes.'

236

'Be a footballer,' put in the boy. 'Thems get loads o' money.'

'That's a thought,' replied Ronny, his hands inert on his (protruding) stomach.

'It won't wash,' said the old man. 'Ye're letting things slip, man Ronny. Ah mean, look at the state of ye. When was the last time ye washed? It's almost as bad as that weed patch o' yours yus call a plot. Ye kna the committee aren't very happy aboot the spreading of that creeping Jenny.'

'That's what ah'll call it,' put in the boy, the wonder of inspiration lighting up his face. 'Creeping Jenny. Me spider.'

Ronny turned to Joe. 'Anyway, the thing aboot me plot being overgrown. Ah'm getting that sorted. Reet at the minute actually.' The goat could be heard bleating once more. 'Ah've borrowed Ginga's goat, one of Terry's ponies, and brought the rabbits from the shop. If a goat, a pony and half a dozen little coneys cannet shift them weeds then nothing will. Mind ye, when ah took the pony, ah had a quick shufty roond Terry's patch. And ah'll tell ye this much, ever since he started seeing that woman from Darlington, it's gone reet doonhill.'

The old man shook his head. 'If ever ah heard the kettle calling the pot black.'

'When ye play pool in the Wheatsheaf on Old Parsonage Road,' said Sonny Gee, 'ye take the fiver if ye pot the black.' He paused before adding quietly, 'Ye can just take the fiver if thems playing are tanked up.'

They sat on for a while, drinking their tea. Getting up, the old man went inside the hut and he brought back a packet of Rich Tea biscuits. 'What, nee Lincolns?' asked Ronny.

'Cheeky,' replied Joe. 'Ye're getting as bad as this one here.' He looked levelly at Ronny. 'Ah thought ye were sweet on Audrey.'

Ronny blushed. 'Ah am.'

'And ah thought ye had it all worked oot. What ye were gonnae say to her.'

237

'Ah did.'

'Well then?'

'Ah couldn't bring meself to dee it. Ah mean, what's a woman like that gonnae see in a man like me?' Ronny shook his head regretfully. 'Ah've been in the pet trade lang enough to kna that a lovebird doesn't share a perch with a pigeon.'

'Well, we'll have to be getting back to it soon,' said Joe, speaking through a mouthful of Rich Tea and gesturing at the trench. He flexed his legs, but having half-heartedly tried to rise, subsided back into the deckchair. 'We'll take another five minutes,' he said, hesitantly.

'Not like ye that, Joe man. Putting a job off.'

The old man stared at Ronny. 'Ah'm not putting it off,' he answered tetchily. 'Who says ah'm putting it off?'

'Sorry ah spoke,' said Ronny.

'Ah'm deein' it for the bairn,' the old man said quickly. 'It's not good for him working oot under the sun. Ye kna me. If it was up to me ah'd get the job finished and done. Ah'm not one to malinger.'

'Mad dogs and Englishmen, eh?' pondered Ronny. He surveyed the plot again, and dunking a Rich Tea in his tea, swallowed the biscuit in one bite. He belched melancholically. 'Aye, aye,' he moaned softly.

'What's the matter with ye now?' demanded the old man.

'Ah'll give ye a hand. With the trench. Take me mind off things. Give ye a rest an' all, Joe.'

'Will ye shut up, Ronny man. For the last time, ah'm not tired.'

'Ye're knackt oot, man lad,' Ronny said, quietly.

Joe bridled angrily, but hid his anger with a laugh. 'Takes more than that to knack me oot. A bit digging. Ah'm a pitman, me.' The old man turned to Ronny with a smile. 'And pitmen are made of sterner stuff. Isn't that right, Ronny?'

'Why aye,' said Ronny, uncertainly.

'Why?' asked the boy.

''Cos they have to be. Deeing the work we dee. It's not for the soft-hearted. Is it, Ronny?'

'Ye have to be lion-hearted,' laughed Ronny, warming to the matter. 'King of the Beasts. That's a pitman.'

'Can ah be a one an' all?' Sonny Gee asked.

'Why aye,' nodded Ronny. 'Ah mean, ye come from pitmen stock, ye.'

'Do ah?'

'Aye,' replied Ronny with a sudden energy. 'Yer granda . . .' He broke off abruptly.

'It's areet,' said the old man. 'Ah've told him. He knas ah'm his granda.'

'A pitman,' began Ronny thoughtfully, 'is someone what knas he's strong when he stands by himsel', but knas he's even stronger when he stands shoulder to shoulder with his marrer. And that he's at his strongest when he stands with *all* his marrers. The women an' all. All the pit folk stand together. Cooperating. Looking after each other. Strength in unity . . .'

'Divven't confuse the bairn,' said Joe. A bitterness settled in the old man's veiny eyes. 'There is nee pitman nee more.'

'Aye, but it's his heritage, man.'

The old man clicked his tongue. 'Some heritage.'

'Why, it's better than nowt,' said Ronny quietly.

'Is it?'

For a while they all listened to the blackbird who was back singing in the fruit bushes. 'He's singing for a mate,' mused Ronny. 'All the other birds have got nestlings. Him, he hasn't got nothing. They sing until they hear a female sing back, and if there's nee female aboot then they just sing and sing. It's unrequited love.'

They sat there in silence until abruptly the boy stood up. 'Ah'll get back to work noo,' he said.

'Take it easy, man,' soothed Ronny.

'Aye, see sense,' said Joe. 'Ye'll get sunstroke. Sit doon.'

'Ah won't dee nee work. Ah'll just look at the trench.' The

239

boy's eyes darted craftily. 'Ah'll sit under that tree.' He pointed at the cherry tree growing close to the leek trench. 'Ah'll just sit there.'

'It cannet dee nee harm,' put in Ronny.

'Whose side are ye on?' The old man looked over at the tree. 'Areet,' he said, grudgingly. 'But ye as much as touch that spade an' ah'll come awer there and . . .'

But the boy had already skipped down the steps of the balcony and was making his way over to the trench. 'Ah've got me hat an' all,' he called. 'Them cooboys nivver got nee sunstroke. Ah'll be a cooboy pitman.'

'He's come on,' said Ronny, nodding appreciatively.

'He's still a argumentative little monkey,' replied Joe. 'He nivver does as he's telt.'

Ronny smiled. 'Now ah wonder who he gets that from?'

The two men watched the boy who was circling the leek trench with a great show of disinterest. 'He has come on, but,' Ronny said softly.

'Aye,' nodded Joe.

Ronny studied the old man's face. 'But ye, man Joe. Ye look all in, marrer. Ye look . . .'

'Ah went to a one of them homes, y'kna,' said Joe, interrupting Ronny.

'Ye nivver said.'

'It was a couple of weeks back.' The old man's jaw clamped tightly shut. Gradually it opened. 'Sunnygarth.'

'What was it like?'

Joe shook his head. A determined glint steeled his eye. 'He's not gannin' into a one of them. Nee way.'

'What yus gonnae dee with him then?' There was no reply. Over at the leek trench Sonny Gee had furtively reached out to the spade which stood speared in the ground. On seeing that the two adults were watching him, he threw a feint and pretended to be swatting flies before wandering conspicuously over to the cherry tree.

'The things ah've seen,' began Joe again after a while, 'since he's been stopping with wor.'

'The bedsit an' that?'

'Aye. But other things. There's a few other things ah've like noticed. Foond oot. Since the bairn came to stop.' Joe trailed off. 'Ah've seen the far end of it all, Ronny lad,' said the old man simply.

There was a brief pause. 'Why divven't ye just let him stay with ye then?'

'Na,' replied Joe.

'Why not?'

'It's impossible.'

'Why?'

'Yus're worse than the bairn with all these questions, man.' The old man narrowed his eyes thoughtfully. 'For a start, what aboot me hands? Ah'm practically disabled, man.'

'Getaway.'

'Ah am.'

'But the compensation'll come through, then . . .'

'What good'll that dee? Why d'ye think that Gemma lass comes to light me fire? For me fashion tips? Ah'm a safety hazard, man.'

'Gemma thinks yus're brilliant with the bonny lad. Elsie thinks so an' all. Why, just this morning jug-eared Walter said to wor: He should just stop there permanent, him.'

'Aye, well, he's a real expert on the matter, him. His idea of babysitting's a bottle o' Broon and ten Senior Service.'

'He's reet, but. The bonny lad should just stop with ye.'

Joe turned to Ronny. He spoke softly. 'Do ye think he could?' Ronny was about to answer when suddenly the old man shouted: 'Hey, lad, ah telt ye, nee gannin' near that spade!'

Over at the trench, Sonny Gee dropped the spade and darted back over to the tree. 'Eh?' the boy called with wide-eyed innocence.

'He loves that spider, y'kna,' said Ronny after a while. 'It was good o' ye to get it for him. But ye didn't have to give wor the money.'

Joe's eyes flashed. 'Ah'm nee borrower me.'

'Ah kna. Ah kna,' put in Ronny hastily. 'What ah mean is that ah could have helped spread the payments oot. So much a week. That type o' thing. Ah could have got half of it an' all. It could have been from both o' wor.'

'Ye dee enough as it is, man Ronny.'

Ronny shrugged. 'A birthday's special at that age, but.'

'It's not his birthday,' replied the old man. 'Ah just got it for the birds. Ye kna, when ah . . .'

'Aye,' nodded Ronny.

'Ah divven't even kna when his birthday is. He won't tell wor.'

'Mebbes he doesn't kna.'

'Eh?'

'Mebbes he doesn't kna.'

'What ye gannin' on aboot, man Ronny?'

Ronny shrugged. 'Mebbes he's nivver had a birthday, or a birthday present. Ah mean, it's not summink yus just kna aboot, is it? Ye need to be told. It's summink others tell ye. Yer family. And he, nee disrespect to your Mary or nowt . . .'

'There's nowt ye could say aboot her that ah wouldn't double,' snapped Joe bitterly.

'Aye, well. The thing is, wor bonny lad hasn't really had much of a family. Ah mean, who would have telt him it was his birthday? Let alone given him a present. From what ah hear, Mary's been strung oot on drugs more than she hasn't, and that Macca . . . Mebbes Sonny Gee's nivver had a birthday.'

The old man's lips trembled slightly. 'Mebbes,' he said.

'Anyway,' said Ronny, taking another biscuit and popping the whole thing in his mouth, and chewing, 'whered'yusget-themoney?'

'What ye on aboot?'

'Themoneyforthespider?' asked Ronny, still chewing.

'Ah cannet hear a word yus're saying.'

Ronny swallowed the Rich Tea biscuit. 'Where d'ye get the money from?'

'What's that got to dee with ye?' demanded Joe curtly. 'Ye cheeky whippersnapper.' A moment passed. 'Ah took a loan oot.'

Ronny stared open-mouthed at Joe. 'Are ye off yer trolley? How will ye pay it back? That's not like ye.'

'Like ye said, man Ronny, he doesn't get many presents.'

They lapsed into silence. The boy got up from under the tree and circled the trench again, but, being observed, slunk back into the shade.

'Hot,' said Ronny, taking out his piece of rag again and wiping away the sweat. 'Hot.' The blackbird fluted loudly. 'Poor bugger,' Ronny said. 'It'd dee owt for a mate.'

'Cooey!' came a sudden cry. It was followed by a loud rapping at the door to Joe's plot.

'Audrey,' Ronny said at once.

'Are ye gonnae let wor in, or is there a state secret in there with ye?'

Sonny Gee ran down the path to let Audrey in. 'It's getting like Casey's court in here,' mumbled Joe.

'But y'kna summink?' said Ronny quietly. 'She's a fine figure of a woman, but. That Audrey. If only she'd gan oot with wor.'

'How auld are ye, man? Just ask her.'

Ronny shook his head hankeringly. 'She looks like a million poond.'

'She's dressed like a dog's dinner.'

Ronny paused reflectively. 'Ah love dogs, me. They're furry, friendly and fun. Ah was just telling the bonny lad the other week that ah was thinking of getting a springer spaniel. Thems are me favourite.'

243

The old man turned to his friend. 'Ye've been alone too long.'

'Dee us a favour, man Joseph. If ye divven't count the hamsters, ah've been alone all me life.' He pursed his lips contemplatively as he watched Audrey. She was talking to the boy, who was pointing the leek trench out to her. 'Put it this way, if Audrey and me had eight legs a piece, ah wouldn't give a toss aboot the empty cage come morning.'

Audrey's movements up the path were restricted by a tight imitation-leather skirt. Her high heels made her totter on the uneven path. Her hair had been cemented into a beehive. She waved a cigarette above her head as though trying to keep her balance. 'Once, twice, three times a lady,' crooned Ronny yearningly to himself.

'Well, noo ah've seen everything,' called the old man. 'Audrey with a bit mud on her.'

Audrey stopped. 'Where?' she demanded.

'Just ye wait,' laughed Joe.

'And top of the morning to ye an' all, ye miserable thing,' Audrey said. She turned to Ronny. 'What are ye looking at?'

'Who knas?' responded Ronny mysteriously.

'And why aren't ye at work?'

'A man is more than his work, Audrey,'

'Ha'way, man,' Audrey laughed. 'Mine's a Castaway if there's booze gannin' roond.'

'Aye, an' ah'll have a lager,' hazarded the boy, coming up behind Audrey. He looked up at the old man. 'Just a half?'

'There is nee booze, man lad. She's just joking.'

'Ah wouldn't mind a drink, but,' said Audrey, smiling at Sonny Gee. She patted his hat. 'And are ye a cowboy today, bonny lad?'

'Ah'm a pitman,' replied the boy.

'So what brings ye doon here?' Ronny asked. 'Where's all yer little cherubs?'

Audrey took a deep draw on her cigarette. The smoke hung

lazily in the air, lifting only slightly as it drifted away. 'Divven't mention them bairns to me,' she said, shaking her head vehemently. 'Toni-Leigh only went and had a barbeque.'

'What's wrong with that?'

'Lit a bonfire in the back lane. Poured petrol on it, didn't she? Nearly set the place alight. Three fire engines arrived. Ah wouldn't mind but she hoyed in twenty poonds' worth o' beefburgers she got from the butchers on credit.'

'Nivver.'

'Ah've had the world and his wife coming roond to complain aboot their washing stinking, and wanting money to put it through the laundrette again.' Audrey rubbed her legs and shoulders regretfully. 'Ah was trying to top up me tan an' all.'

Ronny shivered slightly.

'What d'yus want?' Joe asked.

Audrey paused thoughtfully. 'Well, ah was on me way to Gemma's, 'cos ah'm telling ye, her time's coming. So ah thought ah'd pop in and see ye first. But ye weren't in. Peggy told us where ye were. She doesn't like ye much, does she?'

'So what d'ye want, man Audrey?'

'A chat.'

'A chat?'

'Aye, a chat.'

'Ye've come all the way doon here and ye want a chat?'

'Aye,' Audrey darted her eyes at the boy. 'Ye kna, a chat.' Audrey nodded in the direction of Sonny Gee. 'A chat aboot things.'

'What things?'

'Things.' With a sigh, she pointed at the boy. 'Ah want a chat aboot things.'

'Ha'way,' said Ronny, getting up. 'Ah'll give ye a bit hand with the leek trench, bonny lad.'

'Promise?' replied Sonny Gee.

'At last ah've foond a man with a bit tact,' said Audrey.

'Have ye?' Ronny asked, unable to hide his disappointment. 'Who is he; do ah kna him?'

'Ye, man. Ye,' responded Audrey.

Ronny flushed lobster pink as he followed Sonny Gee. Reaching the trench, the boy pulled out the small spade from the earth. 'This one's yours,' he said.

Ronny lifted both spades up and studied them. 'Ah think ah'd better use the big one, man Sonny Gee.'

'D'ye want wor to tell Audrey that ye fancy her?'

'Areet, the small one'll dee me. Might as well gan the whole hog and be a clown.'

'It's always cloak and dagger with ye, isn't it, Audrey?' Joe said, when the others had started digging.

'And ye have got the hide of a friggin' rhinoceros, Joe.'

The old man began to chuckle. 'Look at that,' he said to Audrey, pointing at Ronny and Sonny Gee. 'He's got the proper one after all.' Ronny worked hunched ridiculously low while the boy struggled with the huge spade. Joe's chuckle turned into a laugh. 'Look at them. He's a bright one that lad, mind.'

Audrey took a final drag on her cigarette, and dropping it on the wood of the balcony, stubbed it out with the point of her heel. 'Ye look knackt, Joe man. Still, ah cannet remember the last time ah heard ye laugh.'

'Make sure yer tab's oot good and proper,' Joe said sharply.

Audrey gestured at the trench. 'Ye haven't done all that the day, have ye?'

'What's it got to dee with ye, woman?'

'Ye're getting too auld. Ah'm sure Ronny'd give ye a hand if ye asked him.'

The old man snorted. 'Ronny's got his own problems.'

'Has he?' Audrey stared keenly at Joe. 'Like what?'

'Ah'm nee gossip, me.'

They lapsed into silence, watching Sonny Gee and Ronny

at work. Audrey smiled and then turned to Joe. 'Well, it hasn't been too bad after all, has it?'

The old man did not look at Audrey. 'Why, should it have been?'

'Just after when ye came roond to see wor. Ah thought ye were gonnae hate him stopping with ye.'

'Did ye?'

Audrey poured herself a mug of tea from the pot. She drank it thoughtfully. 'Then there was the bit trouble with that Walsh lad.'

Joe shrugged. 'Nowt we couldn't handle.'

'Nowt ye couldn't handle? Ye want to be careful. He's a bad lot, that Jimmy Walsh. Moves in dodgy circles.'

Joe snorted. 'Ah'm not scared o' him.'

'Ee, that's what he says.'

'Who?'

'The bonny lad. Ye two are the spitting image, ah swear doon.' Audrey paused. 'Joe, ah've got some news for ye.'

'Have ye?'

'Aye, it's good news.' Audrey took out another cigarette, then on second thoughts put it back in her purse. She looked closely at the old man. 'Ah've been working on Mary.' She waited for Joe's reaction, but his face did not flicker. 'She wants to leave Macca. Decided he's nee good. Seen his true colours at last.' She paused for a moment. 'It won't be lang now, Joe.'

The old man's voice was expressionless. 'What won't be lang?'

'The bonny lad. Ye won't have to have him for much longer. Mary's really . . .'

'And what'll she dee?' Joe snapped suddenly. 'She's nee good for him. She's nee good for anything.'

Sonny Gee and Ronny paused to stare over at the old man's vehemence. Standing up on the wave of his outburst, the old

247

man staggered inside the hut. 'What's the matter, man Joe?' Audrey said, getting up to follow him. 'Joe?'

He did not turn to face Audrey and when he spoke his voice trembled with rage. 'He deserves better than this, Audrey. He deserves better than being passed aboot from pillar to post. And he deserves more than *she* can ever give him.'

Audrey waited a little before replying calmly. 'So what d'yus suggest?' The impassioned clamour of the blackbird could be heard loudly in the silence. 'Are *ye* gonnae keep him then?'

Joe stared at the neat bundle of tools stacked tidily in a corner, the blades glinting with oil. 'Aye,' he said quietly.

'What, ye? Look after the bairn?'

'Me. Why not?'

'Are ye having a laugh or what, Joe?'

The old man slowly turned. His face was set hard. 'Ah've nivver been more serious in me life. Ah'll look after him.'

'But Joe . . .'

'What?'

Shaking her head, Audrey smiled sadly. 'Ye cannet.'

'Why not?'

'Because ye cannet even look after yersel'.'

There was a long silence. The old man licked his dry lips. He spoke quietly. 'In all the time ah've known ye, ah've nivver known ye be cruel before, Audrey.'

'Ah'm not being cruel, man Joe. Ah'm being honest. And if ye cannet look after yersel', then how can ye look after the bonny lad?' Fumbling for her cigarettes, she lit one. The small hut rapidly filled with smoke. 'Are them yer leek sets?' Audrey said gently, pointing past the old man to the pencil-thin young leeks standing in pots on the bench. 'Ha'way, tell us what the secret ingredient is. Everybody wants to kna.'

Joe stared at the seedlings. 'What does it matter?' he whispered. 'What does any of it matter now?'

'Ha'way, man Joe, ah didn't mean anything. We'll work summink oot. If ye've got attached to him then that's good.

Ah was just a bit surprised. Ah thought yus couldn't wait to get shot of him. Ye'll still be able to see him. Ah didn't mean anything by it.'

Joe sighed. Dark shadows had formed under his eyes. All at once he seemed overwhelmed. 'It's all right, Audrey. What ye said was the truth. Ah cannet even look after mesel'. Ah'd probably only end up hurting him. Ah've got to face it. Ah'm finished. There's nowt ah can dee for him.' Joe tried to pick up the young leeks, but his fingers could not grip properly, and he dropped the tray. Soil was sprinkled over the wooden floor as the bulbs of the dropped plants rolled down the slight slope. Joe lifted up his hands, and stared at them. 'The truth is,' he said, 'ah'm a cripple. Just another clapped-oot auld pitman, nee good for anything but the cemetery.' His face was stricken with agony. 'It's too late. It's too late.'

11

Leaving the allotments, Joe took Sonny Gee back up the lane. He walked faster than usual, his boots kicking at the stones, and the child had to trot to keep up with him. The cuckoo was silent; the cows had drifted away on to the lea. 'Where we gannin'?' the boy asked. 'Where we gannin'?'

They emerged from the shade of the sunken lane, and the old man strode on to the Watergate Colliery redevelopment. 'Where we gannin'?' Sonny Gee repeated. Their path climbed through the avenue of saplings and only when he had reached the crest of the rise did Joe stop. Spread out before them, shimmering under the bright sun, was the whole site of the abandoned colliery. The old man stood there a long time staring. There was no sign of it now, no machinery, no coal-blackened tips, no grey, rocky heaps. Only the pitmen's path remained, but taking its way through long grass now. The old man followed the path with his eyes. A small squall of wind blew down past him, and he watched it travel, rippling the flowers and grasses of the newly risen meadows on either side of the path as it combed through them, until it reached the newly made lake which stood at the centre of the redevelopment. Joe turned to the boy beside him. 'Ah worked here. Man and boy for fifty years.' Without waiting for a reply, Joe walked on.

Further along, a cloud of goldfinches lifted on their approach. A skylark ascended. Higher and higher it rose, scattering its song over them, and the higher it lifted, the stronger its song rang out. Head tilting further and further back, the boy followed the skylark's climb until he lost it in the blue of the sky. When he looked down again the old man had walked on. Sonny Gee ran to catch up with him. 'See all of this?' said Joe, wafting his new stick over everything. 'Underneath here is a thousand tunnels. That's where ah worked. That was the pit.' He jabbed the ground beneath his feet with the stick. 'Right under here an' all.'

'To get that coal?' asked Sonny Gee, breathlessly.

'To get that coal, lad.'

They walked on. The old man's face seemed to be burning even more brightly than the sun. 'Why?' asked the boy. 'Why did ye get that coal?'

Joe paused bitterly. 'To make money for other people.'

They continued a few yards. A man pushing a baby in a pram walked past them. 'Why?'

'Why what, lad?'

'Why did yous make money for other people?'

Joe stopped again. 'It's the way the world is, lad.'

'Why?'

Coming to the lake's edge, they began to circle it, sending the ducks drifting to the middle and lifting a solitary sandpiper. The old man pointed at a hump in the land ahead of them. 'That was the pithead,' he said.

'Eh?'

'That was where we got into the tunnel.' Slowly the old man rotated his body in a complete circle, his face hardened. 'Once this whole country was powered by coal. D'ye understand, lad? Once coal powered Britain. But thems what dug it up, why, we were always dirt poor. For hundreds of years people have dug coal here. Dug it oot from under the ground. And they've always had nowt. Everyone o' wor. Wherever ye gan in the world, it's the same. Thems that make the wealth have nowt. That's how it was for me. And me dad and me granda before.'

'Did *ye* have a granda?' the boy asked.

'Aye,' replied Joe simply.

The old man walked smartly over to where the pithead used to be and began to mount the landscaped hump, which nodded with purple-headed clover. He tripped as he climbed, but catching his balance he pressed on. 'Hard work, mind,' said Joe, reaching the top. His breathing, despite the exertion, was even. 'Dangerous. Always risking yer life and limb. Ah worked there, me dad before that, that would be your great-granda, and then stretching all the way back through the generations. There's been people winning coal here for six hundred years. They started with a pick and a shovel. Not much different from what we were using in the allotment. By the time ah was a man we were using a drill. They called it the windy pom.' Holding his hands out, Joe pretended to shudder under the impact of a drill. 'It was that what knackt me hands.'

The boy stared at the hands. 'Will ah be working here?' he asked tentatively. ''Cos ah'll dee it, if ah can help ye. We could have a tunnel for worselves. Ronny can come sometimes, but.'

The old man smiled. 'It's not there any more, man lad.'

'Where is it then?'

'Neewhere. There is nee more mining in Britain. They stopped it.'

'What we gonnae dee then?'

Joe shrugged. His voice grew soft. 'We're damned with it, we're damned withoot it.' His eyes travelled sadly over the panorama. 'Ah can still smell it,' he said. 'They've planted trees here. And let the flowers grow. But ah can smell it.' He broke off, and turning from the old pit, looked down at the boy. 'See, if ah came back here in a thoosand years' time, ah'd still be able to smell it.'

'Ah divven't understand,' Sonny Gee said.

'This,' said Joe, gesturing with the stick over the whole view, 'is your heritage. And ah'm showing it to ye. Ye might not understand it all now, but ye're a bright one, lad, and there'll come a time when ye dee. Well, this is for then. For when ye dee understand it.'

They came to the end of the lake, and the path took them down into Washingwell Woods. High above them, just visible through the canopy of oak trees, stood an old railway embankment. The old man pointed up at it. 'They've ran coal alang there for six hundred years. This is where ye came from, lad. What made ye. Ye're the last of wor. The last of the pit folk. But it's a different world for ye. And it's ye what ah'm thinking on.' Joe suddenly smiled. 'Nothing else matters now,' he said quietly. 'Just ye.'

'Where we gannin'?' said the boy, after they had been walking for a long time through the close woodland which thickly covers the first scars of the Industrial Revolution. A red squirrel watched them furtively as they passed beneath the bough of its larch. When they had gone, it watched them for a little longer, before continuing in its search for food.

'Ah want to show ye summink,' replied the old man.

The path took them through a fir plantation then, leaving it to follow a badger track, the old man and little boy went through an oak glade. They walked slowly and the old man stared ahead all the while. 'It's here somewhere,' he said.

At last they came to a large field, hidden on three sides by the woods. Joe brought the boy to the fence at the edge of the field and then stopped. There before them was the huge skeleton of a Victorian mansion.

Turrets and towers twisted up like a medieval castle, huge clusters of chimneys stood on the still intact roof. Here and there a tree poked its branches from a window. The inside had long been gutted, but the outside was remarkably preserved. The boy's face was filled with wonder. 'Eh?' he whispered. 'It's . . . it's . . .' The words were lost in his awe. 'Is it magic?' he gasped at last. 'Like in a one o' them Disney Singalong videos Gemma's got?'

Joe did not answer for a while. 'Mebbes,' he said. The old man's gaze travelled slowly over the ruin. 'Mebbes.' His eyes narrowed. 'This is where the family lived of the man what owned the coal we dug up.'

Stupefied, Sonny Gee shook his head. 'It's bigger than *all* the bedsits in Bensham!'

Joe nodded. 'Me granda married the girl what worked as a maid here.'

'A maid?'

'She was a servant here, lad. A servant. And she was your great-great-nana.' The old man paused. Bending down, he lifted the fence so that the boy could get under. Then he himself stooped to climb through. But he could not bend low enough. Quickly the boy came over, and without looking away from the ruined mansion, lifted the wire for the old man. 'Ta,' said Joe softly. Crossing the rough pasture, they came to the house. Walking between the tall gateposts, they carried on into the courtyard. Joe stopped underneath the clock tower. A cloud of gnats played in the air, drifting across the courtyard. Tentatively, the old man put his hand out to touch the bricks. He recoiled on the contact.

'It's cold,' said the boy in amazement, also bringing his hand away.

'Ah must have been your age when me granda brought wor here,' said the old man after a while. 'That'd be your great-great-granda.'

'Great-great?'

'And he telt wor summink an' all. Summink ah've nivver forgot.'

The boy's eyes swam dreamily. 'What?'

'He said, if ye ever think ye're clever then come here and take a look at this mansion. 'Cos ye and people like ye built it, with the sweat of yer brows, brick by brick, and yet look where ye're living. That's what he said.'

'Why?'

The old man looked long into the boy's eyes. 'Ah was like ye. Always asking questions. Always thinking of the next

254

thing. 'Cos ah thought ah was clever.' He looked away from the boy to the strangely preserved pile. A heaviness seemed to have fallen over them like a shadow. Through the gateposts, they could see the eaves of the wood stirring slightly in the breeze, but inside the courtyard, only the cloud of gnats moved. From the larch trees drifted the lonely cry of a sparrowhawk. 'Ah've wanted to dee summink since ah was your age an' all,' Joe suddenly said.

'What?'

'Me nana used to sing to wor. All the time, like, but there was one song that stuck in me mind. Lodged there, y'kna. And it was this what ah've always wanted to dee. And now ah'm gonnae dee it.'

For a few more moments the sparrowhawk's call rang out alone, but then it was joined by another voice. The boy's eyes darted urgently around as though he was searching for the voice in one of the glassless windows overlooking them. His eyes came to rest on Joe. It was the old man that was singing. The words came rustily from his gruff throat in fits and starts, creaking like the wincing of old machinery at a long-gone pithead.

> O bonny's my lad as he walks down the street
> With his lamp in his hand, all canny and neat;
> His teeth white as ivory, his eyes black as sloes,
> Ah love my miner lad everyone knas . . .

The old man broke off. He looked about the old house, his eyes squinting as though he were trying to focus on something dazzling. Then breathing in, he began to sing again. It was the tune that he had often found himself whistling since the boy came. Sonny Gee stared at him, wide-eyed.

> Sometimes he has money, sometimes none at all,
> But he'll share what he has, be it nivver so small.

Nee laddie is blither, nee laddie mair kind,
And he'll stand by his word when he's spoken his mind.

Gulping for breath in the middle of lines, pausing lengthily between some of the words, Joe weakened. The effort to sing was draining him, but closing his eyes he continued.

The rich man's pleasure is to blaw the loud horn,
And the farmer is happy a-reapin' his corn;
But the miner must take up the pick in his hand,
For to win all the coal that lies under the land.

The enclosed walls of the once splendid mansion echoed with the broken music; and its rooms, thrown open to the world now as they had never been when its ghosts were living, were filled with a voice worn by a lifetime of hard labour and coal dust. A fragile tenderness had softened the roughness of the old man's singing. But the tenderness came not only from Joe's voice. There was something else accompanying him. A thin, shaky, reedy accompaniment. It was the boy whistling.

We'll build us a castle of highest renoon,
That ladies and masters will nivver pull doon.
The king loves his queen and the emperor the same,
And I love my miner lad, who can me blame?

The last notes of the song seemed to linger over the mansion for some time after the old man and the boy had fallen silent. Joe stood there, face rapt, eyes lively, as though listening to another, distant voice, and then he smiled sadly. 'There,' he said softly. 'That's yer heritage.'

Sonny Gee remained silent, his eyes intent on his grandfather's face. 'Ah can dee it,' he said softly. 'Ah can whistle.'

For a while Joe stayed abstracted, peering into his own beyond, then he turned to the child. The two of them gazed deeply at each other. 'If only ah had a bit longer,' the old man said. 'If only ah could be here for ye. If only me hands were . . .' Breaking off, he lowered his eyes to the ground. At that moment a weasel came running across the courtyard. Seeing the two people, it stopped, and lifting up on its hind legs, watched them. 'Can ye see it?' breathed the old man. 'It's a weasel.' The boy nodded. The little creature ran on, mounting a set of crumbling stairs in a series of zigzag bounds; it stopped halfway up. 'It's got the same colour hair as ye,' whispered Joe. The weasel watched them for a little while longer, its face quick with intelligence, its whiskers glistening. It took one last look at them before disappearing into a hole in the wall. 'The same colour hair,' repeated the old man. Lifting up the boy's cowboy hat for a moment, he stared at the hair. An unusual light sprang up in his eyes. 'D'ye kna summink?'

'Aye,' nodded the boy.

'Before ah lost it all. Me hair. When ah had it. Me own head was as red as yours.'

'Straight up?'

'Why aye.'

'Belter.' They looked up at the clock tower. The face of the clock remained, only the hands had been broken.

Joe reached out and ruffled the boy's hair. 'Ye're a clever lad. Ye're bright. Ye're sharp. Whatever happens, remember that. Always remember that.'

Joe turned and began walking across the courtyard. He led the way back between the gateposts down which the grand coaches used to sweep in a time still linked to our own by spoken memories and song. 'Ha'way, lad, there's one more thing we've got to dee.'

'What?'

'Ye forgetting? We've got to get wor secret recipe for them leeks.'

Even before they reached it, they could see the river shining silver under the sun. The bus dropped them at the Dunston Staithes. 'Have ye got wor bucket?' Joe asked. The boy held it up in reply.

It was low tide and where the River Team guts into the Tyne the mud beds were wide. The wooden vertebrae of an old keelboat lay exposed in the grey gloop. Cautiously the old man began to lower himself down the scree of the steep bank, but, losing his balance, he had to scramble. At a jolting jog he reached the bottom. 'Ye stay up there,' he called, but when he looked round, he saw that the boy was already standing beside him. 'Ye keep beside me then, d'ye hear?' he demanded. 'Yus only gan where ah gan, right?' Sonny Gee nodded. 'It's dangerous. There's been them that have drowned here.'

'Ah'm not scared o' that.'

The wooden structure of the staithes towered above them as they set off over a shingle spit lying across the mud; the pattern of the slatted legs was ghostly; the river running underneath it, restless. 'Where's it gannin'?' the boy asked.

'Eh?'

'All that. Where's it gannin' to?'

'All what?'

The old man turned, and Sonny Gee pointed over to where the river ran between the wide beds of mud under the staithes. 'That,' said the boy.

'The river?'

'Aye, that. Where's it gannin'?'

Joe jerked his head to where the larger flow of the Tyne could be seen through the legs of the staithes. 'Into the bigger river.'

'And where's that gannin'?'

The old man shrugged. 'Into the sea.'

'Why?'

'Ah divven't kna. It just does. That's what rivers dee. They flow into the sea.'

Sonny Gee's voice was suddenly sad. 'Why divven't they stay here?'

'What d'ye mean, lad?'

'Why do they have to gan into bigger rivers and the sea. Why divven't they just stay put?'

The old man shook his head gently. 'Because they cannet.'

'Well, ah divven't like it. Ah wish they'd stop. And if ah was that God gadgie then ah'd make them.'

'But it's the way they are. Ye cannet change it.'

For a while they stared at the restless water of the Team coursing through the mud to its mouth with the bigger river. A row of cormorants watched them from their perch on the railing of the staithe high above, and a kingfisher shot by, its wings splashing colour. Then the old man suddenly began to laugh. 'They think the secret's from the Tyne,' he said to the boy over his shoulder when they came to the end of the little stony outcrop. 'They think it's Tyne mud what makes for the best leeks. But it isn't. It's this . . .' And bending down, Joe plunged his hands into the glutinous substance. Lifting himself again, he brought up two hands full of mud. 'It comes from the Team, man. Team mud. That's what does it! Ye put it in the trench, give it all the care ye can and then hey presto! When the time comes, yus've got prize leeks.'

'Wor secret recipe!' shouted the boy.

'Aye. Wor secret recipe.' Bringing his hands over to the bucket, the old man dropped the mud inside. He took a second handful, and a third. Then he stopped. At their feet, the river passed by, its flow a musical tinkling. 'Funny,' Joe mused. 'Ah cannet feel nowt now. Me hands are numb.' A worry flickered over his face, but he brushed it aside. 'Must be the mud, eh?' he laughed. 'Healing properties, eh?'

Squatting down, the boy scooped up handfuls of the mud, squelching it lovingly between his fingers. 'Belter secret recipe this!' he laughed.

The old man looked up at the staithes. The cormorants

lifted one by one, flapping heavily away, their shapes, broodingly low over the water, strangely prehistoric. His glance travelled the length of the huge wooden platform and then returned to the boy, where it rested. 'They're right. Ye and me. We are chips off the auld block. Looking at ye is liking looking at mesel'.'

Bewilderment filled the boy's eyes. 'Chips?'

The old man did not answer for a while. 'Ye cannet stop with wor,' he said.

A police helicopter scoured the sky above them, circling the sky a number of times before throbbing on towards Lobley Hill. 'What d'ye mean?' asked Sonny Gee.

'Well, ah'm old.'

Sonny Gee shrugged. 'No ye're not. Ye're younger than geet loads of people. Ye? Yus're younger than jug-eared Walter. Yus're only aboot fifty.' Scooping up a huge dollop of mud, the boy patted it between his hands.

Joe shook his head. 'Ah'm old. Proper old.' He paused. 'Ah cannet look after ye. We'll still see each other, mind. Wherever ye gan. We'll still see each other.'

Sonny Gee stopped playing with the mud. 'But the leeks?'

'Ye can still help wor with them.'

The boy's voice rose, and his words went out with the current of the water. 'But ah want to stay with ye . . .'

'But ah'm so old that ah cannet look after ye.'

'Ye divven't need to look after wor. Ah can look after mesel'.'

Joe blinked. 'And anyway ah'm not gonnae be aroond much longer.'

'Eh? Where yus gannin'? Ah'll come with ye.'

'Neeone can come where ah'm gannin'.'

Still holding the mud, Sonny Gee straightened. 'What ye gannin' on aboot?'

'There comes a time when ye have to gan.'

A pained look flooded the child's features. 'Where to?'

The old man hesitated before replying. Then suddenly he raised his voice, and it travelled across the mud to the willow thicket on the far bank of the Team. 'Ah came too late for ye. Ah'm gonnae die, lad. Die. Ah'm gonnae die before ye grow up.'

Sonny Gee looked at the mud in his hands. 'But ah'm grown up noo.'

'Na. Ye're a little bairn, man.'

The mud dropped from the boy's hands and landed with a soft splat. Sonny Gee shook his head, his blue eyes widened. 'What d'ye mean, die?'

There was a long pause. They both stared down at the flowing water which seemed suddenly much louder; only slowly did it fade back to its usual gentle purling. Joe began again. 'When ye're auld ye die. There's nee choice to it. Ye have to gan away. And me? Ah'm getting auld.' He paused again, as though struggling with himself; his face grew animated, before falling expressionless. For a lengthy period of time, it seemed that he had resolved not to speak, but then he broke the silence once more. 'Look. Ah'm too auld. Ah cannet look after ye. Ah care for ye, lad. But ah cannet keep ye. Ah . . . ah really care. But yus've got to gan.'

Sonny Gee gazed at his grandfather in pain. Jerking his head forward, he gnawed at his bottom lip. Blood spurted from it.

'Ee, pet,' said Joe gently. 'Ye've hurt yersel'. Come here, and let wor see to that lip.'

The old man stepped towards him, but the boy pushed him back. He chewed at his lip voraciously for a few more seconds and then abruptly stopped. A dead look came into his eyes. 'Ye're just like me dad, ye,' he said quietly. 'Ah asked him to let wor stop with him. But he wouldn't. He went away an' all. See ye? Yus're just like me dad.'

Joe shook his head. 'It's not because ah want it this way. It's because ah have to. Me hands are knackt, me lungs are . . .' He faltered for a few moments helplessly. 'How can ah look after ye?' Agony flecked the old man's face. 'Ah'm not deeing it on purpose . . .'

'Let wor stay,' begged Sonny Gee.

'Ah cannet. Ah cannet,' said the old man simply.

A cruel glint came into the boy's eyes. 'Ye kna ye, gadgie mista? Ye cannet dee owt, ye.'

Joe looked down at his hands. They lay lifelessly against his side like a clutch of uprooted plants, and the welts raised by the digging were caked in drying mud. The boy took off his cowboy hat and held it out to the old man. 'Ah divven't want that nee more.' He blinked. 'Ah divven't want nowt from ye. Nee hat. Nee leeks. And nee stupid whistling song.'

The boy ran back across the shingle spit. Reaching the bank, he turned. 'Ye promised ah could stay with ye. Ye promised ye wouldn't send wor away until when the time comes. And . . . and . . . ' Sonny Gee pulled himself up the steep bank quickly, scrabbling dextrously up the tree branches. He stood for one more moment, looking down where the old man stood below, and then he was gone.

12

As soon as Joe arrived home, he found the note. It had been pushed through the letter box and lay on the doormat. With a grunt of effort, he bent down to pick it up, but it was tightly folded, and before he had time to read it, there was a knock at the door. Putting the note in a pocket, his old wrinkled face beamed youthfully. 'Listen,' he called, as he impatiently fiddled with the lock and the chain. 'Ah was wrong, yus divven't need to gan neewhere. Yus're stopping here with me. So there's no need for ye to worry . . .' In mid-flow, he threw open the door.

'Areet,' said the woman on the doorstep.

The old man stared across the threshold, disbelief lifting the corners of his mouth as the joy on his face evaporated.

Coming through into the sitting room, Joe slumped into the armchair. The woman sat on the settee. 'Ah won't stay long,' she said.

The old man's visitor watched him for a long time. His eyes were fixed on the far wall, unfocused. 'Ah've left him,' she began. There was no reply. 'Ah'm gonnae gan into a refuge, just until ah get back on me feet.' She breathed in deeply. 'Ah've started on a one of them methadone programmes an' all.'

'Oh aye, Mary?' replied the old man with an abstracted air.

'Aye. It's a new start. Ah'm getting rid of Macca. Ah'm getting rid of the drugs an' that.' Mary fished for a packet of cigarettes. She brought it out, and fiddling with it, her fingers tapped percussively against the box. 'Ah want to be a proper mam to the bairn an' all. Ah want it . . . so that he wants for nowt.' She stared at her father. 'Are yus all right, Dad, ye look proper done in.'

'Mary,' said Joe, speaking quietly, 'how d'ye have the nerve to come here?'

Mary paused. 'Are yer hands areet?'

Joe spoke in nothing more than a whisper. 'There's nee feeling left.' He stared at his hands for a while, gingerly rubbing them together. The mud had dried on the palms and the fortune lines of the old man's life were starkly emphasised. With a baffled air he studied each finger. 'How d'yus have the nerve to come here?'

'Ah kna ah've made mistakes,' Mary put in, quickly. 'Ah divven't say ah haven't, 'cos ah have. But this time things are gonnae change. Ah swear doon. This time things . . .'

Joe shook his head gently. 'Nee more of that now.'

Mary's fingers continued to tap restlessly against the box of cigarettes. Finally she ripped off the cellophane wrapper and took one out. 'D'ye mind?' she asked. The old man shook his head. He watched her as she lit the cigarette, sucking desperately on the filter before exhaling with such force that her whole body leant forward over the edge of the settee. She continued to smoke with an air of almost unbearable need, chewing on the filter and then breathing in as though she might swallow herself. 'Ah've made mistakes,' she said, speaking through streams of smoke. 'Ah kna ah upset ye and me mam. Ah kna that ye divven't approve of wor.' Breaking off, she looked about the room with a puzzled air. 'Where's Sonny Gee?'

Joe sighed. 'Is it only now ye've noticed he's not here?'

'Just did off, did he?' Mary asked. 'He's always deeing that, the little so-and-so. He stayed away a whole night withoot telling us before. Well, divven't worry, Dad. Ah've come to take him.'

As the silence lengthened between them, the ash grew long on the end of the cigarette. Mary smoked self-consciously, her other hand hovering underneath to catch the ash if it should fall. 'Just use the grate,' said Joe at last. There was a profound weariness in his voice.

'Can ah?'

'Or just hoy it on the hearthstone. What does it matter?'

Puzzled, Mary smiled. 'This is the first time yus've let wor smoke in the hoose. Before ye moved in here, in the auld hoose, ah used to have to smoke in the ootside toilet. Mam knew. Didn't she? But she nivver told. Did she?'

Joe sighed.

'So where'd he go then?' she asked. 'The bairn?'

The old man shrugged. 'Ah divvent kna. Ah've been looking for him. Been everywhere.'

Mary nodded. 'Ye divven't need to tell me aboot him. He's always one for gannin' oot, him. Ye just cannet keep him in. He's like a caged animal.' She paused reflectively. 'He'll be areet. The number of times ah've foond mesel' up and doon Old Parsonage Road shouting meself hoarse on him. Ee, ah'm forever finding him where he shouldn't be, an' all . . .'

'Where the hell do ye get the nerve to come roond here?' the old man suddenly yelled. The shout exploded in the room. Left breathless by the abrupt wrench of energy, Joe sat there panting, still staring perplexedly at his hands. When he began to speak again, his voice was a low growl. 'Ah kna aboot the babby. The other babby. Ah kna aboot him.'

Cagily, Mary blew out a chestful of smoke. 'What d'ye mean?'

'Divven't give wor that, man. Ye kna what ah mean.'

'Do ah?'

'Well, if ye divven't, who the hell does? The first babby. The one that stopped with . . .'

'Who's been talking to ye?'

'Does it matter?'

'Aye. If folks are gannin' behind me back.'

'It's ye that's been stabbin' backs, lass.'

265

'Stabbin'?'

'How could ye dee it? How could ye dee a thing like that to yer mam?'

'Ah didn't mean . . .'

'Ye didn't mean nowt. Ye never did.'

An uneasy silence followed this rapid exchange.

'Ye took away yer mam's grandbairn from her,' Joe said at last in a flat, shattered tone. 'And now ye're deeing it all awer again.'

'Eh?'

'Sonny Gee. Yus're deeing it to us again.' His lips trembled as he tried to look at her, but something stopped him. For a few moments he seemed to fear her, and his mouth gaped slightly as though with senility. 'D'yus dee it on purpose? Ruin wor lives? First the babby and now Sonny Gee . . .'

Mary's face puckered with confusion. 'But ah thought ye didn't like him, ah thought ye didn't want him?'

'Didn't like him?' The old man's voice rose again. The fear disappeared in a roar of rage. 'He's me own flesh and blood for God's sake.'

Mary's voice rose also. 'And am ah not too?'

'Ye've nivver acted like it.'

'And ye haven't neither.'

'That's reet, Mary lass, blame others for your troubles.'

'Why not? That's what ye dee.'

They fell silent again. Joe nodded his head exhaustedly. He raised his hands to his face for an instant, then lowered them. He spoke with the weariness of one who has lost everything. 'All that matters is the bairn. Everything else? It's awer and finished with. Only he's left.'

Mary smoked on in silence for a while. 'How's he been with ye, like?'

The old man's breathing began to labour. Slowly it righted itself, but every so often as he exhaled there was a soft, bemused whistle.

Getting up, Mary strode across the room then paused at the door. 'Dad, man . . .' She stared at the old man in appeal, but he did not seem to see her. She sighed, and looking around the room, her eyes came to rest on the sideboard where the spider tank stood. 'What's that?' She went over to it and peered inside. 'A spider? Is it Ronny's?'

'It's Sonny Gee's,' replied the old man blankly.

'He'll love that,' she said. 'He's always gannin' into Ronny's shop. It was good of Ronny to give it to him, but he shouldn't have . . .' Mary broke off, her eyes widened. '*Ye* didn't buy it for him, did ye, Dad?'

'What's so strange aboot that?' said Joe, his wheezing creating a strange sibilance.

'Nowt, but . . .'

'It's only a spider. He wanted a spider. Ah bought it for him.'

Mary paused for a moment. She seemed about to say something then pulled herself up. 'How much was it? Ah'll pay ye for it.'

'It was a present.' Joe blinked weakly. 'Ah divven't want nee money for it.'

The woman gazed at the glowing tip of her cigarette thoughtfully. 'Ah'm surprised he didn't make ye buy him a bird. He's always pestering for a bird.' Mary shook her head. 'Ah bet he asked ye for a bird. He's always gannin' on aboot the birds.'

The old man's weary eyes moved sluggishly with thought. 'He loves them.'

Mary nodded. 'It used to dee me heed in. 'Cos ah didn't kna what he was gannin' on aboot. Ah used to think . . .' She broke off, her lifeless cheeks flushed briefly. 'Ah didn't think he was a divvy or owt. Not proper retarded, y'kna. But ah just thought he was a bit odd. Y'kna. The way he went on aboot them birds. Or whativver else was on his mind.'

The old man sighed. 'Curiosity's a sign of intelligence in a bairn.'

Coming back to the settee, Mary sat down. She leant forward to flick her ash into the fire grate. She missed it. The ash fell on to the hearthstone. Freezing, she stared over at Joe.

'It doesn't matter,' he said without tone.

'Aye, well.' It took Mary some time before she was ready to begin again. She pulled herself upright in the settee a number of times and smoothed her lank hair. 'Ah've worked it oot now,' she said at last.

'Worked what oot?'

'The birds. Ah've worked it all oot aboot them birds of his.' Mary's face twisted with the bitterness of the nicotine as she took another big draw on her cigarette. 'It's his dad.'

Joe stirred bitterly, but did not speak, subsiding into a trance-like stillness.

'He's the only man ah ever did love,' she said. For a while she seemed to lose herself in memories. Only slowly did she pull herself away from them sufficiently to talk. 'It was when he was out of jail last time that we had Sonny Gee. He's back inside noo, but. He lasted nearly four years gannin' straight. The best what he'd ever managed. Ah'd begun to hope it was for ever.' She looked at the old man, but he was gazing expressionlessly ahead, his hands resting on his lap like the mangled wings of a traffic-killed bird. Mary continued, as though speaking to herself. 'We lived in a flat up Beacon Lough way. It was high up, above the trees. Y'kna, right beside the woods there. Just a little wood, but in the spring and summer, ee, ye should have heard them birds singing.' She paused, as though listening to the memory of birdsong. 'He was dead good with the bairn. Loved him to bits. Ah can see the pair of them now. When he was a babby Sonny Gee used to cry and cry. Nowt would stop him, but if his dad picked him up and held him, if his dad went near him, why, he'd chuckle and giggle like a good un. So he used to spend hours just holding him. The soft get. He'd open the window and stand there with the bairn in his arms looking oot. Listening to the birds.' Mary ran a hand over her face, her eyes shone tenderly. 'He'd stand there with him. Chatting. Telling him things. Ye kna, all them daft little things ye whisper to a bairn. And through all of it, the birds would be singing their hearts oot and be forever flying up and aroond.' Mary's face grew resolute for a while, before giving way to reflection. 'Ah didn't think he'd have remembered it. Ah mean, ye wouldn't, would ye? The bairn. How could he have remembered it proper because his dad was arrested again before he was even three year auld.' The woman pulled a rueful smile. 'It's coming off it, ye see. The drugs. Ye start to see things. Ye ramble.' She laughed to herself. 'Ah didn't come here to ramble.'

Joe started. Glancing at Mary, surprise stupefied his features as though he had just noticed that she was there. Slowly he seemed to come back to himself. 'What did ye come for then?'

'The bairn. Ah've come for him.'

The clock ticked loudly in the silence. 'And what makes ye think ah'll give him to ye?' said the old man at last. His voice was strained.

'He's me bairn,' replied Mary with a puzzled shrug.

Joe tried to raise a hand but he could not. 'Na,' he whispered at last. 'Na.'

'But ah telt ye, ah'm coming off all them drugs, ah'll be there for him . . .'

'Ah'll not give him to ye,' roared the old man suddenly, flaring like a fire. 'D'ye hear us? Ah'll not give him to ye.'

Mary pursed her lips sharply. 'Ye cannet stop me, man.'

'Cannet ah?' responded Joe, quickly.

'Na.'

'With all them drugs and the rogues ye hang aboot with, it's a fine life for a bairn that, mind.'

'Ah'm finished with all of that.'

'Are ye?'

'Aye.'

'That's what they all say.'

'It's true. Anyway, come to that, what aboot here? D'ye think ye can give him more? Ye cannet even look after yerself. What ye gonnae give him that ah cannet?'

'Love. That's what ah'm gonnae give him. Love.'

The words shouted by Joe seemed to hang on the air between them. They both seemed bewildered by them. 'And divven't ye think that that's what ah want to give him an' all?' Mary whispered.

The old man and his daughter stared at each other for a long time. Then Joe shook his head. The fire of his energy had burned down, leaving only the cold grey ashes of an expressionless voice. 'Ye gave him away, and now ah've got him. Ye divven't kna the meaning of the word.'

'How d'ye kna?' They were both speaking softly now, as though the terrible storm that had engulfed them had passed on for the time being. 'Ye kna nowt aboot my life.'

'Oh, ah kna areet.'

Mary half rose from the settee as though to reach out to her father. 'Na, ye divven't. Ah love Sonny Gee's dad.'

'Divven't talk daft. He put yus up the spout, and that's it. That's not love, that's . . . that's *sex*.' The unaccustomed word hovered on the air. The old man turned a yearning eye on Mary. 'Me and yer mam. That's love. Together all that time. Fidelity. That's what it's all about.'

Still half-risen from the seat, Mary continued. 'We were together a long time.'

'Mary man, ah'd laugh if it wasn't such a tragedy.'

'He wasn't only Sonny Gee's dad,' she said, and slumped back down.

There was a pause. 'What are ye gannin' on aboot?'

Mary spoke quickly, the words ripping from her. 'He was the babby's dad an' all. The one they all call Sewell. He was the dad of both of them. The bonny lad and me first bairn, they're full brothers. That's what ah mean when ah said ah loved him. Kept to him. Ah wasn't gonnae tell ye, but there ye gan.' Her eyes dimmed for a moment with pain. Her voice grew toneless. 'He was good to me, and the babby. Made sure that the babby was looked after when he went inside. That's why he gave him to his dad. Knew ah couldn't cope. What with the drugs an' all. But he wanted him looked after.' She sighed. 'If only ah'd . . . we could have been like a proper family. All four o' wor. The other pregnancies . . . ah got rid . . . but his two ah had. Because ah love him.'

The old man coughed. He shook convulsively, before seeming to master himself. 'Ah'm an auld man now, Mary,' he murmured. 'Ah cannet take nee more in.' He looked at her properly for the first time since her arrival. His mouth gaped again with senility. This time it stayed open for a little longer. 'Ah'm an auld man now. The bonny lad, Sonny Gee, he's all there is for me now.' He lapsed into silence. The clock ticked. Frequently Joe looked over at the time with an anxious eye. 'He'll be back,' he whispered to himself. 'Any minute now, he'll be back.'

After a long time, Mary stood up. 'Ah'm staying at Audrey's,' she said. 'Ah've left Macca, and ah'm staying at Audrey's place. She's squeezed wor in, just to help me back on me feet. When the bonny lad comes back, will ye bring him there?'

'Yer bairn's wandering the streets o' Gateshead, man Mary man; are ye not gonnae help wor find him?'

Mary shrugged. 'He always comes back.' She crossed the room and opened the door to the passage. 'Ah'll be at Audrey's until ah find a one o' them refuges. Send him when he comes back.'

'He'll be allowed in with ye an' all, will he?'

'Aye.'

An uncharacteristic pleading tone lightened the old man's voice. 'This refuge, is it gonnae be in the area or . . . or are yus

gonnae take me grandbairn away from wor again? Divven't
... divven't ... divven't ...' Joe's mouth opened and closed
decrepitly.

Mary bowed her head. 'Dad man, ah'm sorry,'

'Eh?'

'For what ah did. Oh, ah kna, it wasn't just one thing. Ah
kna ...' She faltered. 'For everything. Ah'm sorry for everything. Well. Ah'll gan now.'

She was nearly at the front door when the old man called
out to her. 'Ah want to kna summink.'

She turned.

Patiently she waited for his breathing to stop wheezing. 'It
was the day yer mam died,' the old man said at last.

'Eh?'

'Just tell wor this last thing, then that'll be it. Nee more.'

'What?' asked Mary breathlessly.

'Yer mam asked for summink. And ye didn't give her it.
And ah want to kna why.'

'What ...'

'It was the only thing she ever asked ye for, and ye didn't
give it to her. After all she'd done for ye an' all.'

'Ah divven't kna what ye are gannin' on aboot.'

'This is what ah'm gannin' on aboot.' Joe inhaled deeply,
but the words were a struggle. 'She wanted to see yus before
she passed on. She wanted us both with her. She had summink
to say. Ah was there. Ye weren't. She asked for ye a dozen
times, but yus didn't come.' The old man stared levelly at his
daughter. 'Ye let yer mother die before she could say her last
words to ye, and for that, God forgive me, ah have not been
able to forgive ye.'

'But Dad,' whispered Mary, 'how could ah have been
there?'

'What d'ye mean? Ah sent for ye. But ye still nivver came.'

'But how could ah have been there?' Mary repeated.

The old man shook his head. His words were almost tender.

272

'Mary lass, it's too late for lies or trying to talk yer way oot o' things. Ah'll be dying meself soon, and before ah gan ah'd like to kna why ye didn't come for yer mam.'

There was a pause. 'Didn't ye kna?' Mary asked. 'Ah thought ye knew.'

Joe shook his head. 'Ah just kna that ye didn't come.'

'But ah was having the bairn.' A silence followed Mary's words.

'The bairn?' mumbled the old man.

'That's why ah couldn't come.' Shivering slightly, she avoided his strange, bewildered expression. 'Ah was on me way to her. Ah swear doon ah was when me waters broke.' Now she looked at her father. 'It was a difficult birth. There was bleeding an' that. Infection. We were in a one o' them special wards. Ah was kept in for days so ah missed the funeral. They didn't tell wor aboot me mam until ah was oot o' danger mesel'. As soon as ah was, ah came to see ye. Ah did, Dad, ah came to see ye. To explain.'

'And ah wouldn't let ye in.' Joe's lips fluttered. 'Ah wouldn't give ye the chance to explain. Ah wouldn't open the door.'

'Aye. When ah came roond to explain, ye wouldn't speak to wor. Ye wouldn't even open the door. But that's how it happened. The bonny lad, it was because of him that ah couldn't come.'

Joe stared at his daughter, his lips trembling. 'The bonny lad?'

'Aye. When she was dying, he was being born.'

'Mary,' said the old man when he could talk. 'Gan now.'

'But . . .'

An unbearable sadness filled his rheumy eyes. 'Just gan.'

When Mary had gone Joe leant back lifelessly against the front door. After a while he trudged back into the sitting room, leaving the door open behind him. He stood in the middle of the room, staring at the red cowboy hat that lay on the table. Walking over to it, he laid a hand on the brim. But there was no feeling in his hand, and puzzled, he removed it from the hat. He looked down at his boots. They were covered in soil from the allotment and mud from the Team.

Angry and puzzled by the dirt, he sat down, and without taking off the boots, began to polish them. But he could not grip the brush with any strength and the bristles brushed uselessly against the leather. With mounting frustration he clashed the brush against them, but it was still no good, and dropping the brush, he scooped his fingers into the polish and began to smear it on the boots. His body jerked wildly as he continued to gouge at the dirt, but he made no impact. His fingers would hardly obey him, and he fell still, gazing down at the encrusted mud in utter defeat.

It was some time later that he remembered the note. Joe reached down but couldn't negotiate his fingers into his pocket. Both hands were as unresponsive as meat, and even when he had struggled to get the paper out, it fell, still folded, from his hand. He stared down at it dumbly. Sighing, he began to lower himself to his knees.

'Ah kna ah'm special, but ye divven't have to bow doon before wor.'

'Eh?'

'Ha'way, man, Joe, what ye deein' doon there?' The face that looked up at Ronny was confused, old and anxious. The tone in Ronny's voice grew serious. 'Are ye all right?'

'What d'ye want?' demanded Joe querulously.

'Ah want to kna what ye are deein' on yer hands and knees.'

'Have ye taken to walking into folks' sitting rooms withoot knocking?' The old man swallowed irritably. 'Help us up then.'

'Nee way,' said Ronny, backing away. 'Ah kna what ye're like if anyone tries to help ye. Anyway, yer front door was open. Ah thought yus'd been done awer again.'

'Forget aboot that. Get us up. Aye, and that piece of paper

an' all.' Shrugging, Ronny leant down. He hesitated, embarrassed by the strange look on his friend's face. 'Ha'way, then,' barked Joe.

'Where's the bonny lad?' asked Ronny, as he hoisted his friend to his feet with a grunt. 'What's the matter with yer hands, man Joe, they've swollen reet up.'

Joe looked down at them. 'They're as dead as ham,' he mused, then added forcefully: 'And the paper. Get us that piece of paper an' all, can't ye? It's probably from that Gemma lass. She's always sending wor notes and that. Reminders she calls them. Things she's noticed ah need.' Joe suddenly grew angry. His voice became tetchy as it grew to a shout. 'But ah divven't need nee help me. Ah divven't need nee nowt! Ah wish they'd just leave us alone. Why won't they just leave me alone?'

Quietening as abruptly as he had been aroused, Joe stared over at Ronny. Their eyes met. The younger man quailed before the blankness which was staring at him in confusion. Joe went into the kitchen.

'Summink's gannin' on roond here,' Ronny called from the sitting room as he picked up the piece of paper. 'Ah met Audrey before, and she was away with it. And now ye. Are ye sure yus're areet?' There was no reply. 'Audrey wanted to kna where ye were. Wanted to kna where the bonny lad was. Heard her knocking at yer door fit to cave it in. Ye must have just missed her. Ah wouldn't mind but ah was gonnae ask her to gan oot to the pictures and she did a runner. Just took off. She was, like, man, wild, y'kna. Can ah use yer facilities?' asked Ronny, stopping abruptly. He belched. 'Too many cups o' tea.'

'Aye,' Joe called back distractedly.

At that moment there was a knock at the back door so faint as to be almost imperceptible. Puzzled, Joe stared at the door, his eyes studying where the wood had been mended after the break-in. Slowly he opened the door.

It had grown darker with the lengthening of the afternoon into evening and at first Joe could see nobody. Then he looked down the yard. There, skulking under the tall wall, with his head down, stood the boy.

For a while neither of them moved, as though they were unaware of each other; then at the same time they both looked up. 'Ye came back,' the old man managed to say at last.

'Aye,' Sonny Gee nodded.

Relief coursed visibly through the old man's body. He had to steady himself by leaning against the door jamb. 'Ye came back.'

'Ah came roond the backyards. Y'kna, like what Audrey does.'

'Ye came back.' A smile softened the worn leather of the old man's face, smoothing away the gaunt, haunted look of senility. The wheezing in his breath eased. 'When ah said . . .' Joe began, 'that yus had to gan. Well, ye divven't. Ah want ye to stop here. Always.' Slowly, the old man walked across the yard to the wall. He stopped a single pace away from Sonny Gee, and lifting a hand, reached out.

Sonny Gee studied the hand carefully. 'That auld coal's knackt yer hands, good and proper,' he said tenderly.

Joe's hand shook badly, the fingers were utterly lifeless. The hand came closer and closer to the boy until at last it was within skin's breadth of his face. A few moments passed, and then the tip of one bent finger touched the child's soft cheek. The finger rested there for a while as the two of them stared at each other. A strange, almost peaceful look transfigured the wrinkles on the old man's face.

'So are ye gonnae tell wor what's gannin' on roond here then or what?' Ronny asked, appearing in the doorway. 'There yus are, Sonny Gee. Will ye tell us what's to do, bonny lad, 'cos ah cannet get nee sense from him?'

With a smile, the old man slowly lowered his hand and walked back across the yard into the cottage, the boy following him. Ronny stood aside for them both. 'Have ah got body odour or what?' Ronny quizzed the yard rhetorically. Lifting an arm, he sniffed his armpit. 'Smells areet to me.' With a shrug he went inside too. 'At least ye're smiling now, Joe. For a minute ah thought ye'd gone a bit funny.'

The old man was sitting in the armchair, the boy on the settee. A calm contentment had come over them both. 'Mebbes this'll shed some light on the matters,' said Ronny, sitting down beside the boy. 'This note. Mebbes it can make sense of it all.' Wafting the piece of paper about, Ronny coughed. 'Ye started smoking, Joe? Stinks of smoke in here.'

'Eh?' demanded Joe suddenly.

'Ah asked if ye'd taken up the tabs . . .'

'Not that,' said the old man, shaking his head. 'The note. What's it say?'

Ronny quickly scanned it. 'It's just short. Not from Gemma.' His face lit up. 'It's from Audrey. Ah can tell by the handwriting. She signs it off at the end an' all, mind.'

'Will ye just read it to wor. Ah'd read it mesel', but ah cannet find me glasses.'

'Well, they're just there,' replied Ronny rapidly, pointing at where the steel frames could just be seen poking from Joe's cardigan pocket. 'Where they always are.'

'Ah cannet get them on, all right!' burst the old man. 'Ah cannet manage them with me hands. So will ye just read the perishing note.'

'Definitely back to normal,' laughed Ronny. He held up the letter. ' "Dear Joe." ' Ronny paused. 'That's how it starts, like . . .'

'Ye are gonnae be the death of me, Ronny man.'

'Give wor a chance, give wor a chance.' Ronny composed himself. ' "Hide the bonny lad. On no account let him come to mine," ' he read. 'Shocking spelling,' he added, before continuing. ' "Don't let him go nowhere." And not much grammar neither . . . "And don't keep him at yours." ' Ronny held the paper up. 'Doesn't give ye much choice there, bonny lad, does it?' Tilting the piece of paper up, Ronny studied it through screwed eyes. 'Hold on, there's two more words. One says Audrey, and the other says . . . it's hard to make out . . . it's underlined twice . . . Whatta. Is that a word, whatta? Or is it Wacca? Aye, mebbes it's Wacca. That's a cricket groond in Australia. What's Audrey kna aboot cricket groonds in Australia? Unless . . . What is this?' Ronny yanked at his ponytail in his confusion, sending it swinging across his shoulder blades like a pendulum. His face darkened suddenly. He threw an anxious glance at Sonny Gee. 'Can ah have a quick word with ye, Joe?'

'Ah wish ye would.'

'No, ah mean . . .' he darted his eyes at the boy. 'It's aboot summink to dee with . . .'

'Oot with it, man, what's the matter with yus?'

'Ah'm not playing nee more games of hide and seek, me,' said the boy, folding his arms.

Ronny yanked on his ponytail with gusto. 'It's feedin' time,' he said with a sudden burst of energy. 'Ha'way, bonny lad. Gan and get them crickets.' The large man bounced over to the spider tank.

'But it isn't a week,' said Sonny Gee. 'And ye said that thems doon at the Spider Society say . . .'

'Stuff thems! They think they kna it all! But ah kna spiders, and wor Creeping Jenny's famished.' Ronny checked himself, and forced a lighter tone. 'Hurry up then, lad.' Opening up the tank, Ronny took out the spider. 'Yer crickets are in the coalhoose, aren't they?'

'Belter,' said the boy, skipping through to the kitchen.

Ronny turned urgently to Joe. 'It's not Wacca. It's Macca. Audrey wants ye to hide the bonny lad away because of Macca.'

'Macca? What does he want with him?'

'Ye kna,' said Ronny. He dropped his voice. 'The muling. He wants him to carry his drugs, man.'

There was a brief, ominous silence, abruptly shattered by the old man trying to push himself with all his might from the armchair. With a wild burst of energy, he managed to lever himself up. Staggering, he was just able to keep his balance. 'Will he come here?'

'From what ah've heard he'll gan anywhere for what he wants.' Ronny suddenly cried out. 'That friggin' spider's got a bite on it like a dog.' Juggling the spider gingerly, he turned to Joe. 'Does he kna the bonny lad's at yours?'

'The world and his wife knas.'

'Ah'll take him to mine then,' Ronny replied. 'He won't kna to look there even if he's foond oot that he's been staying at yours. He cannet stay here because if Macca finds him . . .'

At that moment Sonny Gee walked in. 'Eh?' he asked, clutching the jar of crickets.

Taking the jar and setting it on the table, Joe turned quickly to the bonny lad. 'Gan with Ronny.'

The boy's eyes were wide with incomprehension. 'Ye sending me away?'

'Ye've got to gan with Ronny. But just for a little while until . . .'

'But ah want to stay here,' Sonny Gee said, in his anguish biting his bottom lip.

The old man sighed. 'There's nee time for questions, he could be here any moment. Just dee as ah say.' Joe turned to Ronny. 'Take him to yours.' Having put the spider back in the tank, Ronny took the boy by the shoulders and without a word began propelling him to the passage. 'Hold on,' said the old man. 'Gan the back way, we cannet take any risks. He might be seen gannin' doon the terrace.'

'Ah divven't want to gan neewhere,' the boy said.

'Ye cannet stay here. Macca'll get ye!' bellowed Joe.

A strange look had come into the child's eyes. 'Ah'm staying

here,' he said through clenched teeth. 'Ah'm not gannin'
neewhere. Ah'm not scared of Macca, me. Ah had that lad
from Parsonage Road. Ah panned him in the goolies. Ah'll dee
the same to Macca.'

Ronny shook his head sadly. 'Not gannin' back to yer auld
tricks, are ye, bonny lad?'

The boy began shaking with rage. 'Ah'm not scared of him,
ah'm not scared of neebody. Ah'll get him. Ah'll gan to the
bedsit and ah'll kill him.'

'WILL YE JUST GET RID OF THAT BAIRN
BEFORE AH HAVE TO DEE IT MESELF!' roared Joe.

Stepping over to the boy, Ronny swept him into his arms.
'Ah'm sorry, bonny lad,' Ronny said. 'There's nee time to
explain.'

Sonny Gee wriggled, fought, kicked and bit like a caught
weasel, but Ronny did not let him go. The boy grabbed the
back of the settee and it was dragged across the room. He
clutched desperately at the glass door which crashed against the
wall as he was pulled from it. And his fingers scuttled uselessly
against the draining board as they sought a hold on its smooth
metal. 'Ye said ye weren't gonnae send wor away!' the boy
screamed wretchedly.

'Ha'way,' Ronny grunted as he hoisted the struggling child
into the backyard. 'He's not sending yus away.'

'Let wor gan back then,' wept the boy.

'Ah cannet. It's Macca, man. Ah cannet.'

'Ah'm gonnae kill him,' Sonny Gee sobbed. 'Macca. Ah'm
gonnae kill him.'

Holding him, Ronny climbed over the low walls, down to
his own yard.

'Areet then, Ronny?' called a voice as Ronny gingerly
negotiated the last wall.

Ronny sighed and turned his back so as to conceal the boy,
who was silently, breathlessly weeping. 'Now then, Peggy.'

'Ah thought that was ye gannin' awer the backs.'

'Aye.'

The round shape of Peggy could be seen leaning against one of the yard walls. Her arms were folded over a tightly buttoned housecoat. 'And was that that Joseph O'Brien, shouting fit to wake the dead?'

'Ah divven't kna, Peggy, was it?'

'Well, ye should kna, Ronny, ye've just left him, clattering awer the backs like a flaming donkey derby. And is that cheeky whelp with ye an' all?' Peggy craned to see round Ronny's bulk which was screening the boy from her. 'If ye had any sense ye'd leave that rubbish alone. He's like his granda, nee good for nothing.'

'And ye,' Sonny Gee shot back, darting out from behind Ronny. 'Ah'll dee ye an' all, ye auld witch.'

Peggy paused deliberately and peered down the yards. She sneered. 'Oh, he is with ye, is he? Ah'm sure it was him what helped them rob wor. There's been people looking for him, y'kna. One of them what used to ride the bike. Even been here asking for him. Ah'm just about getting sick of it.' She paused. 'At least now ah kna where he is, so ah can tell him next time he . . .'

'Aye, well, see ye,' Ronny interrupted her in mid-flow, and he began to usher the boy towards his own back door. But the boy twisted free from his grip and threw himself over the wall to the next yard. 'Now see what ye've done, ye hard-faced bitch,' shouted Ronny. Sprinting, he vaulted the wall in pursuit of the child. 'Sonny Gee, come back!'

'Ye'll rupture yersel', ye fat idiot,' called Peggy.

'What aboot Creeping Jenny?' cried Ronny as he chased the boy. 'Come back. We've got to feed Creeping Jenny.'

When Ronny and Sonny Gee had disappeared, Peggy stared curiously down at Ronny's yard. Looking about, she pulled her housecoat tighter round herself, then went inside.

Back in the sitting room of his cottage, the old man had not moved. His eyes darted about wildly, but his body remained still. Then, as though coming to himself, he moved quickly through the room, went down the passage, and pausing only to pick up his new stick, left the house.

He strode down the cut. A fresh piece of graffiti had been daubed on the fence behind the lamp-post. It said: *Mally Johnson The Grass.* Beside it was a little picture of a figure dangling from the gallows. Joe stared at it with uncomprehending eyes as he passed.

The bus came after a longer than usual wait, and Joe was trembling with agitation as he boarded. He walked past without paying. 'Hey,' called the driver. 'Ha'way.' Coming back, the old man just managed to lift his trouser pocket and upend some coins on to the coin tray. 'Charming,' said the driver, bending down to retrieve the coins that had spilt out of the metal plate. 'Hey,' he called, 'divven't yus want yer change then?' The old man did not turn round. Reaching a seat, he lowered himself into it. The driver opened his little door, and came down the aisle. 'Ye ignorant . . .' he started, but stopped abruptly when he saw Joe's hands hanging lifelessly over the little metal bar on the seat in front of him. 'Here's yer change and yer ticket,' he finished with a compassionate smile. Hearing his voice, the old man looked up, glancing at him emptily. 'Ah'll just put them in yer pocket then,' the driver said. Joe watched him expressionlessly, following the coins dumbly as they were put back into his pocket. 'Anyone else what wants to tip wor,' announced the driver as he went back down the aisle and ensconced himself behind the wheel again, 'is more than welcome to dee so.'

Following the old colliery line down the hill, the bus rattled across Gateshead, running under the Dunston Rocket tower block and over the River Team. It was evening and children played in groups beside the road. When the bus pulled in at the parade of shops, the old man was already standing, ready to get off. Mechanically, he waited for the door to shudder open, and then disembarked. At the flats the lift was out of order, so he began climbing the stairs. Every so often the tip of his new stick sounded out forlornly as it brushed ineffectively against a stair. Pausing halfway up, he waited for his breathing to grow steady enough for him to continue, before pushing up again. 'Who is it?' an anxious voice called out after he had rung the bell.

'It's Joe,' he replied.

'Thank frigg for that,' sighed Audrey as she opened the door. Stepping past him on to the walkway, she leant over the parapet and scanned the view. Down below, a group of children were playing hopscotch; an ice-cream van playing 'Greensleeves' cut through the sound of their voices. 'Ha'way in then,' Audrey said breathlessly. Joe followed her inside. 'Where the hell have ye been?' she demanded. She looked past Joe. 'And the bairn's not with ye?'

'He's with Ronny,' Joe replied.

Audrey shot the words like bullets. 'Macca's after him.'

'Aye, so ye said.'

'It's for the drugs. Mary told wor. That's why she's left him. It was to save the lad. She didn't kna that Macca would want him tonight.'

'What we gonnae dee?'

'For a start we've got to keep Sonny Gee hid. Until we work summink oot.' Audrey pulled distractedly at a pendulous pink earring. 'Ye say he's at Ronny's?'

'Aye.'

'And neebody saw him gannin' there?'

'Na. Ah sent him awer the backs.'

'Then we've bought worselves some time.' Audrey went over to the sofa and sank into it. 'Ah've sent all the bairns away. They were here when he came.' Shuddering, she paused. She rubbed her face with both hands. When she looked up, her cheeks were drained of all colour as though from shock. 'He just aboot kicked the door in. And when ah told him that the bonny lad wasn't here, he . . .' Audrey broke off. 'So ah sent them all away, just in case he came back. He means trouble. That's plain to see.' Audrey mused. 'He's evil.'

'But why did he come here?' asked the old man.

"Cos he knew Mary would come here after she'd left him. He thought the bairn'd be here an' all. He wanted to know where he was. Asked aboot ye an' all. Whether the lad was stopping with ye. Where ye lived. Ah said to him, d'yus think an auld gadgie like that could look after that little lad? There's nee way could he. But ah divven't kna whether he believed wor. Ah still wouldn't tell him where ye lived, mind.'

'So he's still looking for him?'

Audrey nodded.

'Reet.' The old man turned and walked back to the door.

'Where ye gannin'?' Audrey asked.

'Ah just came here to find oot what was happening.'

'And noo?'

'Noo, ah'm gannin' back to the lad.'

'But we divven't kna what we're deein'.'

'Ah kna what ah'm deein'. Ah'm staying with the bonny lad.'

'He's dangerous. Macca. He's killed more than one man, ye kna.'

The old man closed his eyes tightly. His face grimaced as he slapped his forehead. Abruptly he opened his eyes. 'The caravan,' he spluttered.

'Eh?'

'The caravan, the caravan!' he exclaimed. 'We've nee time to lose.'

'What yus gannin' on aboot?'

'Yer caravan,' Joe fired back. 'Where is it?'

'Newbiggin by the Sea.'

'That's where ah'll gan. Ah'll take him there tonight. Ah'll take him there noo.' The old man yanked the door open. 'We've got to get him away from Gatesheed.'

'Hold on, hold on,' said Audrey.

'We cannet hold on, man, it's an emergency.' Joe stepped outside.

'Who's gonnae take him?' demanded Audrey, bounding up from the sofa to the door.

'Me.'

'How yus gonnae get there?'

'Bus,' returned Joe, bewildered.

'It's too late. The last bus has already went, man.'

With a shrug, Joe set off down the walkway. 'Ah'll get a taxi.'

'And where ye gonnae get that kind of money from?'

'Eh?'

'It's miles away. It'll cost a fortune.'

'Ronny'll take wor.'

'Ronny?'

The old man turned. 'Aye. He's got a car.'

'And ye think that auld banger'll get ye to the end of the street, nivver mind the coast?'

'Look,' said the old man, desperately, 'ah divven't mind how ah get there. Ah'll hitch-hike . . . ah'll bloody lay doon in the road until someone picks wor up if that's what's needed to keep that little lad safe.'

Audrey's bare feet padded on the concrete as she ran to the old man. 'Think aboot it, man Joe. And if yus get him there, then what ye gonnae dee?'

'What's the matter with ye, Audrey?' His voice rose. 'Anyone would think that ye wanted Macca to catch the bairn!'

'Ah'm just trying to be practical,' replied Audrey, her own voice growing loud in turn. 'Ah mean what yus gonnae dee once ye get up there? It's not exactly a palace that caravan, ye kna. In fact, it's knackt oot. How ye gonnae keep warm at night, what ye gonnae eat? It's nee place for an auld man and a bairn. One of the windows is smashed, there's a leak, and the toilet's miles away . . .' Breaking off, Audrey stared at Joe.

'What else can ah dee?' he asked helplessly, then he began walking again.

Audrey watched him until he reached the end of the walkway. 'Give wor a second, cannet ye?'

'Eh?'

'Ah'll come up with ye. Ah'll just get ready.'

'This is nee time for make-up, man Audrey. Macca might be at the cottages reet noo.'

Audrey disappeared back into the flat. Tapping the stick impatiently against the concrete of the walkway, Joe leant against the parapet and looked down. The ice-cream van had driven away, but its music could still be heard playing faintly. The children played on, their voices clear in the evening air.

She came back with a bulging bin liner. 'Ah've brought a few things.'

Joe had already reached the stairs. 'Ha'way,' he called. 'Let's gan.'

They were running: Audrey's heels clacking and the old man's boots thudding on the pavement. A bemused dog watched them pass, and then trotted after them for a few yards. When they reached the bus stop, Audrey brought out a mobile phone. 'Ah'll give the bairns a quick ring. Lucky ah got mesel' a one o' these, like. Just got it yesterday.'

'Where they stopping, like?' gasped Joe, out of breath.

'At Gemma's. Ah'll work oot what to dee with them tomorrow. They'll be areet for the night. And ah gave Mary a key. She'll be able to let herself in when she comes back from looking at that refuge. It's the bonny lad we need to get sorted.'

'Audrey,' said Joe quietly. 'Ta.'

Taking off the false nail from her forefinger, Audrey dextrously punched in a long chain of numbers. 'Neebody's answering,' she said, her face twisted with worry. 'Mebbes they've just popped to the shop or summink. Ah'll ring them

286

again in a minute.' Clipping the nail back on, she pondered the mobile phone anxiously.

The bus came, and the two of them boarded. The bus rattled its way back to Lobley Hill. For a long time the old man's breathing rasped from him with the effort of running. The bus stops were thronged with people dressed for a night on the town. The men were dressed in short-sleeved checked shirts hanging loosely outside their trousers, the women beside them wearing the merest belt of a dress, the stitch of a top draped over anatomies showing orange after hours spent standing in tan-tubes. They were in high spirits anticipating the frenzy of the night ahead. Joe looked at them through the window as they passed, his eyes glazed with confusion. 'Sometimes ah wonder what country it is ah'm living in,' he said slowly, when he could talk. 'Everything's changed. Ah feel like a foreigner.'

'Ah wish ye'd forgive Mary,' Audrey said.

'Ah've outlived me time,' said Joe simply.

'Na,' said Audrey, shaking her head. 'Times divven't change. People stay the same. We're all still gannin' aboot the exact same business, we've just got slightly different ways of deein' it, that's all.' She paused to study Joe. 'Life's too short. And in the end folk always need to forgive and forget.'

'All ah need is to get that bairn to the caravan.'

'He means the world to ye, doesn't he?' said Audrey, narrowing her eyes.

Joe looked at her solemnly. A smile played about his pale lips. 'Na, Audrey, he means more to us than that.'

In the long silence that followed, Audrey took out the mobile phone, and having once more detached the nail, again punched in the numbers. Her eyes darted anxiously as she waited. 'Still neeone there,' she said, puzzled.

Having climbed the hill, the bus skirted the redeveloped colliery land over which the darkness of night was gathering, and then turned the corner where the church stood. Getting out, Audrey and the old man reached the cut. They walked without speaking, anxiously casting about for any sign of Macca. At the lamp-post, Audrey paused. 'That was what happened to the last one,' she said, gesturing at the freshly daubed graffiti: *Mally Johnson The Grass*.

'Eh?' asked the old man.

'The kids told us aboot it. That Mally lad with the bike, he's in hospital with two broken arms. Wanted to get oot of it all. But ye divven't get oot.'

Emerging out of the cut, they walked down the row of cottages. Audrey was about to carry on past Joe's home to Ronny's, when the old man restrained her. 'Gan through mine and then doon the backs, man.'

'Bang gans another pair o' me best stockings,' joked Audrey.

Joe hadn't opened his door before they heard the shouting. They turned. Ronny was sprinting heavily up the row towards them. 'He's gone,' he gasped, reaching them. 'Ah've been after him, but ah couldn't catch him. He went up the cut and . . .' Ronny was barely able to get his breath out. 'The bonny lad. He's gone.'

13

Sonny Gee sprinted down the row of cottages and into the cut. Reaching the lamp-post, he threw his arms around it and sobbed violently. Chest heaving and gulping at the air, the boy sank to the ground. 'Ah'm gonnae kill him,' he whispered in between sobs. 'Ah'm gonnae kill him.' Fumbling with his sock, he brought out the lighter and flicked its flame into life. 'Ah'm gonnae kill him,' he repeated as he stared at the light, the words toneless as a mantra. The shadow cast by the flame climbed the fence. The words: *Mally Johnson The Grass* flashed in the unsteady light, while on the gallows the little figure seemed to jerk fitfully. 'Ah'm gonnae kill him,' he repeated.

Suddenly there was the sound of a foot scrunching on the ash of the path. Slipping the lighter back into his sock, Sonny Gee listened to the noise for a moment, and then darted behind the wheelie bin with animal agility. The steps were heavy, and getting closer. Sonny Gee held his breath and waited motionlessly. The footsteps reached him and then passed on. The boy did not move. The footsteps built again as the solitary walker came back. He paused under the lamp-post. Then set off again. Peering out furtively, the boy recognised the shape of Ronny disappearing round the corner. But still the boy did not reveal himself. He waited again until he was certain that he was alone and then emerged from his hiding place. 'Ah'm gonnae kill him,' he whispered.

'Areet there, bonny lad,'

Jumping with shock, Sonny Gee turned to face the person speaking to him. There was a silence as he gazed at the body blocking his way up the cut. The face was hidden behind a slash mask. Utter terror coursed through him momentarily, then he set his face hard and pulled himself to his full height. 'Ah'm not scared of ye,' he spat out.

'Ah kna someone who wants to see ye.'

'Ah'm not scared o' nee Springy Jack lad. Ah can have ye any day.'

'Ha'way, dee yersel' a favour and make it easy on yersel',' said Jimmy. 'There's already one doon.' He gestured at the graffiti on the fence. 'Be a good mule.'

The boy stepped back, but before he could run, he found his arms pinioned behind him. He screamed, but rough hands covered his mouth and his struggle was silenced by a powerful blow to the head. Rigid with horror, he allowed himself to be taken down the cut to where the motorbike was waiting. 'Ye taking wor doon the pit, Spring Jack?' Sonny Gee asked.

'Aye, reet doon to the pits,' replied the masked youth as the engine of the motorbike roared into life.

Hoisting the boy in front of him, Jimmy spurted the bike off down the road, its engine shrieking. A bus pulled out from a stop and the motorbike just managed to dodge it. Revving and spluttering, the bike wove through traffic and juddered its way down Lobley Hill. Then abruptly it swerved off the road and headed across the old coke works. Night was already falling over this wasteland, but Sonny Gee's eyes darted about the darkness with the swiftness of a trapped animal. He was waiting for the precise moment before jumping.

He watched the place approach where, fed by a leak from a culvert, the grass grows tall and soft, and the hardness of the earth is cushioned by ferns. Falling inert but tensing his legs on the fuel tank, Sonny Gee felt Spring-heeled Jack's grip slacken on him. The bike bounced over the earth ramps made by local children for their pushbikes to jump, and the grip on the boy grew even slacker. Just as the bike was sailing over the largest ramp, Sonny Gee leapt.

The wind was knocked from his body as he hit the ground.

He rolled for a few yards over the soft grass, then sprawled himself to the entrance of the culvert and pulled himself inside. The engine of the motorbike could still be heard for a while and then it fell silent. Jimmy's frustrated voice echoed after him.

It was a long tunnel, but he knew it well, and when it began to narrow he fell to his hands and knees without a moment's pause and crawled. Hauling himself over any obstacles, he moved quickly, not stopping at the squeaking of rats, which ran just ahead of him. He was soaked when he reached the other end, and the head and face which emerged were grazed where he had misjudged the height and width of the tunnel.

The pipe of the culvert hung out over the River Team. The dark water flowed past ten feet or so below, while above it, the top of the vertically excavated concrete bank could just be seen. Gingerly, Sonny Gee peered out, his head framed by the mouth of the pipe. For a few moments he seemed daunted and closed his eyes. Then, wriggling free, he hoisted himself on to the pipe, and sitting astride it, inched his way towards the bank. Having pulled himself on to his feet, he began to clamber up the bank, his feet scrambling for toeholds in the smooth concrete, his hands flailing at the roots of the profuse vegetation.

At the top he rested for only an instant before he pulled himself to his feet, scaled a security fence and landed on a pavement at the other side. Back on the road once more, he climbed Bensham bank. It was night now, but the close-built houses, each one divided into the Tyneside Flats that are home to two families, and the narrow dusty streets of Bensham still held the heat of the day. Little groups of people lolled on the pavements outside their doors, arms and necks red after a day exposed in the sun. Their voices and the music of their radios hung heavily in the hot air, mixing with the sour tang of lager; no one seemed to notice the child slipping past them purposefully.

On reaching Old Parsonage Road, Sonny Gee burst into a sprint, not slowing down again until he had concealed himself once more in the deep shadows of the back alleys, where he threaded his way resolutely through the derelict houses.

He came to an overflowing skip. Climbing up on to it, he rifled through the rubble, scrabbling deeper and deeper, casting aside the pieces of concrete, the pram wheels and the sawn birch tree branches which grow in profusion between the splintering joins of old walls and glassless windows around about. At last he emerged from the rubble with an old sheet. Carefully, he ripped three pieces from the sheet, and then jumped from the skip.

He shot down a narrow passage between two garages, and emerged on to an unlit alley. The three strips of sheet fluttered as he ran down past the backyards.

When he reached one of the few backyards which still had a door, he stopped. He pushed his hand against the door, but it was locked. His eyes darted about quickly and spotting a wheelie bin he pushed it against the wall. Jumping on to it, he boosted himself on to the wall. Crouching there above the narrow alley, he was bathed in bright moonlight. The moon had risen high, forming silvery pools on the broken black tiles of the run-down houses. For a few more moments Sonny Gee was picked out by the moon's rays as he straddled the top of the wall, then he was gone into the shadows.

He landed skilfully on bent legs and ran across the yard to a little brick outhouse. The door was fitted with a hefty padlock. The boy lifted himself up on his tiptoes and pressed his face against the window to stare inside. A moment later a tinkle of shattering glass filled the yard. With a wary glance over his shoulder up at the house, he hauled himself through the broken window.

There were a number of large petrol cans stacked inside. Sonny Gee unscrewed the cap of one and lowered a strip of the sheet inside. Bringing the strip back out, he dangled it until the petrol had stopped dripping and then dipped a second piece in the container. He did the same thing with the third. Somewhere in the distance a dog began to bark. When he had dowsed all three strips of sheet in petrol, he stuffed them up his T-shirt and climbed back out of the window. Sliding the bolt from the door, he slipped back into the alley.

The barking of the dog faded as Sonny Gee carried on down the alley. The roofs of a large terrace came into view, the moonlight etching their stark silhouettes on the darkness. The boy slowed to stare up at them. Then squeezing through a narrow gap in the hoarding which blocked up a ground-floor window, he moved through a gutted house, emerging in an overgrown garden. There was no moonlight here. The gardens along the length of the large terrace formed a continuous thicket of scrub. Instinctively, Sonny Gee crouched low as he passed down them, the foliage touching and scratching at his face like strong, thin fingers. Above him towered the terrace whose house fronts seemed to glower down stiffly like the faces of the dead stacked rigid in a mortuary. Coming to an ancient holly tree, Sonny Gee hid himself beneath it. It was Clareville Place.

For a long time the boy stared up at the very top of the building in front of him. Time passed and his breathing eased, and still he gazed up patiently at the attic room of the house where a lone light burned. An owl hooted, its call a ghostly sound. And then at last he saw what he had come for. A heavy-set man appeared in the light of the attic room. The man stood there for a while, framed in the window, gazing out on to the night before disappearing back into the room. 'Ah'm gonnae kill him,' Sonny Gee hissed.

Breaking cover, Sonny Gee ran down the garden path of broken concrete slabs and reached the door of the bedsits. Silently, he pushed it open and slipped within.

There was not a sound. The silent darkness hung as heavily as the dust. From outside, the owl continued to hoot and then abruptly fell quiet, deepening the stillness yet further. On his tiptoes, Sonny Gee began to climb the stairs. Pressing himself closely against the wall, he slowly mounted the building. Only at the very top of the house was there any light. It was shining from under the door at the top of the last landing, and reached the lower stairs as a glimmer. The boy moved up through the darkness towards it, drawn like a moth.

He paused on the last step and stared at the light under the door. The light dimmed for a moment as somebody inside the room walked in front of it. Then it sprang back out again. A mobile phone rang out, the notes of its call skeletal. A voice answered. The boy took out the strips of sheet doused in petrol, and inched across the landing. Reaching the door, he laid the strips carefully against it, and then took out the lighter. 'Ah'm gonnae kill ye,' he breathed to himself as he flicked the flint of the lighter. The cold tongue of a flame licked the darkness.

14

'He just ran,' explained Ronny as he bumbled into the old man's sitting room behind Joe and Audrey. 'Ah've been up and doon the cut, but he's gone. It was when Peggy . . .'

'Peggy?' Joe interrupted him. 'What d'ye mean, Peggy?'

Ronny pulled nervously at his ponytail. 'She saw wor.'

'Shit cakes,' Audrey said. 'That's the last person we wanted to kna.'

'What's gonnae happen?' asked Ronny.

Joe shuffled over to the settee. Stooping, he picked up the red cowboy hat that the boy had left there. He stared at it for a few moments and then walked heavily over to the door. 'Hey,' called Ronny. 'Where ye gannin'?'

'To find him,' replied the old man simply.

'Where ye gannin'?' asked Audrey, following him down the passage. 'Hold on, man Joe. We need to plan this. Be systematic, like.' Joe turned. 'Ah'll pop next door and tell Elsie to stop in here in case he comes back,' Audrey said.

'And ah'll gan to the allotments,' put in Ronny. 'He likes it there.'

'There's nee time,' said Joe. 'Ah've got to find him.' Without another word, Joe opened the front door and stepped over the threshold. He was carrying the cowboy hat.

'Where are ye gannin'?' Audrey demanded.

'To get the bairn,' replied the old man, walking up the little path.

'Where ye gannin', but?'

'Wherever he is,' he called back.

'We need to kna where. Just in case . . .'

Joe did not stop as he hobbled up the terrace.

'Joe man,' cried Audrey. 'Ye'll dee yersel' in. Ye cannet keep this up.' Audrey turned to Ronny. 'Stop him.' But the old man had disappeared into the cut.

'Brilliant,' said Audrey to Ronny. 'If Macca gets hold of him, he'll kill him. That's two of them in danger noo.'

Just then the mobile phone rang, playing a metallic version of the theme tune from the film *Titanic*. Audrey grabbed it. 'Hello?' she bellowed, even though the phone was pressed hotly to her mouth. 'Why the frigg haven't ye been answering the phone?' she demanded. Without appearing to wait to hear the explanation, she continued breathlessly: 'Is everything all right? . . . Good.' She sighed deeply with relief. 'Where are yus then?' Suddenly, panic overwhelmed her. 'What's that ye're saying, yus're in the hospital? Yus're *all* in the hospital?' For a brief moment Audrey's arm fell limply to her side and with it the mobile phone. Rallying, she lifted the receiver back up to her face. 'Put yer cousin on. Put yer flamin' cousin on. Toni-Leigh, if ye divven't get yer cousin on that phone this instant then ah'll . . . is that ye, Terri-Leigh? Now what's happened? What are yous deein' in hospital?' Audrey's eyes bobbed apprehensively as she listened to Terri-Leigh's explanation. Relief flooded her features, followed by wonder, until her eyes closed with awe. 'Aye,' she said eventually. 'Stay there until yer mam comes for yus. Yus've already rang her? Good lass.' With a profound smile, Audrey put the phone away. She turned to Ronny. 'Gemma's had a little girl,' she said, her eyes glistening with happiness.

'That's nice,' grinned Ronny.

'Aye, in the middle of all of this, summink good's happened.' Audrey paused. 'He's a great-grandad then,' she said.

'Eh?'

'And the bonny lad's an uncle.'

'How's that?'

'How's that? Are ye on the same planet or what? Gemma's just had a little girl.'

'Ah kna, but what's that got to dee with owt?'

Audrey stared at Ronny. 'Ye mean ye divven't kna? Sometimes ah think men are a different species.' She took out a cigarette and lit it thoughtfully. 'Gemma had been seeing Sewell. Sewell's the father. Sewell, man. Ye kna, big lad Sewell. Him what did the newsagent.' Blowing out smoke, Audrey studied Ronny carefully. Ronny shrugged. 'Sewell's Joe's other grandbairn.'

'His other grandbairn?'

'Aye. Mary's first baby. Didn't yus even kna that?' Audrey tutted. 'Ye're a bit of an innocent, ye, aren't ye?'

Ronny pulled bashfully at his ponytail. 'Did Joe kna he had another grandbairn?'

Audrey shook her head. 'Joan didn't neither. Ye see, Mary telt wor and ah couldn't . . .' Audrey broke off. 'We've nee time to stand aboot gabbing. Ha'way, is that car of yours working?'

'Why?'

''Cos with that new babby now there's even more reason to save that little lad, and his great-daft-granda.'

They swept down the cut at the far end of the cottages and came out on a piece of rough ground on which stood three old garages. Ronny lifted up one of the garage doors and went inside. Audrey followed him, climbing into the car as Ronny opened the passenger door for her. Jumping into the driver's seat, he turned the ignition key and the engine spluttered fitfully into life. 'Audrey,' said Ronny, fiddling with the gears and beginning to back out of the garage. 'Ah kna this isn't the time, but ah want yus to kna that there's more to me than just exotic pets.'

Something twinkled in Audrey's eye. 'And Ronny, there's more to me than just looking after a tribe o' bairns.'

The car chugged down a narrow track and juddered on to

the road. 'Doesn't this gan nee faster?' demanded Audrey, anxiously drumming her fingers on the dashboard as the car shuddered past the red-brick church.

'Just be thankful it's gannin' at all. Any road. Where d'yus want wor to gan?'

'Ah divven't kna, just drive, and ah hope to God we find them.'

They drove on for a while aimlessly, up and down streets, turning back at blank ends, slowing as they passed waste ground, then abruptly Ronny stood on the brakes. The car phutted to a halt. As he turned the steering wheel, Ronny berated himself. 'Ah should have known.'

'What?'

'They're gannin' to Macca's, man. That's where the lad's gannin', and Joe an' all. Ah should have realised it earlier.'

'How d'yus kna?'

'They'll be there. Both of them.'

'But how d'yus kna?'

'He kept on saying it, didn't he? Ah'm gonnae kill him, ah'm gonnae kill him. Look, it doesn't matter. Just say ah've got bush eyes.' Ronny finished executing the hasty three-point turn and began motoring back the way they had come. 'We've got to get there first. If we divven't . . .' Ronny broke off. 'Cannet this thing gan nee faster?' he demanded in frustration.

'Take the dual carriageway,' said Audrey. 'It's quicker.'

The indicator light ticked as Ronny joined the dual carriageway. A heavy-goods vehicle thundered past, shaking the small car. They motored on. 'Frigg this for a game of soldiers,' said Ronny, his foot pressing down on the accelerator. The needle on the speedometer suddenly began to shake and the engine pink. A few moments later, the power failed and the car slowed. With a wail of exasperation, Ronny steered it on to the hard shoulder. It came to a stop twenty yards further on. 'Friggin' hell,' he shouted.

'That's it then,' said Audrey abruptly. 'Ah'm gonnae dee it.'

'Eh?'

Audrey took out her mobile phone and punched in three numbers.

'Who yus ringing?' Ronny asked.

'Pollis,' replied Audrey.

Ronny reached over and snatched the phone. 'Have ye gone mad? Ye kna what he does to grasses.'

A lorry thundered by and the features of Audrey's face were briefly illuminated. They were set hard. She took back the phone. 'What other choice have we got?'

'Ye've seen doon the cut,' spluttered Ronny. 'If ye gan to the pollis then Macca'll dee yus. He won't forget aboot it. He won't give up. He'll dee ye.'

'There's a new babby come into this world the day,' said Audrey softly. 'It's for her and the bonny lad that summink's got to be done. For her and all the rest of wor bairns. It's time someone took a stand.' The mobile phone bleeped as Audrey pushed the buttons. 'Hello?' she said. 'Aye, the pollis please.'

Jumping out of the car, Ronny went to the open bonnet. Heavy traffic sped by. With a sigh, Ronny began fiddling with the engine. 'Ha'way,' he pleaded. 'Ha'way. Big Al said yus'd just been serviced when ah bought ye. Ha'way.'

The old man had waited for a while at the bus stop, but no bus arrived, so he began walking. Constantly looking behind himself as he went, he descended the other side of Lobley Hill. He crossed the dual carriageway through the dank corridors of the subway, his breathing echoing in the long concrete tunnels, while the strip lights flickered above his head. On the fluorescent tube somebody had written: *Kaela 4 Swanny 2 gether 4 eva 4 years 2 come 2 young 4 sex 2 late its done.*

The old man had just reached the Team Valley when he heard the bus coming up behind him. He turned, and lifting his stick, waved it above his head in large circles. The bus slowed, but did not seem to be stopping, so he stepped out on to the road.

'What the hell ye deein', man?' the bus driver demanded as Joe clambered on board.

'It's supposed to be a hail-and-ride, isn't it?' he replied quietly.

'Aye, but ye divven't just step oot in front o' wor.'

'Ye weren't gonnae stop. Ah had to make ye stop.'

'Ye'll kill yersel' another time, man.'

'Ye stopped. That's all that matters. Ah had to make ye stop.'

The old man stared fixedly through the window as the bus bore him across the Team Valley. The windows rattled with the gradient of Bensham bank, and the engine juddered. Even the red cowboy hat vibrated slightly where it lay across his knees. Joe got out at Old Parsonage Road and walked right to the end of it. Without a moment's pause, he turned down one of the alleys. It was dark, but the moon lit his way. His breathing was shallow and painful, he was sweating profusely. He looked about uncertainly as he walked, but the network of lanes and small roads was like a maze, and after a while he seemed to lose his way. He carried on for some time, but when he found himself passing the same hulk of a burned-out car, he stopped in confusion. The moonlight caught his face as he stared around, his bewilderment mercilessly exposed in the cold silvery beams.

He had lost track of how long he had been wandering, and when the large terrace of bedsits suddenly loomed up harshly before him, towering above the shadow scrub of the gardens, he sighed in relief. A light shone from the very top of number 9. From somewhere in the midst of a group of tall lime trees, an owl called. Joe shuddered at the sound and stood there motionless. Only when it had fallen silent did he carry on down the path of broken concrete. Then he reached the building. The door was unlocked. Feeling the brim of the cowboy hat gently for a moment, he went inside.

15

There was a crash from downstairs and Sonny Gee jumped back from the door. The sudden sound echoed shockingly in the silence. He eased the pressure on the lighter's gas feeder and the flame died. The whites of the boy's eyes showed in the gloom as they stared fearfully across the landing. He waited anxiously, but he could hear nothing more. Still he waited, but the quietness had returned to the building.

He stared down at the three strips of sheet uncertainly, listening at the door for a long time. There was a click as he flicked the flint and the flame sprang out once more.

Suddenly Sonny Gee froze. There was someone slowly mounting the stairs. With incredible rapidity, the boy stuffed the pieces of sheet up his shirt and placed the lighter down his sock.

As though uncertain of the stairs, the steps paused below. There was no more movement for a long time and the boy began to think that they would come no higher. A whole minute passed, but then the footfalls began again. A quiet, cautious, inexorable tread on the uncarpeted wood. Sonny Gee's eyes darted strickenly as he looked about the little landing, but it was too late, the steps had reached the top floor.

It was Jimmy. The two of them stared at each other for an instant, then Sonny Gee bolted.

Taking him by surprise, he managed to knock the youth to one side, but was dragged to the ground by him. He flailed wildly and almost shot past him when a blow to his stomach immobilised him. Gasping for air, Sonny Gee peered up at the teenager. 'Ye're a proper divvy, ye,' said Jimmy. 'Ah thought ah was gonnae have to stand in for ye. But ye came here anyway.' He laughed, relief flooding his infantile features. 'Talk aboot dial-a-mule. Ye've delivered yersel' reet to the hoose.'

Dragging the child over the landing and up the last few stairs to Macca's door, Jimmy knocked softly. There was a pause. 'Who the frigg is it?' Macca demanded edgily.

'Room service,' called Jimmy. 'One mule.'

The door was thrown open. 'Ah thought yous'd shot through,' Macca said. He was wearing no shirt, and his upper body was broad in the darkness. 'Ah was just working oot which hand to break first. Or mebbes ah'd cut yer balls off.'

'Nee bother,' put in Jimmy.

Macca took out a wad of notes from his back pocket, he peeled off one and gave it to Jimmy. 'There ye gan. Now frigg off oot of it.'

Macca turned to Sonny Gee. He gestured at the room with his head. Standing up, the boy tensed his body. For a moment he appeared to be about to hurl himself at Macca. But the huge man threw out a hand and grabbed him by the wrist. Pulling him into the room, Macca closed the door, and turning the lock, put the key in his pocket. Without a word, he pulled the child across the room to where the cot stood. 'In ye gan,' said Macca, hoisting Sonny Gee up and placing him inside the cot. 'Doon,' he growled. The boy did not move. 'Ah said doon.' Macca picked up the wardrobe door which was propped up against a wall, and pressed it down on the boy's head. Sonny Gee raised his arms to push up against him but the force was too great and, his knees buckling, he dropped down as the door was placed on top of the cot. 'Listen,' said Macca, squatting down to face him through the bars. 'Ye stay in there until ah get yus oot. Then ye come with me and dee as ah say when ah say. If ye divven't . . .'

'Ah'm not scared o' ye,' hissed Sonny Gee.

Macca smiled. In the half-light, the marks of his neck tattoos appeared even more like the weals raised by a hanging rope. His eyes were lifeless.

Standing up, Macca went over to the bed and picked up a large joint of cannabis. He lit it and inhaled deeply. 'We've got a few hours. And ah divven't want to hear a squeak from ye. Understand? Ah said understand?' Reaching into a corner, Macca took up a metal mop bucket and put it on top of the cot. 'Ye kna how it gans,' he said. 'If ah hear so much of a rattle from that, then . . .' Macca broke off. 'Only this time it won't just be ye. It'll be that auld grave dodger an' all. Yer granda.' He picked up the mop, its wiry material flopping about like the hair of a head as he mimed throttling it. Holding it rigid for a moment, he then threw it down. 'Lie doon there, granda,' he smirked.

Although his body stayed still in its cage, a desperate rage flared in the boy's eyes as he watched Macca walk over to the bed. Lying down, the heavy man smoked his joint. He cradled a bottle of whisky, and every time he took a sip, his lips smacked loudly. 'Ah'll hear ye,' said Macca suddenly, his speech beginning to slur a little. 'Divven't think ah won't. Ye move a muscle and ah'll hear ye. So let's keep everything sweet? Areet. Keep everything sweet.'

Some time later the mobile phone rang again. Macca answered it. 'Nee bother,' he said tersely. 'Ah said friggin' nee bother, the mule's sorted.'

For a long time the boy remained crouching in the trap, all the time watching Macca, then very slowly he straightened his body out so that he was lying down. Motionless, he stared at the figure on the bed. The rage in his eyes had cooled to an icy determination.

'This is the worst bit,' said Macca after a while. 'The waiting. It's not so bad when ye're moving. But it's when ye've got time to think.' When he had finished one joint, Macca reached out for another. The springs of the bed creaked restlessly beneath his constantly shifting body as he smoked.

'Just remember, divvy, if ye divven't dee as ah tell yus . . .'
Gradually, the springs fell silent.

When the breathing had grown heavy, Sonny Gee pulled himself slowly back into a crouching position. Carefully, he tested the door above him. The handle of the bucket clattered. The boy held his breath and stared over at the bed. But the deep, even breathing continued.

Moving only an inch at a time, Sonny Gee painstakingly shunted the door along the top of the cot until there was a gap for him to squeeze through. The space was just too small. He tried to push the door back a little further, and the metal bucket teetered ominously, its handle clattering once more. With a silent gasp the boy froze. Macca stirred in his sleep and Sonny Gee pressed himself into a corner of the cot, terror on his paralysed face. But Macca fell motionless once more, and slowly the boy moved out from his corner. Lifting himself up to the gap, he tried to push himself through again. His eyes continued to blaze with resolution.

Inch by inch he emerged, breathing in each time he pushed. He was halfway out of the cot, perched astride it, when he looked over at Macca. The deep, even breathing was punctuated by a snore that rattled the big man's teeth. The snoring repeated itself at increasingly frequent intervals and with mounting horror Sonny Gee waited for the slumbering man to wake. There was one final immense grunt, but when that had receded, Macca's breathing calmed and he fell into an apparently deeper sleep. Gently, the boy lowered himself to the ground.

Taking out the strips of sheet, Sonny Gee crept purposefully across the room. He placed one of the doused rags against the curtains, wedged another between the bars of the cot, and with the last one clutched tightly in his hand, he approached the bed. Careful not to disturb the sleeping man, he laid the rag at his feet. He then went over to the corner where a pile of *Gateshead Herald* free newspapers was stacked. Swallowing anxiously, the boy took a page from a paper and began to screw it into a ball. The noise it made seemed to surprise him, and he stopped instantly. But still Macca slumbered on, so he carried on making the ball, crumpling the paper with infinite care. The boy stared constantly at the bed as he took out another sheet and rolled it up. A bead of sweat dropped into his eyes, and he paused to flick it away. Taking out a third sheet, he screwed that one up and then stopped. Gazing at the sleeping man with deadly hatred, Sonny Gee took three deep breaths. Macca's sprawling body seemed to fill the bed. The boy bent down to take out the lighter.

Lighting one of the balls, he turned calmly to the curtains. The lit paper was lobbed through the air, landing on the doused rag. Instantaneously, flames shot up the curtains. Moving swiftly now, Sonny Gee lit the second ball of paper and dropped it into the cot. Lighting the third one, he advanced to within a yard of the bed. After a moment's hesitation, he threw it at Macca's feet. Brushing a toe, it missed the rag and fell to the floor.

The boy sprinted to the door. The curtains were already two pillars of fire and thick smoke was beginning to fill the room. Macca stirred heavily as Sonny Gee pulled on the door. It was locked. He twisted the handle frantically, but it would not open. He whimpered as he stared at the door in puzzlement. Harder and harder he yanked at the door, his body lurching as though in a fit. Then he suddenly stopped. He had remembered where the key was.

Hurling himself over to the bed, he stared at Macca who still slept despite the growing fire. Carefully, he tried to reach for the key, but it was trapped in Macca's back pocket. He tried to roll the sleeping body over, but it would not move. With increasing force he pushed at the body. 'What the friggin' hell . . .' yelled Macca, coming round to see the boy on top of him. Stunned for a few moments, he gaped at the cracking, growing flames in disbelief, his small nostrils flaring as he breathed in the thickening smoke. Then he sprang up and grabbed Sonny Gee. 'Ye mad fuckin' bastard! Ye mad fucking bastard!' he yelled. Jumping from the bed, he carried the child a few steps across the room, but Sonny Gee was now struggling madly, pummelling and biting ferociously at Macca. The man stopped. With a roar he hurled the boy against the wall by the door. Sonny Gee landed heavily, his head bouncing against a skirting board.

One of the curtains fell. The wood of the cot began to crackle. Coughing, Macca blundered over to the door, his arms waving protectively above his head. He pulled out the key, unlocked the door and left the room.

The old man was on his way up to the top bedsits when he was knocked to the ground. He felt himself hit the hard wood of the stairs, and then, a moment later, the red hat came to rest too, settling close to him, the white braid within reach. Macca paused for an instant to stare down at Joe as though puzzled by the collision, then he carried on, crashing down the stairs. The door to the bedsits slammed loudly as he left.

The smoke, billowing from the open door, had begun to drift down the stairs and it hung in the air above Joe's motionless body. He lay there for a while, bewildered. Then, raising his head a little, he looked down the stairs as though expecting Macca to reappear at any moment. Taking a deep breath, he smelt the thick smoke, and coming round, hoisted himself to his feet. His breath wheezed agonisingly from him. The effort needed to climb each stair wrung a convulsive shudder from him that threatened to unbalance him and pitch him back the way he had come.

The fire had taken hold of the far side of the room, and Joe staggered under the surge of heat as he stepped over the threshold. He glanced wildly about the room. In the searing light of the fire, the features of his face seemed to melt and his head was reduced to a skull as, mouth gaping, he searched for the boy. After an agony of scouring the room, he saw the fallen body behind the door. 'Sonny Gee, Sonny Gee!' he roared as he fell to his knees. The boy did not reply. Even when he shook him, Sonny Gee did not reply. 'Sonny Gee. Ha'way, Sonny Gee!' shouted Joe, his words drowned out by a sudden crack of the fire.

With a strength born of desperation, Joe lifted Sonny Gee into his arms. Marshalling all his remaining vitality, he staggered through the door and across the landing. He had managed to descend the first few of the steep stairs when he felt his vigour ebbing. He bellowed, trying to rally himself, and he managed a few more stairs, but then he knew he could not go any further. His shoulder crashed against the wall as he reeled. For a few moments he remained upright, then his legs began to fold underneath him. Cushioning the boy from the impact, he fell.

They lay there, side by side with the fire roaring behind. Again and again Joe tried to lift himself but his body would no longer respond. Along with the din of the fire, he could hear the creaking of his own wheezing breath. He felt detached from himself so that even keeping his eyes open was a losing battle. Struggling no longer, he gazed at the face of his grandson. The blue eyes were shut tight. The flawless skin was darkened with smoke. With a final sigh darkness closed over the old man.

The next thing he knew was a movement at his side. A light, fluttering disturbance, like the flapping of a butterfly. It grew in strength, until he found himself wondering what it might be. His senses were locked in silence and he was no longer aware of the fire or even the stairs. He wanted the movement to stop and leave him alone. That was all. But instead it was becoming more and more insistent.

Then all at once the present moment exploded back into life. The din of the fire deafened him. Its smoke choked him. And its light lit up the urgent face of Sonny Gee. The boy was kneeling over him, tugging at his sleeve. 'Ye've got to come, Granda,' he was pleading. 'Ye've got to come.'

Joe looked up. His lips trembled as he tried to speak, but no words came out. He tried to lift himself, but no power had returned to the rest of his body. 'It's nee good, lad,' he managed to say at last.

The boy was shouting something, and although the old man could not hear the words, he could feel his own body vibrating with the sobs that were ripping out of his grandson. 'Listen,' said Joe, with a strange calmness now. 'Ye gan and get help.' The boy shook his head fiercely. 'Aye,' insisted the old man, almost peacefully. 'It's the only thing ye can dee.' He paused. 'Ha'way, lad, yus've got to gan. Ah cannet get up.' He tried to reach out and somehow his hand responded. He laid his gnarled fingers on Sonny Gee's hand. 'Ha'way, son,' he said. 'Gan and get help for yer granda.'

Standing up, Sonny Gee bounded down a few stairs and then stopped. 'Na,' he screamed.

'Aye,' insisted the old man.

Confused and terrified, the little boy tore down the stairs.

The old man's lips trembled. 'Goodbye lad,' he whispered.

When Sonny Gee had disappeared from view, the fire suddenly grew, and like a flood breaching a dam, its din crashed over Joe. He could hardly breathe now. And his face was seared with the increasing heat. A deep drowsiness was settling over him. He saw the red of the cowboy hat, still lying where it had been knocked from his hands. It seemed to bob slightly like a piece of wreckage on the sea. He tried to reach out to it, but couldn't.

Sonny Gee stumbled out into the night. A knot of people was gathered in the garden. 'Another one's run out,' someone shouted. 'Is anyone else inside?'

'Must be the last!' someone else replied.

'It's the bonny lad.'

'Some old man went inside.'

309

'Are yus areet, Sonny Gee?'

'Did ye see someone else in there?'

'It's too dangerous for anyone else to gan in now.'

'What took yus so long?'

'Who started it?'

Overwhelmed by coughing, Sonny Gee fell to his knees. The bodies gathered round him.

'Are yus areet?'

'Can ye breathe?'

'Pick him up.'

'Put him down.'

'Has neeone sent for a fire engine?'

'And a ambulance?'

As he retched, the boy glanced up at the faces which had converged on him. Helplessly, he pointed at the door through which he had come. 'There,' his voice rasped. 'There.'

'What's he saying?'

'What does he want?'

'Divven't push, give him room.'

'He's in a state of shock.'

Sonny Gee's body shuddered convulsively as he continued to vomit. He gesticulated desperately at the door.

'Let wor through please,' Ronny was calling. He and Audrey were running down the broken concrete blocks of the path. He tried to get through the crowd but it was too tightly packed round the boy. 'Ha'way,' he pleaded.

Audrey arrived at his shoulder. 'Bonny lad!' she exclaimed, seeing the boy. 'PISS OFF OOT THE WAY!' she shouted, shouldering and tearing a way through the gathering. The bodies stepped back. 'Christ!' she whispered as she dropped to her knees to cradle the boy. 'Are yus areet, Sonny Gee?'

'Granda!' the boy was able to gasp.

'Where?' Ronny asked, pushing in through the gap created by Audrey's presence. The boy gestured at the door. 'Reet,' said Ronny, turning.

'Where ye gannin'?' Audrey demanded.

'In there,' he returned.

At that moment there was an immense crash and part of the roof caved in. Audrey's face was lit by the orange glare of the fire as she stared at Ronny. 'Ye cannet, man. It's too . . .'

But Ronny had already pushed his way back through the crowd. 'What aboot Macca?' Audrey screamed. 'Watch oot for . . .'

'He's gone,' a voice announced from the periphery of the crowd. 'Ah saw him legging it off up Old Parsonage Road.'

'Hey,' someone said to Ronny as he ran to the front door of the bedsits. 'Ah wouldn't gan in there, if ah were ye.'

Just as Ronny entered the burning building, something toppled from the roof, scattering burning fragments through the night. The crowd broke as shards peppered the garden about them. Everyone froze as though mesmerised, staring at the scatterings. Springing to his feet, Sonny Gee ran to the door. Stumbling on her high heels, Audrey caught him. 'No,' she said, holding him close to herself. 'No.'

'But . . .' The boy's eyes were agonised.

'No, bonny lad.'

Sirens were sounding in the background. The crowd had fallen into a strange, passive state, each face lifted to stare at the fire. The boy's weeping was soft as the flow of water.

Someone ran into the garden. 'Fire engines are coming,' they announced. 'Ambulances and the pollis.'

'The pollis?'

'Aye, the pollis.'

'Who rang thems?'

'Divven't kna.'

'Wasn't me.'

The minutes passed agonisingly. The fire continued to rage, its flames spreading through the fire trap of the bedsits. Audrey stared at the front door. Sonny Gee's eyes were fixed there too, his bottom lip was bleeding where he had bitten into it.

'That old gadgie shouldn't have gone inside.'

'And that fat gadgie was mental.'

'Aye. There's nee way he's coming oot o' there.'

'The whole place is gannin' up.'

The fire brigade had arrived and had begun to push back the growing crowd into some kind of order. Suddenly a figure stumbled from the door. It was heavily stooped. It was a man. The smoke hid him from the view of the crowd, but as he staggered across the garden it became apparent that he was wearing a cowboy hat and was carrying someone.

'It's the fat gadgie.'

'He's areet.'

'He's got someone with him.'

'The old man?'

'Is he alive?'

'He's a goner.'

'Aye, he's deed.'

'It's the auld fella. And he's deed.'

'Na. He isn't, he's alive. He's areet.'

'Is he hell, man, he's deed.'

Slipping Audrey's grip, and evading the firefighters' cordon with an agile writhe of his body, Sonny Gee ran to the old man. Joe had been laid on the ground. 'Granda!' the boy cried.

The fire was roaring out of control. Its flames cut a livid scar on the night sky. The old man opened his eyes.

Suddenly, a gasp ran through the little crowd gathered in the garden. Cinders were falling. White and feathery in the orange flare of the flames, they fluttered down, flitting and dancing in the air. The people had fallen silent, and all at once everything was hushed and stilled. On the embrace of the old man and the boy the soft ashes were settling like an unseasonable snow. 'Me bonny lad,' smiled Joe. 'Me bonny, bonny lad.'